GRIMNIRS

(A Runes Book)

Ednah Walters

Published by Firetrail Publishing

Firetrail Publishing
P.O. Box 3444 Logan,
UT 84323

Copyright © 2013 Ednah Walters
All rights reserved.
ISBN: 0983429790
ISBN-13: 978-0-9834297-9-1
§
Edited by Kelly Bradley Hashway
Cover Design by Cora Graphics. All Rights Reserved.
No part of this book may be used or reproduced in any manner
whatsoever without permission, except in the case of brief
quotations embodied in critical articles and reviews.
First **Firetrail Publishing** publication: Dec 2013
www.firetrailpublishing.com

ALSO BY EDNAH WALTERS:

The Runes Series

Runes (book one)
Immortals (book two)
Grimnirs (A Runes book)

The Guardian Legacy Series:

Awakened (prequel)
Betrayed (book one)
Hunted (book two)

The Fitzgerald Family series (Writing as E. B. Walters)

Slow Burn (book 1)
Mine Until Dawn (book 2)
Kiss Me Crazy (book 3)
Dangerous Love (book 4)
Forever Hers (book 5)
Surrender to Temptation (book 6)

DEDICATION

This book is dedicated to my parents, Walter & Jane Margaret. Thank you for instilling in me the confidence to go after my dreams. May you rest in peace.

ACKNOWLEDGMENTS

§

To my editor, Kelly Bradley Hashway, thank you for
Weeding out the unnecessary words. I am so lucky to have found
you. To my beta-readers and dear friends, Catie Vargas and Jeannette
Whitus, you ladies are amazing. You pushed and pulled me when I
faltered. This book would not have been completed without you. You
girls rock!! To my dearest friends, Katrina Whittaker and Jowanna
Delong Kestner, thank you for always being there whenever I want to
vent. Friends like you are hard to find!
To my daughter, MJ, thank you for listening to my crazy ideas
and showing me how to bridge the gap between our generations.
To my critique partners, Dawn Brown, Teresa Bellew,
Katherine Warwick/Jennifer Laurens, thank you
for being there when my muse takes a vacation.
We are more than writing partners.
To my husband and my wonderful children,
thank you for your unwavering love and support.
You inspire me in so many ways
Love you, guys.

TRADEMARK LIST

Google
Nikon
Mercedes
Electra
Sentra
Harley
Chex Mix
Vampire Diary
Supernatural
Lord Sesshomaru
Portland Art Museum
Tasmanian Devil
Warner Bros
Twizzlers
Baked Lays

GLOSSARY

Aesir: A tribe of Norse gods

Asgard: Home of the Aesir gods

Odin: The father and ruler of all gods and men. He is an Aesir god. Half of the dead soldiers/warriors/athletes go to live in his hall Valhalla.

Vanir: Another tribe of Norse gods

Vanaheim: Home of the Vanir gods

Freya: The poetry-loving goddess of love and fertility. She is a Vanir goddess. The other half of the dead warriors/soldiers/athletes go to her hall in Falkvang

Frigg: Odin's wife, the patron of marriage and motherhood

Norns: deities who control destinies of men and gods

Völva: A powerful seeress

Völur: A group of seeresses

Immortals: Humans who stop aging and self-heal because of the magical runes etched on their skin

Valkyries: Immortals who collect fallen warriors/soldiers/fighters/athletes and take them to Valhalla and Falkvang

Bifrost: The rainbow bridge that connects Asgard to Earth

Ragnarok: The end of the world war between the gods and the evil giants

Artavus: Magical knife or dagger used to etch runes

Artavo: Plural of artavus

Stillo: A type of artavus

Hel: The Goddess Hel in charge of the dead

Hel: Home of Goddess Hel, dead criminals, those dead from illness and old age

Nastraad: The island in Hel for criminals

Prologue

Eirik

I couldn't move if I tried. I was stuffed and exhausted. Being the guest of honor wasn't all that it was cracked up to be. A week had passed since I arrived in Asgard, and the gods were still celebrating. I was flattered, but enough was enough. They used every excuse to keep the party going.

Day and night, the younger gods jousted and competed in every imaginable game. When not gaming, Immortals entertained us with dances, served endless supplies of food, and kept the drinks flowing. Since we were in my grandfather's home, or hall as they called it, the older gods and their servants watched the games then went back to their own halls every night, only to return the next day. Their children didn't seem to get tired or have duties. They partied, disappeared with different women every night, slept, got up, and partied some more.

Someone slapped my back hard. "Hey, Uncle Eirik."

"Enough with that uncle crap," I mumbled and glared at Viggo, son of Forseti—God of Justice. He'd been my shadow since I arrived in Asgard. His father and I were half-brothers, and he got a kick out of calling me uncle, even though we were around the same age.

Viggo laughed, sat, and slapped my shoulder again. It stung. He was a few inches shorter than I, but built like a bulldog.

"I told you to call me Eirik," I added.

"Hey, I'm just giving you the same respect I give my other uncles."

Except they were older and more powerful. Viggo didn't slap their backs or force women on them. "Yeah, I've noticed."

He grinned and ran his fingers through his hair, which was perfectly mussed as though he'd just woken up. He probably had. Last night, he'd disappeared with an Immortal after introducing me to her friend.

"So, did you hook up with Lei or what?" he asked.

"Nope."

"Why not? She thought you were... beautiful. Heck, almost all the women want a piece of you. Maybe you're into guys." He hadn't bothered to lower his voice, and several young gods turned to look at us.

Heat crawled up my face. "I'm all about chicks, dude. My quarters are down the hall from Alfadir," I said, using Odin's preferred name in Asgard. It meant "all father" since he was the oldest and leader of the gods. "I'm not comfortable making out with a girl while that close to him."

I glanced at the table, where Odin calmly watched the hall's occupants and the entertainers with his one good eye. His wife, or Grandmother Frigga, sat on his right, and Goddess Freya sat on his left.

"He won't mind," Viggo said. "He knows that making love is our favorite pastime."

"I'm going to need more than a week to get into the game." I missed Kayville, my friends, even my parents. No matter what everyone said, Earth would always be my home.

"You're still pining for the Mortal you left behind."

"Her name is Cora," I said slowly, trying not to snap. I didn't like the way he dismissed humans.

"Do you want to see her?"

"Sure, but I was told I can't use Bifrost without permission from Heimdall, and he's always busy."

"I don't mean visit." Viggo's eyes went the table where the twelve higher gods were busy having a heated discussion. "From Alfadir's high seat in the throne hall, we can see all the realms," Viggo said. "Since he's here, he won't know."

Tempting idea. "That's okay. I'll see her when I go home."

"Asgard is your home now, my friend. Follow me if you want to see her." He got up, and I knew he was headed to the throne hall.

I glanced around then jumped up and followed him. No one would think it odd that we were leaving together. Viggo had been my tour guide since I got here. When I glanced at the high table, Odin's good eye was on me. He stroked his long beard and nodded. I had no idea what that meant so I nodded back and hurried out of the hall, where Viggo waited with a smirk.

"I knew you'd not resist," he said. He led the way down a broad hallway.

"What if the ravens are back?" I asked. Odin's ravens were smart and observant and never missed a thing.

"They're busy gathering information for Alfadir and won't be back until nightfall," Viggo said confidently.

The hallway was endless and curving. Through a doorway, I spied Valkyries serving soldiers. We passed minor gods' halls, the names on their doors written in the runic alphabet. The major gods and goddesses had their larger halls in different parts of Asgard. We finally approached the massive entrance to the throne room, and Viggo's cockiness drained away. He slowed down.

"What is it?" I asked.

He nodded at the door. "You go first. It will recognize your essence and open."

"I told you I'm not special."

He rested his hand on my shoulder and smirked. "You are the one, Eirik, whether you like it or not. I heard my parents discuss you. Why do you think Alfadir keeps you close to him and is always watching you?"

"Because I'm new here." And Loki was my maternal grandfather, so I could easily be an evil trickster like him. On top of that, I had evil runes on my body, courtesy of my mother. All the gods had a reason to be wary of me. Just because they'd welcomed me didn't mean they were happy to have me here.

Viggo slapped me on the back. Again. "No, my friend. You are the one the *Völvo* said would inherit Alfadir's throne after Ragnarok."

"I'm not buying it," I said.

"Then prove it. Walk to the door. If it doesn't recognize your essence and open, I'll tell all my friends the old geezers got it wrong and you are just like the rest of us—like me, a minor god."

I wasn't like Viggo. He hadn't been raised on Earth among humans, or Mortals as they called them. He hadn't been lied to for seventeen years about who he really was, only to discover he wasn't even human. He didn't have to deal with the fact that his mother was the Goddess Hel, ruler of the Underworld, or that his grandfather was the famous Master of Magic, Loki. But the most important of all, he didn't know what it meant to be in love with one person. To think of no one else but her. To fantasize about being with her. Viggo, like most of the Asgardians, had many women—Immortals, Valkyries, and even other goddesses—vying for his attention. He slept with a different woman every night, while all I wanted was one girl.

Cora Jemison.

I didn't buy into this future leader of the gods crap Viggo kept yapping about, but I wanted to see Cora. "Okay, let's see if you are right."

I stepped forward, and the door to the throne hall flew open.

"I told you," Viggo said.

"You told him what?" a voice boomed from behind us.

We froze, looked at each other, and turned. Odin stood behind us, his hand on his spear, his wolves at his heel.

"Alfadir," Viggo mumbled, his chin dropping to his chest.

"What mischief are you up to now, young Viggo?" Odin bellowed.

"Nothing, Alfadir," Viggo said again, his voice barely above a whisper.

Odin focused on me, his eye blazing like the sun. Of all the gods, I found him the most interesting. He was the oldest and the wisest of the gods, the seeker of knowledge. He willingly gave up an eye to acquire great wisdom and hanged himself for nine days on the World Tree to gain knowledge of runes. Every action he took was to learn new concepts and ideas, which he passed on to humans.

"Eirik?" he asked, his voice softening.

"We were going to check out your throne," I said.

"Why?"

I glanced at Viggo, but his eyes were on the floor. Most young Asgardians were in total awe of Odin. Once again, Odin's eye focused on me.

"I want to see my friends back home."

He glanced at the golden throne then back to me and Viggo. "Okay. You have my permission."

Viggo and I exchanged a look.

"Really?" I asked.

Creases folded the corners of his eyes as he grimaced or smiled—I couldn't tell. "Your grandmother told me you would miss your friends and would want to go back before you start your training."

I frowned. "How could she have known?"

"She gets premonitions. Come along." He walked ahead of us, a hulking figure in a blue and green robe, winged helmet on his head, white hair flowing down his shoulders, and a beard reaching his chest.

I kicked Viggo. He snapped out of his terror and followed us. The throne room was long, and the silver ceiling reflected the spotless marble floor and the golden pillars around the room.

"Does she know *when* I'll go back?" I asked.

"You can never go back, Eirik," my grandfather said firmly. "If you do, you will be lost to us again." He climbed the steps and sat on the golden throne. Runic writing covered the back and arms of the chair, and a fur blanket cushioned the seat. He indicated the step under his feet. "Sit."

We sat and waited. Nothing happened. I glanced at Viggo. He shrugged. A quick glance behind us and we saw why. Alfadir had dozed off. Was he supposed to push a button or wave his spear to get things going?

"Is he asleep?" Viggo whispered.

"I don't know." I studied my grandfather's face. His good eye was closed. I stood and waved a hand over his face. He didn't move. Now what?

"I knew it was too good to be true," Viggo whispered. "No one has ever seen the realms through the eyes of the ravens. Not even my father, who is just and fair."

"I don't care about the other realms. I just want to see Earth." I turned to sit down and froze. The hall disappeared, along with the throne and Odin. I appeared to hover in the air, except my feet were on something solid.

"Holy crap," Viggo whispered.

Holy crap? Hearing a modern phrase from the mouth of a god sounded weird. Viggo appeared to be seated in the air at my feet. I slid down and sat beside him. Okay, so the steps were there, just invisible. Cool. I looked down and grinned. I could see land as though I was a bird, but we were too far up in the air to see clearly.

Where was Kayville?

The land rushed toward us as though we'd zoomed in.

"Whoa. Did you do that?" Viggo asked.

I didn't care how it had happened. I could see familiar landmarks. My high school. The Hub. Jump Zone. "That's Kayville, my hometown," I said, grinning.

"It's a village," Viggo said.

"Shut up." I elbowed him. Where was Cora's farm?

We zoomed in on Cora's farm. Her Elantra was parked outside, and there was movement in her room.

"Is this her house?"

"Yes. She lives on a farm with her parents."

"Looks like they have visitors," Viggo said.

A familiar SUV pulled up beside the Elantra, which meant Raine was coming to visit Cora. Raine was my childhood friend and the girl I thought was *the one* before Cora. It took me a long time to get my act together and see she was just a friend, an honorary sister. The vehicle stopped, and a dark-haired guy got out. Torin. He was Raine's boyfriend.

"I know him," Viggo said. "He's a Valkyrie."

Torin walked around and opened the door for Raine. He lifted her down, wrapped his arm around her waist, and said something. They both laughed. Damn it! I needed sound. As though my thoughts switched it on, Raine's laughter, mixed with Torin's deep chuckle, reached me.

Viggo leaned forward. "Who is she?"

"My best friend and someone you shouldn't be looking at like that." Torin and Raine started for Cora's front door.

"She's beautiful for a Mortal," Viggo said. "When you use Bifrost to visit, I'm coming with you. Maybe she and I—"

"She is Torin's, *and* she's not a Mortal."

"A Valkyrie? I've never seen her before."

"She's much more," I answered absentmindedly, my focus on the door. *Come on, Cora. Open the door.* I wanted to make sure she was okay. That was it. I could see movement at her window.

"I'm a god," Viggo bragged. "No one is more desirable or powerful than a god."

I laughed. "She is more powerful, dude. She's a *Völva*."

"No freaking way. *Völur* are extinct. The remaining ones are old and useless."

"She's the last of her kind. Grandmother told me." The door opened, but instead of Cora, her father stood in the doorway. The conversation between him and Raine was brief. Cora wasn't home. She'd gone to the store with her mother—yet someone was in her room.

Ignoring Viggo, who was still complaining about the *Völur*, I focused on Cora's bedroom window. I needed to see inside. The next second, it was as though her roof became transparent.

Cora wasn't in her room. A man was. He was dressed in a black hooded duster, so I couldn't see his face. "Is that a—"

"Grimnir," Viggo said. "You know what that means?"

Cora was about to die. I wasn't letting that happen or letting her soul be taken by my mother's soul reaper.

1. Souls

The woman reached up to stroke the cashier's hair. Her hand went through his head and dropped to her side, tears filling her eyes. Another ghost. I looked down before she could catch me watching her.

Hollywood got it all wrong. Ghosts weren't white blobs floating around aimlessly and helping people. Nor did they flicker like holograms on a drug trip. No gaping wounds or half-chopped limbs. They weren't even freaking transparent. They looked real, solid, like you and me.

I focused on helping Mom with the groceries, one item at a time. It looked like we were having tacos tonight. I loved tacos. Maybe I'd help her cook.

Thinking about food didn't help. I could still see the crying ghost from the corner of my eye. I didn't want to feel sorry for her, but I did. Why couldn't they just move on already? What made them linger? Unfinished business? I stole a glance at her again and caught her staring at me.

Please don't approach me, or touch me, or follow me around.

Ghosts were persistent, but I had to be careful acknowledging them or telling them to leave me alone. The conversation was always one-sided, and people noticed. The month I'd spent in the psych ward was enough. I was never ever going back. The psych ward had the most annoying ghosts. The people might have been crazy when they were alive, but they were crazier dead.

My heart pounding, I kept my head down as I plucked items from the cart and put them on the conveyor belt. This ability to see ghosts was a curse. A big, fat, ugly curse I was struggling to deal with and failing miserably. I still didn't know how or why I could see dead people. It started three months ago, the night lightning hit the pool during a swim meet at a local university and killed my fellow high school swimmers. A few of us had survived, but something happened to me that night. I actually saw my friends' ghosts and the angelic glowing beings that had led them away.

My mistake was telling my parents. They'd contacted Dr. Wendell and the hack had convinced them to have me committed to a mental institution. It didn't help that Uncle Hack was related to Mom.

I shivered again and rubbed my arms.

"Cold?" Mom asked.

I gave her a tiny smile. "A little. I should have brought a jacket."

Mom started to shrug off her coat. She and I were the same height, though she was slightly heavier, so I knew her coat would fit me.

"No, Mom. Don't give me yours." It was November, and the temperature around Kayville was in the forties. I should have known better than to wear a short-sleeved shirt without a jacket. "I'm fine. Really," I added when she shot me a skeptical glance.

"Okay. Should we have tacos for dinner tonight?" she asked.

I didn't care. I just wanted to go home. Not that the ghosts left me alone there either. But at least I had the means to get rid of them in my bedroom.

"Or maybe lamb chops and baked potatoes," Mom added, her voice upbeat.

I loved lamb chops too, and she knew it. She was trying to butter me up before hitting me with the bad news. I'd overheard her and Dad discussing me this morning. They wanted me to be homeschooled. Who got homeschooled in their junior year of high school? They might as well tattoo "freak" on my forehead.

I mean, seeing ghosts made me a freak already. There was no need to let the entire world know by homeschooling me *after* I'd already spent a year and a half in high school. I hadn't minded being homeschooled when I was younger. I never even found it weird that my parents had a problem with me, their only child, attending Kayville Elementary School when they'd taught there.

No. I planned to finish high school like a normal person. Screw the ghosts. They were not stopping me. I was not letting them win. I'd already missed six weeks of school because of them, a month of that in Providence Mental Institute. If anyone at school knew about PMI, my social life would be yesterday's news.

My eyes drifted to the ghost. She was still staring at me. I glared back this time. No matter how often I tried to ignore them, they always knew I could see them. I didn't know how.

She smiled, and I cringed.

"Can we have lasagna tonight instead, Mom?" I asked, hoping she'd send me to get cheese or spinach and give me a chance to get rid of the ghost.

Surprise flashed in her honey-brown eyes. We both knew I didn't like her lasagna. She used too much spinach, and I hated spinach.

"Sure, hun." Her eyes swept the contents of the cart. "We'll need ricotta cheese—"

"I'll get it." I took off.

"Don't forget the spinach," she called out, chuckling.

Waving, I hurried toward the dairy section. When I glanced back, the ghost was following me, her expression hopeful. That would turn to frustration then anger when she realized I couldn't help her.

I turned the corner and groaned.

A middle-age ghost with greased-back black hair and swarthy complexion was walking backwards in front of a young couple pushing a cart. He gestured wildly, mouth opening and closing. One moment, he flicked his chin with the tip of his fingers, the next he pressed his hands together as though praying. He was definitely a father not too happy with his child's choice in a spouse.

This was a sucky day to be me, but then again, ever since I started seeing ghosts, my life had gone down the toilet. The guy I'd loved since elementary school but basically treated me like his annoying younger sister forgot about me. I forgave him for choosing my best friend because you didn't cherry-pick who you love. But for the two of them to write me off just because I was admitted in a psych ward? That was unforgivable.

To add insult to injury, I got the freaking ghosts. They weren't just in hospitals and cemeteries. They were attached to people, buildings, and objects. And lately, it seemed like they were attached to me. Or attracted to me.

I picked up a pint of ricotta cheese, turned, and smothered a screech. The woman ghost was so close I almost walked through her. I took a step back. I'd walked through one of them and put the experience under never-to-be-repeated. It had felt like being dunked in a murky, icy pond. Totally gross.

Her mouth opened and closed.

"I can't hear you, so go away," I said through clenched teeth.

She kept talking, gesturing wildly. I tried to walk around her, but she blocked my path.

"Leave. Me. Alone," I snarled then glanced around to see if anyone had heard me. The few shoppers hadn't noticed my odd behavior yet. "Shoo."

I turned to go the other away, but the angry father was watching us. His eyes narrowed as though his humans-who-can-see-ghosts radar just clicked on. He started toward us.

I searched for the nearest metallic object. *Thank you, Dean and Sam Winchester.* The fictitious brothers used iron to disperse ghosts in the hit TV series *Supernatural.* The crap actually worked. I'd used a fire poker on one that had wandered into my room a few days ago, and it caused her to disappear.

I grabbed what looked like a cheese grater from the shelf and hefted it. It was heavy, which meant it had more iron than whatever other crap they'd used to make it. I waved the cheese grater around like a ninja with a dagger and hoped no one saw me and called Mom.

I shuddered. No more psych ward. No more meds. As much as I'd hated being committed, the meds had been worse. They'd made me act loopy.

The female ghost watched me warily. At least she'd stopped opening her mouth like a fish. Yeah, I bet she knew what iron did to her kind. The angry dude was closer now, and he wasn't alone. Two other ghosts had joined him, all eager to chat.

Damn it! I hated when they ganged up on me. A wave of iciness drifted from them, and I shivered. *Yeah, come on. Come on, you bodiless, icy bastards, and taste the iron.*

"Hey," a commanding voice cut through the air. "You guys are with me, not her."

Different expressions crossed the ghosts' faces—annoyance, terror, defiance. The angry Italian's eyes darted left then right.

"Don't even think about it, Morello," the voice snapped. "If you make me hunt you down again, I will make the rest of your existence so miserable you will beg for a second death. *Capisci?*"

I turned to look at the speaker, but the only person there was the old woman, who looked petrified. I didn't blame her. That voice was terrifying and irritating. I hated bossy people.

"Sally, you've had your twenty-four hours. Time to go," the voice continued, and then he stepped from behind a rack.

Whoa. Leather, leather, and even more leather, way too much to be fashionable. Unless it had become the "in thing" while I was gone.

His voice said he didn't bend or bow to anyone or anything, so I doubted he cared about fashion trends.

The hooded, ankle-length black leather duster was tailored to fit his tall body and broad shoulders. It hugged his upper torso before flowing to the floor. Ringed and tattooed fingers peeked through fingerless gloves, but as I watched, the tats disappeared as though absorbed into his skin. Weird. Leather pants and boots finished his attire.

My eyes moved up. Even his shirt was made of leather. I reached his face and blinked. Or maybe I should say I reached where his face should have been. There was nothing but darkness under the hood, yet the store was well lit. I peered at him but still saw nothing. A scarf of some kind covered his neck. Surely, it was too early to be dressed like an Eskimo. Besides, this was Kayville, Oregon. We didn't get snow until late winter.

Then weird things started to happen. Something glowed under his hood. I expected to see a skull head or a big gaping hole. Instead, I noticed skin. The glowing things didn't last long enough for me to see his entire face.

Were they tattoos? It was hard to tell. They kept appearing and disappearing as he barked orders at the ghosts. I caught a glimpse of sensual lips and a strong jaw line. I was close to giving up when more tats lit up his entire face.

My jaw dropped.

Good Lord, he was gorgeous. Chiseled cheekbones with a shadow, arched eyebrows, and those totally kissable lips. But his most unusual features were his eyes. They were golden with a ring of green. Like that famous Afghan girl on the cover of *National Geographic*.

The glowing tats added to his striking features instead of distracting from them. I thought I saw locks of shaggy dark hair on his forehead before the tats dimmed, but I could have been mistaken.

What was he? A ghost hunter? The ones who'd taken my dead friends during the meet had lit up like light bulbs too, but the glow had covered their bodies. And they didn't dress like him.

"Let's go before you really piss me off," he ordered. "Jonas, you shouldn't even be here. No, big guy, she cannot help you. Time's up."

The shoppers in the fresh food section didn't turn to look at him when he spoke, which meant they couldn't hear him. He looked at me then at the cheese grater in my hand and chuckled.

The sound sent a warm tingle down my spine, and my breath caught. So not fair. Not only was he hot, but he had a breathtaking smile. I wanted to grin back, stand there like an idiot, and ogle him.

"Put that thing away before you hurt yourself, sweet-cheeks," he said in a condescending tone. "No one, not even you, messes with my work. In fact, if I catch you dispersing my charges again, I will haul your pretty ass to Hel's Hall myself. "

For seconds, my mind went blank, but then anger flashed through me. Sweet-cheeks? How I disliked arrogant, smart-mouthed pretty guys. They should keep their mouths shut and just... just look pretty. This one carried himself like he was commanding an army.

Yeah, an army of ghosts.

I flicked my chin the way the ghost of Morello had done. I knew the gesture was disrespectful and was rewarded when Ghost Hunter's eyes narrowed, the yellow cores intensifying like a wolf's. I think I pissed him off. Good. I laughed.

A humph came from my left, and my head whipped toward it. A woman selecting fruit from a display rack gave me a funny look and shook her head. Yep, I could just imagine how I looked standing there with a cheese grater, gesturing to no one, and laughing like a demented idiot. She probably thought I was on drugs or something. It was time for me to leave.

I turned.

"What was that?" Ghost Hunter asked. "I hope it was a thank you for not telling everyone where you are, Cora Jemison. Back with your parents so soon? You're not going to get better at your job if you keep running home."

I froze. Job? What job? How did he know my name? And why was he acting like he knew me? Frowning, I continued walking.

"So I'm getting the ice princess treatment again? Fine. We'll see how long you last this time."

I glanced back, once again dying to say something. He smirked as though waiting for me to speak. I wasn't stupid enough to try it.

"Still don't know how to engage your runes and become invisible? Well, keep working at them, doll-face." He winked. "If you need pointers, try to be nice to me. Really nice and sweet."

His voice was suggestive and sexy. This time, I fought its effect.

"Oh, and stop hurting my souls," he continued in that annoying voice. "I wasn't joking about hauling your pretty ass to Hel's Hall. And that's saying a lot because I love your ass, sweet-cheeks. If you want to get my attention, you know where to find me."

Love my ass? Nice and sweet to him? It was obvious he was confusing me with someone else. What was he anyway? A grim reaper? Angel of death? Or a ghost hunter?

He reached under his duster trench coat, and my grip tightened on the cheese grater, my eyes not leaving him. I braced myself for the worst, but all he pulled out was a stick. No, not a stick. A scythe. It was so puny I wanted to laugh.

Then the tats on his fingers returned and the scythe elongated, the same markings on his fingers appearing on its shaft.

Okay, he was definitely *the* grim reaper.

Morello's ghost took one look at the scythe and bolted. The reaper pointed the blade at him. "Stop!"

The fleeing ghost froze, terror in his eyes.

"Didn't I say no more running, you piece of filth? Want me to use this on you?" The reaper marched to him, grabbed him by the collar, and slashed the air with the scythe.

A gray mass appeared out of thin air. It looked like a thick smoke or a dark cloud. It started to move in circles, churning faster and faster until it formed a tunnel. I couldn't see what was at the other end of the tunnel, but it was dark and the cold draft I had felt earlier swept the store again.

I shivered.

He threw Morella into the tunnel. One by one, the other ghosts—no, he'd called them souls—followed, disappearing inside the murky interior. The last one was the woman, Sally. She said something to the reaper, but he shook his head. She gestured toward me, her mouth opening and closing.

"I'm not promising anything," he said, his voice losing its annoying arrogance. He glanced my way and added, "Later, gorgeous."

The tunnel closed behind him, and I released a breath. A hand landed on my shoulder, and I jumped.

"Mom? You scared me."

She smiled. In her hand were two bags of frozen spinach. "I knew you would forget these. What are you doing with that?" She pointed at the cheese grater.

My face burned. "I thought we might need a new one."

"No, the one at home still works," my ever-thrifty mother said firmly.

I placed the grater on a shelf by the boxes of un-popped corn and followed her. What would she say if I were to tell her what I'd just witnessed? She'd probably call Dr. Wendell again. My mother was a practical woman. Unlike my father, who was an author, she didn't believe in anything she couldn't see. As she used the self-checkout to pay for the cheese and spinach, I kept an eye out for more ghosts. Souls. I had to get used to referring to them as souls.

She placed the new purchases on top of the others and pushed the cart out of the store. I followed slowly, staying vigilant in case more souls appeared.

***

I saw a few souls here and there on our way home. They all stopped and stared at our car. I slid lower in my seat and wondered whether the arrogant reaper would collect them, too. Maybe he was here to clean up our town. I hoped so. I was tired of being a target.

"You've been quiet since we left the store," Mom said as we got closer to home. We were on Orchard Road, the street that split two of the largest vineyards in Kayville. "Are you okay?"

I shrugged. "Yeah."

"You know, you can talk to me if anything is bothering you."

Talking to her was out of the question. Dr. Wendell might prescribe more psych meds or insist on having me admitted again. "I heard you and Dad talk about me this morning. I don't want to be homeschooled, Mom. I'm going back to school on Monday."

"Sweetie—"

"No, Mom. I'm better, and I want to do this."

Her lips pinched in annoyance as she turned onto the road leading to our farm. "Let's discuss it after dinner."

Her firm voice said the discussion was closed. I leaned back against my seat and stared out the window. My parents had had me later in life and tended to be overly protective. Most of the time, I listened to them. Not this time. This might be the beginning of a trend. First, homeschooling. Next, not going away to college. The only college in town was a private one, and I planned to go as far away from Kayville as I could. There were way too many bad memories here.

Mom brought the car to a stop beside my Elantra, and I jumped out. I didn't speak as I helped haul groceries inside. Dad glanced up from his computer, his long graying hair disheveled as though he'd run his fingers through it.

He pulled glasses from the dangling chain around his neck and adjusted it on the bridge of his nose. He was far-sighted and wore round glasses, which had gone out of style eons ago. Dad didn't care about style. If he weren't an author, one would confuse him for an absentminded professor. He wrote sci-fi books for middle graders and had seriously loyal fans. Unfortunately, he hadn't won me over. I found it hard to get into his books. Still, I was proud of him.

"That was fast," he said, standing.

I shrugged and kept walking to the kitchen.

When I crossed the living room, Mom was by Dad's desk, the two of them talking in whispers, probably discussing me. Mom looked even shorter beside Dad. He was tall with graying hair and beard, and twinkling gray eyes I'd inherited. The rest of me came from my mother, including the big boobs and the blonde hair. Hers had more gray now though.

I ignored them and went back outside. I brought in more bags of groceries and almost bumped into Dad.

He scratched his beard and studied me. "You okay, muffin?"

"Yeah."

He grabbed most of the remaining bags. Dad carried his weight around the farm and was fit for his age. He usually woke up early to write and then helped Mom afterwards. He also tended to write late at night and was known to take odd naps in the afternoons. He was one of those dads who was around a lot but wasn't really there. How had he put it? His characters talked to him all the time.

"Your mother said you want to go back to school on Monday," he said as we started for the house.

I nodded. He often let Mom make most decisions about my life, and he went along with them. This time, I wanted him to take my side.

"Can you talk to her, please? It won't feel like I've recovered if I don't do normal things like normal kids. Being homeschooled will only remind me of PMI. Please, Dad. Please."

He sighed and nodded.

Mom glanced up when we entered the kitchen, her eyes volleying between us. "I think I'll make ground turkey lasagna without spinach today."

I placed the bags on the counter and eyed her. "You are buttering me up, Mom."

She smiled, a twinkle entering her honey-brown eyes. She always looked younger and less tired when she smiled. "No, I'm not. We'll still have spinach as a side dish and some green beans. Dinner will be ready in an hour."

"About school…"

"Not now, Cora," she said.

"Let her go to school, Penny," Dad said. "She's better now. That means doing normal things with her friends."

Mom frowned. She looked ready to argue.

"Remember what Wendell said, dear," Dad continued. "She must go back to doing normal things."

Mom sighed. "Okay, she can go, but on one condition."

"Yes! Thank you, Daddy. You are the best." I gave him a hug and ran to give Mom one too.

Mom chuckled and exchanged a look with Dad, who was putting groceries in the fridge. "You haven't heard what it is yet," she chided.

"Hey, you always say I have to learn to compromise. I get to go to school so…?"

"If anyone gives you a hard time about your stay at PMI, we want to know about it. Students can be cruel," Mom said firmly.

Like I was going to tell them things that happened at school. That would be so lame. They'd stopped fighting my battles when I started public school in junior high. In public school, you either swam or sank, and I'd floated to the top with the help of… I wasn't going to think about them. I wasn't going to think about Raine or Eirik.

"Deal," I fibbed.

"We mean it, Cora," Dad added. "I have no problem calling Raine and grilling her about what's going on at school if you keep things from us."

Heavy silence followed.

Raine was one name we'd avoided mentioning around my house since I came back. Raine Cooper was… No, Raine and I *had been* inseparable since she found me crying my eyes out in junior high, until she'd decided I wasn't worth her time. I hadn't heard a peep from her while I was in the psych ward. She never visited or called to see how I was doing, until I came home a week ago. Then she'd stopped by. Thankfully, Mom had known I didn't want to see her and told her to take a hike. Raine hadn't tried to see me again.

I'd thought we were tight, that nothing could ever come between us. Obviously, I was wrong. She hadn't wanted to be associated with a mental case. Like I said, I forgave her for dating Eirik, but this…

Thinking about her hurt and pissed me off at the same time. I started for the stairs. "I'll be in my room."

"Sweetheart, wait!" Mom called out.

Sighing, I turned.

"Give Raine a chance to explain when you see her. I was a bit hard on her when she stopped by."

I didn't want to hear this.

"And she swung by while you two were at the store today," Dad added.

I wanted to ask him what she'd said, but I clammed up. There was no excuse for the way she had behaved. Friends were supposed to be there for each other through the crappy times and good one. Raine had kicked me to the curb without a thought.

"Can I go now?" I asked.

They exchanged a look, and then Mom nodded.

"And can I have my electronics back, too?" When they exchanged another look, I groaned. "I'm just following the doctor's orders. You know, doing normal things. It's been a week already. I want to vlog and text Raine," I lied again. I had no intention of ever talking to that bitch.

"Okay," Mom said, smiling. "Dinner will be ready in an hour."

Dad walked to his desk, opened a drawer, and removed my laptop and phone. "Ease back into things, muffin."

"I plan to." I kissed his cheek, waved to Mom, and raced upstairs. I tried to turn on my cell phone, but the battery was dead. I plugged it in, booted the laptop, and sat at my desk.

My first concern was what my friends had been saying about me while I was gone. People in high school could be cruel, especially girls. On a given day, I'd stand toe-to-toe with any one of them and win. I didn't take crap from anyone. Things were different now. I had a horrible secret to hide. No, I had secrets. Secrets that could ruin me. I had been admitted at PMI, and I could see souls.

I visited social websites and checked my friends' updates. No one mentioned my absence. No one had missed me. Phooey. But I was tagged on pictures of Raine and… her new boyfriend? What happened to Eirik? Did she ditch him for the new guy?

Poor Eirik.

The more I read, the more I realized my friend… my *ex*-friend had changed. She was dating a quarterback. She didn't even like football. He was hot. I mean, model-like, drool-worthy, lip-smacking hot. Going by the pictures and comments, I wasn't the only one who thought so. They raved about his everything—hot bod, hair, eyes, accent. Even more interesting were the changes I saw in her.

Raine was naturally beautiful with gorgeous skin, thick luxurious hair she didn't need to style often, and the perfect body. She wasn't disproportional like me. I had big boobs. Add my hair color and everyone assumed I was a dumb blonde. The funniest thing was Raine didn't even consider herself beautiful. I'd never thought freckles were cute until I met her.

Before the tragic meet and my trip to PMI, her idea of makeup had been gloss and occasional mascara. From the pictures, she was curling her hair and wearing lipstick. She looked radiant.

There were pictures of her and her man on almost all the social websites I visited and some of just him and the team. According to the Kayville High grapevine, he was the reason the football team might make it to state this year.

Once again, I was envious of my best friend. And maybe a bit annoyed. She'd dumped Eirik fast. Was he heartbroken? Maybe I had a shot with him now. Nah, I didn't want him anymore. He had a chance to be with me and blew it.

Feeling crappy, I clicked on my vlog. I'd missed vlogging and interacting with…

No, this couldn't be right. I checked the date again on the video. The last vlog was posted a little over a week ago. I clicked on it, and my face filled the screen.

"Okay, guys, Hottie of the Week should be known to all of you. Six-foot-three, moves like a dancer, a six-pack you can bounce a quarter off of, and a body like a well-oiled machine." I fanned my face to the camera. "I know what you are thinking. How do I know? That's for me to know and you to guess. He has gorgeous, black wavy hair that comes to his shoulders and impossibly blue eyes any girl could stare into forever. If you still haven't guessed who he is, he rides a Harley and has the most amazing accent. If you haven't seen his pictures online, you're missing out. Let me know what you think. Till next time."

Nothing made sense. When did I post the video? How could I have made it or posted it? The date at the corner said it was posted ten days ago. I was still in the crazy house ten days ago.

I clicked on the next vlog entry, then the next one, my stomach churning. They'd been posted every week I'd been away. Had I sneaked into the doctor's office and used his computer while in a drug-induced haze?

I re-watched the first video, studying my body language and clothes. I didn't act drugged, and the pink silk shirt was mine. I didn't remember taking it with me to the hospital. I jumped up and checked my closet. The shirt was there along with the dresses and jackets I wore on the other videos. Another thing caught my attention. The background in each video was the same. I'd taped all of them here in my bedroom.

"Are you editing another video or do you just like watching yourself?" a familiar voice mocked from behind me.

My heart tripped then started to pound. The reaper from the store was in my house. In my bedroom. What was he doing here?

2. Echo

Before I could turn, a hand pushed my hair away from my shoulder and warm lips kissed my neck. Sensation slammed through me, and my breath caught. I froze, even as my body reacted and trembled. Hands slid down my chest and cupped my breasts with such ease, as though he'd done it before.

I gripped his hands and yanked them away from my chest. "Get your filthy hands off—"

He moved fast and covered my mouth, swallowing the rest of my words, his tongue sliding between my lips in a kiss that drove all thoughts from my head.

My world exploded, blinding sensations surging, swelling, and crashing through me. I mumbled a protest. At least, I think I did, but he angled his head and deepened the kiss, his tongue boldly caressing mine.

Holy crap! Was this the kiss of death? Was this how he yanked people's souls from their bodies? I tried to resist, but I was no longer in control. He'd taken over every one of my senses and had me completely under his power. Dizziness washed over me as I floated away to a place where nothing mattered but his mouth and the way he made me feel.

There were worse ways to die, I decided. At least this way, I'd go happy. As though he'd heard me, he lifted his head. I pried my eyelids open and stared at him.

His face slowly came into focus. His hood was down, baring his face and hair. His skin was tanned and smooth, the shadow on his chin making him look even sexier. His golden-green eyes flashed with a naughty gleam as though he was thoroughly enjoying himself. His shaggy dark brown hair was cut in an asymmetrical style, low on the sides and longer on top. The style looked too tame for a leather-wearing reaper, even though he'd changed his leather shirt for a black T-shirt. I'd expected him to have longer, unkempt locks. Up close, his face was even more beautiful, and he smelled so good.

"I love it when you lust after me," he said in a husky voice. "I've missed you too, sweet-cheeks."

Sanity returned.

"What... what do you mean?" I managed to whisper, my lips still tingling from his kiss.

"It amazes me how you can be so devious and twisted, yet look so sweet and innocent." He kissed me again, laughter rumbling through his chest and vibrating through my body.

I wasn't ready to die yet, damn it. No matter how intoxicating his kisses were. And I wasn't twisted. Nothing he said made sense.

I brought my teeth down hard on his lower lip. More laughter came from him. Then he leaned back, licked the drop of blood, and exposed the teeth marks I'd left on his lip.

My eyes widened when the cut slowly disappeared. He self-healed? Of course, he did. He was the grim reaper. I opened my mouth to ask him how long I had left, but he spoke first.

"You want play rough?" he asked. "Good. That's just how I like it."

"No. Don't—"

He scooped me up and moved so fast my room was a blur. One second I was on the chair, the next flat on my back on the bed. Panic coursed through me.

"What are you doing, you sick bastard?" I snapped.

"Playing your game." A wicked smile lifted the corner of his lips.

I scooted to the other side of the bed, but he was there, blocking me.

"Where are you going when I came here specifically for you, Cora?" he said.

My heart threatened to leap from my chest. "Right now?"

"Yes. Right now. I want you, Cora." He went into hyper-speed. When he stopped, he was coatless and shirtless and straddling me, most of his weight on his knees.

My head spun, and I was so confused I just stared at him like an idiot. I didn't understand why he had to be shirtless to take my soul, but I guess if I had to die, I didn't mind being escorted by a shirtless hunk.

He had a broad, masculine chest covered with black tattoos. The tats, glowing and dimming, continued down between his rock-hard abs and disappeared under the waistband of his pants. The leather pants stretched across his thighs and hugged his...

"Keep looking at me like that and the game ends now," he said in a husky voice.

I dragged my eyes away. What in the world was I doing ogling *him*, the being about to yank my soul from my chest. I should be screaming. Begging for mercy. No, I wasn't going to beg, and if I screamed, my parents would rush upstairs. I didn't want my parents to find my lifeless body upstairs.

Maybe I could reason with the reaper. Buy more time. "Can I have more time with my parents before…" My voice trembled to a stop. I cleared it and finished, "you take me away?"

He cocked his eyebrow.

"Please," I added.

He chuckled and ran a finger down my neck to the top button on my shirt, leaving behind heated flesh. "Begging, Cora? That's new. You can have tonight and the whole of tomorrow." He undid the top button of my shirt. "I'm not taking you away. You're coming with me. We all have jobs to do."

I grabbed his wrist. "So I can have until tomorrow night?"

"Sure." He studied me with narrowed eyes then smirked, reached behind him with his other hand, and pulled out a weird-looking knife. It wasn't the mini scythe. This one was different. It had a thinner blade and a ridged handle as though it was specifically made for his long fingers. I swallowed, staring at the blade and then his face.

"I'm done playing games, sweetheart," he said. "I want you now." He lowered the blade toward my heart. I stopped breathing.

"Please," I whispered. "You said I had—"

"The begging is a nice touch, but you're overdoing it," he mocked, sliding the blade under my shirt. "You don't want to bore me, Cora."

Part of me wanted to close my eyes and let him finish me off, but another part refused to cower. Let him look me in the eyes as he killed me, the jerk. How could he promise me more time then change his mind? Was this how he did things? Gave false hope to the dying? I hoped my face haunted him for eternity.

I glared at him, and our eyes locked as I braced myself for the pain that was sure to follow. Instead, the buttons on my shirt flew across my room as he cut them off in one clean sweep. Cold air rushed to my skin. Instinctively, I pulled at the gaping fabric and tried to cover myself.

"You don't want to do that either, doll-face," he warned.

I held my breath again when the cold tip of the knife touched my skin. Any moment, I expected him to yank my soul out with the blade.

Hadn't he pointed his scythe at Morello's soul and caused him to freeze?

"I want to talk to my parents first," I demanded. At least that was what I'd meant to do. My voice came out shaky. Totally pathetic.

"Now?" The blade moved toward my heart.

"Yes. To say good... good..." Tears rushed to my eyes, and I couldn't finish the sentence. Not wanting him to see them, I closed my eyes and braced myself again. Once again, the pain didn't come. I opened one eye then the other.

He was staring at me with a frown.

"Are you okay?" he asked.

I started to nod, but then shook my head. "No."

"You're crying. What's wrong?"

What did he expect? That I should laugh in the face of death? "I don't want to... to..." I couldn't bring myself to say "die".

He shifted, so he was kneeling, though he still straddled me. "Why didn't you just say so? I would have stopped."

I blinked. My voice shook as I mumbled, "You would?"

"Of course." He shoved the knife somewhere behind him. "What's the fun in foreplay when you're not enjoying it?"

Enjoying it? What kind of a sick bastard toyed with people before killing them? Trying not to lose it, I narrowed my eyes at him. "Do you mean I have to show you that I'm scared before you kill me?"

He looked at me like I was the village idiot. "Kill you? What are you talking about?"

"Just now. You were about to kill me and take my soul."

He laughed and gracefully got off the bed. "Nice comic relief, sweet-cheeks." He bent and came up with his T-shirt.

"I'm a Grimnir, not a killer. There are rules and there are *rules*. I might break and bend a few, but I don't cross some lines. I don't kill my people. Where have you been the last week?"

Now I was the one confused. His people? "Last week?"

"You were supposed to meet me, but you just disappeared. What happened?" He pulled on his shirt, tugging it over his broad chest, his movement graceful. The sleeves hugged his hard chest and masculine arms. By the time he covered his ridged abs, I was sitting up and trying, unsuccessfully I might add, not to drool while pulling my button-less shirt across my chest.

"Meet you?" I asked. My thought process had slowed to a snail's pace. "I've never seen you before until today at the store. I think, uh, you are confusing me with someone else."

"Oh, sweetheart." He reached out and twirled a lock of my hair around his forefinger. "I'd never confuse you with anyone else. I know you in the only way that matters. Intimately. Talking is for those who lack imagination, and the little games we play are just, uh, foreplay." He caressed my lower lip. "Spices things up."

"Cut that out." I swatted his hand, heat rushing to my cheeks. Needing space, I scooted to the other side of the bed. "You are mistaken. I've never…"

"Never what?"

I couldn't just blurt out I was a virgin. That I'd been waiting for Eirik, the guy I loved, to one day wake up and notice me.

"Never mind. So what you're saying is that the entire time I thought you were about to kill me, you were playing a game?"

"Foreplay, doll-face." He wiggled his brow. "That's how you like it."

"Are you nuts? You scared the crap out of me, and over what? An imagined relationship between us?"

"Imagined?" He appeared beside me in a flash. I took a step back, but he followed. His earthy scent and warmth swirled around my senses, screwing with my thoughts. "Would you like a blow-by-blow description of what you and I have been doing the past several weeks? How much you like it? How often you—"

"No," I snapped, my cheeks burning. "Stop it! I don't want to be part of your twisted game, reaper. What? You're bored escorting souls, so you have to find people to screw with?"

His eyes narrowed. "Are you serious?"

I wanted to claw his eyes out. Right at that instant, I didn't care that they were gorgeous or that he had the most incredible lashes I'd ever seen on a man. I wanted to neuter him.

"Do I look like I'm having fun?"

"Then tell me how I know personal things about you, Cora Jemison," he said, leaning in. "Born on December sixteenth in Portland, natural blonde, curtains and carpet." He grinned when heat rushed to my face. "You wear bra size 30 D, hate spinach, but love Hawaiian pizza. Your best friend is Raine Cooper, and until I came along," he paused and smirked, "you thought you had a crush on Eirik Seville. The god-child didn't deserve you."

"It isn't a crush. I love Eirik."

"No, you don't. I could tell you a thing or two about him that would make you run—"

"Not interested. He's perfect. And Raine is no longer my BFF." Gripping my ripped shirt, I moved as far away from him as I possibly could. "You could have gotten that information from my friends or my vlog."

His arched eyebrows shot up. "Okay, let's move on to intimate details. You love it when I kiss your neck. Makes you purr like a kitten. You have two distinct birthmarks: one on the underside of your left breast and the other on your inner thigh, where only a lover would know. You want to cover both with tattoos but you're scared of the tat guy getting too close."

How could he possibly know such things? Covering my birthmarks was something I'd never discussed with anyone, not even Raine. No, that wasn't true. The topic of body mutilation had come up during a group session with Dr. Wendell at the psych ward, and I'd mentioned wanting to ink myself.

"GAH! You are a sick, perverted jerk! You had your souls spy on me. No wonder I'd wake up and find them standing over my bed."

"Listen, baby-doll. I love playing games with you because it makes sex great between us, but this is ridiculous." He moved away and snatched his duster. "Stop pretending you don't know me. If you want to end things, just say so. It's obvious you'd rather be a Mortal than…" He looked ready to grab me and shake some sense into me. "Forget it."

"Than what? Be with you, someone who's obviously insane?" I pulled a hoodie off the peg on my wall and yanked it on. "What kind of a reaper goes around making up stories about people? Kissing them like… like…"

"Like what?" he asked, the annoying smirk back on his face. "Like I know you? Like I know what you like and how you like it?"

"Like you want to suck their soul, you jackass." I snapped and tried to zip up the hoodie, but my hands were shaking too much. "You want my soul, take it, but don't go around claiming we are lovers when I've never seen your smug, condescending face from wherever hellhole you crawled up from. If this is some kind of reaper joke because I dispersed a few souls, then hardy har har. The joke's on me. Now get out of my room."

He stared at me as though I'd lost my mind, and then he chuckled.

"Jerk." I grabbed a pillow and threw it at him.

He caught it and threw it on my bed. Then he opened his arms. "Come here. I should be consoling you, not giving you a hard time. The Norns must have erased your memories. That's why you can't remember me."

"Norns? I don't know what those are or care. Just. Get. Out." I grabbed the nearest thing, the poker I'd used to disperse ghosts, and threw it at him. He didn't even attempt to block it. It bounced off his chest and landed on the floor with a thud.

"Don't worry, sweetheart. I'll find out why and help you remember everything." His glance went to my bed, and he gave me a slow smile, the implication clear.

"In your dreams, *reaper*," I snapped, making the word sound like something that had crawled out of a sewer. "Leave."

He stopped smirking, his tattoos appearing and starting to glow. "Someone is coming." He angled his head and listened. "Heavier footsteps mean it's your father. I'm a Grimnir, not grim or reaper. Grimnir." He moved fast and was in front of me before I could blink, his hand cradling my head, his lips an inch from mine. "And you and I are lovers."

"No, we're not." I tried to push him away, but it was like pushing a wall. A warm wall with a pounding heart and scents designed to mess with a girl's head. His eyes went to my lips. "Don't you dare," I said through gritted teeth.

"Oh, but I do." Then he kissed me.

I'd expected an invasion of my senses. Instead I got gentleness and something I couldn't explain. My hands stopped pushing him away. My fingers curled and bunched his T-shirt. I wasn't sure what I meant to do. Pull him closer, perhaps. All I knew was the fight had left me.

He lifted his head, saving me from humiliating myself. Then he opened his mouth and spoke. "You want me, Cora Jemison. Your mind might not remember, but your body does."

I wanted to knee him hard, but he was already moving away.

"If the Norns did a clean sweep, you don't remember my name. It's Echo. Don't forget it, because you and I have a good thing going here, Cora. I'm coming back for you."

That sounded ominous. "Don't bother."

"When it comes to you, nothing is a bother." He stopped next to the full-length mirror on my closet door, his eyes not leaving me, his smirk in place. The surface of the mirror changed texture, growing grainy then cloudy just like the cloud I'd seen him conjure in the store. It churned and formed a tunnel to nowhere. Probably to hell.

Echo winked just as the door flew open and my father stood in the doorway with a worried expression.

"Later, doll-face," Echo said.

Dad didn't seem to hear him or see the portal on the mirror. "What's going on, Cora? We heard you yell." He glanced around as though checking for an intruder.

"I'm fine, Daddy." I searched for an excuse and remembered the laptop. "I was online and, uh, kind of overreacted to something I read. I'll keep it down."

He frowned, his eyes on the laptop. "What was it about? You?"

"No-oo." I laughed, though my voice sounded shaky. "It's the stupid fashion trend. I have no idea who comes up with what's in and what's not." I rolled my eyes and gave a fake shudder, then glanced at him from the corner of my eye. He was still frowning, obviously not buying my act. "Leather is big this fall, and I absolutely loathe the feel of leather on my skin, unless they are boots, which reminds me I have to go shopping. I need a new jacket and sweaters and, oh, pants. Several pairs." Dad winced. Fashion wasn't his thing. "You or Mom can drive me into town, since you won't let me drive."

"I, uh, your mom can take you." He started to close the door. "Dinner will be ready in fifteen minutes. Come downstairs and help your mother set the table."

"I'll be down in a minute." The door closed behind him, and I slowly exhaled.

I sat on the bed and stared at my reflection. What was going on? I jumped up and stripped. The birthmarks Echo had mentioned were still there. Either someone was playing a cruel joke on me or I'd entered an alternate reality where I was having an affair with an annoying, arrogant grim reaper.

I'd take the cruel joke any day.

3. Two Places or Two People

The closer I got to my school, the more nervous I became. The last two days had been a nightmare—worrying about school, Echo returning with more outlandish stories, watching the videos on my vlog over and over, and trying to find anything that made sense.

The annoying reaper didn't come back, and I didn't find anything useful online. It was me on those videos, not someone impersonating me or a doppelganger. The mannerism, facial expressions, even the laugh on those videos said it was me.

But how had I sneaked out of the psych ward? Had I created a portal through a mirror the way Echo had done, but had been too pumped full of psych meds to remember? The problem was I didn't sound drugged or look loopy in the videos. Not knowing how I'd recorded them was driving me nuts.

For two days, I'd researched supernatural phenomena. Astral projection was a possible explanation. I could see souls, so it wasn't a stretch. Echo flashed his tats and became invisible, so my astral image could have hooked up with him.

Right. It sounded like something straight out of a fantasy novel. I would have remembered Echo. Making out with him. I just hated the idea of having had sex with him. How could I have forgotten my first time?

Dad stopped at the stop sign, and I pulled up behind him. I'd insisted on bringing my Elantra even though he and Mom had caused a big stink about it. How the heck was I going to go back to being normal when I couldn't drive myself to school? After clothes shopping with Mom yesterday and souls following us everywhere like zombies, I knew I couldn't let her chauffeur me around. She'd almost caught me glaring at a soul.

A sudden cold draft filled my car as I stepped on the gas. I smothered a scream and slammed on the brakes when my eyes met Echo's in the rearview mirror.

"Where did you come from?" I screeched.

Echo grinned at me from the back seat of my car. "Morning to you too, doll-face."

"How did you—? Never mind. You probably walk through metal, too." His tats were glowing again.

"Yes, I do," he bragged.

"What are you doing here? Didn't I tell you to leave me alone?"

"Didn't I tell you I can't? I miss you." He draped his arms around the headrest of my seat and scooted forward.

Heat rushed to my face. The thought of him as my lover filled my insides with butterflies. That it wasn't nausea annoyed me. He was the grim reaper, damn it. A being I was supposed to fear and revile, not... I wasn't sure what I felt when he was around. Annoyed was at the top of the list.

"I told you I don't know you and we are not..."

"Lovers? I know. That's new."

"What?"

"The blush. You never blush, even when I do the naughtiest—"

"Oh shut up, you letch. It's like you have a one-track mind."

"That's not my fault. You never wanted to talk. Not that I minded. I loved having you rip off my clothes."

"Don't worry; it won't happen again," I shot back as my body heated with images his words evoked.

"Want to bet?"

A car honked, and I realized I hadn't moved since he appeared in my car. There was a long line of cars behind me.

"Now see what you made me do." I eased off the brake. Ahead, Dad's truck was nowhere in sight.

"Sorry about that," Echo said, but he didn't sound or look it. He reached out and lifted the hair on my right shoulder.

I swatted at his hand. "Stop that."

"Can't help it." He planted a kiss on my neck. The car swayed as I momentarily lost control.

"I'm serious. Quit messing with me, Echo."

"You smell amazing." He trailed kisses up my neck to my ear and inhaled.

The sensations that invaded my body were downright frightening. Not even Eirik had ever made me feel like this. If I could forget Echo was a lunatic and I was losing my mind, I would have enjoyed the sensation.

I reached up and tried to push his head away, but it was like moving a boulder. Worse, my hand sunk into his hair. It was silky, and for one brief moment, I wanted to run my fingers through it, maybe hold his head in place and savor the moment.

He bit my ear. I squealed and, once again, lost control of the car. "Dang it, Echo. We could get into an accident."

"But we self-heal."

I self-healed, too? Nice. No, not nice. I refused to start buying into his crazy assumptions. "I could hurt someone."

"There're just Mortals. If it's their time to go, it's their time to go. No force of nature can stop that. No, that's not true. Norns could. You look breathtaking this morning. Love that shade of red on you. Very vampy. What is it you once told me? Red gives you the extra oomph when you are having a shitty day."

The only person who knew that was Raine. "Who told you that?"

"You, doll-face. Why are you having a shitty day?"

I glared ahead. "Because you are screwing with my head. How come you keep saying things I don't remember?"

"I told you. The Norns put a whammy on you."

"Norns?"

"Deities of destiny. Mean, bitter hags. They control the destiny of all beings—Mortals, Immortals, even the gods. Interestingly, I just found out why they targeted you and erased your memories."

"Why?" Not that I believed his rambling.

"Say please."

I was tempted to ignore him, but something weird had happened to me and I wanted answers. I eased the car into a parking spot across from my school, switched off the engine, and turned to look at Echo. He was dressed in all leather again today. I realized that what I'd assumed was a leather shirt was actually a vest of some kind. Once again, he wore fingerless gloves and silver Gothic rings with weird markings.

"Please," I said through clenched teeth.

He touched his lips. "I want a kiss, too."

I narrowed my eyes. "Why are you such a tool all the time? You think this is fun for me? Not remembering things? Waking up one morning and seeing souls? Ending up in a psych ward, where they pumped me full of drugs, then coming home only to be met by you, a reaper?"

"Grimnir," he corrected then frowned. "Are those the fake memories the Norns gave you? Psych ward? That's just wrong."

"I was in a psych ward," I snapped.

He raised his hands. "Okay. No need to be snippy."

"I'm not—"

He covered my mouth then smirked when I bit his hand. I bore down until I tasted blood. He didn't even wince. His grin broadened instead.

"Drink my blood, doll-face. Bond with me for eternity."

The thought was scary. I pushed his hand away and wiped my mouth. "Ew. Can your blood do that?"

He laughed.

"Will you be serious for even a second?" I asked.

"Don't you want to be mine forever?"

"Ew, no." I made a face. "I don't even like you."

"What's liking me got to do with anything? As long as you want me, I'm good."

"I *don't* want you."

He gave me a slow wicked smile. "Want me to prove it?"

Silence followed, and I could feel heat crawling up my face. He reached out to touch my face, but I dodged his hand.

"Okay, I'm kidding about the blood," he said. "But you can bite me any time." He proudly showed me the bite mark I'd left on his hand. The runes on his hand glowed bright and the wound sealed, the blood disappearing too. "It's nothing my runes can't heal. To bond with me, sweet-cheeks, I'd have to rune you."

"Rune me?"

"Etch these," he pointed at his tattoos, "on you with my blade. Don't say anything. Your father is here. I'll explain about Norns later. Right now, I gotta go. Souls don't wait around forever, you know. They run, and the lucky ones follow hot Grimnirs like you."

I turned to find Dad by my door.

"I'm not a grim," I said through clenched teeth.

"Grimnir, doll-face. Stopping calling us grim. It's insulting. Do I get a kiss before I leave?"

"No."

"Oh, come on."

Ignoring him, I opened the door and hauled out my backpack. Echo was already outside, looking like the angel of death in his black clothes and duster, the only color was his smooth golden skin with glowing tats. No, not tats. Runes.

I glared, but it was wasted on him. He just smirked, leaned against my car, and gave me a slow perusal from under heavy-lidded eyes. I shivered. Did he have to do that? He must have perfected that pose in front of a mirror, but he looked so hot. Ignoring him wasn't easy, but I managed to drag my eyes away. The parking lot was empty except for a few cars, but soon it would fill with cars and bikes. Oregon was a green state and unless it was snowing, a lot of students biked to and from school.

"I'll carry your backpack," Dad said.

"It's okay, Dad. I got it." I locked my door. Echo still hovered.

Dad touched the bottom of my backpack. "What are you carrying? It looks heavy."

I rolled my eyes. "They're just books, Dad. And please, stop treating me like I'm sick. If I can drive myself to school, I can carry my own backpack."

"And if you engage your runes, you can carry him without breaking a sweat, too," Echo added.

I didn't look his way, but I put that information away for later. Not that I had any runes or intention of engaging them. Whatever that meant. Dad still studied me with a frown.

"You've lost quite a bit of weight," he said.

"I agree," Echo said. "I felt it yesterday when I lifted you. I think you were pining for me and refused to eat."

Ignoring him was becoming harder.

"They don't exactly serve large potions at the crazy house," I said.

Dad winced, and I wished I hadn't brought up the mental hospital. He'd looked uneasy whenever they visited me at PMI. It was probably hard for him to accept that his only child had been institutionalized.

"Told you those were false memories from the Norns," Echo interjected.

I wish I could tell him to shut up. I reached up and kissed Dad's cheek. "Love you, Dad."

"How come he gets a kiss and I don't?" Echo asked.

"What was that for?" Dad asked at the same time.

"For being the greatest dad." I started across the street, and he fell in step beside me. Echo flanked me on the other side. He was saying something, but I tuned him out. He talked too much. More cars screeched to a stop behind us. I glanced back, recognizing a few. Soon the front entrance would be packed with students wondering where I'd been. Staring. Pointing. My worst nightmare.

"School," Echo said and shuddered. "Why Valkyries insist on mingling with Mortals in this cesspool boggles the mind. You swore you wouldn't come back here either, but since the Norns screwed with your memories, I suppose you don't remember that."

I let my hair fall forward, so Dad wouldn't see my face, and I glared at Echo. "Just go away," I mouthed. "Please?"

His eyes narrowed. Then he sighed. "Okay, but you owe me."

"For what?" I wanted to ask, but I didn't want to know the answer. His crazy stories were adding to my nightmare. I didn't check to see him disappear, but I knew the moment he was gone. The air was less charged. It was as though he emitted some pulse and I was tuned in to it, which was crazy because every time he appeared, frigid air followed.

We entered the double doors leading to the front office. The secretary waved us into the principal's office. I didn't really want to see Mr. Elliot. A phone call explaining my return would have been enough, but Dad had insisted on talking to him.

"Mr. Jemison," the principal said, standing up. He shook Dad's hand, nodded in my direction, and indicated the chairs across from his.

"So what I can do for you?" he asked, sitting.

"My daughter," Dad glanced at me and smiled, "has missed quite a bit of school, and I'd like to help her catch up. I do not want her to repeat a class or for her grades to suffer."

Mr. Elliot smiled and leaned forward. "That's very admirable, Mr. Jemison. But like I told you in the e-mail, Cora is a great student and will have no problem catching up."

Yeah, right. I was going to have no social life for the rest of the year.

Dad frowned. "You don't think she needs help? She's been gone a while."

Mr. Elliot smiled. "The teachers will give her packets of missed work, and she can take any quizzes and tests she missed. But I don't think she's missed enough for us to worry about. Her grades are good. I checked. If she has problems grasping concepts, the teachers will work with her."

I tuned them out and slouched in my seat. Most students who'd missed weeks of school often struggled to catch up. Raine could help me. No, I wasn't running to her for help. I'd plod through the packets alone. When Dad and the principal stood, I realized they were done talking.

Outside the office, students hurried past, but no one stared or pointed. Dad glanced left and right before turning to peer at me. He looked worried.

"Go," I said. "I'll be fine."

He hesitated. "You sure?"

"CORA!"

I turned and was almost knocked over by a dark-haired girl from my swim team. Hanna Jenkins, swim nickname Kicker. We weren't buddies or even remotely close, so the exuberance was surprising.

"Where have you been?" she asked. She glanced at Dad and grinned. "Hi, Mr. Jemison."

Dad wore a confused expression. Even though he'd attended my swim meets, I doubted he remembered Kicker. We didn't hang out outside team activities.

"I'll see you at home later, muffin," Dad said.

"Okay, Dad. Bye."

I gave him a brief wave, happy to be at school and, at the same time, worried.

Kicker bumped me with her shoulder. "Seriously, what happened to you? You didn't answer my texts or calls. It's like you just disappeared after the game."

"Game?" The last event I'd attended with her was the tragic swim meet.

"You know, the home game. You kissed Drew." She fanned her face. "It was smoking hot. Torin and Raine definitely have competition with you two. I'm amazed you didn't call him. The poor guy kept calling and texting me, asking where you were. He was worried about you. He looked terrible when I saw him at Keith's funeral. I mean, he and Keith were close, so of course he was bummed by his death, but I think he was also worried about your sudden disappearance."

"Keith Paulson died?"

Kicker nodded. "Deidre Fuller and Casey Riverside, too. It was a crazy night."

I remember Deidre, a cheerleader who'd acted like she was above everyone else. Casey had been her opposite. Sweet and nice. She'd dated Blaine Chapman, the former quarterback.

"That's too bad," I said.

"It's like our sports teams are being stalked by death or something. Drew said you were kissing, and then you just disappeared."

There was no way I'd kiss Drew Cavanaugh. He was handsome, popular, and loaded, but he wasn't my type. I didn't date preppy guys.

"Cora?"

I glanced up and realized we'd reached our lockers. Thankfully, Raine wasn't there. Her locker was next to mine. "I'm sorry. I got hurt that night, too, and had to go away for a while."

"Oh, why didn't you tell me?" She peered at me, her voice funny. "No one knew where you were, except Raine."

I frowned. "Raine?"

"I asked her on Monday if she'd heard from you and she acted kind of weird. Then yesterday, she said you were away and would be back soon. When I pressed her for more information, she blew me off."

Raine had lied. Why?

"My parents decided I should stay with my aunt in Portland for a while," I fibbed, putting my books away and selecting what I needed for my morning classes. Kicker kept staring at me. "I hit my head pretty hard and had a severe concussion, so my memories have been a bit off."

She closed her locker and moved closer. Other students were entering the hallway, but they weren't staring at us. Still, Kicker lowered her voice. "You mean you don't remember stuff?"

I nodded.

"Like what?"

"I can't seem to remember the last month or so, including the home game or kissing Drew."

Kicker's eyes widened. "Whoa."

"The doctors said I'll recover the lost memories, but it's going to take a while."

"Dang! That sucks."

"That's why I didn't call you or Drew." We started toward the English wing. Raine and her boyfriend were coming toward us. I saw them first. They were wrapped up in their own world. Behind them were the blonde and the guy with silver hair she'd come with to my house.

Raine looked up and saw me. She smiled and waved. I ignored her and followed Kicker into the hallway to our left, not slowing down when Raine called my name. She and I were so over.

"When was the home game?" I asked.

"Uh, two Fridays ago," Kicker said.

"So I was here at school, except last week?" I asked.

Kicker laughed. "You are really serious. I mean, you're not bullshitting me to spare my feelings or anything like that."

"I'm serious. I, uh, don't remember much."

"The dinners at my place?"

I shook my head.

"The Halloween Invitational when we had a humiliating loss to the Cougars and later ended up at Sondra's, eating cold pizza and watching Psycho?"

Me eating cold pizza? Ew. My astral projection or the other me was either a total loser or a nymphomaniac, if Echo was to be believed. "No, I don't remember any of that."

Kicker sighed. "You were here at school, until after the game. We started hanging out weeks ago. You, me, Naya, and Sondra."

"Raine?"

"She's not swimming anymore and is always with her boyfriend. I assumed you two had a fight or something. You, kind of, stopped hanging out with her, and you never wanted us to invite her."

Maybe I just hadn't wanted to be a third wheel, or Raine had realized I wasn't myself. That didn't explain how I'd been in two places at the same time, because my stay at PMI wasn't a figment of my imagination. I wasn't too sure about the astral projection theory, and my gut instinct told me not to trust anything Echo said. Destiny deities erased my memories—how convenient for him.

"You flirted with Drew a lot, and Eirik too," Kicker added. "He's gone now."

My stomach dropped. "Eirik?"

Kicker nodded. "Of course, you don't remember. His family moved."

I was actually relieved to hear that. I thought she'd meant he'd died. "To where?"

Kicker shrugged. "I don't know. Doc just told the team he was gone. Maybe Raine knows."

I wasn't sure what was more painful: Eirik not visiting me or leaving without even saying goodbye. I must have meant nothing to him all these years.

***

"We missed you last week, Ms. Jemison," Mr. Pepperidge, my English teacher, said, handing me a paper. "Good job on that essay. See me after class."

I glanced down at the paper. A+. The paper was typed, had my name at the top, and was submitted two weeks ago. More proof I'd been in two places at the same time. Maybe taking psych meds had been good for me because I hadn't received an A in English since I started high school.

The class was finishing Scarlet Letter, so I was lost and bored. I waited for the students to leave the room then approached the teacher. My heart pounding, I was sure he was going to say I was a fraud. He handed me a copy of the book.

"Read it and choose two characters or events in the story and demonstrate how Hawthorne describes them from different points of view and how this affects your impression of them. It's nothing big, just a short essay."

"Thanks, Mr. P." I put the book on top of my folder.

He smiled. "I think you should seriously consider taking AP English literature and composition next year. Your writing has improved tremendously in the last month."

"Okay, I will," I fibbed and hurried out of the classroom.

Every class after that was the same. I'd become an exemplary student. A genius. Even math, my most hated subject. I had aced every quiz, test, and homework assignment. The handwriting on handwritten tests was mine down to the way I wrote uppercase L so it looked like the English pound sign minus the short horizontal line.

Either Echo had been right all along and I never really left until last week, or my astral projection had attended classes while I was trapped behind PMI walls. I was going with the latter because there was no way that annoying reaper could have been my lover.

After what Kicker had told me, I was feeling a little charitable toward Raine, but I wasn't ready to be pals yet. Twice, between classes, I saw her, and each time she smiled. I ignored her, or tried to. It wasn't easy. We'd been friends since junior high and had shared so much.

I was putting my books away before heading to lunch when she and her boyfriend cornered me. He was more striking in person than in the pictures online and had amazing blue eyes, yet something in them reminded me of Echo. Maybe it was the alertness or the edginess pulsing from him.

"Hey," Raine said.

I wanted to ignore her again and even tried to leave, but her boyfriend blocked my path. I glared at him. Sighing, I turned and faced Raine. There was no point showing her how much she'd hurt me, and her whipped puppy look was getting tired. She'd never been good at hiding her emotions.

"Hi," I said. "I like your hair."

She blinked as though surprised. "Thanks. I know what you'll say about this. I use a curling iron."

I wasn't ready to be that chummy with her. If she wanted to ruin her hair, I didn't care.

"Uh, this is Torin St. James," she said when she realized I wasn't going to say anything else. "Torin, Cora Jemison, my best friend."

Yeah, right. Some best friend.

Torin smiled and nodded, but he continued to watch me as though he expected me to, I don't know, say something mean to Raine. What would he do?

I gave him a challenging glance and said, "I saw your pictures online."

"It's ridiculous how he always ends up on some girl's page," Raine said. "Alone. Shirtless."

"Actually, the ones I saw were of the two of you," I corrected.

"Oh." She glanced at him and elbowed him when he grinned. She leaned against him and focused on me. "Uh, it's nice to have you back, Cora."

I shrugged. "It's weird."

She exchanged a look with Torin and frowned. "What do you mean?"

"It's like I never left." I waited for her to say something about my psych ward stay, or give me a clue about what she knew. I wasn't sure what she'd told my mother a week ago or what Mom had told her. I hadn't cared enough to ask.

An awkward silence followed.

"We stopped by your place on Friday after school," Raine said. "I don't know if your father told you."

"He did. I meant to call you." I didn't explain why I hadn't.

"Do you want to have lunch with us?" Raine asked tentatively.

I shrugged. "I promised Kicker I'd sit with her and the others."

Raine made a face, not hiding her disappointment. "Actually we were thinking of heading downtown." She glanced at Torin and a silent communication passed between them. "But I'll join you guys. Torin hates school food."

"I don't mind eating it once in a while," he said in a British accent, his voice deep and smooth. No wonder the comments online had raved about his accent. It was subtle, beautiful.

"No, you are going downtown," she whispered to him.

"Trying to get rid of me, Freckles?" he teased, caressing her cheek.

"Yeah. So play nice and go."

"I don't play nice, luv." He glanced at me and smiled. "See you around, Cora. As for you," he touched Raine's nose, "you can't get rid of me that easily." He dropped a lingering kiss on her lips and sauntered away. She watched him. As though he knew she was watching, he turned and winked.

"Show off," Raine muttered.

"Wow, hard to believe you are dating *the* quarterback," I said sarcastically as we started for the cafeteria. "You hate football."

Raine smiled. "I know."

"Do you watch him practice?"

"Yeah." Her cheeks grew pink. "He likes it."

I laughed. "What have you done with the Raine I knew? You know, the one who laughed at girls who did things for their guys and never, ever dressed up for school."

"Don't start. So how is your first day back going?"

I shrugged. "Okay, I guess."

"Do you remember the meet we had over a month ago? You know, when lightning hit the pool and killed some of our teammates?"

Yeah, the day my nightmares started. It was etched in my brain. She'd warned people to leave the pool. Then there was chaos as bolts of lightning rained on the pool. Whoever said lightning didn't hit a place twice had lied. I couldn't remember what had happened to Raine, but I'd seen the glowing beings lead the souls of the dead into a tunnel filled with colors. Three of the beings had tried to lure Raine away.

Not sure why she was asking, I decided to play it safe. "Vaguely."

She frowned. "What do you mean?"

"I don't remember anything, except you warning people to leave the pool just before lightning hit."

Raine frowned. "You don't remember the last six weeks?"

I shook my head, though I was dying to ask her about my behavior during those weeks. "It's all blank. It's like I was never here. How did you know something bad was about to happen at that meet? What happened afterwards?"

She went pale. "I can't explain how I knew. I just did. I was gone for two weeks after that, and when I came back, it was really hard to adjust. People treated me like I had cooties."

"That's awful. Why?"

"Everyone in school was talking about the meet. They labeled me a witch. If it weren't for Torin and Eirik, I don't know if I would have made it through those weeks."

Was that why she hadn't visited me? No, she hadn't visited because I was here, too. Someone shoot me. This was so freaking confusing.

"No one seems to care now," I mumbled.

"Dating Torin stopped the gossip."

What about Eirik? They'd started dating just before the nightmarish meet. Had she ditched him for Torin? Had he left before or after she started dating Torin?

Before I could ask her about Eirik, we turned a corner and I smothered a groan. Drew and a bunch of football players and cheerleaders were by the entrance to the cafeteria. He was the last person I wanted to see.

"What is it?" Raine asked when I slowed down.

"Uh, nothing." As we got closer, Jaden Granger saw us first. I couldn't stand him.

"Look who's back," he said. "Miss Prissy Jemison. You owe me a date, Cora."

In his dreams. Annoyance crossed Drew's face, but he quickly covered it with a smile. He was cute with brown hair and topaz eyes, and I couldn't help wondering what he'd done to make me kiss him. He so wasn't my type.

"Hey," he said.

"Hey." Not sure what to do, I gave him a brief hug. The ankle cast and the crutch made it über awkward. "How's your leg?"

"Itchy. Can you sign it?"

I chuckled. "Sure, but I don't have a Sharpie right now."

"Later then. What happened to you?" he asked.

Raine was busy teasing the other ballplayers about their last game, so they didn't focus on my conversation with Drew. "I needed to get away. Sorry about Keith. I didn't know or I would have called."

"Yeah, a bummer," he said. "He was a nice guy."

"You had to be living under a rock not to have heard," Jaden said, butting into our conversation. "They turned him into a hero. Please. He was an idiot for jumping in the middle of a stupid fight for some chick he wasn't even doing."

"You are an ass, Granger," one of the players said.

"Whatever, dude," Jaden said. "Just sayin'. I gotta get some to care."

"We have to go, Drew," I said, signaling Raine. "I'll see you later."

"Text me," he said.

As soon as they were out of sight, I relaxed. "Jaden is such a tool."

Raine laughed. "And a groper."

"No way."

"Yes way. You, uh, a friend went out with him and he tried to cop a feel under the table. She ditched his sorry ass."

"Only an idiot would go out with him." Kicker, Naya, and Sondra saw us and waved, and suddenly I wished we weren't sitting with them. All they ever talked about were books and their character crushes. They all had blogs and did reviews. "I wish we'd gone with Torin."

"I can text him." Raine pulled out her cell phone.

"Nah. It's okay." I didn't want to be a third wheel.

We got in line and collected our food. We were walking toward Kicker and the others when I saw Raine's father. What was he doing in the cafeteria? He looked thin and pale. The last time I saw him, he'd just come back from the dead. Everyone had thought he'd died in a plane crash, but a captain of a boat had fished him out of the sea and taken him to safety. I never heard the entire story about his rescue, but he'd arrived home the same day lightning killed our teammates.

As I watched him look around, I waited for Raine to say something. She was staring straight at him. He walked right across a table and I realized why. It was not Mr. Cooper. It was his soul. No one had told me Raine's father died. He was always nice to me and often treated me like a daughter.

He stopped in front of me. Like most souls, he tried to talk, but I couldn't hear him. I shook my head. He kept talking. My vision grew blurry as tears rushed to my eyes. When I blinked them away, he'd disappeared.

4. Sad News

"Are you okay?" Raine asked.

"Yeah." I wanted to hug her and ask her to forgive me for refusing to talk to her when she'd come to my house. Raine had been so close to her father. Her mother was great, but she was way out there, a throwback to Woodstock and the hippie movement. Her father, on the other hand, was a down-to-earth guy, and Raine adored him. Now he was dead.

Not sure how to approach the subject of her father without revealing I could see souls, I focused on my food and didn't bother to participate in the conversation at our table. Kicker and the others were discussing some popular book. Raine was a serious reader, but she wasn't obsessed with characters like the other three.

I couldn't eat. My thoughts kept going back to Mr. Cooper. Any second, I expected someone from the principal's office to come for her or the paging system to blast her name and summon her to the office.

Neither happened.

"Are you coming to practice today?" Sondra asked. She was the co-captain of the swim team.

I shook my head. "I don't know. I haven't really thought about it."

"We have a meet next weekend, and Doc will expect you to be there," she added.

I frowned. "I haven't swum in weeks."

They stared at me as though I'd lost my mind. Then I realized what I'd just said.

"Uh, did I miss a meet?" I asked quickly, hoping to distract them.

"No, but we are going against the Cougars again, and the four of us," Kicker pointed at herself, me, Sondra, and Naya, "are in the relay. Just like we did before Halloween Invitational. Hopefully this time they'll catch our bubbles. She hurt her head during the home game and had a concussion, so doesn't remember some things," Kicker explained to the others, who continued to stare at me.

I glanced at Raine. Her eyes volleyed between me and Kicker, but she didn't say anything. It was obvious something troubled her. She was the best sprinter in the group, yet Kicker hadn't mentioned her. She must have no intention of coming back to the team.

I couldn't ask her about it without revealing my ignorance. Not being sure what I could or could not say was starting to give me a headache. Lunch could not be over soon enough.

"How's your mother doing?" I asked Raine as we walked back to our lockers.

"Good, considering." She sounded sad.

"Considering what?"

She stopped walking and looked at me with shiny eyes. "My dad is sick, Cora. He has this, uh, really aggressive brain tumor. They tried to treat it, but..." Her voice trembled to a stop. "He can die any time."

My throat closed, and tears sprung to my eyes. He was already dead. Once again, I couldn't tell Raine the truth without revealing my ability to see souls.

"When did you find out?"

"A couple of weeks ago, but they knew about it before the plane crash and didn't tell me. It's the reason Dad went to Hawaii. He was seeing some specialist." Tears swam in her eyes. "I was so pissed and hurt when I found out. I couldn't look at them without wanting to… scream and yell at them." A tear slipped, and she swiped at it.

"I'm so sorry." I hugged her, wishing I could tell her the truth about her father. I fought tears and lost. I wasn't a crier, but shit kept piling on me today.

People walked by and stared at us. I glared at them, and the few with a sense of decency looked away. The rest of the morons watched us and whispered.

There was weird warmth behind me, and then Torin asked, "Are you okay?"

I looked over my shoulder to find him studying us with concern.

Raine left my arms and walked into his. The envy I'd felt toward her disappeared. The last few months must have been tough on her. First, she almost died because of a weird accident, now her father was dead. The worst part was I couldn't tell her.

Feeling useless and angry with myself, I removed books for my afternoon classes and closed my locker. When I glanced toward Raine and Torin, they were gone. I searched along the students around the lockers. They weren't in the hallway. It was as though they'd disappeared into thin air. Weird.

Shaking my head, I started for my next class.

I was in the math hallway when someone snatched my hand and the hallway became blurry. The next second, I was in total darkness. Only one person could move that fast.

Echo.

Seriously, I should kill him slowly and painfully. The problem was, he'd probably self-heal, or haunt me since I could see souls.

I fumbled for the switch, and my hand closed over his. Light flooded the tiny room. We were in the Kayville High make-out closet. Echo scowled at me. I was used to seeing him smirk, so his ferocious expression seemed odd. Still…

I backhanded his chest. "What's wrong with you? You can't just snatch me in the middle of the hallway like that. People would have noticed."

He snorted. "Like I care what they think."

"I do."

"Since when? You hate this place."

"Since always and I happen to love it here."

"Damn the Norns. You wouldn't be here if they hadn't messed with your memories." He leaned in and pinned me with his wolfish eyes, which were nearly all golden now. He really had gorgeous eyes, the green surrounding the gold changing size with his mood.

"Back to what's important," he said. "Who made you cry?"

"No one." I turned to leave.

He pressed his hand on the door and stopped me from opening it. "Some waste-of-space-Mortal made you cry, Cora, and I want to know who it is so I can gut him alive and personally escort his worthless soul to an island where he'll beg for a second death."

He really was impossible. "Enough with the second death threats. You don't kill."

"There's always the first time," he said without missing a beat. "Who is it?"

I ignored his question. "Can you be killed?"

"By decapitation, but no one would dare tempt it unless they have a death wish."

"Really? I don't have a death wish, and I'm so loving the thought of you headless."

He laughed. "Stop hedging, doll-face. Who made you cry?"

"No one. I saw Raine's father in the cafeteria and she told me he's been diagnosed with a brain tumor and is dying, so I just lost it because he's this amazing guy and she's really close to him…"

My voice trailed off when he pulled me into his arms. For a moment, I let him hold me. He smelled of leather, outdoors, and a musky scent that made me want to burrow in his neck. Last weekend, when I wasn't driving myself crazy, thoughts of his sensual lips and how they felt would mock me. Right now, all I had to do was lift my head and we'd kiss.

"It's okay," he said softly, his warm breath fanning my forehead.

My knees went weak, and my breathing grew erratic. He didn't help matters when he started rubbing circles on my back. I gave in to temptation, turned my head, and buried it in the crook of his neck to smell him better. I inhaled.

He leaned back and smirked as though he knew. "I don't think I understand what seeing him in the cafeteria has to do with your tears," he whispered, "but I promise you, it's not what you think."

He was patronizing me, and just like that, thoughts of kissing him went poof. "I saw his soul, Echo."

"I heard you the first time." He pulled me closer again and rested his chin on the crown of my head.

"That means he must be dead," I said.

"No, he's not."

"Yes, he is."

"He can't be."

I wiggled out of his arms. When he moved closer and I didn't have anywhere else to go, I pressed both hands against his chest. "Stop and listen."

"But I like holding you."

I threw him an annoyed glance. "Don't say things like that. He was trying to tell me something. Then he disappeared."

Echo shook his head, covering my hands with his. "That's impossible. I would have known if a reaper came for him. I was supposed to reap his soul, but I gave him a free pass a couple of months ago. No reaper can touch him now."

I shook my head. "What?"

"He was in some village in Central America dying, but I didn't reap his soul as a favor to a certain Valkyrie, who now owes me." He stroked my hands, distracting me again.

I yanked my hands from his chest and raised them. "Okay, stop. You can't keep throwing words at me without explaining what they mean. It's driving me crazy. What are Valkyries? Norns? Hel's Hall? You can't explain right now, so don't say another word. I'm going to class and after school I'm coming straight home. Be there to explain everything, or else."

He grinned.

"What?"

"I like this bossy side of you. It's very… exciting." His grin turned wicked.

I shook my head. I'd never met a man with a one-track mind. "Just when I'm beginning to see something redeemable in you, you open your mouth and spoil it." I reached for the door, but he pressed on it. "Echo—"

"You can't just step out of the closet into a hallway full of Mortals. They're not only ignorant, they spook easily, like a school of fish. Until you learn to engage your runes and become invisible, I'll help. Come closer."

"Didn't you just say a moment ago that you didn't care what they thought?"

"I don't, but *you* do." He slipped his arm around my waist, pulled me to his side, and smirked when I stiffened. "Trust me."

That was one thing I couldn't afford to do. "For now."

He chuckled, the sound dark and full of mischief. Runes inked his skin. He took the blade from the back of his pocket and sketched on the door so fast his hand was a blur. When he stopped, the door shifted and moved until a portal formed. I could see students hurrying past, some walking toward the cafeteria for second lunch, while the others headed toward the classrooms. No one appeared to notice us.

"They can't see us?" I asked.

"Mortals can't see a lot of things, including portals. Which way are we going?" Echo asked.

"I am going right. You? I don't know."

"I'm going reaping, but first, I'll check on Raine's father. Someone might be playing games. Enjoy the ride." He stepped into the hallway, moving so fast nearby students were a blur. He must have carried me because my feet didn't touch the ground. When he slowed down, none of the students even looked at us.

"Later, sweet-cheeks." He kissed me and was gone. My lips were still tingling when I reached my class.

The rest of the day was a blur. My last class of the day was P.E., and I spied Torin by the entrance of the gym, watching us play basketball.

Something shifted in my stomach. Could Raine's father be dead and he'd come to tell me? I excused myself to go talk to him, but by the time I turned around, he was gone.

Weird guy.

I changed out of my gym clothes then reached for my cell phone as I left the gym. My call to Raine went unanswered. Echo was waiting for me at home with answers, but I couldn't ignore the gnawing feeling in my stomach.

I threw my backpack in the passenger seat and started my car. Instead of going home, I headed east toward Raine's house.

***

It was November and most trees were leafless. Thanksgiving was around the corner, yet some people still had their spooky figurines and lawn decorations out. Orange Halloween garbage bags filled with leaves lined lawns and sidewalks. If only they knew about the beings that walked among them unseen, they would stop with the fake ghosts and monsters.

I pulled into Raine's cul-de-sac. Her car wasn't in their driveway. The house next to theirs must have finally sold. It had a For Sale sign for, like, forever.

As I parked by the curb, Mrs. Rutledge, Raine's nosy neighbor, stepped out of her door. The woman had something against young people because she never warmed to me or Raine.

I went to the door and rang the doorbell, but no one answered. Mrs. Rutledge continued to watch me from across the street. I'd bet she was waiting for me to ask her about the Coopers. I refused to accommodate her.

Instead, I removed my phone and called Raine. When it went unanswered, I texted her then got in my car. Mrs. Rutledge's narrowed eyes followed me as I drove past. I waved. If Echo wasn't waiting for me at home with answers, I would have gone to the Coopers' shop. Raine's family owned a shop that sold mirrors and framed portraits.

Butterflies flitted in my stomach the closer I got to home. Mom was baking. I could smell pies before I parked my car. She supplied local shops with pies and organic fruit. When it was warmer, she sold some of the produce at the Farmers Market. We had so many apple, peach, and apricot trees.

My parents used to be elementary school teachers before Granny died and left them the farm. While Mom turned her attention to organic farming and baking pies, Dad chose to chase his dream of becoming a writer. They were both successful, and I was rather proud of them.

"How was school, sweetie?" Mom called out when I stepped inside the house.

"Okay." I dropped my backpack on the living room chair and joined her in the kitchen. She stopped whipping the pumpkin batter, hugged me, and leaned back to study my face.

"I'll ask again. How was school?"

I grinned. "Tough, but I'll be okay."

Mom's eyes narrowed. "Your father said the principal acted weird."

I tasted the batter. Mmm. Good. "He wasn't acting. He *is* weird."

Mom pinched my nose playfully. "What a terrible thing to say."

"Is there cooled pie?" I asked.

"Apple?" Mom teased.

I shuddered. She knew I couldn't stand apple pie. We ate so many apple products the sight of apples gave me a bellyache. "Pumpkin."

"Check the fridge. Dinner won't be ready for a while."

"That's okay. I have tons of homework." I opened the fridge and removed the pie and two cans of pop. Echo had better be upstairs. I cut a huge chunk of pie and got two forks. I slipped one in the pocket of my jacket just in case Mom asked.

"You must really be hungry," she commented as I walked passed her.

"It was mystery meat today."

"If you need help with anything, bring it downstairs."

"Sure, Mom." I grabbed my backpack and hurried upstairs, my heart pounding. I pushed open my door, peered inside, and sighed with disappointment.

Of course Echo wasn't in my room. He'd appear when I least expected it. Arrogant reaper.

I did my homework, but I kept checking the clock and my cell phone in case Raine called back. Four o'clock came and went. Five. I put aside my homework and turned on my laptop. Instead of waiting for that flaky reaper, I could do my own investigation, starting with a familiar word—Valkyries.

Females from Norse mythology. Choosers of those killed in battle. The Valkyries walked through the fields of the dead fighters and chose those who lived and those who died. Half of the dead went to the God Odin in Valhalla, while the other half went to a Goddess Freya in Folkvang. The fighters trained daily for the final war between the gods and the evil giants.

The more I read, the more questions I had. Soon I was reading about Norse pantheon, the nine realms, and the gods and goddesses. Hel was the name of the goddess of the underworld. She had a huge hall and watched over those who died of old age and diseases. No wonder Echo kept mentioning Hel's Hall.

Next, I researched Norns, female deities who controlled destinies like the Fates in Greek mythology. They always appeared in threes. The most famous Norns were maiden giantesses. Their arrival in Asgard ended the golden age of the gods. Norns also arrived when a child was born to determine his or her future. Some were good and protected humans, while others were bad and caused most natural disasters.

I jumped at a knock on my door. Echo? No, of course not. He wouldn't knock.

Mom stuck her head inside my room. "Dinner."

"Can I eat up here?"

"No."

I grabbed my math package and headed downstairs. "I need help with a few math problems."

It was another hour before we finished dinner and homework. I lingered, needing to ask my mother a few questions.

"You don't have to do the dishes," Mom said.

"No, it's okay. I don't mind." I rinsed and put the dishes in the washer. Mom wiped down the counters while Dad went back to his writing. "Mom, can I ask you something?"

"Sure, hun."

"What exactly did Raine say when she came here?"

Mom rinsed the rag she'd been using and carefully draped it to dry on a peg by the window, her expression preoccupied. "Why? What happened at school?"

"We talked and made up." Sort of. I closed the dishwasher and pressed the start button. "Raine told me about her father."

Mom moved closer. "They found him in Central America."

"I know, but that's not it. He had, uh, *has* a brain tumor. He's dying, Mom. Raine found out a few weeks ago."

"Oh no." Mom covered her mouth, her expression horrified. She looked toward the alcove, but Dad was already on his feet walking toward us. He put his arms around her. "The poor dear. I feel awful about the way I treated her when she came here. First the accident then this. I thought…" she sighed. "I thought she was caught up in her image and social standing at school, and that's why she didn't try to visit you."

"So what did she say?" I asked.

"She wanted to see you. She didn't know you were at PMI. I didn't see how she couldn't have known. You weren't in school for over a month and she never stopped by during that time."

"She told me her parents took her away for two weeks after the lightning accident," Dad said. "So she was probably dealing with the situation with her father when she came back."

I only partially listened to Dad. Raine didn't know I had been at PMI, so she must have seen me at school every day like everyone else. I was back to the astral projection theory.

"How's she doing?" Mom asked.

"Not so good. Thanks, Mom." I kissed her cheek. "Goodnight. Night, Dad."

Upstairs, I entered my room and froze. Echo sat on my writing chair, demolishing the rest of the pie I'd left by my laptop. He pointed at the screen. "Were you reading this inaccurate crap?"

I closed the door. "Where were you?"

"Working." He swiveled the chair around and studied me. "Miss me?"

"No."

He chuckled. "Come here."

I ignored him and put my math folder on the table. "We agreed you'd be home when I got here."

"No, we didn't. You ordered me to be home, so I went home. *My* home. Next time," he pointed the fork at me, "be specific. I was waiting for you. Then I remembered your memories were gone and you didn't remember our little love nest in Italy. Next time, say your bedroom. Come here."

I didn't buy that crap about his home, but I needed information locked inside his arrogant head. "I need information, Echo, so stop playing games."

He put the bowl down, used his legs to propel the chair to where I stood and studied me with a lost puppy expression. "I'm sorry I was late. I just came back from escorting some souls. Do you know how many people die per minute? Thousands."

"Are you the only reap—Grimnir?"

"No, but I'm the best." I rolled my eyes and tried to walk around the chair, but he stuck out his leg. "Not so fast, doll-face." He pulled me down on his lap and wrapped his arm around me before I realized his intentions. His clothes were cold, his cheek freezing against my arm.

I shivered. "Why are you so cold?"

"Hel is frigid. Nonstop blizzards. No natural light. No amount of clothing stops the cold from sipping under your skin. That's why I always look forward to coming back to Earth and warmth." His hands slipped under my shirt.

"Whoa! Your hands are like icicles." I gripped his wrists, pulled his hands from under my shirt, and trapped them between my hands.

"I need your warmth, Cora."

If I wasn't holding his hands, I would have thought that was another cheap come-on. Slowly, I rubbed them. He still wore the fingerless gloves and silver Gothic rings with runic etchings. "You should invest in some serious winter gloves, not these."

"I can't. There must be skin contact with the scythe for me to engage its runes and use it." He slid his hands under my shirt again to warm them against my skin. This time I let him.

"So Hel really exists?" I asked.

"The goddess *and* the place, yes." He explained who Hel was, daughter of Loki, sister to some serious shape-shifters, and ruler of the land of the dead. "They say her giantess mother is more evil and devious than Loki, and that's why Odin decided to give Hel a realm to rule so she wouldn't get into mischief. It backfired of course. Her loyalty is to her father, and she'll fight with him before the world ends. She even kept Baldur, Odin's beloved son, after the gods begged her to let him go."

"Doesn't that make her and you, by association, evil?"

He chuckled and rubbed his cheeks against my arm. I seriously loved that sexy chuckle of his. "That's like saying the police and jailers are evil for rounding up scumbags and keeping them behind bars. It's just a job."

"I read that you only reap the sick and elderly?"

"And bad people. You know murderers, thieves, and other sociopaths." He rolled us back to the desk.

"But won't you be on Hel's side during the final battle between the gods and the giants?"

"Nope." He buried his face in my neck, his warm breath teasing my senses. I shuddered. I wanted to hold him longer, but I knew I shouldn't. He was distracting me from my goal to pump him for info.

I pushed his head away and angled my body so I could see his face, which didn't help. He really had the most incredible lips ever. Think lower lip and perfectly shaped upper lip. So kissable. The corners of his mouth lifted in a smirk, and my eyes flew to his.

"You keep looking at my lips like that and we'll be over there," he nodded at my bed, "making up for lost time."

My cheeks burned. What were we discussing? Ah, the war of the gods. "So what side will you support?"

"Neither. According to the prophecy, which is annoyingly vague, most of the fighters, the gods, Valkyries, Grimnirs, the Immortals, Hel's army of misfits, and the giants will die. I intend to survive, so I will fight for me. That's the beauty of immortality, doll-face. If you can survive getting your head severed, you live to see another millennium. You can fight by my side. I'll protect you."

The look in his eyes said he was about to do something outrageous. In fact, his hands were no longer cold. They'd inched up and were busy tracing the edge of my bra. From the sexy, hooded look in his eyes, he wanted to slip under the silk material and caress my chest intimately.

"You are warm now." I stood and moved away from him, straightening my top. "And shameless."

"For putting my well-being first?" He picked up the bowl with the pie.

"Among other things." I went and sat on my bed.

He forked the last piece of pie and ate with utter delight, closing his eyes and humming. His ridiculously long lashes formed a canopy on his chiseled cheekbones, and his shaggy brown hair was carelessly styled. "That's the best pie I've ever eaten. Can I have more?"

I made a face. I needed answers, not to march up and down the stairs getting him food.

"Please." He picked crumbs with his finger and licked them off.

"Fine, but when I come back, I want to know everything about Valkyries, Immortals, and Norns, especially Norns and what they can do, because nothing that happened at school makes sense."

"What happened?" He stood and followed me to the door.

"I've been gone for weeks, yet everyone acted like I only missed one week of school. How could I have been at school *and* at PMI? My friends talked about meets I attended and teachers gave me back homework I did. I've never aced math tests or essays in my English class, but I'm getting A-pluses. History is my worst subject, yet the research paper I wrote covered things I've never read. Oh, and I kissed a football player during the last game and he's not even my type."

Echo's eyes narrowed. "You kissed someone? Who?"

He sounded outraged. I laughed. "That's all you got from what I just said?"

"Who did you kiss, doll-face?"

"Drew."

"Does Drew have a last name?"

Okay, maybe his reaction wasn't funny. "Leave him alone."

"When was this kiss? Where was I? No one is supposed to mess with you except…" He glowered. "No one."

I rolled my eyes. "Except *you*?"

"That's right. Just because you don't remember what happened between us doesn't mean I don't. We made a pact."

"Quit making up things as you go, Echo. I would know if I was no longer a virgin." Heat rushed to my face when I realized what I had said.

"Sweet-cheeks, you weren't a virgin when we hooked up."

For a moment I just stared at him, then anger spread through me like wildfire. "You're such a jerk. I've never been with a guy that way and… and…" I growled. "Stay away from Drew. He's suffered enough." I shook my head. "What am I talking about? You don't even go to my school."

Echo's eyes narrowed. "That could change."

"Well, how about this? I don't want you there." I left the room before he could say anything else. I refused to believe I let that arrogant man touch me. Of course, his story about us could be pure fabrication. Or not. Maybe things like virginity didn't manifest themselves in astral images. How dare he say he wasn't my first?

Believing in astral projections would have been a stretch, but my perception of reality had shifted when I started seeing souls. I had a smoking hot reaper in my bedroom who had just returned from the realm of a goddess called Hel. Norse freaking gods really existed. Dad would have a field day with that kind information. He could write bestsellers based on just reapers alone.

Downstairs, my parents were on their respective computers. They looked up. Hoping my face wasn't red, I said, "I need more pie."

"I told her she'd lost weight, and she said they didn't feed her at PMI," Dad teased.

Was I really at the mental hospital, or did Norns also erase my parents' memories?

"I was teasing, Dad." In the kitchen, I cut a huge chunk of the remaining pie and scooped it into a bowl. Our first floor had an open floor plan with arched doorways separating the kitchen from the living room and the living room from Dad's writing cave. Mom often conversed with Dad while cooking in the kitchen. "I missed Mom's pies."

Mom chuckled. "Thanks, hun. Make sure you bring down the bowl, okay?"

"Promise."

Back upstairs, Echo was on top of my bed as though he belonged, the laptop on his chest. He'd removed his jacket and only wore the leather waistcoat and a long-sleeved cotton shirt. With the leather pants hugging his thighs, he looked so tempting.

I knocked his booted foot with my knee. "You're making my covers dirty, reaper."

He looked at his boots then at me. His expression said he knew I was being a bitch over nothing. There was no dirt on his boots. He sat up, put the laptop next to him, and took the pie.

"I'm sorry today was rough on you," he said.

I shrugged. "Until I understand what happened to me during those weeks, it's not going to be easy."

"Norns plant false memories in Mortals' heads all the time. They don't mess with us, but I guess your situation is different."

"What do you mean?"

"You were training to be a Norn, Cora."

What I'd read about Norns flashed through my head. The good ones helped humans, while the bad ones were behind most natural disasters. "Good one?"

Echo smirked. "No, doll-face. You are bad-ass."

"That doesn't sound like me. Why would I want to be an evil Norn?"

"I don't know. But you changed your mind and decided to join us. You chose to be a Grimnir."

Reaper of scumbags, the sick, and the elderly? From online pictures, Valhalla looked like a palace. Why would I choose to be a Grimnir and not a Valkyrie?

I didn't realize I'd spoken out loud until Echo stopped in the process of putting a chunky piece of pie in his mouth and shot me an annoyed glance. "Inside Hel's Hall is not so bad. She has a nice court, even though it is cold and a little depressing. Valkyries are wussies. Every time one of them is sent to Hel's Hall, they whine like babies."

"You hate Valkyries?"

He smirked. "Hate takes energy. I don't care about them one way or the other. I just don't like them stealing my souls."

"Yet, you let Raine's father go." Then I remembered. "Oh, Crap. Mr. C. What did you find out about him? Is he okay?"

Echo frowned. "He had a stroke this morning and flat lined around noon."

"That's about the time I saw him." I reached for my jacket and car keys.

"They resuscitated him, but he's in a coma at the local hospital. Kayville Medical Center. Where are you going?"

"The hospital. Raine must be devastated. No wonder she hasn't returned my calls or texts."

"You want to go now? It's late to be driving anywhere. Use a portal."

I glanced at the mirror and wished we could. "I can't. My parents might wonder where I've disappeared to when they swing by my room and find it empty."

"They check on you before they go to bed?"

"Every night. The first few days when I came home, they did it several times. Drove me crazy." He had that look on his face. "Don't say anything about false memories. I was in that psych ward." I paused before opening the door. "Come on. I want to hear why the Norns erased my memories."

"We can talk in the car, but I can't come inside with you. The Valkyries around here don't like me, so don't tell them anything about me." He walked toward the mirror still wolfing down the pie.

I stared after him, wishing I could use the portal. What Valkyries was he talking about, and why would I mention Echo to them? I didn't know them.

5. Valkyries

"Isn't it late to be going out now?" Dad asked, standing. "You could always go tomorrow."

"It's only," I glanced at my watch, "eight, and Raine would be there for me if it were you in the hospital, Dad."

He reached for his jacket. "I'll come with you."

"No. I'll be fine. I'm picking up a friend on the way. Go back to your work. I'll call you when I get to the hospital and when I'm on my way back."

He glanced at his computer. "No, I'm not letting you drive anywhere alone, muffin. I'll tell your mother where we are going."

Arguing with him was pointless once he made up his mind. "I'll be by the truck. I want to get something from my car first."

Outside, I saw Echo in the front passenger seat of my car. I opened the car door and peered at him. The runes on his body glowed. "My dad insists on taking me."

"Good. We'll finish our conversation later. Remember, your memories are gone because Norns erased them and replaced them with fake ones. When you get them back, it will all make sense."

"You said the Valkyries don't like you. Why?"

"I didn't reap Mr. Cooper as a favor to Torin St. James, so he owes me. Valkyries don't like owing us favors."

I'd gone into selective listening at the name Torin St. James. "Raine's boyfriend is a Valkyrie?"

He nodded. "Yep. He's a hard ass, but a good soldier. We tend to steer clear of each other. Andris is young and an idiot." He touched my cheek. "Go. Your parents are coming. Oh, don't forget. No mentioning my name to anyone."

That again? "Why would I do that?"

He smirked. "Because girls love to talk about guys they're crazy about."

I laughed. "You are one person I try not to think about."

"You can try, but you can't help yourself, doll-face."

Talking to him was useless. I turned to see Dad coming toward me. Mom was locking the door. When I glanced back at Echo, he was gone.

"Your mother is coming, too," Dad said, stating the obvious.

I wasn't surprised. My parents didn't socialize often with Raine's parents, but they were friends. We had potluck a few times a year, and Raine's dad often came to the farm to buy fresh fruit and vegetables and visit with Dad. I slid in the back seat and checked my cell phone. There was still no text from Raine.

"How did you find out about Tristan?" Mom asked as we left the farm.

"A friend texted me," I fibbed. "Mom, did you guys see Raine's family while I was away?"

"Not really. We were so busy, and with Raine not coming to visit you, I thought it was best we keep our distance. I had no idea they were going through so much." Mom sounded calm, but I knew she felt guilty. Dad took her hand and squeezed it.

"I'm sure Raine's mother will appreciate seeing you at the hospital," I said.

The drive to the hospital reminded me of our mad dash after Raine had injured herself. Eirik had driven like a maniac, hardly stopping at stop signs. Eirik. Funny I hadn't thought about him in the last few hours. When did his family move away? I was hoping Raine would tell me.

Kayville might be a small town in wine country Oregon, but we had an amazing hospital with great staff. We didn't airlift patients to bigger hospitals in Portland or Salem. After the lightning accident, Kayville Medical Center had taken care of all the students. Even Raine had been treated here after she received a head injury.

We entered through the ER and headed upstairs to the ICU. Torin and a blond couple stood somewhere ahead. The same couple had come with Raine to my home after I came back from the hospital. Runes covered their faces and arms.

Valkyries.

Did Raine know about them?

The ICU had open visiting hours, but only relatives were allowed. Dad convinced the nurses to get Raine and her mother to come out. I left my parents waiting at the nurses' station and found the perfect seat to observe the Valkyries. I picked up a magazine, lowering it so I could study them unnoticed.

The girl was gorgeous and frail-looking. From the way she was looking at the silver-haired guy, she was totally into him. The guy had the same alert look in his eyes as Torin and was equally good-looking. Maybe runes gave them model-worthy looks, or being exceptionally good-looking was a criterion for becoming a Valkyrie.

I pretended to read when Torin glanced my way. In a few seconds, my heart skipped with dread. They'd decided to join us. My parents were still by the nurses' station. Maybe I should just join them. The Valkyries took the empty chairs across from mine. My heart pounded so hard I was sure they could hear them.

No, I'm not going to look at them. I'm not... I'm not...

"Maliina got a few things wrong," the silver-haired guy said. "She's hotter."

"Shut up, Andris," Torin said firmly.

So that was Andris. Were they talking about me? And who was Maliina?

"Do you think she's faking?" Andris asked. "Her mother said she had a breakdown and claimed she could see us and souls."

They were definitely talking about me.

"Can you hear and see us, Cora Jemison?" Andris asked, confirming my suspicions.

"Leave her alone," Torin said in a firm voice. "I'm sure it was a one-time thing."

Was that why he'd been in my P.E. class? To confirm whether I could see him? He didn't have runes at the time, but... dang it. I hated not being able to look at them. And I agreed with most comments I'd read online. Torin's British accent was sexy.

"Maliina marked her," the girl said in an accent I couldn't place. "She was never patient, so maybe she mixed up the runes. Gave her temporary abilities."

Maliina again. Who was she?

"I can prove she's faking." Andris stood and walked toward me.

My heart picked up tempo. What was he going to do? So what if they found out I could see them? Who was Maliina? I kept my eyes glued to the pages of the magazine, but I could see him coming closer and closer.

"Enough!" Torin snapped, appearing beside Andris.

"Ooh, why do you always spoil my fun?" Andris griped, but I could hear the laughter in his voice. "You can't be everywhere, big bro. I'll corner her at school when you're not around."

"Hel's mist, Andris," Torin snarled. "If you are bored, find a freaking distraction. A girlfriend or a boyfriend. Just leave her alone. She's Raine's best friend, which means you don't mess with her."

"Boys. Boys. Fighting over me again?"

Echo. I almost turned. I blew a shaky breath and bit my lower lip to stop myself from smiling.

"What are you doing here, Grimnir?" Andris snarled.

"Always nice to see you, *Andy*." Echo bowed to Torin. "*My Lord* St. James, Earl of something-something. No, you lost that title along the way, didn't you? In the most humiliating—"

"Shut up, Echo," Torin said. "You are not supposed to be here."

Echo chuckled. "Really? Last time I checked, hospitals are my hunting ground, which makes you bitches trespassers."

Someone growled. Probably Andris since I couldn't see Torin losing control like that.

"Outside, Echo," Torin snapped. "Now!"

"Since you didn't say please... Who's this beauty?" He came into my line of vision and studied me. It took all my effort not to kick him.

"Don't even look at her wrong or you'll have Raine to deal with," Andris warned.

"Torin's mate?" Echo asked, reaching out to touch my hair. Torin grabbed his wrist. "Völur don't scare me."

"You should be scared," Torin added slowly. "Her powers are emerging fast. Within a year, you'll tremble in her presence."

Echo sighed melodramatically and studied my face, his unusual eyes gleaming. "So you're saying I can't have this one?"

"You don't touch her. Ever. Let's go."

Echo laughed. Then he was gone. The other two Valkyries followed him. I didn't look, but I felt rather than saw them leave. I blew out air.

The blonde who'd stayed seated during the entire exchange, got up and walked toward me. She stopped by my chair. "I saw your face, Cora. I know you can see and hear us. Don't be scared. You're not going crazy or anything like that. I want to help you."

"Why?" I heard myself ask and cringed. I didn't dare look at her.

"My sister did this to you. If she hadn't marked you, you wouldn't be seeing us now."

Marked me? I looked up and our eyes met. Hers were filled with pity, which annoyed me. I hated being pitied.

"Why would a Valkyrie mark me?" I asked.

"She was an Immortal, like me, not a Valkyrie. I'll text you," the girl said.

"Cora?"

Raine! I whipped around and saw her. She looked terrible, her eyes red and hair a mess. She wore the same clothes she'd worn to school. I jumped to my feet, rushed past the blonde, as though she wasn't there, and hugged Raine. Had she seen me talk to myself? I leaned back and studied her face.

"How's he doing?" I asked.

Her chin trembled. "He's still in a coma. He looks bad. Really bad."

I held her and fought my own tears. Damn my tear ducts. Through a haze, I saw Raine's mother talking and smiling with my parents. What the hell was wrong with her? How could she be smiling at a time like his? I never understood her. No one could be this chipper all the time. Even when Raine's father had gone missing, she'd carried on like he'd gone on an extended vacation or something. When our eyes met.

"Thanks for coming," Raine mumbled after what seemed like forever.

"You'd do the same if Dad was…" I sighed. No need to spell it out. "Do you want me to get you anything?"

"No. I'm just happy you came." She glanced over my shoulder, and I followed her gaze to see the two male Valkyries walking toward us. They didn't have runes this time, but their hair looked disheveled. Andris had a rip on his shirt. A hollow feeling settled in my stomach.

Where was Echo? What had they done with him? If they'd ganged up on him…

I sighed. There was nothing I could do now without letting them all know my secret. I should have told the blonde not to say anything. Mom's voice cut through my thoughts.

"Raine can come home with us, Svana," Mom said.

No, I wanted to protest. Echo wouldn't visit me if Raine was around. As soon as the thought crossed my mind, I realized how selfish that sounded.

"You should, Raine," I repeated Mom's offer.

Raine shook her head. "I can't."

"That's nice of you to offer, Penny," Svana Cooper said, "but my sister arrived this evening and will keep an eye on her. In fact, the boys should take her home now." Raine's mother waved to the Valkyries.

In the years I'd known the Coopers, I'd never heard her or Raine mention her family. "You have an aunt?" I asked.

"More like a half-sister of my mom's. They were estranged, but they recently made up."

"Could you take Raine home, Torin?" Mrs. Cooper asked.

"Yes, ma'am," Torin said, but Raine was already shaking her head.

"No," Raine said. "I'm not leaving until Dad wakes up. I have to know that he's going to be okay."

"Oh, sweetie," her mother said, cupping her face. "I know how you feel. I'm going to be here keeping an eye on him. Nothing is going to happen to him without me knowing. And the minute he regains consciousness, I'll call you."

Raine glanced at Torin, and a silent communication passed between them. She must have seen something in his eyes she didn't like because she made a face and said ungraciously, "Fine, but I'm coming back first thing in the morning."

Her mother smiled. "Of course. You and Lavania can stay with him while I go home and change." She kissed Raine's cheek then patted Torin's arm.

We didn't stay long after Raine and Torin left. I avoided eye contact with Andris and was surprised he and the girl remained behind. I hope she wasn't going to tell him I could see them. Were they after Mr. C's soul?

Outside, I searched the parking lot for Echo. Maybe he'd be in my bedroom when I got home. We left the town behind and entered Orchard Grove. It was narrow with leafless trees hulking above us like something from a horror movie. Our headlights barely penetrated the bushes at their base. A movement on our left caught my attention, and I peered for a better look.

Suddenly a thump rocked our car, something hitting us on the left.

Mom screamed and reached in the back in an instinctive protective move to stop me from flying forward. Dad cursed as he struggled to control the car. We spun around, our back tires ending up in a ditch.

"Honey, you okay?" Mom asked in a high-pitched voice.

I nodded.

"I think we hit something," Dad said, starting to get out.

No, something hit us. "Don't get out!" I cried.

"It's okay, muffin. If it's an animal, we'll have to put it out of its misery."

Swallowing, I peered outside, searching the shadows. Something was out there. The thought barely crossed my mind when a shadow zipped past. Another followed. They darted across the vineyard. They were fast, and the darkness made it hard to see what they were. One of them shot up in the air. Then there was a burst of light zipping across the field to where it had landed. A bright spark then nothing.

I was shaking, my mouth dry, my heart pounding. The only being that could move like that was supernatural. Grimnirs. I jumped when the front car doors opened and my parents got inside the car. I hadn't even noticed Mom leave the car.

"That's strange," she said, shaking her head.

Dad nodded, sliding behind the steering wheel. "Maybe it limped off."

"No, I'm talking about the car. There's no dent, but we hit something."

"Very strange." Dad shifted the gears from park to drive. The wheels churned before gaining traction. As we pulled away, someone whizzed from the bushes, stopped in the middle of the road behind us, and watched us drive away. He wore a long coat.

Echo?

At home, I stepped out of the truck and stared in shock at the huge dent on the side and runes drawn all over it. How could my parents not see the dent or the runes? I knew runes were powerful enough to make people invisible. Obviously, they also made people not see things.

Mom put her arm around me. "It's amazing, isn't it? No mark on the car after we almost landed in a ditch."

No marks indeed. I wished my parents goodnight on the run, needing to be in my room. *Please, let him be there.* I pushed open the door and looked inside.

It was empty.

"Echo?" I called out, but there was no response.

Disappointed, I got ready for bed, fought sleep, and waited for him as long as I could. Where was he? Was he the dark figure in the middle of the road? Had one of his people tried to kill us? Why had an Immortal marked me?

***

My alarm went off, yanking me from sleep. I was alone in bed. Somehow, I'd expected Echo to be lounging around, ready to drive me crazy. Last night's events rushed back and, immediately, a hollow feeling settled in my stomach.

Where was he? Was he hurt or off somewhere reaping? Who was warming his hands and face when he came back from Hel's Hall?

Even as the thought crossed my mind, I wanted to kick myself. I didn't care if he had women in every major city of the world. He and I weren't lovers, no matter what he'd said. I could walk into my doctor's office and ask her to confirm my virginity, but that might lead to embarrassing questions and innuendos.

I got up, showered, and got dressed. I felt like slapping myself when I peered into my bedroom and searched for Echo before stepping out of the bathroom. Seriously, I needed to get a grip. Echo thrived on being unpredictable. He'd appear when I least expected him. I headed downstairs for breakfast.

"I want to go back to swimming," I said as I forked a piece of pancake.

Mom looked up with a frown. "Why?"

"Because it's something to do in the evenings and it's normal."

"What about your homework? You have a lot of catching up to do, Cora. I don't want you spreading yourself too thin and making yourself ill."

If she only knew. "I'll have time to do my homework too, Mom. I promise I'll finish everything in a few weeks. Raine promised to help me. It will give her something to focus on."

Mom couldn't argue with that without coming across as insensitive. She gave in, though she didn't look happy about it. I'd talk to Dad later and get his support. He was the only one who could stop her from complaining.

Outside, I stared at our truck. The dent was gone, but the runes were still there. They were different from last night's and covered the entire truck. I tried rubbing one off, but they appeared imbedded in the paint. What did they mean?

Echo had been here, fixing things with runes. Why hadn't he awakened me?

I left the farm, eager to get to school and talk to the blonde Valkyrie about her sister marking me. Maybe Echo would pull me inside the make-out closet again. He had a lot of answering to do. He was the one on the road last night. I just knew it.

Flashing police lights ahead forced me to slow down. Cops scoured the grounds at the scene of last night's incident. What were they searching for?

Even as the question flashed through my head, I noticed the rows of flatted vines on both vineyards. They looked like weird crop patterns conspiracy theorists blamed on aliens. Deep fissure were also visible on the ground, and several trees were down as though ripped from their roots by giant hands. It would take superhuman strength to do this kind of damage. Or aliens called Grimnirs. I knew they were fast, but were they strong, too? I didn't recall seeing the trees fall last night, which meant more fighting must have happened after we drove away.

An officer indicated that I move along. Now I was worried about Echo. At every stop sign, I expected him to appear in my car.

The first person I saw when I parked at the school's parking lot was Kicker. She waved and hurried toward my car.

"We missed you yesterday at the pool. Are you swimming today?"

"Yeah. Got my stuff." We started across the parking lot when I noticed her T-shirt. It had the silhouette of three guys and a girl.

"What's that?" I pointed at her shirt.

She looked down at her chest and grinned. "Reapers? The hottest band ever."

I frowned. Reapers? "How come I've never heard of them?"

She laughed. "You have to live in a major city across the globe and attend rave parties to know about them. They are ravers' best-kept secret. They appear out of nowhere, perform, and leave. No one knows who they are or where they come from, but people love them. They symbolize what raves are about."

All I knew about ravers was that they did drugs. "What?"

"Spirituality, intimacy, letting go of society's shackles. They don't care about money or fame."

Sounded like something a real reaper would do. "I never would have imagined you as a raver, Kicker."

"Me neither. My cousin who's a serious raver invited me to a party a few months ago in Portland, and Reapers made a surprise appearance. That's what they do. They come unannounced, which is totally cool. They gave out these T-shirts for free."

"Do you know the names of the band members? What they look like?"

"No. They always wear masks, but you can tell they are young and hot. I mean, they are seriously buff and ripped. Since they've been around since the eighties, some ravers believe they get new members every ten years. Others believe they are more than one group. You know, like a hundred members of the band, because they've monitored and timed their performances down to seconds. They perform one night a month in a span of twenty-four hours across the globe. There's no way they can move from city to city in minutes."

If they used portals they could. We entered the school and moved past people standing in groups catching up on gossip.

"The fact that they can do that only makes them more mysterious. My cousin's dream is to be a member of the Reapers."

I could easily see a bunch of reapers taking one night a month to release steam, performing to underground groups. Maybe Echo knew them. Drew was near my locker when we entered the hallway.

"Are you two back together now?" Kicker asked.

One kiss didn't an item make us. On the other hand, the one from Echo had made an impression and left me hungry for more. I didn't answer Kicker, choosing to focus on Drew.

"Hey," I said, slowing to a stop near him.

He grinned and dangled several Sharpies, including a pink one. I chose a pink and a black one, squatted, and wrote my name, making O a heart and coloring it with pink.

"Want to hang out after school?" Drew asked.

With his leg busted, he wasn't playing football anymore, which meant he had more free time and no friends to pass it with. I glanced at him and smiled. He was so sweet, just not my type.

"I'd love to, but I can't. I have swim practice. Then I promised to stop by Raine's. Her father had massive stroke and is in a coma." I stood and pushed the lids back on the Sharpies. "She's not taking it well."

"That sucks. I, uh, I'm thinking of throwing a party for Keith on Friday. It would have been his eighteenth birthday. Can you come?"

"Sure." I put my stuff away and picked up my folder. "When and where?"

"At my place. Come on, I'll walk you to class."

I chuckled. "You do know my first class is English and it's on the west wing of the school. Upstairs."

"I know." He flashed a boyish grin. "You'd be amazed at what I can do with three legs."

"Okay." But I slowed down to match his gait. I had no idea what he had in the first period, and I didn't want to ask in case it was something I should already know. Somehow, I must find a way to let him know I wasn't interested in him. Maybe during his party.

"Hey, dude, have you seen St. James?" a jock asked Drew as we left the locker area.

"No. Why?"

"Coach wants to see him."

"That's terrible about Raine's father," Kicker said. I'd completely forgotten her presence. "She must have cracked a mirror or something. First, her father's plane crashed, then the accident at the pool, which people blamed her for. Then when she came back to school, everyone drew horrible things on her locker and yours, and now this."

I stopped walking. "People did what?"

Kicker's eyes widened, and even Drew stared at me with a weird expression. Then I realized what I'd said. Dang, another thing I should have known about. Seriously, I should just keep my mouth shut when people talked about what had happened the last several weeks.

"What? That's messed up," Drew said and I realized they were talking.

"I know," Kicker said. "I was shocked when she told me."

"You seriously can't remember anything that happened?" Drew asked, staring at me and standing smack in the middle of the hallway. Students were forced to walk around him.

I shrugged. "The doctors said everything would come rushing back whenever."

"It's my fault," Drew said.

"It's no one's fault. Things happen." Especially when the supernatural are involved. "I have to go. I don't want to be late for class."

He grabbed my arm. "You don't understand. We were, you know, kissing after we won, and I didn't realize the crowd was surging toward us. One second you were in my arms. The next someone pulled you away while others pushed me down. I tried to find you. I should have tried harder or held you tighter or—"

"Don't say that. I'm sure it was a crazy evening, and no one is to blame."

"I agree," Kicker added.

Drew smiled at her. He walked me to class and somehow ended up inviting Kicker to his party, too. The look on her face was comical. She'd never hung out with football players.

For the rest of the morning, I searched for the Valkyries and hoped Echo would do his appearing act. I was beginning to worry about him, even though I knew I shouldn't. He could take care of himself.

Still, he'd better show up soon. I had enough crap to deal with without worrying about him. When I didn't see Raine near our lockers, I sent her a text message.

During lunch, Kicker filled me in on everything I'd "missed" and it wasn't pretty. My anger shot up as they talked and laughed about someone defacing Raine's locker and people treating her like crap because she'd known something bad was about to happen during that disastrous meet. Apparently, Eirik and the other me were the only ones who'd stuck by her. That they found that amazing made me want to smack them.

"What's wrong with you guys?" I asked, glaring at Sondra, then Naya, and finally Kicker. "This is Raine Cooper we are talking about. The nicest person you bitches know."

Sondra's jaw dropped. "You didn't just call us the B word."

"Shut up, Sondra," I snapped. A few students at the neighboring table looked at us. I glared at them until they looked away. Focusing on the three girls at my table, I added in a lower voice, "You know and I know that Raine would never knowingly hurt anyone. How could you not stand by her?"

"Come on, Cora. It was kind of spooky the way she knew things," Kicker said defensively.

"I saw her too, Kicker. I thought she'd lost it, but I would never think she's a witch," I retorted, seriously thinking of bitch-slapping them into next week. "Or are you guys forgetting she had an accident and almost died, and maybe, just maybe, the accident messed with her head."

"She levitated, Cora," Naya piped in. "Jocelyn saw her float above the water."

"And the disappearing thing," Kicker added. "One second she was there, the next gone."

I must have missed that while I was busy staring at the Valkyries and the souls. When I hadn't seen her, I'd just assumed she'd run out into the changing rooms like the other students.

"Jocelyn lied," I said, enunciating my words. "With the chaos, people running and screaming, the lightning, anyone would have imagined anything. Or lightning shooting through her caused her to appear to levitate." I stood and glared down at them, daring them to contradict me. When they didn't speak, I turned and walked out of the cafeteria.

Of course, they'd seen Raine appear to levitate, or carried by beings no one could see. I blew out a breath, feeling terrible. School must have been a nightmare for Raine.

After her father's crisis was over, she and I were going to have a long talk. There must be a reason why she'd known about the pool accident before it happened. Maybe she was a witch. If I could be in two places at the same time and Valkyries existed, my best friend could definitely have premonitions. And she had to know Torin was a Valkyrie. One second in Echo's presence and I'd known he was different.

Where was that reaper? I was going to make him sorry for making me worry about him.

***

I didn't hear from Raine until after lunch. She hadn't come to school. And from the looks of things, neither had Torin, Andris, or the blonde.

At the pool, I basically ignored Kicker, Sondra, and Naya. They were on my dislike list until I felt they'd done their penance. I wasn't sure what that was, but I could be creative.

After practice, I headed straight to Raine's. Her text said she was at home. A tall woman with a porcelain complexion and pitch-black hair answered her door. Except for the black hair, I didn't see any resemblance to Raine's mother.

"Cora, how nice to finally meet you," she said, planting a kiss on my cheeks then giving me a hug.

I wasn't sure how to respond, so I returned the hug. She leaned back and studied my face as though searching for something. I gave her a tiny smile.

"I'm Lavania, Raine's aunt." She squeezed my arms and stepped back. "Come inside. Everyone is in the kitchen."

Everyone? She led the way, her walk graceful, her dress a free-flowing piece that reached her ankles and was cinched at the waist by a bejeweled belt. I tried to see over her shoulder, but she was tall.

"I've heard so much about you, of course," she said.

"Oh." Finally, I could see "everyone". Torin was chopping something on the kitchen counter. A fallen angel in an apron. Looks and talented with his hands, lucky Raine. Andris and the blonde sat in their kitchen nook, sipping soda. Raine was missing.

"Eirik talks about you all the time," Lavania said.

My feet faltered. "I didn't know you knew Eirik."

She turned and faced me. "Oh, dear. Raine didn't tell you? His new home is just a block from mine."

The blonde choked on whatever she was drinking. Andris slapped her back, but his eyes were on us. Torin had stopped chopping. They were all staring at Lavania in utter shock. What? She wasn't supposed to tell me about being neighbors with Eirik?

She faced them and waved toward the kitchen table. "Sit, Cora. Torin and I are cooking tonight, so I insist you join us for dinner."

"Sorry, I can't. My parents are expecting me. Is Raine home?"

"Upstairs sleeping," Torin said, pointing up with the knife.

"Thanks." I waved to Andris and the blonde.

Andris got up, a mocking grin curling his lips. "Nice to see you *again*, Cora."

Remembering my gaffe this morning, I decided to play it safe. "Again? I don't think we've met. You are?"

"Andris." His eyes narrowed as he closed the gap between us. "We met months ago."

I shook my head. "Sorry, I don't remember."

"And last night at the hospital."

Had the blonde told him my secret? Our eyes met, but I couldn't read her expression. "Yes, I remember that. You and Torin came to the ICU just before we left."

Andris chuckled. "You are good, sweetheart, but I've been playing games for centuries."

"Leave her alone, you naughty boy," Lavania warned, but there was no censure in her voice.

"Aye, aye, *Mother*," Andris said. "Have you met Ingrid?"

Mother? I shook my head.

"Cora, Ingrid." He waved toward the blonde. "Ingrid, Cora."

"Nice to meet you, Ingrid. I'll just head," I pointed up, "upstairs."

Andris pointed at his eyes with two fingers than at me. Yeah, whatever, Valkyrie. I imitated his gesture.

Lavania chuckled. "Don't mind him. He likes to act outrageous when bored. I keep hoping someone will keep him preoccupied." She shot the blonde a pointed look.

The girl blushed and looked down. Then I remembered something. "Uh, your coach was looking for you at school today, Torin. I don't know if your teammates texted you."

Torin frowned then shrugged. "No, but that's okay. Thanks." He didn't sound bothered about it.

"Dude, you missed practice and semi-finals are in two weeks," Andris said.

"Screw football," Torin retorted.

"Watch your mouth, sonny." Lavania smacked Torin on the back of his head. "You know better than to use that kind of language around me."

Okay, the dynamics of relationships in this house was weird. She was so at home in Raine's house. Red flag number one. She and the Valkyries talked like they'd known each other forever. Red flag number two. She called Torin "sonny" and Andris called her "mother". Flaming red flag number three. On the other hand, Raine's mother was just like that. Outgoing. A knack for treating people like they were lifelong friends and making them feel at home. So maybe my lie-radar was off.

I headed upstairs, knocked slightly on Raine's door, and opened it when I didn't get a response. I peeked inside. She was curled on top of her bed, fast asleep, a crunched tissue in her hand. There were several used ones in the basket by her bed. Poor Raine.

I decided not to wake her, turned to leave, and saw the blown-glass ornaments. They were beautiful. I picked them up one at a time and studied the designs. One was of a rainbow. Giving Raine one last glance, I put it down and let myself out of the room.

Downstairs, Lavania saw me and frowned. "Leaving already?"

"She was still asleep, and I didn't want to wake her. I'll text her later."

"See you at school, gorgeous?" Andris called out.

"You too, handsome." Laughter from Lavania and Torin followed me.

Outside, I turned the corner and almost bumped into Ingrid. "I looked for you at school today."

Ingrid shrugged. "We were at the hospital with Raine and her family."

Didn't they realize their behavior was odd and would draw attention? People didn't skip school to hold their friend's hands at the hospital. Or was Mr. Cooper's soul that important?

"Why?"

"Because Raine is special and important, and when Torin needs our help, we give it. What I said last night about my sister—"

"Maliina," I interjected.

She nodded. "She marked you with runes. Because of that, you can see us and souls."

"Why did she mark me? What did I ever do to her?"

Ingrid grimaced. "Maliina was Andris' first mate, but she was never completely sure about his feelings for her. You know, not like Raine is with Torin. When we first came here, Andris had shown interest in Raine. He was just playing around, but Maliina didn't think so. She went after Raine." Indris shook her head. "When Torin told her to stop, she did. Instead, she marked you to hurt Raine."

I laughed. "Are you saying my entire life is messed up because some stupid girl—"

"Immortal," Ingrid corrected.

"I don't care," I snarled. "She did this to me over that self-absorbed..." I pointed toward the house and barely stopped myself from saying Valkyrie. The curtain at Mrs. Rutledge's house fell into place as she stopped spying on us. Taking a deep breath, I asked in a low voice, "Where is she now?"

Ingrid shook her head. "We don't know."

Stupid Immortal. "When did she do this to me?"

"About two months ago?"

"Why don't I remember you or meeting her?"

Indris shrugged. "Your memories were probably erased by Norns." She searched my face. "You know who Norns are?"

"Yes." Echo had been right. I wanted to see him. Needed to see him and listen to everything he had to say with an open mind. "Thanks, Ingrid. I have to go."

6. The Party

As I drove home, I noticed the trees near the accident site were gone, but the vines weren't salvageable. The farmers would have to do some serious replanting. I parked outside my house and hurried inside. As usual, the scent of fresh baking greeted me.

Mom looked up from the stove. "Hi, honey. How was swim practice?"

"Good."

"Did you hear the news?" Dad asked. "The police are looking for vandals who uprooted trees and destroyed vines from the Tolbert and Melbeck farms."

My heart dropped. "Did they talk to you guys?"

"Oh yes," Mom said, switching off the stove. "We told them about the accident and how there was not a scratch on our truck."

"Aliens did it," Dad said, grinning. "I've never seen vines flattened like that."

"Don't start with that, Jeff," Mom said.

"Think about it, Penny. We get hit, but there's no dent. Huge fissures appear on the ground, yet there are no tire tracks. Trees are uprooted, and no one can explain how it was done. Vines are flattened like crop circles..."

I grabbed two nectarines and headed upstairs. Dad was enjoying this too much. I could see him starting a series based on what happened last night.

Echo wasn't upstairs.

The next day, I worried and waited. I needed answers and Echo went and pulled a freaking disappearing act? Raine came to school, but she might as well not be there. I couldn't talk to her because she was always surrounded by the Valkyries. Torin acted like he'd kick anyone's ass who dared to bother her. I hated waiting for answers, but I had no choice.

Andris kept his distance, but I could tell he was dying to screw with my head. I couldn't figure him out yet. He hanged out with the dope heads and skater dudes, and the next he was with the hipsters. Rumor had it that he was dating some guy, while another rumor linked him with Ingrid. It didn't take a genius to see that the Valkyrie liked him. During lunch, she sat with her fellow cheerleaders at a table, but her eyes kept straying to his table.

By Friday, I was cursing Echo. I didn't even enjoy the pep rally they had at the end of the school day. If he made an appearance, I was going to rip him a new one. Not only did I need answers only he could provide, but the souls were starting to come to the farm again. I had to disperse a few. I'd actually hoped doing so would draw Echo's attention and bring him back.

I rolled down the window and waved to Drew. He was one of the few students who drove a brand new car, an SUV. The parking lot was packed with clunkers and students yelling out weekend plans. Most were going to watch our boys play in the quarterfinals.

"See you at seven," I called out to Drew.

He grinned. "We are playing the Shithawks tomorrow afternoon, so the guys need to blow off steam tonight," he said, and the two jocks beside him back-thumped him.

Blowing off steam meant booze and hookups, a coach's worst nightmare. The Shithawks were actually the Skyhawks, Southridge High School in Beaverton. Somehow, I had a feeling the party was going to be about football, not Keith's posthumous birthday. We'd never made it this far in football. In fact, I couldn't remember if we ever made it to the quarterfinals, yet we were going against one of the top schools in the state.

Kicker was waiting for me by the lockers when I arrived at the pool. I wanted to ignore her, but she had the lost puppy look and was wearing the Reapers T-shirt again. Seeing it reminded me of Echo and how much his disappearance bugged me. I hated admitting it, but I kind of missed him.

"Okay, don't bite my head off until I finish," Kicker said. "Naya talked to the team, and after practice, we are heading to the hospital to show our support and prove to Raine that, despite not being on the team, she's still one of us."

It was brilliant, the kind thing I would have suggested if my life wasn't so effed up. "That sounds good."

"So can we hitch a ride to Drew's party?"

"We?"

"Naya, Sondra, and me. Naya's brother was going to give us his Jeep, but he and his friends went to Portland after school and won't be back until later tonight. He'll give us a ride home afterwards. We just need a ride there."

I shrugged. "Okay. Where do I pick you up?"

She laughed. "My house."

"The address, Kicker?" I asked when she started to walk away. She always forgot I couldn't "remember" some of these mundane things.

After practice, the entire swim team piled up in their cars and drove to Kayville Medical Center. Even Doc, our coach, came with us. The nurses didn't seem surprised to see us. Our team had a reputation for keeping vigils at the hospital.

Raine's expression made my calling the three girls bitches worthwhile. She fought tears and mouthed, "Thank you."

Her mother was more vocal. While she voiced her thanks and told us how wonderful and supportive we were, I pulled Raine aside.

"Did you do this?" she whispered as we hugged.

"No. Kicker, Naya, and Sondra came up with it. It's their way of apologizing for the way they treated you after the accident. Dubbing you a witch was stupid. Defacing your locker was unforgiveable."

"You know about that?" Raine asked, eyes wary.

"Yep. Kicker told me."

"Then she called us bitches for not sticking by you," Kicker said, having moved closer to us without me being aware.

Raine laughed, glanced at me, and cocked her eyebrows. "You did not."

I shrugged.

"I've missed your craziness, Cora." She hugged me again.

"Me too. Missed my crazy side, that is. How's your dad doing?"

"Didn't you hear what her mother said?" Kicker said, butting in again. "He came out of the coma this afternoon."

It was another hour before we left the hospital. I noticed a few more ghosts than usual. Once again, I found myself going over what had happened the last time I saw Echo as I drove along Orchard Grove. As if I couldn't help myself, I tried to remove the runes on my parents' truck again, even used my nails. Why had Echo drawn them? Assuming he was the one who had done it.

"You're still trying to find a dent on that old thing?" Mom called out. She was walking toward me from the barn.

I smiled and waited for her.

"Your father has come up with a new theory. It was an air pocket shot by a high-velocity air shooter that caused the accident. The air flattened the vines and yanked the trees from the ground. He plans to test his theory with a modified leaf blower."

"So who created the high-velocity air thingamajigger?" I asked.

"The military of course." She shook her head. "That imagination of his never ceases to amaze me."

"Or his fans," I said.

Mom chuckled and looped an arm through mine. She was carrying a basket of eggs on her other arm. "How was practice?"

"Good. The team decided to stop by the hospital after practice to visit Raine's dad and be there for her. We found out her father came out of the coma this afternoon."

"That's wonderful. I know Svana will be relieved."

"Will she?" I asked before I could stop myself and cringed when Mom stopped and studied me with narrowed eyes.

"You don't think she's grieving?" she asked.

I shrugged. "She's always so upbeat, and that didn't change when he was missing or when we saw her at the hospital."

"Oh, honey." She palmed my face. "There are so many faces of grief. Svana Cooper is the most amazing woman I know. She knows she must stay strong for Raine. That's what parents do. If she cried or doubted he was alive when his plane crashed, she did it privately. Anyway, I'm happy the team went to support Raine. That's one thing I've always liked about your swim team."

"Good, because a bunch of us have been invited to a party tonight. Can I go?"

She pushed open the door and walked ahead of me. "I guess if you're going to parties things are back to normal."

"So I can go?"

She pressed her lips to my temple in a gentle kiss. "When does it start?"

"Seven, but I'm picking up a bunch of girls who are driverless."

"Who is driverless?" Dad asked, coming downstairs.

"Swim friends going to a party," Mom said. "Be home by twelve."

"Mom," I protested.

"Ease back into your social life, muffin," Dad said. "We don't want you doing too much too soon. Twelve is reasonable. Unless you prefer eleven-fifty-nine… forty-five…"

"Hardy har har," I said and punched his arm as I passed him at the foot of the stairs.

"Make sure you eat something before you leave," Mom called after me.

She said the same thing every time before I left for a party, even though I never ate anything. Excitement and nervous energy tended to mess my appetite. I hoped Raine would be there. I hadn't dared to ask her anything when we were at the hospital, but Torin was the QB. No team party happened without the quarterback.

I didn't expect Echo to be in my room, yet I felt his presence the moment I opened the door. His intoxicating, masculine scent was unmistakable. My heart pounding, I looked around.

The room was empty.

Damn it. I missed him.

My dresser was exactly the way I'd left it this morning, a total mess, but my bed looked rumpled and there was an indentation on my pillow. He'd lain on my bed. Then I saw the glove. Right there in the middle of the bed. Had he left it behind or forgotten it?

Anger surged through me. "Stay in Hel, Echo."

I marched to the bed, grabbed his glove, plumped my pillow, and straightened my bed. I was not playing his stupid games anymore, and I had a party to go to, where there were going to be normal guys.

In the bathroom, I threw the glove in garbage, stripped, and got in the shower.

An hour later, my nails and my hair were done. I stepped from under the hair dryer and removed the curlers. I had lost weight while at PMI, so most of my favorite pants were a little loose. I decided on a mid-thigh stretchy skirt. The top was just the right length and displayed my cleavage to the max. I studied my reflection then sat in front of my dresser to apply makeup and brush my hair.

Happy with the results, I slipped on ankle boots, grabbed a jacket, and left the room. Two steps and I whipped around, went back to the bathroom, and fished Echo's glove from the garbage. On a whim, I slipped it on.

It was made of soft leather and hugged my hand. Smiling, I headed downstairs.

***

I drove slower than usual on Orchard Grove, but nothing weird happened. Kicker lived on the other end of the town. I noticed a few souls wandering around. As usual, they stopped whatever they were doing and stared after me. Seriously, I didn't understand their attraction to me. I now carried a fire poker in my car, just in case I had to disperse a few.

Naya and Sondra were at Kicker's when I arrived. They must not have gone to their homes after swim practice. Worse, they weren't ready. Their level of excitement surprised me. Being invited to Drew's party was a shortcut up the social ladder, where jocks and cheerleaders reigned supreme.

"You look amazing," Kicker said. She pointed at Echo's glove. "I love that. Where did you get it?"

I didn't get a chance to respond.

"How do you make your hair look like that?" Naya asked.

"Curlers." I just wanted us to leave, but they needed help with their makeup. And their hair. Naya's hair was naturally curly, but she'd blow-dried it. I knew the kind of girls who attended Drew's parties. Catty with each other, but downright cruel to girls they believed were socially beneath them.

"I like your makeup," Kicker said.

"I can finish applying yours if you like," I offered, picking up the makeup case on the dresser.

Kicker glanced at the other two and giggled. "I was done, but if you can make me look like her," she grabbed a magazine and showed me a picture of an actress with her coloring and hair color, "I will love you forever."

Forever. Echo had jokingly asked me to be his forever. Annoyed that I was thinking of him I again, I ground my teeth and answered Kicker. "Okay."

She sat and tilted her head back. I studied her face.

"FYI, you are more beautiful than Jen," I said, inclining my head toward the magazine.

Kicker grinned. I gave her pointers as I applied the makeup. When I finished, Naya and Sondra wanted theirs redone, too. I ended up curling their hair with a hot iron. I hated hot irons and the damage they did to hair. I mentioned that and explained how I always used curlers and a hooded dryer. From their expressions, I might have just converted them.

While they dressed, I texted Raine. "Are you going to Drew's party?"

"Wanted to, but don't feel up to it," Raine texted back. "Torin will stop by. Have fun."

"When is your dad coming home?"

"Tomorrow. We're turning the den into his bedroom."

"Need help? I might need a place to go if the party blows."

"Drew's parties never do, but feel free to stop by. I'll be home. Got Torin and Andris doing the heavy lifting right now. I heard you and Andris hit it off."

"He's an ass."

Instead of a text response, my phone went off. I brought to my ear. "Hey."

"I was laughing so hard the guys wanted to know who I was texting," Raine said. "Andris says hi."

"He's still an ass."

"I know. Where are you?"

"At Kicker's. They... she, Naya, and Sondra are getting ready." I looked up to find the girls watching me. "Just a sec." I cocked my brow at Kicker.

"We're ready," she said.

"Oh, good." I got up and started out of the room, the phone back on my ear. I wish Raine were with me. She, Eirik, and I often did things together. "Can I ask you something?"

"Shoot," Raine said.

"Have you heard from Eirik since his family moved?"

There was silence on the line.

I unlocked my car and slid behind the wheel. Still no response. "Raine?"

"A few times."

She sounded funny. "Where is he?"

"He, uh, moved up north," she said vaguely.

"North where? Seattle? Canada?"

She laughed. "I wish. Listen, Cora. Eirik is coming back. He said he'll explain everything when he does."

I frowned. "Explain what?"

"Why his family left. You were all he could think about before he left."

I laughed. "He had a funny way of showing it. One, he left without saying goodbye. Two, he didn't visit me—" I stopped when I remembered I wasn't alone and there was just so much I could reveal to anyone. "Forget about him. I mean, we were just friends. You were the one dating him."

"Biggest mistake. He was crazy about *you*," Raine said.

"Sure he was. I gotta go."

"Cora," she said.

"Seriously, let's *never* discuss him." Thinking about him still hurt. Getting pissed with myself, I turned the key and pulled out of Kicker's driveway.

"Eirik never said goodbye?" Naya asked.

"Naya! Remember what I told you?" Kicker asked.

Naya frowned, then her mouth formed an O. "Oh, yeah. The concussion!"

"You and Eirik did everything together, Cora," Kicker said.

"We did?" I asked.

"You'd come to the pool to watch him swim and leave together before you decided to rejoin the team. We thought you rejoined because of him. At least that's what we concluded." She turned and glanced back at the other two. "Right?"

How had I juggled three boyfriends—Eirik, Drew, and Echo? I must have been the most unfeeling astral projection in the world. I kept my mouth shut for the rest of the drive.

The driveway to the Cavanaugh's home was lined with cars, the clunky pickups from kids from across the railway track and the expensive foreign models favored by his closest friends—sons and daughters of vineyard owners and other upper elite Kayvillians. The place was packed, and people were still arriving. The party was on the pool deck, and people were dancing to the music blaring from speakers on the large wooden porch. The benefit of living in a huge vineyard was no angry neighbors ordering you to lower the volume. Drew's parents were often out of town at wine shows, and his sister never seemed to be around whenever Drew threw a party.

Some people sat around on pool chairs and lounges while others played in the swimming pool, but majority stood around the wide porch in groups, talking or swaying to music while sipping fruit punch. Knowing Drew, the punch was mixed with some of his family's favorite brews.

"Cora!" he called out.

I waved. He was holding court away from the dancers on the right end of the pool. He gave me a once over and grinned with appreciation. Most of the people around him were jocks, cheerleaders, or members of the drill team. My vlog had given me a free pass into their inner circle, even though I wasn't really "one of them".

Fulton, a blond wide receiver who could pass for a surfer dude, jumped up and offered me the lounge next to Drew.

"Thanks, Fulton."

"Want something to drink?" he asked, his eyes on my cleavage.

"Sure." As he took off, my eyes met Leigh Haggerty's. Her fake smile didn't fool me. She'd been after Drew for, like, forever. She was seated on a deck chair behind him, stroking his hair. He didn't seem to mind. Another girl, Pia Gunter, sat on the lounge on his other side, scratching the skin under his cast with a cast scratcher. She was in my English class and was a total airhead.

"Did you bring *them*?" Leigh asked, nodding at Kicker and the other girls. I almost laughed at the annoyance in her voice. The swimmers were talking to some jocks and were, therefore, considered a threat.

"Yes. Why?" I cocked my eyebrows, daring her to say something mean about my teammates.

"They shouldn't be flirting with Rand. He is Kenzie's boyfriend," Leigh said.

"Hmm, maybe Rand shouldn't flirt with them since he's the one with a girlfriend," I said. Guys were so easy. Fix your hair a bit, slap on makeup, and they acted like they'd never seen you before.

"I've never seen them before," Pia said with a bored air.

She never noticed anyone who wasn't in her circle of friends. This party was going to get boring fast. I glanced at Drew and found him studying me. He smiled. I smiled back. One hour, then I was leaving.

"Is Torin coming tonight?" someone asked, and just like that, the conversation switched to tomorrow's game and the Skyhawks—because it was a football party.

"I recorded their last three games," Drew said. "It's on DVR, so if you guys want to watch…" There was mass exodus of most players from around us and the ones in the pool followed. A few clingy girlfriends went with them.

I sipped my drink and nibbled on a slice of pizza. The music was loud, the drinks and food plenty. This was what I needed. Normalcy. Hanging out with people my age. Indulging in a little underage drinking. No more thoughts about Echo or Eirik, souls or reapers. I didn't even care that a few gate crashed the party and kept staring at me. I wasn't dealing with souls or the supernatural world. Tonight, I was just a teenager trying to have fun.

Drew's arm came to rest on the top of my lounge, and he gently stroked my shoulder. His touch was pleasant. There was no zing or the urgent need to touch him back. No charged moment when our eyes met. He was a handsome guy, and I might even let him kiss me again tonight.

I was laughing at something someone said when there was a reduction in the noise level. The people on the porch seemed to lose interest in dancing. The ones in the pool stared and whispered. A sliver of awareness scuttled under my skin.

Echo. Somehow, I knew it was him before I turned.

"Who is that?" Leigh asked with awe.

He stood at the entrance of the back door, hands in the front pockets of his pants, his piercing eyes scanning the crowd. I could feel his impatience. He didn't return smiles or nods.

He found me, and a lazy grin lifted one corner of his lips. My heartbeat shot up, a mixture of excitement and anticipation shooting through me. His wolf eyes held me captive, his bone-melting smile making my insides gooey. He started forward, his walk lazy.

"He's coming this way," Pia whispered excitedly.

He looked amazing. His duster was unbuttoned and revealed jeans and a gray T-shirt. It was the first time I'd ever seen him dress so casually, and he looked hot. The pants hugged his powerful thighs, and his shirt hinted at the masculine body underneath it. I wanted to yank off the duster and feast on him. Stand up, run to him, and touch his face. His shaggy hair had that messy look he pulled off so seamlessly, and he'd shaved. Another first. No guy at the party could touch him on hotness.

"Who is he?" one of the girls asked.

Every mother's worst nightmare.

Ignoring everyone, he offered me his hand. The left one with the other glove. "Dance with me, doll-face."

My anger with him for disappearing melted away. One second I was on the lounge; the next I was walking beside him, my gloved right hand in his. Since when had I become this easy? Probably since I'd met the gorgeous reaper.

Echo slipped an arm around my waist and pulled me close. I trembled when the full length of his hard body pressed against mine. He interlaced our fingers, his eyes not leaving mine.

"I'm happy you wore the glove tonight," he whispered in a husky voice.

"You knew about the party?"

"Yes. Did you miss me?"

I had. "No. Where have you been?"

"I missed you, too." He pressed his cheek against mine.

He was warm, which either meant he hadn't come from Hel or someone had warmed him. I hated the feeling that washed over me. Jealousy was ugly. I refused to let it consume me the way it had when Raine was dating Eirik.

"Where were you? I thought Torin and the others hurt you. Then I was sure you were on the road uprooting trees and destroying grapes."

He chuckled. The sexy sound rumbled through his chest and mine, doing things to me that defied description. I wanted to purr.

"I was watching out for you. Which one is Drew?" he asked, swinging me around so he could look at the group I'd been sitting with.

"Leave him alone, Echo."

"Kiss me and I'll play nice." He dropped a kiss on my neck.

Heat shot through me, and a low moan of pleasure escaped my lips. Gah, I wanted to kiss him so badly. Devour him. "Behave!"

"I will once you tell me which one is Drew."

"You don't need to worry about him."

"I'm not worried. I just want to tell him to forget about you in the nicest possible way." He stepped away from me, and I knew he'd humiliate Drew in front of his friends and not care.

I grabbed his shirt and pulled him back. The T-shirt rode up and revealed his ridged abs and the intriguing line of hair disappearing under his waistband. I drooled a little. Okay, a lot. He chuckled, and my eyes flew to his. The smile disappeared from his face.

"A kiss it is," he whispered, cupped my face, and lowered his head. "I need to kiss you."

I expected him to take over my senses like before, bending me to his will. Instead, the kiss was gentle. He rubbed his lips across mine as though waiting for my permission to deepen it. I sighed and invited him to take more. He did, nibbling my upper lip then lower. I trembled, but frustration washed over me. He was holding back, while I wanted more. Needed him to make me remember what it felt like to be in his arms.

I reached up, grabbed his coat, and pulled him closer. At the same time, I flicked my tongue and tasted his lips. The dam broke. He groaned, angled his head, and took charge of the kiss. The earth fell from under me. I clung to his shoulders so sure I'd fall if he let me go.

Sensations crested and exploded through me. The music disappeared into the background. Where we were and who might be watching ceased to matter. All I cared about was Echo. His lips. His tongue. The feel of his body against mine.

He broke the kiss. More like yanked his mouth from mine and muttered, "Hel's Mist."

The smoldering look in his eyes had me wishing we were alone. I looped my hands around his neck and buried my face in his chest, my heart threatening to burst.

He moved his mouth to my ear. "Now he knows you're not available," he said in a husky voice, his arms tight around my waist.

Sanity was slowly returning. My body still hummed, and my lips tingled. "You're a jerk."

He chuckled. "I know, but you still want me."

I did. Too much. "Shut up."

"I'll see you later tonight. Okay?"

Surely, I hadn't heard him right. I leaned back, my eyes narrowing. "You are not leaving me here."

He glanced at the other students and smirked. "I wanted to make sure you didn't forget me. Now be a sweetheart and go have fun with your Mortal friends."

"In your dreams, buster. You are not going anywhere until we talk." We couldn't do it in the middle of Drew's deck with everyone watching. It was time to say my goodbyes. "I'll be back."

Echo pulled me back into his arms again and peered into my eyes. "I have to go, Cora."

"Why?"

"I'm trying to stop Hel's private army from finding you." He winced as though he hadn't meant to say that.

"Finding… What?"

He touched my cheek and chuckled. "Sorry, I didn't mean to drop it on you like that. I meant to explain everything last time after your trip to the hospital, but a couple of my brethren were on your tail and had to be stopped. Now, give me a kiss before I leave."

"You're not doing that to me. Not again."

"Doing what?"

"Leaving without an explanation. I was worried when you just disappeared." I glanced around. We were the center of everyone's attention. "Don't move."

"Cora—"

"Do. Not. Leave." I marched to where Drew sat. "Sorry, I have to go. Something's come up."

Annoyance flashed in his eyes. He opened his mouth to say something, but then he glanced behind me and clammed up, his jaw tense.

"See you around," he said through clenched teeth. He looked pissed. I guess that meant this was the last party I'd be attending here. Oh, well.

"Yeah, see you around." I turned, expecting eyes to be on us. Instead, they were on Echo. The attention didn't seem to bother him. He stood in the middle of the deck like an island and watched me with piercing eyes, leaving no doubt in anyone's mind that he was only there for one thing. Me.

"Let's go." I grabbed his arm and tugged. He allowed me to pull him along. Just before I entered the house, my eyes met Kicker's. The expression on her face was comical. I waved.

"You know what everyone is thinking, right?" Echo asked.

"I don't care."

"That you can't wait to get me alone."

"I *can't* wait to get you alone."

"Rip my clothes off and have your way with me," he added, smirking.

I threw him an exasperated glance. He wanted honesty? He was about to get a bucket load of it. I was done pretending I didn't want him. "I'd like nothing better than to do that, but first we talk."

He cocked his eyebrows. "Rip my clothes off?"

"Uh-huh." We left the house and headed toward my car. I unlocked my car, but before I could slide behind the wheel, he gripped my hips and turned me around.

"You mean it about us and clothes off?"

I touched his cheek, his lips. "We've done it many times before, right?"

He nodded, a heavy hooded expression settling on his face.

"Then it's no big deal." I reached up and pressed a kiss to his lips. "Let's go." But before I could turn, he palmed my face, eyes blazing under the moonlight. He wanted to kiss me. My pulse raced. Knowing he wanted me was thrilling.

"I want you." He pressed me against the car door, one thigh pushing my legs apart. He settled between my thighs, pressed closer. "I stayed away, hoping I'd get you out of my mind, but the longer I was gone the stronger my craving for you became."

Holy crap! What had my admission unleashed? "I thought you were stopping Hel's army from coming after me."

"Hel's army doesn't stand a chance against me." He rubbed his cheek against mine. Inhaled deeply. "I missed your smell. When I'm away from you, I dream about holding you, touching you, making you happy." He kissed the corner of my eye. "When with you, I want you in my arms."

"That's because you remember what we had."

"No, it's more than that. There's something different about you. I feel it whenever we... Before, we'd have sex and I'd leave without a single concern. Not caring if you went back to Eirik or a Mortal."

His hand crawled under my top. I trembled when his fingers caressed my side. His skin against mine was stimulating. I stopped breathing when his touch became intimate. I knew we'd done this before, but it all seemed new and exciting. Part of me wanted to tell him to stop, but I was curious, so I didn't push his hand away. Worries about privacy flitted in my head. We were away from the house, and darkness hid us from prying eyes. His duster also gave us some cover.

Thoughts of lack of privacy became unimportant as his caresses grew bold. I wanted to say something, but speech was beyond me.

"Now I want to punch every Mortal that looks at you. I want them to know you might live among them but you are mine."

The possessiveness in his voice should've bugged me, but all I felt was elation. Then I realized his hand was on my leg, inching up under my skirt. Now was the time to tell him to stop.

"I've tasted every inch of you, doll-face, yet this all feels new, like I'm rediscovering you. You want to know why?" he whispered in my ear and nipped my earlobe.

I trembled, my mouth too dry for me to speak. Worse, his hand was under my skirt, on my thigh, hip, slowly creeping to the front, totally driving me crazy.

"Your kisses are different, your responses natural." He kissed my neck then moved to my shoulder. "You taste so sweet. Every time your eyes widen or your breath catches, it makes me feel invincible." He moved to my jaw, punctuating each sentence with a kiss. "It makes me want to please you more. Keep you with me always."

Our lips connected. Once again, the kiss was gentle, worshipping. When I sighed with pleasure, his tongue slipped between my lips to caress mine. The tempo of the kiss changed, and he became demanding. Lost in sensations, I clung to his shoulders.

A rumbling groan vibrated through his chest as his fingers tugged my thong. The material rubbed intimately against me, and the intensity of the pleasure stole my breath away. I pressed closer to him. I wanted his touch. Needed to remember what it felt like to have him make love to me. Every fantasy I'd ever had about being intimate with a guy ceased to matter. He was my fantasy.

He let go of my lips to trails kisses along my neck, nibbling and suckling.

"If you want me to stop…" His words came out disjointed, his voice husky and ragged.

"Don't," I gasped.

His fingers slipped my thong aside and touched me intimately. His touch was electrifying, the feeling mind-numbing. I strained against him, needing more.

He looped his free arm around my waist and lifted me up, using the body of the car and his thighs to anchor me in place. I wrapped my legs around his waist as each movement of his fingers pushed me higher and higher, the intensity of the pleasure increasing with the number of the runes appearing on his body.

I heard something rip, and then cool air rushed on my chest. My silk bra didn't stop Echo. The heat from his mouth replaced the cold.

Pressure built. My body became a fine-tuned instrument at his hands, until something beautiful unfolded in my core and spread through me like a wild fire. I cried out, but he kissed me and swallowed the sound.

7. Breaking Rules

My world would never be the same again, I thought dreamily. *I would never, ever be the same again.* Echo didn't stop kissing me. His kisses became slow. He was taking his time, as though giving me a moment to recover. Didn't the reaper know a kiss from him always had the opposite effect?

"Wrap your legs around me." I tightened my arms around his shoulders and my legs around his waist. Echo secured me against him by crisscrossing his arms under my butt. He started around the car to the passenger side of the car.

"You know I can walk."

"I'm not ready to let you go." He stopped by the passenger door, propped me against the car body, and started shrugging off his coat.

"What are you doing?" I asked.

"Stripping just for you."

Oh, baby. The visuals were enough to make a girl drool. "Cute."

"Your shirt is ripped, and I don't want anyone looking at you."

Heat rushed to my face. There were a few students, some making out, others walking to or from their cars. Had they seen us? Echo had ripped my shirt. I still couldn't believe what we'd done. What I'd let him do. Should I offer to return the favor? Even now, I could still feel the evidence of his need pressing against me. My legs tightened around him, and he groaned.

"Did I hurt you?"

He chuckled. "No, but you could."

I frowned. "What do you mean?"

"Forget I said that." He lowered me to the ground and pressed against me, sandwiching me with the car. He ran a finger down my neck. I shivered. He smiled, pleased with my reaction. "Engage your runes and fix your top."

"What?"

"Use the right runes to fix your top."

I shook my head. "How do I do that?"

He cursed softly under his breath. "That really pisses me off."

"What?"

"The way the Norns erased all your memories you can't even remember simple runes." He shrugged off his coat and held it up.

I shoved my arms through the sleeves. "So, uh, did you write the runes on our truck?"

"Yeah. I hope you don't mind."

"Why should I? What do they mean?"

"They are protection runes against car accidents. Your parents will be safe now. And before you ask, I didn't etch them on yours because I assumed you were covered, that you could engage healing runes and self-heal. You are going to need a crash course on runes, doll-face. Once you know them, you can visualize them and make them appear on your skin whenever you want." He started buttoning the duster. "There are runes for healing, speed, strength, protection, guidance..."

Something pressed on my left ribs. I reached inside, pulled it out, and frowned. It was his scythe.

"My artavus." He took it and touched the tip. "Sorry I forgot about this. You don't want this cutting you. It is sharp and cuts deep."

"Is artavus another name for a scythe?"

"No, artavus just means magical blade, which is what a scythe is to a Grimnir. Our most important magical blade. You might disperse a soul in this realm with a metal rod, but the scythe does it *and* inflicts excruciating pain. That's why souls freak out when they see it. It also opens a portal to Hel's Hall. The scythe, like any artavus, is sacred to its owner." He shoved it somewhere in his back pocket, helped me with the buttons, and looped the chains on his coat. The duster was longer on me and dragged on the ground.

"I look like a clown," I said.

"You look dangerous. My kind of girl." He opened the passenger door. "Get in. I'm driving."

"Oh no, you're not." I started around the car, but he grabbed my hand.

"I need to focus on something else, Cora, not you or how amazing you smell or how you felt in my arms a few minutes ago. I need to stay preoccupied or I'm not going to keep my hands off you while you drive."

Put that way, who was I to argue? I opened the door and settled into the passenger seat.

"No snarky comment?" he teased.

"No." Until I knew how to engage my runes and self-heal, I was playing it safe. "But I'm happy to know you can't keep me out of your thoughts and dreams, or keep your hands off me."

He chuckled and ran his knuckles down my cheek. "That mouth of yours drives me crazy. Do you want to head to your place and talk?"

"No." I shook my head. "If I go home now, my parents will want to know why and start worrying that someone said or did something to make me leave the party early. I have until midnight, and I know the perfect place to go for our little chat. It is quiet, and with Drew's party here, no one will be there to bother us."

"Good." Echo ran around to the driver's seat, slid behind the wheel, and studied the dashboard.

"You do know how to drive, right?" I asked.

He chuckled and extended his hand toward me, palm up. I dropped the key in his hand. "I've been driving for centuries, doll-face. From steam to electric cars." He started the car and eased out of the spot.

I couldn't remember details of industrial revolution. Steam engines were used in the 1700s. "How old are you?"

"Old." He reached for my hand, interlaced our fingers, and pressed a kiss to my knuckles. "At least much, much older than you."

"Where were you born?"

"France."

"So you are French?"

"You could say that."

I sighed. For someone who talked a lot, he was being stingy with information. "Okay, Echo. Hide your identity. Continue being Mr. Mysterious. Turn left ahead." I waited until he turned. "Stay on this road then turn right at the light."

"Tell me again where we're going?"

"A scenic overlook. It's quiet, and the scenery at night is breathtaking. It is only five minutes from town. Right turn's coming up."

Silence filled the car. Soon were headed out of town on I-5.

"About my past," Echo said, "I'm not trying to be mysterious. I just hate dwelling on it."

The wariness in his voice surprised me. Echo wasn't the type to be so cagey. "Why? What happened?"

He let go of my hand and gripped the steering wheel. "Long story."

"We have…" I peered at the time on the dashboard. It was a little after nine. "About three hours and I'm a good listener."

More silence. Okay, this was out of character. Echo was cocky, bold, badass, and unstoppable. He was Hel's best reaper. What could have happened in the past that was so horrible he couldn't share?

I took his hand, wrapped it between mine, and rested my head on his shoulder. "It's okay. Talk to me when you are ready. Just know that I won't judge you or anything like that. I'll just listen and keep my opinion, good or bad, to myself. Of course, you must also know I hate people who keep secrets from me and I'm not a strong believer in double standards."

"You didn't want to talk about Eirik before," he reminded me.

"Yeah, well, that's because he's not important. You are."

He chuckled. "Are you trying to manipulate me, Cora Jemison?"

"Of course. How else am I going to get you to talk to me? Seriously, what's so bad that you can't tell me? I swear I won't laugh or joke about it. If it's sad, I'll keep my tears to myself."

He chuckled again. "You are amazing."

"I know."

He laughed. "I came from a Druid family."

"See, that wasn't so bad." I knew next to nothing about Druids, except what I'd read in fiction and watched on TV. They were a magical people. "What were the Druids?"

"We *were* a priestly race during the Iron Age. Very spiritual. We sought knowledge and enlightenment. Respected nature and tried to learn from it. Our scholars were respected and revered. In fact, rulers could not make decisions or maintain order without our help."

"You also used magic," I said.

"To do good, not hurt people. During the peak of the Iron Age, we were everywhere—Britain, Ireland, Gaul, and Celtic Europe. My family came from Gaul."

"We're almost there. The sign is on the left. Where's Gaul?"

"A region that covered most of western Europe, present day France, Luxembourg, Belgium, Switzerland, northern Italy, Netherlands, and Germany. My father was an important official, so I became a novice to a priest at a young age. It helped that the head of the Druids at the time was my uncle. By the time I was seventeen, I had learned all the verses by heart."

"Verses?"

"Sacred teachings passed down from Bards, Ovates, and Druids to novices. We weren't strong believers in keeping records or writing down our practices. Everything was oral. Spells, charms, incantations— they were all memorized. When Rome attacked Gaul, I was eighteen. We were a peaceful people. We didn't even join the military, but the Romans were determined to destroy us." His hands flexed on the steering wheel. "Once they conquered Gaul, they slaughtered my people and outlawed our religious practices. I think they targeted us out of fear because the Gaullish society was dependent on us, yet our teachings were sacred and not shared with non-Druids. Is that the sign?" he asked.

A white sign with the words "Kayville Point" was ahead. "Yes. Go on with your story."

"Some of us were forced to fight back using magic. The scholars took to the forest, hiding and moving from place to place. My group managed to survive for two years when a traveler from Otherworld visited."

"An alien?"

He laughed. "That's a more recent term."

He pulled up on the gravel embankment with parking spaces clearly mapped. Only one car was parked in the area, its windows foggy.

"Is this the go-to place when students want to make out?" Echo asked.

It was. "Yes and no."

He switched off the engine and faced me. Runes appeared on his body, a few lighting up his face and the interior of the car. I could never get enough of looking at him when his runes were engaged. He looked beautiful, yet dangerous. Then I noticed his narrowed eyes. It wasn't the I-can't-wait-to-kiss-you look he'd worn at Drew's place. "What is it?"

"You come here a lot?" he asked.

"No, just a couple of times. The football team holds crazy parties up here after games. They don't come for the view, even though it's amazing." I pointed to our left. "There's a sharp drop over there with more beer bottles than the city dump."

Echo's eyelids dropped as he pushed his fingers through my hair and gripped the back of my head. "You and Drew ever drive up here, doll-face?"

He spoke softly, but I heard the jealously in his voice. "No. We didn't have that kind of a relationship. I mean I kissed him, but it was a one-time thing."

He studied me as though trying to see if I'd lied. "Eirik?"

He's coming back... You were all he was concerned about before he left... "No. We, uh, I don't want to discuss Eirik. Tell me about Otherworld."

Heat flashed in Echo's eyes. "What happens if he comes back?"

I shrugged. "I don't care. He's not who I though he was."

"Yeah, he's a freaking god among Mort—"

I pressed a finger to his lips. "Let's not talk about Eirik, okay. He never understood me, and he wasn't there when I needed him. You get me, and you are here."

He kissed my knuckles and smiled.

"Yes, I get you. Just a second." He stepped out of the car, pulled the blade from his back pocket, and went into high speed. I got out of the car and watched him, but he was a blur, so I focused on what he was drawing on my car. He was etching runes. So many of them.

"Excuse me?" a guy said behind me, and I whipped around, my stomach dropping. The couple from the other car peered at me.

"Cora?" the girl asked.

I recognized her from school. Kendra something or other. Her date looked familiar, but I couldn't place his face. "Hi, Kendra."

"What are you doing up here alone?" she asked, studying Echo's coat curiously. She didn't introduce her date, and I didn't really care.

"I'm not alone." I glanced at Echo, who as still scribbling. Of course, they couldn't see him. He slowed down, and I caught his smirk before he disappeared inside the car.

"So are you guys just hanging out?" I asked lamely and tried not to cringe.

Kendra looked at her date. "Yeah."

Her date peered at the car. Thankfully, the door opened and Echo stepped out.

"Oh, there you are," I said with relief.

He completely ignored the couple. "Come on."

"Nice seeing you again, Kendra." I opened the passenger door and slid inside.

Echo opened the back door and fumbled with the driver's seat until it folded, creating more space. "Back here. If we're really going to talk, let's get comfortable."

I tried climbing over the tray with the coffee holders, but the duster kept getting in the way. Growling in frustration, I sat back in my seat and opened the door.

Kendra and her friend were walking back to their car. They turned and waved. I'd normally be embarrassed if anyone saw me crawling into the back seat of a car with a guy, but not this time. I could make out with Echo anywhere and not feel ashamed. Not that we were planning on making out now.

I got in the back seat and sat on the folded seat facing him, but the duster got caught in the door. How did he move around wearing it? Worse, my car had little legroom.

"Easy, sweetheart. That's my favorite coat." Echo decided to help by undoing the buttons. A grin curled his lips when he spied my ripped shirt.

My face grew warm. "And this *was* my favorite top."

He removed his artavus from his back pocket, lifted my shirt, and etched runes on it. I'd assumed he drew the runes, but it turned out that a light shot from the blade to the fabric. The fabric of my shirt shifted and remolded, until the rip was repaired. It wasn't perfect, but I was covered now.

"That looks awful. I'll buy you a dozen to replace it."

"With what? Mortals don't trade in souls. It takes cold, hard cash to buy goods."

"I have money, mainly in gold." He pulled me down on top of him and stretched his legs over the folded seat. It was a tight fit, but we made it work. He tucked my head under his chin, and I sighed. He smelled amazing, and I loved listening to his heartbeat.

"I want to hear the rest of your story," I said. "You were at the part with the aliens from Otherworld."

"I just told you I have gold."

"And this should interest me because…?"

"You're a new Grimnir and haven't accumulated anything. I've had millennia to collect stuff, properties, money, expensive toys, which means I can give you anything I want. Women dig that stuff."

I opened my eyes wide and fluttered my eyelids. "Oh, Echo, you're so rich. Can you buy me an island?"

"Sure. Which one?"

I laughed. "Quit showing off and tell me about the aliens that visited your people."

He chuckled, the sound vibrating through his chest. I loved that chuckle. It was dark and sexy and never failed to send a shiver of pure excitement through me.

"Not aliens," he said. "Beings from other worlds. We believed that other realms existed. What I didn't know was how often they—Valkyries—recruited from among my people. The secret was well kept. The selected few went through intense training, learning about the realms and magical runes. I was twenty when I became an Immortal. It usually took years of training before one started reaping, but my case was unusual. Within a year, I was reaping souls for Valhalla."

"You were a Valkyrie?"

"Yeah, but not for long. My people were still in hiding, still being hunted down like animals. My sisters…" He released air. "Died horribly, stoned to death when they weren't even sorceresses."

My heart squeezed. He stared bleakly into space, but I could see him struggle to gain control. I touched his face, wanting to comfort him, but what words could convey how horrified I was by his story? So I let my lips speak for me.

I kissed him. Gently at first, then deeply, trying to absorb his pain. Make him forget even if for just a moment. I didn't stop until he took over. His lips eased from mine and pressed on my forehead.

"The Roman emperors were wussies, scared of old men and women, novices too young to shave," he said, speaking slowly. "We couldn't be Druids and Roman citizens. I was in a position to rescue as many of my people as I could, so I came up with a plan and rallied the support of a group of Valkyries, all former Druids, and told them what I'd planned. I didn't give them a chance to refuse. I told them they owed it to our people, that we were Druids first and Valkyries second. We started rescuing our people. I might have said before that there are rules I break and those I don't, but the circumstances were different then. We bent some and broke quite a few." He became quiet.

I lifted my head and peered at him, the runes on his forehead gave a soft glow that made him look even more exotic than usual.

He smiled. "Actually, we broke a lot. The dying ones, we took their souls to Valhalla and Falkvang. We didn't care whether they were fighters or not. The rest we marked with healing runes and turned into Immortals. It is against the Valkyrie laws to turn Mortals into Immortals, not without proper training and the right artavo."

"Is artavo like artavus?"

"Artavus is one. Artavo is plural. I became friends with dwarves, makers of weapons, and convinced them to make us more artavo, which we used to turn my people. When the gods discovered what we'd done, we were hauled before the Council. The sentence was harsh. We got Hel duty for eternity."

I studied his face, the furrows of his brow, and the downward turn of his sensual lips. At first he couldn't meet my gaze. When he finally did, I sucked in a breath. There was so much torment in his eyes.

"You did the right thing, Echo."

"Did I?"

"Of course, you did. Your people were being slaughtered. You did what you had to do to save them. So you broke a few rules…"

"I forced my friends to follow me, Cora, and condemned them to eternal servitude to Hel."

"They didn't have to follow you. You didn't threaten them with bodily harm."

The laugh that escaped him was derisive. "Actually, I did. The ones I couldn't guilt into joining me, I threatened."

Of course, he had. He wouldn't be Echo if he hadn't. "What are a few bruises among Valkyries. They self-heal, don't they?"

"True, but they're not happy serving Hel."

"Then they are a bunch of wussies," I retorted.

"They hate me. I started an underground band, and until recently, I was the lead singer. Things got so bad I decided to quit."

The Reapers. No wonder Kicker almost recognized him. I'd so love to hear him sing. "Their loss."

He chuckled, lifting my leg over his hip and running a hand up and down my bare thigh. My skirt had ridden up under his coat. "I killed two of them."

He spoke so softly I thought I misheard him.

"Two of what?"

"Druids. Well, Grimnirs. Even after a couple of millennia, I still think of them as Druids, which is rather funny because I've given you a hard time over calling us grim or—"

I gripped his face and forced him to look at me. "Why did you kill them?"

"They were coming after you, Cora."

Wow. He'd killed his own people for me. How was I supposed to process that? It was obvious he felt terrible about it. His golden eyes were shadowed. I'd noticed how they became golden when he was excited or aroused, but the green ring grew larger when he was sad. "I don't know what to say."

"You don't have to say anything. I couldn't let them take you from me."

It wasn't just the words, but how he said them, with unwavering conviction, that had my insides turning into warm goo. I loved the feeling, but at the same time, it was scary. No one had ever made me feel like he did. "Will you get in trouble?"

"Only if the goddess finds out."

"Why did they want me?"

He was silent.

"Echo?"

"Goddess Hel had sent you on a secret mission, something she does with us whenever she's interested in a particular soul. Usually, she calls one of us to her throne room for a private meeting. In your case, you approached her while you were still with the Norns and asked to work for her. That's how we met, in Hel's Hall. You seemed out of place, cold, and angry. She hadn't decided to trust you, but then again, she has trust issues." Echo paused and frowned. "Was that your stomach?

My stomach growled again. Heat crawled across my face. "Don't mind it."

"Have you eaten?"

"I had half a slice of pizza at Drew's, but food can wait." I made a deal with Hel? What was I thinking? "I can't believe I'm evil."

"I wouldn't go as far as to call you evil. You seemed driven when we first met. Norns rarely associate with the gods or work willingly with them. None ever dared approach Goddess Hel. Even Valkyries hate working for her. That's why quite a few of her reapers are old and ghostly. She recruits Grimnirs among the souls under her care, which explains the depiction of reapers in Mortal folklore."

I heard him without commenting. There was something wrong with me. How could I have made a deal with Hel? What was I thinking? "What was my mission?"

"I don't know. I asked around the last few days, but no one seemed to know anything. When you failed to deliver, the goddess sent Grimnirs to find you. Two succeeded, and I had to take care of them. I distracted the others, but they'll be back. Grimnirs are resourceful."

I knew I could be a bitch, but there was no way I could be evil. Or maybe the Immortal Maliina had done something to make me evil. Whatever the reason, I was being hunted now. No wonder I was back at home with my parents. A thought flashed through my head. Could I be putting them in danger by staying with them? Echo was already breaking laws to help me.

I sat up, completely straddling Echo. He circled my waist and pulled me closer until our hips locked. The position was intimate despite his jeans, so I wasn't surprised when his body responded.

"What are you thinking about?" he asked.

"Nothing." I shrugged his coat. It was too bulky.

"You're not a 'nothing' kind of girl. You spit and scratch. You…" His lips brushed against mine in a gentle exploration, as though he was savoring the texture of my lips, memorizing it. Then he moved on to the moist interior as his tongue darted between into my mouth. "You are full of surprises," he whispered against my lips. "A week ago, I'd never have imagined this."

I shook my head, not understanding. "What?"

"Holding you in my arms. Telling you my darkest secrets. You weren't a talker or a listener. We had sex and played mindless games. I don't know what happened, but I like the new you. You are sweeter. You make me wish—"

"Yes?"

He twirled a lock of my hair and smiled. It was a sad smile. "It doesn't matter. I will protect you and help you finish your mission. Once we do, Hel's fury will disappear and we can go on with our lives."

We? I liked it. Obviously he saw a future for us. I put my arms around his neck and wiggled on his lap. He groaned, and I grinned.

"And who will protect you, Echo?"

"You, *Cora-mio*. We are a team."

I loved the way he said my name and liked the idea of protecting each other. "How does one kill a Grimnir?"

"I told you before. Decapitation or you yank the heart out of his chest." His arms tightened around my waist, his fingers grazing my skin. I shivered.

"That sounds gruesome," I mumbled. "Can Grimnirs do that to Mortals?"

"No. Valkyries and Grimnirs can't kill Mortals without being punished. The ones who attacked you and your parents weren't playing by the rules and deserved what they got. When I followed them from the hospital, I thought they were out to settle old scores. You know, going after mine to get to me. After they bragged about their mission, I couldn't let them go through with it. No one goes after what is mine and gets away with it."

Mine? Did that make him mine, too? I hoped so, because I didn't mind claiming him. I forced myself to focus on our conversation. Despite his assurance, he had killed his own people to protect me. That couldn't be good.

"Maybe I should go home now," I said.

"Maybe you should not." He slipped his hands under my shirt and stroked my back, his eyelids drooping. The warm pressure of his palms sent anticipating through me.

"Why not?"

"Because I want you. First, we're going to my place, where I'm going to feed you so your stomach can stop growling every few seconds. Then you can have your wicked way with me. When you are done, it will be my turn."

Heat crept up my face. He had a way with words, and I loved it. Despite my heated cheeks, I was drooling with anticipation. "Do we have time?"

"Your parents don't expect you home for several more hours. Second, I will not allow you to run and hide at home because Hel's private army is after you. You are not a coward. You wouldn't be with me if you were."

He made it sound so simple. He was used to bending and breaking rules while I… Yeah, what about me? Miss Make-a-deal-with-Goddess-Hel. I was just like him. Gah, I wished I could remember what the Norns had taken from me. Remember what I was thinking when I chose to go to Hel's Hall and offered her a deal. Remember my past moments with Echo.

I touched his face, the chiseled jaw and the sensual lips. He didn't stop me, just watched me with hooded eyes. "You and I are alike," I whispered.

He cocked his eyebrows. "How do you figure?"

"We live by our own rules. Good or bad. One day we'll cross a line." I already had. "The Norns probably erased my memories because I'd betrayed them by joining forces with your goddess."

"They did." A smile tugged the corner of Echo's lips. "But you're nothing like me, Cora. I'm a total screw up. I tend to act first and ask questions later. Been doing it for centuries and will probably continue doing it for the rest of my miserable life. You barely became a Grimnir. You are allowed to make a mistake or two."

"Miserable life?" His head rested on the headrest, his eyes almost closed, but I knew he was studying me. "What's there for you to be miserable about? You're going to live forever, you don't age, and you are loaded."

"The wealth means nothing to me, and being young forever is overrated."

"What would make you happy?"

"You."

Okay. Not what I was expecting. "You have me."

"Do I?" He leaned in and trailed kisses along my neck to my ear. "I like being this close to you, holding you in my arms. You are warmth, Cora. Light. Pure sweetness. You make me feel things I never felt before."

I giggled. "Good or bad things."

He nuzzled my neck. "I haven't decided yet. It's unsettling, yet I still want you. I want to do naughty things with you. Things we've never done before, but at the same time I want to just hold you and feel your soft breath against my skin."

His warm breath fanned my skin, and I shuddered. Focusing on our conversation was getting harder. "Didn't we cuddle before?"

He nibbled on my shoulder, shooting heat through my body. "You weren't interested."

Weird. I loved to cuddle. I'd imagined cuddling with Eirik for so long I'd felt deprived. Yet now I didn't want to be in anyone else's arms but Echo's. "Maybe I had more evil deals to make with other goddesses."

Laughter rumbled through him. I gripped his head and directed his lips to mine. The world tilted as we kissed, our breath mingling, hearts pounding. When I bit his lower lip, he shuddered and let out a low growl. He pulled me tightly against him, his hardness sending pleasure through my body.

I didn't want to wait until we went to his place. Already, I was getting lost in his kisses and the sensual haze we were creating. When he nipped on my lower lip, I grounded against him. We both moaned and strained against each other.

Gripping his face, I pulled my lips from his.

"Don't ask me to take you home again, Cora," he whispered. "Not yet. I want you."

"Then have me." I pulled off my shirt and threw it aside. Reaching behind me, I unclasped my bra.

Echo sucked in a breath. I've always complained about guys ogling my boobs instead of listening whenever I talked, and yes, I'd used them to my advantage on an occasion or two. But this was the first time I was proud to have someone stare at them. Watching Echo drool was a big turn on. The awe in his eyes. The tremor in his hand as he reached out and cupped their undersides as though seizing them up. Then he lifted his head and our eyes locked.

"You are so beautiful," he whispered in a voice gone husky and stroked my skin. My body trembled.

"So are you," I managed to say.

He grinned, leaned forward, and nuzzled my chest. Then his mouth replaced his fingers. Moans of pleasure escaped me as sensations washed over me. More runes appeared on his body, glowing and dimming, sending a surge of new sensations through me. Whatever the runes were doing, I wanted more of it. More skin contact. More connection.

I pulled and pushed his T-shirt over his head, needing to touch him intimately, too. I caressed his abs and pecs, ran my hands over his shoulders, defined arms, and down his back. His muscles flexed under my palms. The skin on his back was a bit bumpy as though scarred, but he didn't give me a chance to explore it.

He kissed me hard, bending me backwards and curving into me as though he craved skin contact, too. Then he froze.

Sure I had done something wrong, I cringed. "Echo?"

He smothered a curse, forked his fingers through my hair, and fused my mouth with his again. The thrust of his tongue was urgent, demanding, consuming. I grabbed his shoulders and held on for dear life. When he tore his lips from mine, I moaned in protest.

He was breathing hard, his eyes more golden than green. "Stay here while I get rid of him." He lifted me off his lap and onto the seat. "Don't move."

I couldn't move if Hel's army was attacking. Through the tinted window of my car, I could see one bright light. When the roar in my ears subsided, I realized it had been mixed with the sound of a motorcycle.

8. Not Worthy

The voices were muted, but I knew an argument when I heard it. Had a cop pulled up on a motorcycle? They often came up here to disperse parties. Echo arguing with him wasn't going to help matters.

I felt around for my bra. It was dark inside the car, but I refused to turn on the lights when I was naked from the waist up. From the raised voices, Echo was probably pissing off a cop and buying us one-way tickets to the county jail. He really was a hot head. Why had I thrown the damn bra and shirt? I found my top and pulled it on. I patted around the tray and something sharp sank into my hand. Pain shot up my arm.

Crap. Echo must have put his artavus there.

I lifted my hand and warm blood rolled to my wrist. That was heavy bleeding. I

turned on the car's interior lights and saw my hand. The cut was long and deeper than I'd thought, and it was bleeding profusely. Outside, the voices grew louder.

Dang it. What was Echo doing now? Ripping off the head of a local cop? And where were my healing runes when I needed them? I reached in the glove compartment, grabbed wads of tissue, and pressed them against my palm.

A loud roar came from outside, and my car shook and rotated as though something had hit it in the rear. Not something. Someone not human. More crashes followed.

I grabbed Echo's coat, shrugged it on, opened the door, and stepped outside. My eyes widened at the scenes of mayhem. Echo was fighting someone or something, their movement so fast, they were blurs of light as their runes glowed and dimmed. They collided and rolled on the ground, leaving fissures on the parking lot like a freaking volcano.

Didn't these people ever talk? Not sure what to do, I kept low and followed the body of the car while peering at them. Was it one of his Druid Grimnirs? They slowed down long enough for me to see the face of his attacker. I gasped.

Torin? Why was Raine's boyfriend fighting with my Grimnir?

They were back on their feet, circling each other, hands clenching and unclenching. I opened my mouth to yell stop, but then I saw the smirks on their faces. They were enjoying this. The two idiots were actually getting a thrill out of pounding each other and destroying everything around them.

"I told you to leave, Valkyrie." Echo's voice shattered the silence.

"And I said I wasn't leaving without her."

Her who? Me? Even as the questions flashed in my head, the two charged each other, shifting into hyper speed. I screamed, but the sound was swallowed by the thud of Echo's fist connecting with Torin's body. The force threw Torin backwards and into the air, across the parking lot and the road to the trees on the other side.

A crack filled the air, and I winced. More uprooted trees and no explanation. The people of this town were going to believe we'd been invaded by aliens.

"Stand down, Valkyrie," Echo yelled, turning around slowly, piercing wolf eyes studying the surrounding darkness. "Go home to your—"

Torin flew across the parking lot in swirls of flashing lights and caught Echo on the side. The force of his attack knocked Echo backwards. He slammed into Torin's Harley, which broke his momentum. His hands and fingers dug into the ground, leaving grooves.

"STOP IT!" I yelled. "ECHO!"

But I might as well have been talking to myself. He propelled himself forward like a sprinter, but Torin was ready. Their bodies slammed, the sound like a cannon going off. They rolled across the parking lot and disappeared over the side of the mountain, taking down half the wooden security fence with them.

I ran, almost twisting my ankle in the fissures they'd left behind, fear clutching my stomach. There was no vegetation down there to break their fall, only broken beer bottles students had chucked.

I peered into the darkness. There was nothing but the sound of the rushing river at the bottom of the canyon.

"ECHO?" I yelled. The sound pierced the air, but the only answers were tremors from below as they continued to rip each other apart. "TORIN!"

Getting pissed, I turned and marched back to my car. The huge dent on the rear end of my car only made me angrier. Hand still hurting, I found the key on the tray next to the cup holders, where Echo had put his blades and started the car. Turning on the headlights, I hit reverse, almost running over Torin's Harley, which had toppled on its side. I was surprised it wasn't totaled.

The car rocked as it hit the cracks. My hand throbbed and continued to bleed. I brought the car to where the fence gaped like something from a haunted house and flashed the lights.

Please, let him be okay. Please, let him be safe.

I rolled down the windows and screamed again, "ECHO! TORIN!"

Echo appeared suddenly in front of headlights, looking like something out of a horror movie, blood on his chest and face. I forgot about my hand and slammed it on my mouth. Pain shot through my arm, and I cried out.

Echo peered at the car as though he'd heard me. He started toward me, but Torin appeared behind him, his T-shirt ripped, leather jacket dirty. Relief that they were both fine left me dizzy, but it was short-lived. Their arms shot out toward each other, and I lost it.

I grabbed Echo's artavus, yanked the door open, and jumped out. "I swear if you two don't stop this stupid fight, I will personally decapitate both of you right now."

Their heads whipped in my direction.

I brandished the blade with my good hand. "I mean it. Stop it or I'm coming after both of you, and I'll win because I'm pissed and I fight dirty, and you can't fight back because I'm a girl."

"Sweetheart," Echo said.

"Don't sweetheart me. I can't just sit here while you two try to kill each other over… what? Some stupid ego crap? The worst part is you are enjoying it while I'm bleeding to death."

Echo raised his hand in a placating gesture. "It's okay, doll-face. We're not fighting anymore."

"You're… not?" I stared at them. Their hands were clasped as though they were about to arm wrestle. They patted each other's shoulders in a manly hug. The gesture looked staged because they were both stiff as though waiting for the other to attack.

"See? We made up." Echo moved toward me, his eyes moving from my face to my hand. "You engaged your runes."

I stared at him stupidly. "Huh?"

"Your runes. They're glowing."

I looked down, trying to see them under the glare of the headlights. I had runes on my arms. Not a lot, but still… I had them. They dimmed and disappeared. I opened my palm to check on my cut. It didn't hurt as much, but the cut was still there.

"Echo, those are not regular—"

"Shut up, St. James," Echo snapped, but his hand, when it closed around my wrist, was gentle. He pried the blade from my hand, saw the bloodied tissue in my other hand, and turned pale. "Are you bleeding? Did you cut yourself?"

I shook my head, trying to process many things at once. I had engaged my runes, but they hadn't healed me. Torin was trying to warn Echo about something. Me? My runes? Why would he come for me? For that matter, why didn't Torin want Echo to be with me when he had Raine? It wasn't fair.

"It was an accident," I said, searching Echo's face. "I was looking for my, uh, things and cut it on your artavus." His face was bloody, but I didn't see any open wounds. Not on his chest or his abs. He'd run out shirtless. "Why did the runes take away my pain but not heal me?"

"Because you don't have the right—"

One second Echo was beside me, the next he was by Torin, the artavus he'd taken from me pressed against Torin's throat.

"I'm tired of your bullshit, Valkyrie. I want you to listen very carefully because I'm only going to say this once. I know her. She's not some Immortal bitch with a vendetta against your people. She is Cora Jemison, and she's mine. One more word out of you and your head says bye-bye to your neck," Echo snarled.

Torin smirked, and I realized why. His hand was pressed against Echo's chest. "We'll see who is faster, Grimnir," Torin retorted. "If you weren't so irrational and stubborn, you'd see that I'm right. Or make an effort to confirm it."

Tired of their crap, I marched to where they were facing off and pressed my hands on their chests. "You two have way too much testosterone to be rational. Echo, put the blade away. Torin, hands off his chest. You hurt him and I will come for you."

Torin cocked his eyebrows and smirked.

Of course, I had no chance of ever hurting him. "In your sleep when you are vulnerable," I snapped.

Torin stopped smirking while Echo chuckled.

I glared at Echo. "And you, no more warming you and no more kisses for a week if you don't stop."

He stopped smiling.

I pushed on their chests, but I might as well have been trying to move a wall of reinforced steel. Worse, the blood from my hand was leaking onto Torin's shirt.

"Back down, boys. Now."

"Anything for you, doll-face." Echo removed the blade from Torin's neck and slipped it in whatever hiding place he had in the back of his pants. Torin's hand fell from Echo's chest.

I stepped back, wooziness threatening to suck me under.

"Seriously, you two act like little boys when you are, like, what? Gazillions of years old?" I snapped.

"Actually, I'm—"

"I don't care, Torin. Just play nice." I stepped away from them, so exhausted I just wanted to go home. Worse, tears rushed to my eyes. I turned and stumbled on the uneven ground. Arms wrapped around me.

"I've got you." Echo lifted me up and cradled me closer to his chest.

I studied his face. His beautiful face. "You look awful."

"All the cuts are healed." He walked around the car, opened the front passenger door, and sat with me on his lap and his feet on the ground. "Let me see the damage you've done to yourself." His hand was gentle as he probed my palm. Funny how it looked ghastly yet I felt no pain. "What idiotic Valkyrie turned you without giving you healing runes?"

"Maliina."

Echo stiffened. "How do you know?"

"Ingrid told me. Maliina is her sister, and she is not a Valkyrie. She's an Immortal. Can you give me healing runes?"

"Hel's Mist!" he swore and glared at Torin, who was watching us with an unreadable expression. "Get lost, St. James." Torin turned and walked away. "Damn Andris and his idiotic habits. I'm so sorry, doll-face."

The distress in his voice didn't make sense. "It's just a cut."

Echo sighed. "No, it's more than that. You're not self-healing for a reason. St. James was right."

"About what?"

"You." Anguish flashed across Echo's face, and with his runes glowing, I didn't miss a thing. His eyes darkened, the green swallowing the gold. He dropped the bloodied tissue, reached down on the floor, and came up with his T-shirt. He wrapped it around my hand, his movements slow and gentle. "The things I've put you through. I shouldn't be calling Andris an idiot. I'm the idiot. I should have seen it. Should have listened to you, but you look just like her. No, she looked just like you. There were subtle and obvious differences, but I wanted you and didn't care. I liked the changes in you. You were sweeter and nicer, and I wanted it all. I'm so sorry." He kissed my wrapped hand. "You need stitches on that cut." He pressed his lips to my temple. "Hel's Mist, this is my worst screw up yet. I'm so sorry."

I wished he would stop saying that. My fear had morphed into a full-blown panic. "What are you talking about? Who is like me? And why do we have to go to the hospital?"

He stood, easily carrying me, then walked around to the other side of the car and reluctantly set me on my feet. His hands, when he cupped my face, were unsteady. His face was gray under the runic glow. He brought my head toward his until our foreheads touched. Then he closed his eyes, his ridiculously long lashes forming a canopy on his chiseled cheekbones.

"I don't think I can explain anything right now without going over the edge," he said slowly as though he was in extreme pain. "I need to think. Confirm a few things."

He opened his eyes. The wildness in them said thinking or confirming anything was the last thing on his mind. He looked ready to kill someone. Level a mountain or something.

"Echo—"

"Just know that I wanted to be with you, so I ignored the signs. I want you, Cora, not anyone else. You. Your warmth and sweetness."

"I know." I searched his face, my heart pounding with dread. "But you're beginning to scare me, Echo. Nothing you say is making sense. Please, tell me what's going on. Who is like me? What signs are you talking about?"

"Signs that you are not meant to be mine." His voice was now a husky whisper of pain and self-recrimination. Blood roared past my ears, muffling his voice and distorting his words because there was no way he'd said what I just heard. "You never were."

The ground gave out under me, and I would have fallen if he hadn't wrapped an arm around me and held me up. I gripped his arms to steady myself.

"No," I protested.

"Yes. I'm sorry."

"Stop saying that. Tell me what's going on."

"I don't want to let you go," Echo whispered, arms tightening until there was no space between us. I didn't even care that he was smearing blood all over me. My body recognized his, and my heart pounded in perfect unison with his.

"Then don't let me go," I begged, not fully understanding what was going on.

"But I must. It is the only decent thing to do." His mouth ground mine, and a shudder rocked his body. My body echoed it. His teeth sunk into my lower lip and bore down as though he meant to leave me branded. I cried out and wrapped my arms around his neck, holding his head in place as his tongue soothed the pain then slipped inside my mouth to find mine. I got lost in the heat of the moment. Got lost in his arms. How could he deny that I was his and he mine?

He wrenched his lips from mine. "I can't do this. I have to go."

My body ached and screamed in protest, but my heart... my heart felt like he'd reached inside and yanked it out of my chest. Nothing made sense.

"Please, don't leave without explaining what's going on. Don't do this to me."

Echo shook his head, his eyes fierce. He and the body of the car behind me were the only things propping me up. If he let me go, I was sure I'd crumble where I stood. As if he knew it, he slowly backed away, his hands gripping my arms to steady me against the car.

"Echo, please."

"I'm so sorry, Cora. I should not have let my feelings get in the way of my thinking. St. James," he called out and Torin moved closer. "I will explain everything to her personally. You open your mouth and I'll make it my personal mission to make your life miserable. For now, take her to the hospital."

"No," I protested.

"Yes." Echo let go of me and shuffled backward, his eyes not leaving mine. He was still shirtless and I had his duster, but that didn't seem to bother him. He pulled his scythe from behind him, runes crisscrossing his bloody arms, chest, stomach, and face as the scythe elongated to its real size. He looked so beautiful, like an ancient warrior, a fantasy, and he was breaking my heart.

"Tell me what's going on," I begged.

"I'll explain when I come back, after I confirm a few things. For now, just know that you and I can't be together. For both our sakes, accept it." He sliced the air to his right, and the portal started to form. I found my legs and started toward him.

"I will not let you leave, Echo. If I have to follow you the coldest halls of Hel—"

"Don't, Cora. I'm not worth it." The defeat in his voice sent anger through me.

"Don't tell me what to do. And you are worth every—"

He went through the portal at a run before I realized what he had planned. I ran forward, but the gateway closed behind him.

Too shocked, I stared in dazed confusion, trying to wrap my head around what had just happened. I reached up and pressed my hand against my chest.

Something was squeezing it. Crushing it. It hurt to breathe. To think. So this what a broken heart felt like? Like the very air I breathed couldn't reach my lungs.

I started to shake. My vision grew blurry.

First Eirik. Now Echo. What was wrong with me that guys had no problem walking out on me? Tears burned my eyes.

I will not cry. I will not… will not…

That would be admitting it was over, that I'd given up. I titled my head and blinked hard. I was Cora Jemison. I could see souls. I had been admitted to a freaking psych ward and had my memories erased by some badass Norse deities. There was nothing on earth that could make me cry because the man I was crazy about just walked out on me. He was probably going to Hel.

Shirtless. And he'd probably catch a cold.

Why was I focusing on such a mundane thing? He wouldn't die from cold. Echo had been going to Hel's Hall and back for centuries. He was Immortal and probably hadn't caught cold a day in a millennium. Fact was he had left me. Just like Eirik had. I blinked harder.

"Cora?"

Torin's voice reached me as though from afar. I refused to look at him until I had my emotions under control. Until I stopped shaking. As though he understood, he left me alone.

Echo wasn't gone. He'd be back. He must come back.

Tremors shook the earth under me, and I turned. My headlights were still on, so I could see the parking lot and the overlook. Torin was erasing Echo, I thought irrationally. The fence was whole as though it had never been broken. The ground no longer had fissures. It was as though he and Echo never fought. Even the dent on my car was gone. If it weren't for his coat, which I still wore, I would have thought I'd imagined Echo.

Tears rushed to my eyes, and I blinked hard.

Torin stood to the right side of my car, frowning. He didn't look like he wasn't going anywhere without me. I didn't want to go anywhere with him. Because of him, Echo had left.

"Why did you do it?" I asked.

"I had to tell him the truth. I didn't think he'd take it so hard."

My anger rose.

"What truth?" I yelled.

Torin stayed silent.

"I want to know what happened here tonight, Torin, and I want to know *now*," I yelled. "You had no right to come out here and interfere with us. When you finish talking, you go find Echo and bring him back."

Torin sighed. "Let me take you to the hospital; then we'll go to Raine's. She'll explain everything to you."

"No, you start talking. Right now."

"Echo's threat was real, Cora."

"Then deal with it," I snapped.

He smiled, and I wanted to smack him.

"I can stand up to Echo any day, but I have people who depend on me who will be caught in the crossfire. Andris. Ingrid. Raine. Souls destined for Valhalla who will end up on Corpse Strand instead. I cannot risk Echo's ire, not even for you." His British accent had grown more distinct. "Raine will explain. He can't touch her without evoking the wrath of the gods. She's worried about you. She's the one who sent me to find you after we went to Drew's party and found out you had left with someone. The description they gave us matched Echo's."

I had gone into selective listening as soon as he'd mention the wrath of the gods. "Raine is a Valkyrie, too?"

"No, she's something else. Something more powerful and rare. I'll drive you to the hospital," Torin said, indicating my car. "Raine will tell you everything you need to know."

Only things I *need* to know? We'll see about that.

I sat in the front passenger seat and buckled up. Echo's gloves, including the one I'd worn, were on the tray between our seats. I picked them up with my good hand and pressed them against my chest. Once again, the urge to cry washed over me. I closed my eyes and fought the tears.

Torin backed up and took off toward downtown Kayville. I started in on him again.

"Why is it okay for you to be with Raine, but I can't be with Echo?"

***

"How did this happen, honey?" a woman asked.

I blinked and looked around. I must have blacked out during the ride and the registration at the ER because I was already assigned a room. Torin sat on a chair on the other side of the bed, his concerned eyes not leaving me.

"Cora?" the woman asked again, consulting her notes. Her tag said Dr. P. Satchel. Something about her reminded me of Naya. Maybe it was the honey-brown skin or the shrewd brown eyes.

"I cut it on a knife by accident," I murmured.

She probed the cut, her glance sliding to Torin. "Is this the first time this has happened?"

What? Did she think I'd cut myself on purpose? Sure, the cut was close to my wrist, but still… "I did not hurt myself on purpose, if that's what you're asking, doctor," I said rudely.

She studied me, then Echo's coat and frowned. "Can you show me your other hand, please?"

Torin reacted, one second he was in his seat; the next he'd drawn runes on the doctor's arm and returned to his seat.

"Why did you do that?" I asked in a whisper.

"She asks too many stupid questions. The nurses at the front desk did, too."

The doctor sutured my wound without asking any more questions and added steri-strips. Her glance kept going to Torin as though she couldn't help herself. Maybe she felt he wasn't human or she had lust on her mind. At the moment, I didn't think he was that hot. He was just the jerk who'd caused Echo to leave.

Dr. Satchel finished with my hand. "The nurse will give you a list of instructions on how to take care of your wound, Cora. If you see red streaks, swelling, pus, or have a fever, contact your primary physician." The doctor consulted her notes again to see who my primary physician was. I was still seeing my pediatrician, Dr. Olsen. "I also want you to follow up with Dr. Olsen on Monday. In the meantime, don't get the sutures wet in the next twenty-four hours. After that, you can shower and wash the area with soap and warm water."

"When can I go back to swimming?"

"After it heals. Dr. Olsen will remove the sutures and tell you when you can go back to swimming. The wound wasn't deep, so it should heal quickly. If you don't aggravate it, that is. If you are in pain, take ibuprofen. Any questions?"

I shook my head. Torin didn't react. I could feel his impatience. The doctor smiled at us one last time and left the room. A nurse walked in and gave me a printed list of instructions, which were basically what the doctor had told me.

"That was fast," I said as we left.

"I hate hospitals," Torin ground out.

Weird attitude for a reaper. I spied a few souls loitering around. They stared, but kept their distance.

"Did you rune me on our way to the hospital?" I asked.

He shrugged. "I wanted you to rest and stop giving me a hard time."

"If you can rune people like that, why didn't you just heal me?" I asked when we reached my car.

"There's a big difference between focus runes I used back there, or rest runes I etched on you, and healing runes. Healing runes are bind runes. They are powerful and long lasting. They give people the ability to regenerate new cells, so they self-heal and stop aging. It is against the law to use them on a Mortal. The ones I used on you only last a few minutes. Thirty tops."

"Which ones did Maliina give me? How long are they going to last? And how could you let her do this to me?"

Torin frowned, opening the passenger door. "We don't know what she used, Cora. We didn't even know she'd runed you until the night of the home game two weeks ago."

Everything always came back to that night. Tonight, I was getting the answers. "I wish she hadn't runed me. I don't like seeing souls. I hate that I can't go anywhere without one approaching me. I can't even go to sleep without waking up and finding one staring at me. Why are they attracted to me? Why not to you guys? You are the reapers."

"I don't have all the answers, Cora. If I were to guess, I'd say Maliina marked you with special runes." Torin walked around the car and slid behind the wheel. "Have you ever thought of asking the souls what they want?"

"What do you think?" I stared into the night as he took off, noticing a soul here and there. I guess now that Echo was really gone, they'd come back even in greater numbers.

Sighing, I gave Torin a glance from the corner of my eyes. I should stop acting like a bitch toward him. It was counterproductive. He was my best friend's boyfriend. Besides, it wasn't his fault Maliina had runed me. He might have facilitated Echo's sudden flight, but he didn't throw him through that portal. Echo chose to leave.

"I've tried to ask them what they want, but it's not easy when I can't hear them," I said, speaking slowly. "It's like being inside a silent horror movie. A few of them touched me, and it was cold and icky."

"If it's okay with you, we can use special runes on your home and around your farm to stop them from coming inside."

I'd rather have Echo as my shield. "That would be nice. Thank you."

"We'll take care of it tonight," he said.

Maybe he wasn't such a bad guy. "I'm just going to lay this out there before we get to Raine's. I wish you hadn't come looking for us tonight and made Echo leave."

Torin chuckled. "Cora, no one makes Echo do anything. He's stubborn, opinionated, a total pain-in-the…" He shook his head. "I apologize."

Echo was all of the above. "That doesn't explain why he couldn't heal me."

Torin pulled up outside Raine's house and switched off the engine. "He has a thing about never turning Mortals into Immortals, which is completely out of character because he thrives on breaking rules."

Maybe I was the only one who knew about his past. Turning his people was the reason he'd ended up on Hel duty. Torin opened the door, and I stepped out of the car. We didn't talk as we headed toward the front entrance of Raine's house.

Raine opened the door, and her eyes went to my hand. "What happened?"

I glanced behind her to make sure we were alone. "My world collided with yours; that's what. What are you? And were you ever going to tell me the truth, you," I pinched her arm, "traitor."

"Ouch!" She rubbed her arm and stepped back. "Why am I a traitor?"

"We made a pact we'd never keep secrets from each other." I followed her. "How could you? The last week you knew that… that bitch everyone thought was me wasn't really me, and you said nothing."

She grimaced. "We didn't really have time to talk. You know with Dad's stroke and all."

I pinched her again. "Don't use him as an excuse. It takes seconds to say, 'Hey, Cora, I know the truth, so don't stress out.' I thought I had astral projected while in the crazy house or something."

Raine laughed. "Astral… that's ridiculous." She jumped back when I reached out to pinch her again. "Enough with the pinching already. I was going to tell you everything. I needed the right moment and, you know, to confirm you could still see souls." She glanced at Torin, who smirked. She glared. "It's not funny. I told you she'd be pissed when she found out."

He lifted his hands. "Don't include me in this mess. I'm going to pick up Rod then head home. I'll be there if you need me, but I can't be here when you two talk."

Raine grabbed his hand. "Why not? You explain some things better."

He glanced at me. "I can't. But I'll be home when you are done." He kissed her and walked away.

"Home as in Asgard?" I asked after he disappeared around the corner.

Raine laughed, closing the door. "No. Next door."

"He lives next door? How convenient. Now start talking. I'll ask again. Were you ever going to tell me the truth?"

"Eirik was."

My jaw dropped. "He's one of you, too? No, don't answer that. I want to know everything from the beginning." I pointed at her then upstairs. "Let's go."

"Do you want something to drink? Does your hand hurt?"

I glared. "Do I look like I want a drink or need pain meds? The stupid runes Maliina etched on me take away the pain. Don't know how long the effect will last. Don't really care right now. I. Just. Want. Answers." Lifting the hem of the duster so I wouldn't trip on it, I marched upstairs.

By the time Raine entered her bedroom with two bottles of water, I was settled on her bed with piles of pillows behind me. She put one water bottle within my reach and took a chair. When she opened the top and took a sip, I wanted to snap at her to hurry up.

She put the water on the table and moved her chair closer to the bed. "Well, it started the day Torin moved in next door."

"Where was I?"

"Upstairs vlogging. I was down here doing my homework, so I answered the door. You don't remember any of this because the Norns erased your memories."

"So he was right about that."

"Who?"

Echo. Even thinking his name hurt. "Never mind. Go on."

Raine nodded and continued. The story was like something straight out of a fantasy. From Torin healing her to her nightmare cat and mouse games with Norns to discovering her mother was also a former Valkyrie. If I couldn't see souls, I wouldn't believe anything she'd just said.

"Eirik is what?" I asked.

"A god. Grandson to Odin and Loki."

No wonder Echo had called him a god among Mortals. I'd just assumed he was being sarcastic. My stomach started to growl, but I ignored it. I snapped the lid off the bottled water Raine had brought for me and sipped. My hand tightened on the bottle when she mentioned Maliina.

"She was back, but we didn't recognize her. Norns can change their appearances on a whim. She used her new Norn powers to create a disguise, the perfect disguise to infiltrate us. She chose you."

I frowned. "What do you mean?"

"She knew you were at PMI, Cora. We didn't. She changed her appearance to look exactly like you. Act like you. Speak like you. She knew things only you would know, which is possible because Norns know everything. I even came to your house to pick her up once and she met me at your door as your mother. Then she used a portal and was waiting for me in your bedroom as you. She had us all fooled. I mean, there were a few moments here and there when she acted odd, and my trainer, Lavania, didn't like her from the first moment they met, but no one thought she was Maliina."

My stomach churned as everything fell into place. While I was in the crazy house, that Immortal bitch had stolen my identity, taken over my life. My friends. My vlog. My house, since my parents often came to PMI to see me and would stay for days. Oh God...

She'd slept with Echo. No wonder he'd assumed I had. She'd had my Echo.

Nausea rose to my throat, and I jumped out of Raine's bed. I barely made it to the toilet and dropped on my knees. The water I'd drunk a few minutes ago spewed out of my mouth. Dry heaves raked my body, my eyes watering.

Echo had thought I was Maliina. His lover. The one he'd played sex games with. I had just been a substitute. A freaking substitute. No wonder he'd taken off after learning the truth.

Torin must have told him and I'd confirmed it when I couldn't heal and mentioned Maliina. That was the point he'd looked like someone had gutted him. How humiliating. I wanted to disappear in some dark corner of human existence and never resurface.

Raine held my hair and pressed a wet cloth to my forehead. "Are you okay?"

What do you think? I wanted to snap. I took the cloth from her and wiped my face. I closed the toilet bowl and flushed. Our eyes met. She was sitting on the edge of the tub, hands on her knees, her hazel eyes filled with worry.

"I'm okay. You blindsided me with Maliina. I knew she'd marked me, but this..." I shook my head. "What else did she do?"

"She spent a lot of time with Eirik."

"Why couldn't he tell she wasn't me? Why couldn't *you*? Her sister has an accent. Didn't she have one, too?"

Raine sighed. "Yes. But when she came back as you, she spoke like you, Cora. Lived in your house, wrote on your vlog, had your cell phone, and swam with the team."

"She aced every class, too," I wailed. She was better than me at everything. Because of her, my GPA was above 3.9. That only made me hate her more. She'd had Echo. I didn't care that I now knew the truth, that I hadn't astral projected from the psych ward. The Immortal who'd ruined my life also had the man I wanted.

"She played mind games with Eirik because she wasn't really working with Norns as they'd thought. She'd made a deal with Goddess Hel, who wanted Eirik."

No wonder Hel's army was after me. Maliina had failed in her mission to lure Eirik to Hel, and now Eirik was with his grandparents. The good grandparents—Odin and Frigga. Pretty boy Eirik was really a deity. Not surprising.

"We learned who she was that evening we came to your house and your mother told us to leave. I'd seen you, uh, *her* the night before, etching the runes on Eirik, and we came to your house to confront her. You have no idea how relieved and happy I was when your mother told me about PMI."

I cocked my eyebrow. "I was in a nut house, Raine."

"I didn't care. I would not have cared if you'd really been crazy," she said, laughing. "You are my best friend. Crazy is better than what Maliina was... what she is—pure evil. If we had known you were at PMI, Cora, Eirik and I would have been there every weekend. He's crazy about you."

"Are you sure? Maybe it's Maliina he's crazy about. If he and Maliina spent time together, they probably slept together."

"No, I don't think so. She drew evil runes on Eirik to turn him evil. Then she played games to make him jealous and force his evil side to take over. Like kissing Drew the night of the game and flirting with jocks when we'd go out. Eirik was consumed with jealousy because of his feelings for you, not her."

It was too late now. I didn't want Eirik to want me. "Did he know the truth before he left?"

"Yes. He was devastated that we hadn't known about PMI. He said he'd come back just to see you."

"He shouldn't," I whispered.

"Don't say that," Raine begged.

The physical attraction I'd felt toward Eirik was nothing compared to what I now felt toward Echo. Thinking about Echo hurt, but I still wanted him back. I stood and rinsed my mouth with water and mouth wash.

"Call your parents and tell them you are staying here for the night," Raine said. "I'll get you something to eat."

I'd forgotten how bossy Raine could get sometimes. "I don't feel like eating and, uh, how did you know I didn't want to go home?"

"Because I know you, Cora Jemison."

I made a face. "Yeah. Right. An evil imposter fooled you."

"Have you seen her vlog entries?" Raine rolled her eyes and imitated my voice. "'Hey, Hottie of the Week is smoking hot shirtless. Don't ask how I know.' Sound familiar?"

"Shut up."

"I'll get the food from Torin's place. He cooks the most amazing dishes." She glanced out the window and waved. I checked at what had her riveted. Torin. "Before you say you're not hungry, we still have some talking to do. I want to hear about you and the souls and PMI."

Thank goodness she didn't mention Echo. I wasn't ready to talk about him. I watched as Raine stopped in front of her mirror and it dissolved into a portal. When it closed, I could see her in Torin's room. She had her man right across the lawn while mine was in Hel's Hall. No, mine was no longer mine. He was never mine. He was Maliina's.

For the first time, I wanted to cry. Just curl up in bed and cry until I was exhausted.

No, no more jealous thoughts. My best friend was a powerful seeress. A young one but one day she would become a force of nature. Maybe she could foresee my future.

9. Outsourced

I overslept. I couldn't remember the last time I'd had a sleepover at Raine's. Norns probably took that memory when they scraped my mind. They were way up there on my hate list, along with Maliina.

I stretched and winced at my throbbing hand. Guess the effect of the runes had waned. Did I have to make them appear on my skin for them to work? Did I even want to? I sighed and looked around.

Echo's coat was draped over the back of a chair. Relief washed over me, the ache of losing him settling deep in my chest. He could easily have come for it while I slept. I was happy he hadn't. I wanted to see him again, even if to say goodbye or yell at him for leaving without explaining everything.

I sat up and adjusted my top—Raine's stretchy pajama top was more like it. The bottoms fit, but the top was tight. She and I had talked late into the night and pigged out on finger foods Torin had delivered. The man could cook. Lucky Raine. She got the whole package in that man.

Yawning, I swung my legs onto the floor and slipped on the slippers Raine had loaned me. I padded out of the room. Noises filtered upstairs, but I couldn't tell who was talking. I'd walked halfway down the stairs, when Andris walked past the stairs on his way to the kitchen, saw me, and backtracked. Smirking, he openly ogled me, his eyes lingering on my chest. I didn't care enough to get insulted.

"Seen enough, *Valkyrie?*" I asked.

"No. The top is in the way."

I smirked. "Bet that line has gotten you a lot of *nothing* in the last century alone."

"No, it's gotten me plenty of play. So you want to take it off? It's been a while since I visited a strip joint."

"Why are you such a letch so early in the morning, Andris?" Raine said, coming from behind him. She smacked the back of his head. "Get out of here. Mom just called. They'll be here any second."

"I want to welcome your dad home, too," he griped. "And Cora was just about to make my morning."

I stopped on the last stair and really studied him for the first time. Valkyries must recruit from young up-coming models because the combination of silver hair and melted chocolate eyes, androgynous face and his dressing style made Andris a hottie in his own way. Unlike Torin and Echo, who looked like they'd kick ass without breaking a sweat, Andris had softness around the edges. He would pass for a rich artist or a hipster.

"You are staring, Mortal," he said.

I gripped the edge of the tank top. "What would you do if I removed this?"

"Try and see. I happen to love Mortals."

I lost interest in baiting him. He'd turned Maliina. "So I heard."

The smile disappeared from his face. "I'm sorry about what Maliina did to you. I had escorted a swimmer to Falkvang and was delayed. If I had been around—"

"It's okay," I said. "She screwed me over, not you. You might be guilty of turning her, but we all do stupid things when we are in love."

"You just became more interesting, Cora Jemison," he said. His eyes went to my hand. "What happened to your hand? And what stupid thing have you done in the name of love?"

Fallen for a reaper. No, not fallen. I wasn't in love with Echo. I just wanted him.

"We're not discussing me." I walked past him. My hand was throbbing. The sweet aroma of freshly brewed coffee welcomed me to the kitchen, where Raine was clearing breakfast stuff. Several covered pans were on the stovetop.

"I need coffee," I murmured and reached for a mug. "And pain meds."

"Ibuprofen?"

"Two."

She reached up for the cupboard above the fridge and pulled out a plastic container with all sorts of over-the-counter meds. "Dad hasn't used these in a while, so I hope we have some that haven't expired." She found the Ibuprofen bottle and checked expiration date before giving me two pills.

I threw them to the back of my throat and washed them down with unsweetened coffee. "Gah, that's bitter."

"Coffee creamers are in the fridge. Torin is gone, so I made breakfast." She pointed at the stovetop. "No snarky comments if the bacon is not up to par."

I mustered a grin, got hazelnut creamer, and poured a liberal amount into my coffee. Raine really sucked in the kitchen. Her dad did most of the cooking. At least he used to. I learned to cook from Mom, who could give Rachel Ray a run for her money, except Mom's dishes were healthier and organic.

"Where is Mr. Perfect St. James?" I asked.

Raine smiled dreamily. "He left with the team for Jeld-Wen. They are playing this afternoon."

"Perfect?" Andris called from the living room. "He's anal, overbearing, and a know-it-all. Live with him for a century and you'll be singing my tune."

"You're just jealous," Raine called back.

Andris laughed. "I so do not want to be him. They are here."

I looked out the window but didn't see a car pull up. Instead, warm air rushed through the room, and I realized they were using a portal. When Torin had appeared around the lockers on Monday, I'd felt the same wave of warm air.

Raine hurried to the living room, and I followed.

Raine's father and mother slowly walked into the living room, the portal closing behind them. She had his right arm looped around her shoulder.

"Daddy," Raine said, rushing to his side. She hugged him. "Are you sure you should be walking?"

"As long as I have strength left in me." He pressed a kiss to her temple, saw me, and smiled. Or at least tried to. He looked bad, just like his soul in the cafeteria.

"Nice to have you home, Mr. C," I said.

His eyes went to my hand. "Thank you. What happened to your hand?"

He couldn't stand on his own two feet, yet he was thinking of me. That was Tristan Cooper, the sweetest man I knew. It was easy to see why Raine's mother gave up a future with the Norns for him.

"It's just a cut. The ER people took care of it."

"Come here, sweetheart." He hugged me and kissed my temple. "It is nice to have you home," he said.

So he knew about PMI. What else? "Thank you."

"If I may, sir," Andris said then looked at Raine and her mother. "Ladies, if you'll excuse us." He scooped up Mr. C as though he weighed nothing.

"You are enjoying this, aren't you?" Mr. C said as Andris carried him toward the den.

"Immensely, sir." I could hear the smile in Andris' voice.

"Don't mind those two," Raine's mother said, giving me a hug. "They are always arguing about something." She leaned back and cupped my face. "Oh, sweetie. I'm so sorry about what my people have put you through. Valkyries and Mortals were never meant to mix. Someone always gets hurt."

"But you married Mr. C," I reminded her.

She laughed. "Yes, I did, and I'd do it again in a heartbeat," she whispered. "Love knows right from wrong." Her eyes grew sad. "Let's talk later. I'll answer any questions you may have. Right now, I need to rescue Andris before Tristan hits him on the head. Andris can be overbearing, and Tristan's tolerance is very low right now." She patted my cheek then hurried away.

"Be warned, there's just so much she can tell you," Raine said, leading the way into the kitchen.

"So the Council hasn't let her back in?"

"Nope."

"Even though you are a vol-whatever?"

She laughed. "*Völva* or just say seeress." She turned and walked backwards. "Or a prophetess."

"You're enjoying this."

She nodded. "Oh yeah. I've started getting visions." She retrieved three plates from the cupboard and scooped eggs onto a plate. "Do you want some of this?"

"Sure." I held the plates while she distributed eggs, bacon, and pancakes. "No pancakes for me."

"You sure? I used Dad's famous recipe."

"The operative word is *his*."

She wrinkled her nose.

"So would you tell me if you saw a vision about me?" I asked.

She thought about it and made a face. "I don't know. I haven't really thought about it. I mean, would you like to know if a bad thing was going to happen to you?"

"Oh yeah. Then I'd do whatever I could to stop it. Wouldn't you?"

"Yes, but unfortunately, I can't see my own future."

"That sucks." I helped her set the tray and started on my food as she took food to her parents. Andris sauntered back into the kitchen, poured himself a cup of coffee, and watched me. I ignored him.

"So, you and Echo?"

My hand froze with the fork halfway to my mouth. Exhaling, I put the piece of egg in my mouth. If he so much as badmouthed Echo, I was going to kick him so hard he wouldn't walk for a week.

"You Mortals know how to pick them, don't you?"

How many Mortals in love with Valkyries or Grimnirs did he know? Not that I was in love with Echo or anything like that.

"He and I loathe each other. Do you know why?" Andris asked.

"You had a crush on him and he wasn't interested?"

He choked on his drink. "He told you that?"

I smiled. The way his voice went pitchy told me I'd hit the mark. "No, an educated guess."

"You are wrong. I never had a crush on him. He hates Romans."

Romans had destroyed the Druids, Echo's people. I studied Andris. "Are you from ancient Rome?"

"And proud of it, which pisses off your Grimnir," Andris said. "Don't know why. He's mysterious and a loner, a total a-hole most of the time. Other Grimnirs are cool. You know, our paths cross and we hang out, compare notes, and even hook up. Not Echo. Some Grimnirs are in awe of him, while others just hate his guts."

Druids. Whatever.

"They told the craziest stories about him. I didn't buy them. Maybe you can confirm some for me. You know, ask him."

I stood, placed my plate in the sink, and turned. "Andris," I said, moving closer and forcing him to lean back. "I'd love to be your go-to girl whenever you want to hook up with a guy or a girl." Gripping the counter, I boxed him in until my face was only inches from his. "But don't ever mention Echo to me again. Okay?"

"You are hot when pissed." He eyes moved to my cleavage. "Are these babies real? They're too perky."

I thumped his forehead with the heel of my palm, picked up my coffee, and started for the stairs. Andris followed me, hands in his front pockets, shoulders hunched.

"Where's Ingrid?"

"Jeld-Wen Stadium. Cheering. She's into someone else, a football player of all Mortals. She went to the game just to cheer for him."

I stopped at the foot of the stairs. He looked so forlorn. "Isn't she a *cheerleader*?"

"Yeah. So?"

"So she has to be there with the squad. And you are acting like a punk."

His eyes narrowed. "Punk?"

He sounded so insulted I grinned. "Yeah, for letting a jock steal your girl."

"She's not my girl," he said, frowning.

Refusing to make his problems mine, I dismissed him with a wave and ran upstairs. Raine was still downstairs when I finished taking a bath. Bathing with one hand while keeping the other dry wasn't easy. I borrowed the biggest sweatshirt she owned and jeggings and called home. The door opened behind me, and Raine entered. I saw her expression.

"What is it? Is your dad—?"

"He's okay. He wants to see you. Alone."

I made a face. "Why?"

She shrugged. "I don't know. He's acting weird. Andris needs to etch pain and sleep runes on him, so he can rest, but he can't until you two talk."

I hurried downstairs. Raine's father was alone when I knocked and peeked inside the den. "You wanted to see me, Mr. C?"

He waved me inside. "Close the door, sweetheart."

My stomach was churning by the time I took the chair by his bed. The room had undergone some serious transformation. The sectional couch that usually dominated the room had been replaced by a queen-sized bed, and the desktop computer that used to sit on his desk was now a large screen TV.

I'd always thought Raine's father was indestructible. With his hearty laugh and love for lengthy debates, he'd challenge us to think deeper about events whenever I visited. Sometimes, I'd go with him and Raine to triathlons. To support them, not participate. Swimming was my only sport.

"I know about your ability, Cora. I was dead for a minute or two on Monday and came to you in the cafeteria. You saw me."

I nodded. "Why did you come to me?"

"I don't know. There was no Valkyrie or Grimnir to escort me, so I was a little confused. I remember thinking I had a few things I needed to say to Svana and Raine, but it was too late. Then I saw you, a light at the end of a dark tunnel."

"What do you mean?"

"The runes on your body glowed like a beacon, Cora. They drew me to you. Maybe this is your gift."

"Being seen and hounded by lost souls? I don't think so, Mr. C."

He smiled. "I meant helping lost souls. I tried talking to you, but you seemed distraught."

"That's because you surprised me, and I didn't hear anything. In fact, I can't hear souls. They follow me around, their mouths opening and closing, but," I shook my head, "that's it. No sounds."

He frowned. "I wonder why?"

"Most of the time, I just want them to go away and leave me alone. It's scary trying to balance the living and… them. And talking to them would only land me in the psych ward again."

He nodded and closed his eyes as though exhausted. Silence followed, his chest rising and falling underneath the blanket. Images of my grandmother flashed in my head. She'd looked just like him before she died. Had Grimnirs taken her or Valkyries? Funny I hadn't thought of that until now.

"I understand," Mr. C said, speaking slowly, eyes still closed. "It is very confusing out there once this world is closed to you. Maybe you should try to be more, uh, friendly, listen with compassion. You could also try luring them away from people so no one can see you talk to them."

Mr. C had lost it. There was no way I'd be buddies with souls. Seeing them already made me a freak. Talking to them? Wasn't going to happen.

"I'll try," I fibbed.

"That's the spirit." He took a deep breath, opened his eyes, and smiled. "Now I need to rest. We'll talk again soon. Hopefully, in this world, not the next."

He was trying to be funny. I reached down and kissed his forehead. "Definitely this one, Mr. C."

***

"CORA!"

Kicker's voice penetrated Jesse James' voice from my smart phone. I didn't need the attention, but I knew this was coming. The looks and the whispers I was getting from people who'd been at Drew's party had warned me. I turned and removed my earbuds.

The soul tailing me was still there, eyes begging, cheap suit rumpled. He must have died in it. Kicker ran right through him, without slowing down, and screeched to a stop beside me, her breathing uneven, light-blue eyes sparkling.

"You missed an amazing game on Saturday," she said.

Okay, I was being totally self-absorbed now. This wasn't about Drew's party. We'd won and that was huge. Raine had texted me after I left her place on Saturday with the news. She and Andris had used a portal to get to the stadium before the game started.

"We are heading back to Jeld-Wen in two weeks." Her voice rose with excitement. "We might make state this year." She did a little dance.

I loved football. Raine and Andris had asked me to go with them, but my sucky mood had killed my enthusiasm for the sport. I'd fibbed and told her I had a lot of homework, but Raine wasn't stupid. She'd seen through the lie.

Fact was I'd hoped Echo would stop by to get his duster. Instead, I'd spent the rest of the weekend reliving our moments together with occasional thoughts about my conversation with Raine's dad. With the runes on my house, no soul had bothered me. For once, I'd wished they would so I could disperse them and piss off Echo. The best part was they were everywhere, like the gray-haired man tailing me right now. Too bad I couldn't carry my fire poker inside the school. It was in the car though.

"So… about the guy at Drew's," Kicker said, her voice low, enthusiasm shooting up a notch. "The one you left with. Who was he?" Then she saw my hand. "What happened to your hand?"

I wished people would stop mentioning it. Mom had fussed over it. Everyone I saw always asked what happened. It was like being constantly reminded of Echo's sudden exit from my life.

"Cora?"

I glanced at my hand. I had to see my doctor today. "An accident."

"Does that mean you can't swim?"

I shrugged. "The doctor said no."

"That sucks. We have a meet on Saturday."

"I'll talk to my doctor and see what he says. I texted Doc too, so he knows about my hand."

Kicker sighed. "Dang it! We were depending... Never mind. About Mr. Trench Coat? Who's he?"

"Someone I met in Portland while I was away."

"So you two are, like, dating?"

"We are, like, over." I didn't want to discuss Echo. I glanced back. The soul was still there.

"How could you let him go? He's hot. And that kiss..." She fanned herself. "You should have seen the look on Drew's face. I bet no girl has ever done that to him. Of course, Leigh was there to comfort him. You two were all everyone talked about after you left. I mean, you and, uh, what's his name?"

"It doesn't matter, Kicker. He's gone."

"But Portland is just an hour away. You can see each other on weekends and..."

"Let it go, Kicker." I pushed the earbuds back into my ears.

The moment I entered the first room, a shiver shot up my spine. The familiar scent was Echo's. I turned and searched the students already seated, my heart pounding. My eyes connected with familiar ones.

Andris in my English class? Since when? And why was he covered in glowing runes? He didn't look happy either.

I hurried past the other desks, leaving Kicker behind, and slid into the desk next to Andris'. "Was Echo here?"

"Good morning to you too, Mortal. Thrilled to be on babysitting duties. Again. Please, try not to look at me when you talk." He slid lower in his seat.

I frowned. "Why not?"

"You'll look like an idiot."

He was such a douche sometimes. "What are you doing in my class?"

"I'm the freaking go-to babysitter whenever your men want to outsource. First Raine. Now you."

"Sounds like insourcing to me, and I'm insulted by the word babysitter. So he was here?"

"Which part of don't look at me while talking didn't you get? People will notice."

He was in one of his weird moods. "So what if they do?"

"I'm invisible right now, Mortal."

Oops. I glanced at the class. A few frowns were directed my way. I lifted my smart phone and adjusted the ear buds. Pia, the airhead from Drew's party, and two cheerleaders chose that moment to enter the class. They saw me, stopped, and exchanged whispers. Giggles and the glances directed my way said they were talking about me.

Yeah, like I cared.

I rested my elbow on my desk, supported my head on the heel of my arm and faced Andris, or the empty seat next to mine. "Okay, I'll pretend to be texting a friend or... we could just text each other. Do you have a cell phone?"

He pulled one from the pocket of his jacket and showed it off. "The best money can buy, but the only Mortals who get my number are ones I'm hooking up with on a daily basis or interested in. And that excludes you. You are taken. Hmm, I wonder who you will end up choosing. Eirik, the perfect son of Baldur or the big, bad Grimnir? My bet is on Eirik. He is royalty among the gods. Mortals tend to marry up, not down."

I didn't want to discuss Eirik or play Andris' mind games. "What did he want?"

"What did who want?"

I glared at him. "Don't mess with me, Andris. I can become a bitch real fast."

"Oh, spare me the teenage drama," he snapped. "He was here to order us around. He didn't even ask. On a good day, I would have told him to screw himself, but big brother was around and wanted me to play nice."

I ignored his rant. "What did he say?"

"He didn't explain. He just said you need to be protected then left. I guess some badass Grimnirs are in town and they're not here for souls."

My heart dropped. He didn't have to spell it out. They were here for Maliina, which meant me. I glanced at the entrance. The soul was visible. "Is the old guy pacing in the hallway one of them?"

Andris studied the man. "Nah, that's a soul."

"Why can't you escort him to Valhalla?"

Andris laughed, studying the soul. "Cheap suit, gaunt face, pudgy stomach, a bit green around the gills—I'd say he died from some serious illness, which makes him Hel bound."

"Cora Jemison!" Mr. Pepperidge called out, and I whipped around. "Turn off your phone or I'll confiscate it."

Students snickered. Usually, teachers didn't tell students to turn off their phones. They just confiscated them until the end of the day. I wondered how long before Mr. Pepperidge started treating me like other students. Probably after he read my next paper, which I hadn't even started writing.

"It's off." I waved the phone then put it and the ear buds away. Andris smirked then closed his eyes. He dosed off during the class. I kicked his feet a few times and was answered with a snarl.

"You were snoring," I wrote on a piece of paper and showed him. He wasn't, but I needed a distraction. Mr. Pepperidge was beyond boring.

The soul was still in the hallway when class was over, but he kept his distance. Torin was waiting for me. At least he was visible.

"She's all yours," Andris said and took off.

I rolled my eyes. "How long are you guys going to do this?"

"For a couple of days or so."

I frowned. "What's happening in a few days?"

"I don't know. Echo sucks at explaining things, and arguing with him is usually pointless. Come on."

"Great game, St. James," followed us. Torin bumped fists with a few jocks as we walked down the hallway. Other students gave him thumbs-up with broad smiles. I couldn't remember a jock being this popular.

"How long has that soul been following you?" he asked when there was a break in the streaming adoring fans.

"Since I got to school. I don't know how to get rid of him. At home I usually use an iron rod to disperse them."

Torin winced.

"It doesn't hurt them, does it?"

"I don't think so, but it can't be pleasant. It takes them a while for their energy to coalesce."

"Oh, maybe I shouldn't do that anymore."

"Maybe you shouldn't. Here we are." He waited until I was seated before he left. He was back seconds later, runes engaged. I guess staying invisible eliminated explaining their presence in classes they didn't usually attend.

By lunchtime, I was used to them in my classes. Torin was cool because he didn't talk much. Andris bitched nonstop. Lucky for him, no one could hear him. Unlucky for me, I could. I had to catch myself from laughing out loud because he could be funny. He said hilarious things about the students in each class.

During lunch, he sent one of his friends, Pretty Boy Roger, to ask me to join them just as I sat next to Kicker and the other swimmers. Raine insisted Andris was just toying with the boy, but I'd seen the way he looked at Roger. There was something there.

"Sorry, Roger. Tell him if I spend one more second in his presence, I'll probably strangle him." I wiggled my fingers at Andris and stayed put. He shot me a mean look.

I grinned. *Yeah, right back at you.*

Hanging with him wasn't so bad. He kept me company when I went to Dr. Olsen's for my follow up. Mom arrived after we did, but I doubted she realized Andris was with me. Afterwards, I told her I was meeting a friend at The Hub, for a homework session.

Turned out Andris was really smart and actually helped me with my work load after he zipped through his. But the surprise was watching him cradle an out-of-print copy of some sci-fi book. It was as though he'd found the Holy Grail.

"I gave up on ever finding an original copy after I lost mine." His eyes narrowed when he caught me watching him. "If you ever tell anyone I love sci-fi books, I will take you out."

I grinned. "You should try my dad's."

Andris frowned. "Try your dad's what?"

"Books. He's a sci-fi author," I told him proudly.

He threw me a skeptical look. "Yeah, right."

"Come on. I'll show you." We went to the section of the store that featured regional authors. I grabbed two copies of Dad's books and dangled them under Andris' nose. "Ta-da!"

He grabbed the books from my hand. "No way. I've read all J.C. Cooper's books. I mean, they're middle grade books, but who cares." He turned them and studied the photograph of my dad on the book jacket. "Are you sure he's your father?"

I chuckled. "What? Can't you see the family resemblance?"

"Yeah, now that you mentioned it," Andris teased. "The beard and gray hair are a dead giveaway. Can he sign my copies? No, even better, introduce us, so I can give them to him and watch him sign them." His excitement was contagious.

"Sure. Once all this mess is over, I will. He might even let you read his next book before it hits the stores."

The look on Andris' face was priceless. "I think you and I are going to be friends now, Cora Jemison."

"You mean we aren't already?"

"No, but don't be offended. I barely tolerate most Mortals. Unless they have something I want."

"Aren't you a walking mass of contradiction?" When he cocked his eyebrows, I added, "You're selfish and proud of it."

He smirked and nodded. His phone beeped. It was a text from Ingrid. She used a portal and joined us, but Andris didn't hear her when she tried to talk to him. She shook her head and came to sit by my side.

"So now you know his secret," she said softly. Her Scandinavian accent was beautiful.

"What do you mean?" I asked.

"Andris guards his nerdy side from everyone except those closest to him. I even doubt *Roger* has ever seen him touch a book." She said Roger's name with distaste. "He disappears in libraries and bookstores whenever he's not reaping, or he buys books online. You should see the den. It's overflowing with his collection of books and comics, some of them so old they belong in a museum. And when he's not reading, he's wiring something." She glanced at Andris, her cheeks turning red. "He's sort of a genius. There's no computer he can't fix or system he can't hack."

Men could be so blind. Despite all his smartness, Andris couldn't see that Ingrid adored him. When we finally dragged him out of the store, he was the proud owner of several books.

The two of them followed me home, but didn't enter the farm. They just made a U-turn and left. They must have believed I was safe with my parents. Obviously, Echo had forgotten to tell them about the attack on us and the dent he'd fixed on our truck.

Echo came to my room that night while I slept. I realized it on Tuesday morning when I woke up after a dream where he was leaning over me and saying, "I'm sorry."

I would have written it off as a dream if he hadn't taken his T-shirt, coat, and gloves. I had washed his T-shirt and left it with the coat and the gloves on my dresser. That he chose to take them without waking me up told me he hadn't wanted to talk.

That hurt.

Andris and Ingrid were waiting outside my gate in their SUV and followed me all the way to school. Then Torin stayed with me most of the day. He and Raine decided to eat lunch at school, so we shared a table with a bunch of jocks and my swim friends. It was an interesting combo. Naya must have hooked up with one of the jocks during Drew's party because they were all over each other.

Torin had football practice, Ingrid had cheerleading, and Raine had lessons with her Valkyrie instructor, so I hung out with Andris again. This time, we went to the Creperie. Once again, Andris helped me with my homework, and then he introduced me to his favorite authors. I loved seeing this side of him. It was opposite the blatantly misogynist, cocky, selfish douchebag he sometimes morphed into.

At night, I tried to stay awake and wait for Echo. Something woke me after midnight. Maybe he'd made a sound or there was a sudden chill in the air. I didn't have to search hard to find him. He was seated on my chair, runes glowing, arms crossed as though he was trying to stay warm. I didn't have to touch him to know he'd come from Hel.

"Echo?"

"Go to sleep, Cora."

"You are cold," I whispered.

"I'll be okay."

I wanted to ask him to come to bed, where it was warm, but I feared he'd reject me, so I got up, went into my closet, and came out with a throw rug. I gave it to him. The gold in his eyes intensified.

"Talk to me, please," I whispered, staring down at him, wanting to crawl onto his lap.

"Go to bed, Cora. I'm here to protect you, nothing else."

His voice was frosty and uninviting. Thoroughly humiliated, I crawled back into bed. Sleep eluded me, and I kept tossing and turning. He must have runed me because I fell asleep suddenly and didn't wake up until morning.

Wednesday night, Andris told me Ingrid had a date. He didn't look too happy about it, but he perked up as the evening progressed. He took me and Roger to dinner, so I didn't come home until late.

Before I went to bed, I left two throw rugs on the chair for Echo. Still, I knew the moment he came into my room, and I pretended to be asleep. He walked to my bed and stared down at me for a very long time. A few times, he reached down as though to touch my face, but each time he stopped. It took all my effort to lie still when all I wanted to do was pull him down beside me.

I was pissed off when I woke up. He must have runed me again because I couldn't remember anything happening after he stood by my bed. The rugs were on the bed as though he'd covered himself with them, and there was an indentation where his head had been.

How dare he rune me and deprive me of the memory of sleeping in his arms?

Pissed-off me was a total a bitch to Andris and Torin. All of a sudden, their presence bugged me. I hated that I couldn't go anywhere without one of them hovering and told them in large letters on a notebook, which I shoved at them.

Drew had kept his distance the last few days, although I'd caught him staring at me with a calculating gleam in his eyes. His pride had been hurt, but he'd be an idiot to try something. Leigh and Pia were beyond stupid and made the mistake of cornering me in the bathroom during lunch.

"Stay away from Drew if you know what's good for you," Leigh snarled.

"Or what?" I asked, eyeing her through the mirror.

"Or I'll bury you," Leigh snapped. "One word from me and the entire school will treat you like slime. Not even your friendship with Raine and St. James will save you."

I laughed. "You think I care about my social status in this school? Not anymore. Besides, Drew likes me. If he decides to talk to me—"

"He won't."

"Not after he saw the type of men you date," Pia pitched in. "Who was the guy anyway? We've never seen him around."

"He's a college student. Unlike you guys, I only date older guys now." I moved closer to Leigh, forcing her to lean back. "Don't ever threaten me again, because you have no idea what I'm capable of." Grinning at their expressions, I left the room.

Andris went with me to Dr. Olsen's for my Thursday checkup and, once again, stayed in the waiting room with his nose buried in an e-reader. He'd hoped Dad would come to the doctor's office with me, but it was Mom who hurried into the waiting room.

"We have a meet on Saturday. Is there a way I can participate?"

Dr. Olsen studied the sutured wound and glanced at Mom. "It's healing well, but I don't think that's a good idea. The last thing you need is an infection."

"I told her the same thing," Mom piped in.

"The team needs me, Mom. Isn't there something I can use to cover it? I plan to swim a few races, and like you said, it's practically healed. No pinkness or swelling. I've been taking good care of it. You know, using antibiotic ointment and wiping the area with peroxide."

The doctor shook his head and exchanged another glance with Mom. "She's still as stubborn as ever."

Mom sighed. "She takes after her father. Is there anything she can use?"

"Of course, but you have to be very careful, young lady."

I left the doctor's office with hydrocolloid adhesive pads. I was so waiting to have it out with Echo that night, but he didn't even show up. Or if he did, he must have runed me again.

***

"It's Friday. Please tell me you're planning on clubbing or at least throwing a beer bong party in the middle of some vineyard," Andris said, sliding beside me, his boy toy Roger by his side.

"I have swim practice. Then I plan on going to bed early."

Andris sighed. "How can someone so hot lead such a boring life?" I was sure he was saying that for his friend's benefit. "Roger, is there anything happening anywhere tonight?"

Roger shook his head. "Geoff is having a Minecraft tourney at his place."

Andris chuckled and touched Roger's cheek. "You know I don't go for those kinds of games. We need to go out and have some serious fun. How about it, Cora? Pick a place. L. A. Connection or Bill's Taproom, the new bar on 8th North."

"Sorry. I have a meet tomorrow morning, so it's early to bed for me."

"What? Where?" His eyes narrowed. "How early is this meet? If I have to get out of bed for you, Echo will owe me."

"Who is Echo?" Roger asked.

"The guy she has a crush on. The reason she's being Miss Goody Two-Shoes. She doesn't know that's not the way to keep someone like Echo interested."

If a glare could kill, he'd be plant food. "The meet is here, and you don't have to be there, douchebag. I don't want you to. And FYI, I don't have a crush on him," I added through clenched teeth. "Oh, and your services are not needed this evening either. Go clubbing or partying for all I care." I exited the building, but Andris was right behind me.

"Wait up, Cora," he said.

I ignored him.

"Okay, I'll apologize. Stop stomping like Attila the Hun. Girls are supposed to glide."

I stopped and turned. "You do know when you piss someone off, you are supposed to apologize, not hurl more insults."

He raised his hands in mock surrender and smirked.

I cocked my eyebrows. "I'm still waiting for an apology."

"Which part pissed you off? The crush, Miss Goody Two-Shoes, or keeping a certain Grimnir interested."

The anger drained out of me. I couldn't stay mad at him no matter how often he pissed me off. He was cute and had been great the whole week. Besides, I loved his snarkiness. "Forget it."

"Now I need a hug. Come here." He extended his hands toward me.

I rolled my eyes and gave him a hug. His hand crept lower. "You touch my butt, Andris, and I'll knee you so hard your jewels will lodge in your throat."

Grinning, he stepped back. "Okay, no need to turn me into a eunuch. Come on. I'll take you to the pool and stick around until you're safe at home. Again. What time is the meet tomorrow?"

"Early. It's okay. I'm going with Raine." Raine had been studying with her Valkyrie instructor after school, so we hadn't hung out, but she had off today. She caught up with us before we reached my car.

"Roger is waiting for you, Andris," she said.

"I know. Isn't he adorable? Are you really babysitting Cora this evening?"

"Babysitting?" Raine and I said at the same time.

Andris took off laughing. "You two be good. Watch out for Grimnirs."

I was beginning to doubt the "presence of other Grimnirs" story Echo had fed Torin and Andris.

"At least you don't have to skip class to *babysit* me," I told Raine and threw my backpack in the back of my car. She added hers and her oboe then sat in the front passenger seat. I cranked the engine. As I backed out, I almost hit a girl. The soul that had been following me on Monday was walking beside her. He shook his fist at me. "Don't your man and Andris care about missing classes?"

"Not really. School is about blending in, not learning. Are you excited about tomorrow's meet?"

"Yep." I always enjoyed meets. Raine liked to say I was an adrenaline junkie, and she might just be right. It might explain why I was lusting after a certain bad boy. "Can you come with?"

"No way. Even coming with you tonight scares the heck out of me. I don't know how the others will react to my presence."

"Oh, please. The way they all came to the hospital after your father's coma scare should tell you the past doesn't matter anymore."

At the next stop, a cold draft filled the car, and I grinned.

Echo.

I turned and groaned with disappointment when I saw the gray-haired soul from school. How did he pull that off? I thought he was attached to the girl I'd seen him with. I studied him in the rearview mirror. He wore an expectant expression.

Why did they always look at me like I was the answer to whatever bugged them? I shivered. And why did they have to be so cold?

"What do you want?" I snapped.

"What?" Raine asked.

"I'm talking to the dead guy, not you," I said, glaring at the soul through the mirror.

Raine whipped around, her eyes wide. "Where?"

"The soul, Raine."

She squinted, her eyes darting around.

"Behind me. Can't you see him?"

She sighed. "No. Why can't I see them? Everyone does except me."

"But I thought you wanted to be a Valkyrie."

"Doesn't mean I can see souls yet. Mom and Lavania keep saying I will when the time is right. That the Veil opens slowly so we are not overwhelmed by what we see. Yours happened too fast and you, uh…"

"Went crazy," I finished, not bothered by my stint at the psych house anymore. "I can see why slow is good. Cerebrum overload is a bitch."

"So what does he look like?" She continued to squint at the soul.

"Old. Graying hair. Potbelly. Wrinkled suit. Andris said it's cheap."

"Andris is a fashion snob. What is he doing now?"

"Talking. I still can't hear the souls." I peered ahead, trying to find the perfect spot to park. I passed business offices and restaurants. All their parking lots were packed with cars. "I need to park somewhere private. Somewhere no one can see us."

"First Presbyterian Church."

First PC was by our school. "That's way back there."

"Make a U-turn. It's secluded, and the parking lot is empty."

And it didn't have a cemetery, so no more souls. I made a U-turned and headed back toward school. I studied the soul through the rearview mirror. He seemed harmless. Just an old dead guy.

"Are you going to disperse him?" Raine asked.

I would if Echo would appear to lecture me about messing with his charges. Unfortunately, Torin's words kept ringing in my head. Then there was Mr. C's advice. I never thought there'd come a day I'd want to be nice to a soul.

"I'm going to show compassion," I said.

Raine frowned. "What?"

"Crazy, right? But someone I respect told me I needed to change my methods of dealing with them."

"Echo?"

"Your father."

"Is that why he called you to the den on Saturday?"

I chuckled at her incredulous tone. I wasn't planning on telling her about seeing her father in the cafeteria after he'd died. "Yes. He said I should embrace my gift."

Some gift. More like a curse. I still couldn't see me embracing it.

I signaled, entered the empty church parking lot, and parked. Blowing out air, I opened the door, stepped out, and waited. The soul followed. Raine opened her door and peered at me from across the hood. Since I was facing the car, if anyone saw me, they'd assume I was talking to her. Heart pounding, I smiled.

"Okay, mister. Tell me what you want," I said, going for calm and confident. Yeah, like I knew what I was doing. This was crazy.

His mouth opened and closed without making a sound.

"I'm sorry, but I can't hear you."

He gestured wildly with his hands, his lips moving fast.

I sighed. "This is ridiculous. I can't hear a thing or read lips."

"New souls are like newborns," Raine whispered. "They don't know how to express their thoughts or emotions properly. Most of the time, the Valkyries do all the talking and the souls do the following. Valhalla is like any military. They train, eat, and sleep… train, eat, and sleep. Same routine without deviation. No time to think for themselves. The souls left behind often find something familiar and become attached to it."

No wonder they were attached to buildings and family members. "Or walk around aimlessly as though lost. Okay, I'm going to try again. Listen, sir. I." I touched my chest. "Help." I pointed at him. "You."

He stopped talking, titled his head to the side, and pointed at his chest then me.

"We're getting somewhere. Yes. I will help you. Tell me what you want."

He pointed at his chest again then me.

I grinned. "Yes."

He moved so fast I didn't realize his intention until our bodies melded. The cold was bone-chilling and smothering. My skin felt clammy and tight. My lungs strained to suck in air, and my sight grew hazy.

"What's happening, Cora?" Raine screamed.

Her voice echoed as though she was talking through a tunnel. I tried to respond, but I couldn't open my mouth. I felt light, as though I was floating away. Hands grabbed my arms.

"Cora! Damn it! Talk…"

Raine's voice faded only to be replaced by another. A man's voice. The soul's? Probably. I strained to understand what he was saying. His voice grew loud then faint… loud then faint…

My head hurt, and my chest burned from lack of oxygen. Darkness tried to swallow me, but I fought against it. Fought and fought… until sounds filtered through.

I recognized Andris' voice then Raine's and Torin's. They were arguing.

"Don't look at me," Andris snapped. "They wanted to do their female bonding thing and told me to leave."

"He shouldn't be here," Raine whispered.

Who shouldn't be here? Andris?

"There's nothing we can do about him now," Torin said reassuringly.

"That's right," a familiar voice said. "You can whine about my presence all you want, but I'm not leaving. Without me, she'd be fighting for her life."

Echo.

My heart pounding, I opened my eyes. He might have sounded amused, but anger burned in the depth of his golden eyes as he studied me. I grinned.

"And she smiles. What are you doing, doll-face?"

10. Close Encounter

I hated that name. It was probably Maliina's nickname.

"Checking how comfortable the ground is." I moved my legs and arms. No broken bones. Raine must have broken my fall. "Very comfy. What are you doing here during the day?"

He squatted beside me, bringing with him raw sensual energy and his tantalizing scent. I wanted to inhale him and soak him in. Then deck him.

"Rescuing you from a soul. Again. Are you okay?" He touched my head.

"Gah, your hand is freezing." I sat up. "Did you just come back from Hel's Hall to brag? Or..." I remembered our first meeting. "You knew what they wanted, didn't you? The first time we met. You knew."

Echo nodded.

"Does *she* attract souls, too?"

His eyelids dropped. "I don't know. Our interaction was limited to... other pastimes. Thank you," he added, studying me through the canopy of his ridiculously long lashes.

"For what?" Reminding him of Maliina and that all they did was have sex? I hated her.

"For warming my hand," he said softly, a sexy smile tugging the corner of his lips.

My eyes flew to my hands. I had his trapped between mine, instinctively warming it. I let him go, heat rushing to my face.

"What you did today was very dangerous and reckless, doll-face. Do you know what happens to Mortals who are possessed by a soul?" he asked.

"No, but I'm sure you are going to tell me in excruciating details. And please, don't call me doll-face."

"Have you watched Poltergeist?" Echo asked.

"Yeah. So?"

"Poltergeist is nothing compared with real possession. You could easily go crazy, hurt yourself, or worse."

Wasn't he the bearer of gloom? And since when did I become so easy? I was supposed to be pissed with him. Instead, my heart pounded with excitement, and the urge to throw myself into his arms threatened to overwhelm me.

"If you're here to lecture me, then leave. I was trying to help a soul find closure. Something I'm sure you wouldn't understand. And no more watching over me while I sleep either. You rune me again and I'll make you sorry in ways you couldn't possibly imagine." I was being a total bitch now, but I didn't care.

"Who said it's your job to give them closure?" he asked, ignoring the last things I'd said.

"Me, and there's nothing you can do about it."

Laughter came from my left. My head whipped toward it, and I caught Andris' smirk. Even Torin was trying hard not to smile. Raine was the only somber one. She looked shaken.

"Your presence is upsetting Raine." I got up and walked to her. We hugged. "I'm sorry," I whispered.

"He's not scaring me. *You* did. And you shouldn't be listening to my…" she glanced at Echo. "He is right. You should never do this again."

"What happened?" I asked.

"You went into a trance. You know, eyes rolling into the back of your head, body shaking. I barely caught you before you fell. Then you started talking in a strange voice. Finally, you blacked out."

I frowned. I thought I hadn't blacked out. "How long was I out?"

"About ten minutes."

That was long. "And, uh, what happened to the soul?"

"I happened," Echo said, sounding close.

He must have taken it to Hel's Hall, which would explain his cold hands. I turned around to face him. "You ordered it out of me?"

Echo nodded. "Lucky for you, I knew his name. He had no business possessing you."

I frowned, hearing the concern underneath the anger, or maybe I wanted to hear it. "He wanted me to pass a message to someone called Clare Bear. Something about a safety deposit box at Key Bank. The password is her name, Clare Bear." I walked around him to my car, opened the back door, and reached for my folder. It was already open. Weird. I didn't recall opening it. I sat in the back seat with my feet on the ground and started writing down the names and numbers.

"What are you doing?" Raine asked.

I looked up to find the four of them staring at me "Writing down what he told me. I hope I remember everything."

Raine waved a notebook. "You already wrote them down."

I stared at the notebook in her hand. The exact same number and words I'd just written were scribbled over and over again on a piece of paper. Some were initials. SDB instead of safety deposit box. KB instead of Key Bank. PW instead of password. The handwriting wasn't mine. "I did that?"

"You demanded in the weirdest voice that I give you a paper and pen. When I did, you wrote this." She tapped at the page.

After what Maliina did to me, I should be pissed or maybe even leery of someone using me. Instead, I was excited at the possibility of what I might do with my weird ability. I could actually help someone find closure. Maybe this was what Mr. C had meant—find out what they wanted. The soul had given me a message.

"You can never do this again, Cora," Raine said. "It's too dangerous."

Torin nodded. "Too many Mortals have gone insane from possession. For centuries, powerful high priests and priestesses have cleansed the possessed by ordering the soul to leave. They don't always succeed."

"But that means you guys can order them out once I joined with them, right?" I gave them a sweeping glance. Torin's expression was unreadable. Andris smirked while Raine still looked worried. Knowing her, she was probably blaming her father for this fiasco. The soul had blindsided me. Next time, I'd be prepared. "I mean, Valkyries and Grimnirs are crème de la crème of high priests and priestesses." I slanted Echo a look. He was frowning, yet his people were priestly. "Right?"

"I think you and I should discuss this privately," he said slowly.

"That's not going to happen," Torin said.

Something lethal and deadly flashed in Echo's eyes, but his gaze didn't leave mine. "Stay out of my business, Valkyrie," he warned softly.

"I told you, you are not using her while we are around," Torin retorted.

"You don't matter in the grand scheme of thing, St. James. She does." Echo grinned and gave me a slow perusal. I was wearing my swim team sweatpants and jacket, but from the heat in his eyes, I might as well be sitting there naked. His voice dropped an octave and became husky. "Besides, 'using' is such a misunderstood term."

The timbre of his voice stroked my senses. Even when he pissed me off, I still wanted him. Torin moved to stand beside me like a guard and faced Echo, who was holding the car door. I was still seated in the back seat with my feet on the ground. They were acting ridiculous. Echo would not hurt me. Not physically anyway. And Torin's antagonistic behavior didn't make sense.

"I know you, Echo," Torin said. "You never do anything without a reason."

"And it's always for your goddess," Andris added. "Isn't that why you are her favorite? The guy she goes to when she wants a job done?"

A spasm crossed Echo's face as though Andris had hit a nerve, but he recovered fast and smirked. "Hel's favorite? You have been reading up on me, pretty boy. How flattering." He finally dragged his eyes from me to Andris and then Torin. "I'll say it again. Step down, Valkyries. I appreciated the fact that you watched over her while I couldn't, but I'm back now. This is between Cora and me."

Torin casually placed his hand on the hood of my car and leaned back as though he had no intention of leaving. He was wearing his football gear, which meant he'd left practice to come here.

"Anything that concerns her concerns us," Torin said.

I had enough of their performance. It didn't make sense. "Let me butt in here, boys, since you are about to have another brainless testosterone showdown and I don't plan to stick around and stop it this time." I pointed at Torin then Andris. "You two guarded me this week because Echo asked you to and now you're turning against him because...?"

"He never asked," Torin said. "He said you were in danger and left."

I shook my head. "I'm confused. Doesn't that make him a good guy?"

"No," Andris and Torin said at the same time. Echo just smirked.

"We didn't see any Grimnirs while he was gone," Andris said.

"Maybe I took care of them," Echo said, sounding indifferent, as though he didn't care whether they believed him or not.

"Maybe there weren't any Grimnirs to begin with," Andris snapped. "Maybe the broken trees and ruined vines near Cora's home were staged to make her think she was in danger."

"And you wouldn't kill one of your own without facing Hel's wrath," Torin retorted. "You are here on a job, and it involves her. So I'll say it again, leave her alone or deal with us."

If everything they said was true… No, I wasn't going to start believing everything they said, and I didn't like the way they were ganging up on Echo.

"Whoa, slow down, guys." I stepped away from the car and went to stand by Raine who hadn't spoken since the guys started their little fight. "Thanks for keeping an eye on me, guys. Whether you had to or not, I still appreciate it, but it is not up to you to decide whether I talk to Echo or not."

Echo smirked.

I glared at him. "You had your chance to explain things, but you walked out on me instead. And every night since then, you had a chance to talk to me, but you slipped me sleeping runes instead, so I'm not ready to listen to anything you have to say. In fact, I don't know if I trust you enough to believe anything you say now."

Eyes shadowed, Echo walked to where I stood. He was so close the heat from his body leaped between us and wrapped around me. Part of me wanted to put some distance between us, but another part wanted to grab him and hold him close. Forgive him for his shitty behavior the last week.

He didn't speak, letting his eyes speak for him. He was sorry, they said.

"You can trust me, Cora. I'd never lie to you. *You*, Cora, not Maliina. She doesn't matter or mean anything to me. They," he waved toward Torin and Andris, "don't matter. You do." Heat flashed in his eyes. When his eyes moved to my lips, they tingled as though he'd kissed me.

It was time to create some distance between us.

"Don't ever mention her name to me again." I shuffled sideways and hurried to my car. When our eyes met, there was pain in his eyes. He had no reason to be hurt. I was the one he'd wronged. "Coming, Raine?"

Raine kissed Torin then ran around to the front passenger seat. I backed out and took off. I could see the guys in the side view mirror. They were still standing where we'd left them. Torin's Harley and the SUV Andris usually drove to school were parked a few feet away.

"Do you think they'll be okay?" I asked, my eyes returning to Echo. He was watching us drive away, his expression hard to read.

"Yeah. Andris hates to fight and will stop them if things get out of hand."

"I don't understand why Torin dislikes Echo when he did him a favor—uh, never mind." She might not know about her father's soul.

"You mean when he chose not to reap my father's soul?" Raine asked.

"Oh. So you know."

"Torin doesn't keep secrets from me. Torin owes Echo a soul, and Echo plans to collect." She made it sound like Echo was wrong.

"It seems fair to me," I said defensively. "A soul for a soul."

"Or he could let it slide. I mean, it's just statistics to him. I'm happy you told Echo to take a hike. He's no good for you. Torin and Andris don't trust him either."

"I know."

"He's an odd ball, you know. A lot of Grimnirs can't stand him."

The details of Echo's story flashed in my head. "Druids," I muttered.

"What?"

"Nothing."

"I asked Torin why the Grimnirs hate him, but he doesn't know," Raine continued. "Chances are the Grimnirs who came after you were out to hurt him. That is assuming the story he told you is true. He was once a Valkyrie, you know, but he did something so horrible they kicked him out of Asgard and placed him on Hel duty—permanently."

I hated the way she gleefully listed Echo's faults. "I know about that, Raine."

"You do?"

I glared at her. "Yes, I do. Echo told me. He doesn't keep secrets from me. It is the same reason his fellow Grimnirs hate him. He did something noble, and those who disagree with him are idiots."

Silence filled the car as I entered University Boulevard, the road that ran in the middle of Walkersville University. I glanced at Raine and caught her grin.

"What?" I asked.

"I knew it." She laughed. "I was wondering how long you were going to let me hate on Echo before you told me to shut up. I watched your reaction when Torin and Andris were ganging up on him and when you were warming his hand. You are so into him."

"No, I'm not. He's an arrogant know-it-all, who seems to think he can do whatever he likes and get away with it just because… because he's hot."

"And you are so into him," Raine added.

I sighed. "Am I that obvious?"

"Only to me. So, on a scale of Drew to Eirik, where does he fall?"

"You mean when he's not driving me nuts and making me want to knee him?" Raine laughed, and I grinned. "Way, way above Eirik. Drew doesn't count."

"Aw. Poor Eirik."

"I feel bad for him too, but Echo caught me by surprise." I parked the car in the university parking terrace, and we started toward the Draper Building, Walkersville's sports and recreation complex. "I can't help how I feel."

"I know. What did you mean by he runed you to sleep?"

I quickly explained about Echo coming to my room at night to keep an eye on me.

"How sweet. Are you going to forgive him?"

"Eventually. Right now, let him stew. He acted like I'd hurt him, when it's the other way round. I'm pissed and hurt."

"I don't think he's going to make it easy for you to stay pissed because he is here."

I followed her glance and sighed. Echo watched us from the entrance of the building and completely ignored the college students who kept turning to check him out. Even the guys found him intriguing. How could they not when he looked like a fallen angel in his black clothes, duster, and those unusual eyes?

"Please, don't mention our conversation," I whispered.

Raine shot me an annoyed glance. "Really? You really think I would?"

"He can be very charming and persuasive."

Raine rolled her eyes.

Echo straightened when we approached the door, but I ignored him. Raine slowed down.

"See you after practice, Raine."

I ran inside, almost bumping into students. The building tended to be busy this time of the evening. I showed the girls at the recreation service desk my school ID then ducked into the changing room. Warm-ups had already started when I entered the pool deck. Coach waved me over.

"Are you sure you should be swimming?"

"My hand is healing fast." I showed him the hydrocolloid adhesive pads. "The doctor said this should keep the water out."

"All right. Use the fourth lane and see me after practice."

"Okay." I went to my lane and checked the bleachers to see if Raine and Echo were there. They weren't. Frowning, I dove in. Warm-ups were often intense, but Doc kept them short. He always made us taper down before a meet. If a swimmer pulled a muscle or got injured, we'd be in trouble. As it was, we were short on faster swimmers.

We lined up to race. Kicker was with the team on the lane to my left. She winked. "So it's over between you and Mr. Hottie-in-a-Trench-Coat, huh?"

I shot her an annoyed look. "Yes."

"So then why is he here?"

I followed her gaze to the bleachers, and my eyes met Echo's. He winked. Where was Raine? I almost missed my turn and dove into the water seconds late. I pushed myself, kicking and pulling, happy as a clown. Echo was here. Watching me. Maybe I *was* going to listen to what he had to say.

I finished the lap and pulled out of the pool.

Doc checked his stopwatch and gave me a thumbs-up. "I want to see that drive tomorrow, Jemison. You just dropped nine-tenths of a second."

I smiled and looked toward the bleachers. Echo got up, and my stomach dropped. Dang it. He was leaving. Instead of walking away, he moved closer to the pool and sat down again.

Smiling, I went back to practice. He was still there when I finished.

Doc pulled me aside when practice was over. He checked my hand. "Did it hold?"

"Oh yes." I wiggled my fingers. "I'll be here tomorrow."

"How is Raine doing?"

I shrugged. "Okay."

"Do you think she'll come back to the team? We could really use her."

Raine was too busy with her after school activities to swim. "I can talk to her, but I'm not making any promises. Her dad is pretty sick, and he's all her family is focusing on right now."

"I see," Doc said, bending down and picking up a pair of goggles a swimmer had left behind.

"Like I said, I'll talk to her." I left him doing rounds, collecting things students forgot. I carried my stuff in a mesh bag and disappeared into the showers.

"So you two are back together?" Kicker asked as we changed.

I didn't understand her obsession with Echo. Why should she care whether we were back together or not? "No."

"I want to know where he bought his coat. It's exactly like the one worn by the lead singer of the Reapers."

"Oh. I'll ask him if you like."

She gave me a thumbs-up and disappeared with Naya. I finished getting dressed and grabbed my bag. Echo stood by my car when I entered the parking terrace, and he wasn't alone. A girl was talking to him.

The green-eyed monster reared its ugly head somewhere deep inside me. I fought it. I refused to be one of those girls who became jealous just because her boyfriend said hi to another girl. Not that Echo was my boyfriend or anything like that.

He saw me and started forward, the girl completely forgotten. She stared after him and then at me, shrugged, and walked away. The monster quieted down.

I slowed down as he got closer. "I'm still not ready to listen—"

He wrapped his arms around me and pulled me close, swim bag, wet hair, and all.

"I'm sorry I hurt you, Cora," he whispered. "I didn't mean to. I'd do anything to undo the way I behaved. I want a chance to explain, and if you decide never to talk to me after that, I'll completely understand."

The timbre of his voice washed over my senses in such a delightful way that I shivered. He sounded really sorry, and it felt wonderful to be in his arms. Funny how warm he was when he hadn't visited Hel.

He leaned back and studied my face with such intensity I started to fidget, my heart tripping with anticipation and apprehension.

"I didn't mean to leave you the way I did last weekend," he said, stepping back and taking my gym bag. He gripped my arm and nudged me toward to the car. Instinctively, I pressed the button to unlock the car. "I should have stayed and tried to explain, but reasoning went out the window when I realized what I had done to you. I was pissed. Shocked. In denial. I made a terrible mistake."

His words hit me hard like a brick wall. "I was, uh, a mistake?"

"No, sweetheart. Not you. You are the most honest thing in my life right now. You told me you couldn't be the person I claimed you were, but I refused to listen or even consider you could be right. I had all the evidence that I was dealing with two different women, but—"

"What evidence?"

"You. Maliina might have looked like you, but she could never be you. I noticed a few minor details." He glanced at my chest and then my face and grinned. "Yours are perkier and bigger and… more responsive than hers."

My face grew hot. "You have a one-track mind."

"No, I don't. Just stating the obvious. But beyond the physical, there's… you. You are stubborn, opinionated, and take such pleasure in pissing me off."

I grinned.

He sighed. "It's not funny. Women adore me."

I rolled my eyes. "For an apology, yours sucks."

He winced. "You are also giving, loving, and an amazing listener. From the first kiss, I noticed the difference in the taste and texture of your lips, but I wanted you and couldn't believe I hadn't noticed…"

"That I wasn't Maliina?" I whispered.

He lifted my chin with his forefinger and studied my face, eyes blazing. "The gem hidden underneath the vampy exterior, except I was dealing with two different women. You are the gem. She is the vamp." He tucked strands of my wet hair behind my ear and moved his hand as though to cup my face. He stopped, fisted his hand, and let it drop by his side. "St. James was right about me. I use people and discard them when I'm done. I play dirty and don't care who gets hurt in the process as long as I win."

"But—"

He placed a finger on my lips. "Let me finish. I've been doing it for centuries, and I don't think I can change. I'm no good for anyone, least of all you, doll-face."

"Don't say that!" I whispered.

He closed his eyes, and when he continued, his voice was heartbreakingly sad. "I will bring you nothing but misery and heartache,

Cora. Believe me. I know what I'm talking about." He opened his eyes and ran his thumb across my lips. His head dipped as though he was going to kiss me, but he stepped back, arm dropping to his side. "I shouldn't even be touching you. Come on. I'll escort you home." He reached for car door and indicated I enter.

I pushed the door shut. "What do you mean by you know what you're talking about?"

"It can't work between us."

"Why not?"

"You know why."

The pain from a week ago returned. This time, it was worse. "Because I'm not Maliina? I'm not tough like her and would get easily hurt by the big bad Grimnir?"

Echo sighed. "This has nothing to do with her. Please, get in the car."

I didn't budge. "Is it our age difference? Raine and Torin are making it work."

"Our age difference doesn't bother me. You are Mortal, Cora, while I'm a Grimnir. I deal with the dead."

"So do I."

"It's not the same. Our worlds are not supposed to mix."

"Raine's mother and father made it work," I said.

"And see what's happening to him and Raine."

"What do you mean?"

"The Norns and the Valkyries, even the gods, never forget. How do you think her father, a man who took care of himself physically and watched what he ate, got cancer at such a young age? That's the Norns doing. I'd hate to see you hurt because of my choices."

I laughed. "You'd hate to see me hurt? What do you call what you are doing right now, Echo?"

"Doing the right thing."

"For you, not for me." I yanked the car door open and got behind the wheel. He gripped the door when I would have slammed it. "Let go."

"I'm sorry."

"Whatever makes you sleep at night, pal." I started the car and backed out, forcing him to jump back. He moved to the other side of the car, opened the door, and sat beside me before I switched gears. "Get out of my car, Echo. Let's make this break clean and final."

"I can't do that. I need to explain why I came to your bedroom that first night."

"That's self-explanatory," I snapped and hit the gas. "You thought I was Maliina, and you came for a booty call."

"That's not true."

"Oh, please. Do I look stupid to you? I was there. You practically mauled me."

He closed his eyes and sighed. "There's a reason I was there, Cora, and yes it had to do with her."

I stopped at the parking booth and handed the guy the correct amount of money. "I don't want to discuss her or that night, Echo."

"Then listen."

"Don't feel like doing that either." So hurt by his attitude I couldn't think straight, I stared straight ahead and stepped on the gas when the parking bar lifted. I careened around a corner without slowing down.

"You may want to slow down before a cop sees you," he warned.

I hated that he was right. I slowed down and took a calming breath. It was over between us. I had to accept it. Move on.

"About that night, you see—"

"Don't. I don't think I can take any more confessions from you today. Please."

Surprisingly, he became quiet. I focused on getting home in one piece. What was involved in moving on once a guy dumped you? Hook up with a new guy? Forget about dating and focus on school? No, I was never big on sitting around and nursing my wounded pride. I needed a new boyfriend. Someone hotter than Echo. Someone who'd never hurt me.

"We still need to talk," Echo reminded me when I pulled up outside my house.

"Not now." I jumped out of the car, but he was faster. He blocked my path, runes glowing. The look in his eyes was heartbreaking.

"Can I come upstairs, so we can finish this discussion?"

I blinked. "Are you serious?"

"Yes," he said. "I'll wait in your room until you are ready to listen."

"No. I don't want you anywhere near me, Echo."

He winced. "Okay."

"Fine. Goodbye." I took off and didn't look back.

My parents were downstairs, and chances that they'd seen me talking to myself were high. They didn't say anything though. We went through my usual afterschool ritual—they asked about school and swim practice and I gave them vague answers, grabbed something to eat, and headed upstairs.

For once, I didn't search for Echo when I entered my bedroom. He was leaning against my car as though he planned to stay there the whole night, his eyes on my window. My heart tripped. Stupid heart.

11. Searching for Maliina

Echo was still outside when I went to bed, but I knew the moment he appeared in my room. Awareness zipped up my spine. Too tired to fight, I ignored him. Or tried to. Surprisingly, I fell asleep.

He was gone the next morning, the throw rugs on the chair telling me he'd slept there. Mom was already in the kitchen, a hearty breakfast on the stove. She still wore her pajamas and her graying blonde hair was mussed from sleep. It was my first meet in weeks, and my stomach churned. I always got nervous before a meet.

"Can't eat?" Mom asked, placing a lunch bag with my usual swim energy supplies—banana, granola bars, and bottled water—on the counter.

She knew me too well. I gave up the pretense of eating and put down the fork. The weather didn't help either. It was raining hard. The situation with Echo and the Grimnirs made things worse.

Mom gave me a hug, and I let my head rest on her stomach and wrapped my arms around her waist. I needed a mommy-and-me moment. I needed to feel loved.

"Are you coming to the meet?" I'd never asked before.

She chuckled. "What a silly question. Of course." She dropped a kiss on the crown of my head. "When does warm-up start?"

"Eight." I looked at my watch and sighed. "I'd better get ready."

"And I'll wake up your dad. He had a late night, but he's looking forward to watching you swim. We'll be there before the meet starts." She poured a cup of coffee and paused in the process of leaving the kitchen. "Make sure you have extra—"

"Goggles and caps, I got it, Mom." I gave her another hug, put my plate away, and carried my snack bag. Doc always provided sandwiches and drinks, which I never ate. They got their sandwiches from a local store, and I hated limp lettuce and the bread they used. If I needed more munchies, I knew exactly where to go. This was a home meet, and I knew where all the vending machines were in the building.

My bag packed, I pulled the hood of my raincoat over my head and hurried to my car.

Echo wasn't there. Somehow I'd expected him to be inside the car. Neither Andris nor Torin was waiting to escort me like they'd been doing.

I threw my gear in the front passenger seat and cranked the engine.

A chill crawled under my skin when I hit Orchard Drive. I wasn't alone, and it wasn't Echo. I checked the rearview mirror, but there was no one in the back seat. My head whipped left and right, but I couldn't see anything. It was raining too hard.

Then I noticed the vines on either side of the road rustling in one direction as though something invisible was running through them.

Grimnirs in freaking hyper speed. Crap!

I reached for my cell phone and floored the gas. My heart pounded, my hand shaking so hard I almost couldn't punch the numbers. Any minute, I expected the Grimnirs to hit the car and squish me like a bug. Raine didn't pick up her phone.

I yelled something into the phone and dropped it, my hand returning to the steering wheel. The Grimnirs stayed with me, inching closer. They were now on the grass and bushes, blurry mini twisters from Hel. Shaking, my chest hurting with each breath, I ran a stop sign and entered another street, tires squealing. Lucky for me, it was Saturday and the traffic was nonexistent. And only a fool would run in this downpour.

A shadow appeared in the back of my car. No, not a shadow. The beginning of a portal. One of them was trying to get inside my car. Echo's words screamed in my head. They had no problem attacking a Mortal.

Where was Echo? I deliberately swayed, making the car zigzag so they wouldn't create a portal. My eyes darted around between the road, the Tasmanian devils racing my car, and the rearview mirror. My windows frosted and a chilling draft filled the car. My crazy driving hadn't stopped them.

A scream filled my car.

I didn't realize it was mine, until Echo's voice reached me from the back seat. "It's me," he said calmly. "Stop the car."

I slammed on the brakes. The tires screeched in protest, and the back wheels turned and skidded as the car swerved and rotated until I was facing the opposite direction. I brought us to a stop on the side of the road, almost landing in a ditch. Frantically, I searched the hedges.

"You okay?" Echo asked.

No. I opened my mouth, but my teeth were chattering so hard I couldn't speak. He moved to the front passenger seat.

"You are going to reopen your wound," he warned, gently prying my fingers from the steering wheel. He was cold—his clothes, his skin, his hands—but those arms never felt safer or more comfortable when they pulled me into his chest. His face, when he buried it in my neck, was arctic too, but I welcomed it. It was familiar.

"I'm sorry I wasn't here. I was only gone for a moment and didn't think they'd come after you right after I left. Luckily, I heard you."

He didn't make sense. How could he have heard me when I'd never called him? But his breath was warm on my nape. Another familiar thing. My heartbeat slowed down, and I opened my eyes.

"Did... did you stop them?" I asked.

"They're taking care of them."

"Who?" As the question left my lips, Torin appeared from the other side of the road and sauntered across the street. The rain didn't seem to bother him. He wore sweatpants and his leather jacket only. He was also barefoot.

Torin opened the door and slid in the back seat. "We got them."

"Good. We are even now," Echo said.

"I didn't do this for you."

"It doesn't matter. Your debt is repaid," Echo added firmly as the other door opened and Andris joined us, his silk pajamas plastered to his body.

"Hel's Mist! It's cold out there," he griped. "Next time you feel like racing Grimnirs, Mortal, make sure it's in the afternoon or far, far away from this stupid state and weather."

Echo stiffened.

"I have to go," I murmured. "Warm-up will be starting soon."

"Are you serious?" Andris asked. "After being chased by Hel's private army you still want to go to that stupid meet?"

Echo growled. "Shut up, Andris. You talk to her like that again and I'll..."

"You'll what?" Andris asked.

Torin gripped Andris' shoulder. "Easy, bro."

"You should be apologizing, not pissing me off, Valkyrie," Echo warned. "I told you the Grimnirs were after her."

"Except you haven't told us why," Torin retorted. "Two dead Grimnirs doesn't make you innocent." He used an artavus to etch runes on the car door and a portal appeared. I didn't see where it led, but as soon he stepped into it, I heard Raine's voice.

Andris looked at us and smirked.

"You're trying my patience, Valkyrie," Echo said.

"It's going to take a lot more than a few dead Grimnirs to convince us you've changed, Echo," Andris retorted.

"Too bad I've no interest in convincing you of anything. Cora is in this mess because of your idiotic decision. Get out of here before I forget she needs me."

"Bring it on," Andris snapped.

"Leave him alone, Andris," I cut in. "Just go."

A snicker escaped Andris. "Maybe you two deserve each other." He created his own portal and left.

"You defended me," Echo said, his voice softening, his breath warm on my nape.

I stared at our linked hands. His larger ones swallowed my smaller ones. He wasn't cold anymore. "I hate it when they treat you like that. It's also not Andris' fault Maliina turned into a psycho. You should cut him some slack."

"He's an idiot. He turned her using his artavus, after I warned him not to."

"He was in love and made a mistake." I turned my head and our gazes met. His eyes were warm and hypnotic. I wanted to grab his face and kiss him, make him want me.

"Are you warm enough to let me go?" I asked, even though I knew the answer.

"Yes. Are you calm enough to drive?" His voice had gone smoky. Sexy.

"I'm good."

He didn't move. Neither did I.

"Your poor hand." Without breaking eye contact, he brought my injured right palm to his lips and pressed a kiss to the healing wound. My breath caught. His eyes dropped to my lips. My teeth sunk into the soft flesh of my lower lip and he groaned. My eyes flew to his. I held my breath and waited to see what he was going to do.

"Cora," he said.

The way he said my name in an achy I-want-to-kiss-you-so-badly voice had my heart leaping and warmth unfurling in my stomach. "Yes?"

"Drive."

I blinked. "What?"

"Start the car." He spoke through clenched teeth, his voice curt.

"But—"

"Now."

He didn't have to snarl. I got it. He didn't want me. He was here to protect me. Nothing more. Nothing less.

"I get it," I snapped back, turned away from him, gunned the engine, and took off. He leaned back and took his warmth with him. Funny, how fast he went from cold to warm to hot. And I wasn't talking about his skin.

Pissed with myself for letting my guard down, I repeated, *he doesn't want me… he's here to protect me…* over and over, until I entered University Boulevard.

School buses were in the parking lot outside the Draper Building, but the students were already inside. It was a quarter past eight, and Doc was probably thinking I'd missed the meet.

I parked and glanced back at the brooding reaper in my car. Golden flames leaped in his eyes, but all he said was, "Go. I'm right behind you."

I grabbed my bag and headed for the building, not looking back until I was inside. My car was visible, but I couldn't tell whether Echo was still inside. Having him around was both frustrating and reassuring.

He doesn't want me. He's here to protect me. I kept repeating that as I changed and headed to the pool.

***

I didn't see Echo on the bleachers during the meet, but I felt his presence. Mom and Dad were hard to miss. Dad cheered the loudest, his voice following me out of the pool.

"Way to go, Cora!"

"That's my girl!"

The good thing was he cheered just as hard for the other Trojans. Most of our students were used to him and just smiled. Others even waved. He did have quite a local fan base in the valley. It didn't take the visiting team long to connect me to him. They stared as though he was a whack job and then smirked.

How I wished Raine were still with the team. Her parents had been just as bad as my father, and we had suffered the embarrassment together.

"Please come rune my father and make him invisible," I texted Raine.

"I don't think I'd know how," she texted back.

"You are a seer. Use your powers."

"I'm using what I know to make myself invisible, smarty pants. I suck at it."

"Why do you say that?"

"The guy on my left is onto me or something. It was nice to see others catch your waves during the last heat."

I glanced at the bleachers, but I didn't see any glowing beings. "Where are you?"

"The hallway."

I looked up the wall adjacent to the bleachers. The hallway's glass wall was another viewing area, even though there were no seats. I saw her and almost waved. "You sure you don't want to join my parents? You might calm my dad."

"I'm about to leave. Just wanted to make sure things were okay."

My stomach dropped. "Are the Norns around?"

"LOL," she texted back. "Nope, thank goodness."

"Have you seen Echo?"

"Briefly when I got here, but he's gone. Gotta go, Cora."

"I have two more heats. See you at your place later. Start working on my lost soul."

"Okay. Will need to hear more on this morning's mess, too. Torin was sketchy with the details."

"Thanks for sending them."

"That's what friends are for. Later." She disappeared from the window. I put my phone away and refocused on the meet. A few times, I found myself searching for Echo, and each time I wanted to slap myself.

It was over between us.

Seven schools were at the meet, most of them not top contenders for state championships. It was obvious some came out of curiosity to see the pool where lightning had nearly decimated our team. A few guys from the other teams even asked outright which one of us was the girl who'd had the premonition.

The meet ended at two. We got second place, while the guys placed third. Majority of us dropped time, so it was all good. In the changing rooms, I got more questions about the tragic Lightning Meet, as everyone was now calling it, and furtive glances. Some big mouth from my team had told them I was tight with Raine.

I stared down a few, but it didn't stop them. I didn't bother to change, just pulled on my sweatpants and jacket, grabbed my stuff, and took off.

Outside, the rain had stopped, but the sky was still overcast.

Kicker and her dynamic duo besties caught up with me just after I exited the building. We'd won the relays, and they were stoked.

"We're headed to my place to hang out and watch *Supernatural* reruns," Kicker said.
"Want to come?"

I loved *Supernatural,* but I didn't feel like hanging out with them.

"I can't. I'm so tired I just want to go home and crash." I waved to my parents who were waiting for me. "If I change my mind, I'll text you."

I hurried to my parents, while Kicker and the others headed in the opposite direction.

"You kids were amazing," Dad said, giving me a bear hug.

I wrapped an arm around his waist. "And thanks for embarrassing me again. One of these days they'll throw you out for being too loud."

Dad laughed. "Let them try. It's my right to root for my daughter."

"So we'll see you at home?" Mom asked.

"Later. I promised Raine I'd stop by for a visit." I searched for Echo.

"When will you be home?" Mom asked.

I shrugged. Raine and I had plans. "I don't know, Mom. Raine is going to help me with my homework."

More hugs and they left.

I headed for my car, unlocking it as I got closer. Heart pounding, I opened the door and peered inside. No Echo. Disappointment washed over me.

I hated how my emotions were tied to whether he was around or not. Somehow, they were slow at getting what I already knew. He was not for me. Grimnirs didn't date Mortals.

"I like your dad."

I whipped around, almost banging my head on the doorframe. Echo was leaning against the car, arms crossed and eyes on my parents, who were pulling away. He had runes all over his body, so I knew they didn't see him as they waved. I waved back.

"I didn't see you inside."

"I was around. I saw your reaction when you finished the breaststroke and saw the board. How many seconds did you drop?"

I completely forgot about everything else as we talked. He took the passenger seat while I slid behind the wheel. We were still talking about the meet when I pulled up outside Raine's.

"What are we doing here?" Echo asked.

I shrugged. "I'm going to hang out with Raine for the rest of the day."

His eyes narrowed. "Why?"

"Because there's nothing to do at my place but sit around and wait for Grimnirs to attack."

He chuckled. "I was hoping you'd want to eat or catch a movie."

My heart leaped at doing something with him. To be able to pretend we were normal, act like young people on a date would be wonderful. No, that was a lie. It would be terrible. He'd look at me the way he'd done earlier, as though he couldn't wait to devour me, then turn away. I wasn't strong. One more rejection and I'd crumble.

"I'm not hungry," I fibbed. "And I really think the less time we spend together the better."

"Cora—"

"In fact, I don't need you to protect me here," I continued quickly. "I'm sure Torin can keep an eye on us for the rest of the day."

Echo smiled. "Whatever you say, doll-face."

I grabbed my gym bag and stepped out of the car, feeling bad for turning him down. But it was better this way. I could feel his eyes on me. Goosebumps spread across my skin, yet heat pulsed in my veins. It was peculiar the way I reacted whenever he looked at me. Hot and cold. Angry with him yet wanting him. Pushing him away but longing to hold him closer.

I didn't look back, even though I was dying to. Raine opened the door before I reached it, and we hugged. I dropped my gym bag by the door.

"Where's Echo?" she asked.

"Gone," I fibbed.

She frowned. "Hmm. Okay. How was the meet?"

"We got second place. The boys got third." Sounds came from the den, her parent's new bedroom. "We need more serious swimmers. Doc even asked if you'd come back to the team."

Raine laughed. "With all the stuff I do? I don't think so."

I followed her to the kitchen. "I'm starving."

"We have leftover stir-fry from last night or a sandwich."

"Stir-fry. I want something hot."

I got myself bottled water while she warmed the stir-fry. "So what did you find out about our soul?"

"A lot. His name is William 'Bill' Burgess. He had a heart attack last Sunday while on his way home from a business trip. He was driving, the poor bastard. He's survived by three older sons from a previous marriage and a teenager daughter, Victoria, from his second wife, Clare."

"Clare Bear," I whispered.

"That's right. Victoria Burgess is a sophomore at our school." Raine placed a steaming bowl of yummy looking chicken stir-fry in front of me. "Want to know how I did it?"

"Okay, Sherlock. How?" I got a fork and twirled the spaghetti.

"I started with online obituaries for Bear. Checked Kayville then the county. There was no one by that name who'd died in the last week. I went back weeks. Nothing. Then going by your description, I studied the pictures instead and found photographs of a younger and older Burgess." There was a pile of newspapers on the counter. She pulled out the one on top. "Dad reads papers from cover to cover. You know, out of boredom. Here's William 'Bill' Burgess." She tapped at an article.

It showed a picture of the soul from school and the story about the accident. I skimmed through it as I ate. "It doesn't say where they live?"

"Newfort. I called Defoe Funeral Home and pretended to be a pharmaceutical salesman, a former associate of Mr. Burgess. I must have been convincing because the funeral director told me the wake was on Wednesday night and the funeral was two days ago."

"Dang! We could have mingled with guests at his wake and slipped the envelope with the safety deposit box info in among the condolence cards."

Raine pursed her lips in thought. "Actually, this might work better. The man was a salesman. We could say he dropped the piece of paper when he stopped at our house to sell his products and we just heard he'd died."

The perks of having a brilliant best friend. I grinned. "I like it. Did you get the address?"

"Oh yeah."

"Great! We can leave after I finish eating. This is really good." The garlic sauce was creamy. "Torin's?"

"No. One of Lavania's special dishes."

"What does she do when not working with you?"

"She visits Asgard and prepares my lessons." She rolled her eyes. "Sometimes, I wonder about this seer thing. All I want to be is a Valkyrie, but she keeps saying not yet. Not yet. Not yet. Not freaking yet. I have a feeling she's getting orders from someone up there."

"Goddess Freya?" I asked. "She is in charge of that kind of magic, right?"

Raine nodded, grinning. "I'm so happy I can discuss these things with you. I talked to Lavania about your possession issue, and she said I should be able to help when the guys are not around. They use their artavo, like Echo did, and command the souls by calling out their names, while I use incantations."

I paused in the process of putting a piece of chicken in my mouth. "Like Dean and Sam in *Supernatural?*"

She laughed. "Yeah, except I'll use the Old Language."

"Which is what?"

"I don't know. Old Norse, I guess. Lavania dishes out information like it is a rare element. Maybe Echo might know. You should contact him. We might need him when we go to the Burgesses' home. Torin and Andris went reaping. Don't know where or when they'll be back. I can protect you if we are attacked, but I'm not as skilled as the guys, so you might get hurt. What? Why are you looking at me like that?"

"I don't know where Echo is either."

"Why not? How do you contact him whenever you need him?"

"I don't. Usually, he just, uh, appears."

Raine grinned. "Torin, too. He insists he can *feel* when I need him. Obviously it's the same with you and Echo."

That would be cool. If we were a couple. "I don't know about that."

"Did you see him after the meet?"

"Yeah." I ate another forkful. "He came here with me."

"And?"

"I left him in the car."

Raine's jaw dropped. "Cora! You should have invited him inside."

"I didn't know Torin and Andris were gone. I didn't think we needed him, and he understood. Kind of."

"You two fought?"

"No. We are in perfect agreement about everything. He's here to protect me. Nothing more. Nothing less."

Raine's eyes narrowed. "What? So you are not going to be, you know, together?"

"Nope. He's a Grimnir and I'm Mortal. The two don't mix."

Raine sighed. "Torin played that card, too. I'll be right back." Raine disappeared toward the front entrance, and I went back to my food. I knew she went outside, and I waited to see whether she'd come back with Echo or not.

The door opened and Echo's laughter drifted inside.

"Hungry?" Raine asked, entering the house.

He followed her inside. "Famished."

Our eyes met. I looked away, feeling a little guilty for leaving him outside. Okay, not a little.

"I make a mean sandwich," Raine said, opening the fridge door. "We have bologna, chicken breast, or beef."

"Just throw everything in. I'm not picky." He paused by my stool. "Hey, doll-face."

"Don't call me that." He took the stool beside mine, facing Raine with his back to the counter. He was so close his thigh brushed my hip.

"I forgive you," he whispered.

"For what?"

"Leaving me."

I made a face.

"Feeling guilty yet?" he asked.

I was and he knew it. "No."

He moved closer, close enough I could count his ridiculously lush lashes. I moved back and dropped my arm onto my lap. He chuckled. "So, what's the plan?"

Refusing to play his childish games, I stood. Raine was watching us with a knowing grin. "I'm going upstairs to change."

"Why? You look perfect the way you are," Echo said.

I ignored him, even though the compliment was nice. "Call me when it's time to go."

"We are going to the Burgess after this," Raine told him as I walked away. "Remember the soul that possessed Cora?"

"He's wishing he hadn't," Echo said in a harsh voice.

"What do you mean?" I heard Raine ask.

"There's this island in Hel called Corpse Strand, where souls are subjected to the most excruciating pain…"

I didn't hear the rest of Echo's answer. I grabbed my bag and disappeared upstairs. Echo was angry with that soul for nothing. Burgess had asked if it was okay to possess me, and I'd agreed. Of course, I had no idea what I was agreeing to at the time. Echo and I were going to have a little chat about the guy.

Upstairs, I replaced my sweatpants with skinny jeans, loafers with boots, and my sweatshirt with a long-sleeved flannel top. Mascara and lip-gloss came next. I studied my reflection and sighed. My hair was a mess. Weeks at PMI meant I had serious split ends. Sighing, I brushed my hair then slipped my bag of toiletries back into my gym bag.

Raine walked in just as I finished. "Ready?"

"Yep."

She picked up her lip-gloss and applied it, but she studied me through the mirror.

"What?" I asked.

She shook her head. "Nothing."

"I hate when you stare at me like you're dying to say something but you don't because you don't want to hurt my feelings." I rubbed the moisturizer on my hands and waited. She didn't speak. "Seriously, Raine. Say it or—"

"Fine." She finished with the gloss and put it down. "Echo is not exactly what I expected."

I braced myself to defend him if she said something mean. "What do you mean?"

"He's charming."

I relaxed. "He's not that charming."

Raine laughed. "He is and you know it. You just hate it 'cause he gets to you. He does the same with Andris and Torin. Do you know where he was last week?"

"I really don't care."

"He was searching for Maliina."

"Why?"

"I asked, and he just smirked. You should ask him."

Yeah. Right. We started downstairs. "Where is he?"

"In the car. He insisted. Go and keep him company before Prune Face Rutledge decides to call the police. She was peering at him from the safety of her curtain like he was about to pillage our cul de sac."

I'd so love to rune Mrs. Rutledge. She had a thing against teens. Or was it younger women? I had a feeling she'd never liked Raine's mother either. "Okay, I'll be in the car."

"No fighting with him," Raine warned.

I stuck my tongue out at her before closing the door. Mrs. Rutledge watched me from behind her curtain. I waved and gave her a big smile. The curtains fell back. A blast of cold hit me when I opened the car door, and I expected to see a portal to Hel's Hall in the back of my car again. Instead, Echo sat in the back as though he hadn't left, the front seat folded to give his long legs more room. Memories of the last time we'd folded that seat had my pulse leaping. His uneaten sandwich and bottled water was on the seat beside him.

I slid behind the wheel, and our eyes met in the rearview mirror.

"Not going to join me back here?" he asked naughtily, the timbre of his voice sinfully sexy.

"No."

"But I need your warmth and sweetness."

Sweetness? I cringed. "I'm not sweet."

He pretended to think about it. "No, you're not. I've watched *your* vlog entries and social network updates. You are a little spitfire." He gave me a slow smile. "It makes your sweetness, when you choose to show it, even more special. Please, come back here, Cora." He patted the seat beside him. "I just came back from Hel's Hall and need you."

"Last night, we agreed we'd keep our distance," I reminded him.

"We did? You said a lot of things last night and didn't give me a chance to respond. I want us to be friends, doll-face."

Friends? Was he crazy? I couldn't be friends with a guy I wanted to deck one minute and kiss the next. "Sure, Echo. We can be friends. Start by not calling me doll-face."

"Maliina hated that name, too."

"Oh. Then I like it."

I didn't realize I'd spoken until he chuckled. "So will you come back here and warm me, a cold, miserable friend?" He gave me a fake lost puppy look. "Please?"

Part of me wanted to ignore him. I should, but I had questions. It was a little cooler inside the car, so he might really need me. I touched his duster. It was cold. "Who used to warm you before me?"

He grinned. "You don't want me to answer that question."

Probably Mortal women. "Why did you go to Hel's Hall anyway?"

"To check if they knew two more Grimnirs were missing. I checked earlier during your meet, but they didn't know anything then. Now they do." He extended his hand toward me. "Please."

I started the car and hiked the temperature. "There you go. So what did Torin and Andris do with the Grimnirs' bodies? I mean, they didn't just leave them out there in the vineyard."

Echo shrugged. "I'm sure they took care of them. As for you, you are developing quite a reputation."

"Me? Why?"

"Everyone thinks you are the one taking them out."

I cocked my eyebrows. "Don't you mean Maliina?"

He rubbed his hands and blew into them. Sighing, I stepped out of the car, ignored the peeping hag across the cul-de-sac, and slipped beside him. He scooted to create more room for me, wrapped his arms around me, and dropped his cheek on my neck. He was really cold.

I rubbed his hands. *I'm an idiot.* "Why do they still think I'm Maliina? Didn't you tell them the truth?"

"No." His breath teased my ear, and my body responded.

I fidgeted. "Why not?"

"I have a plan," he said. "Remember I told you yesterday that there's a reason I came to your place that first night. If you are ready to hear that story, let me know. But you should know that, to the Grimnirs, you are a means to an end, namely giving the goddess what she wants. As soon as I find Maliina, I'll fix up this mess and you'll be safe."

I still didn't want to discuss Maliina. "So no one knows about you, Torin, and Andris hurting Grimnirs?"

"No. I've made sure the Grimnirs who came for you didn't report back to the goddess. Otherwise we'd be on the hit list, too."

Instead, I was the target. I shivered. At least he and the others were safe.

"Hey," Echo lifted my chin, "they won't get you as long as I'm around."

Looking into his gorgeous eyes reminded me why I'd agreed to warm him. He was irresistible when he turned on the charm. And no matter how much I wanted to pretend things were over between us, they weren't. I saw it in his heavy-lidded eyes. Felt it in the heavy pounding of his heart and the change in his breathing. My hands tightened around his.

"Cora," he whispered. His head started a slow descent, and my breath caught. I wanted to kiss him so badly it hurt. But I couldn't. I didn't want to invite more heartache. Maybe it was time to talk about the Immortal who screwed me over.

I turned my head. "Do you know where Maliina is hiding?"

There was silence. I stole a glance at him and caught the heated look in his eyes before he shielded it with his lashes.

"No. I've checked most of the realms, except Muspell and Asgard. I'm persona non grata in Asgard, so Torin and Andris are checking there now. If she's not there, she's with the Norns in Muspell."

I frowned. "Don't the Norns live in Asgard?"

"The good ones do. The evil ones are in Muspell, the land of the demons and fire giants. No one has ever gone there and made it back to talk about it."

"Then what are we going to do? I can't be hunted by Grimnirs forever."

"You won't. She'll soon hear about how she's being blamed for the disappearance of Grimnirs and come out of hiding. No one wants to piss off Hel. Maliina already did that by failing to deliver Eirik. Killing Grimnirs will make her the most wanted woman in history."

"In the meantime, your people will continue to think I'm Maliina and keep coming after me." I sighed. "There must be a way to force her out of hiding."

"She could help." He glanced outside, and I followed his gaze. Raine was walking toward us.

I frowned. "Raine?"

"She's a powerful seeress, and her powers are tied to the Norns. She can summon them, hear them, and when possible, see what they see."

"Yikes. No wonder they want her."

Raine opened the front passenger door and peered at us, grinning. "Cozy?"

"No," I said.

"Yes," Echo said at the same time.

"Do you think you guys can go without me? Mom needs my help with something."

I wiggled out of Echo's arms and got out of the car. "Is your dad okay?"

Raine sighed. "Today has been rough on him, so we need to sit with him." She glanced at Echo, who'd gotten out of the car and was walking toward the front passenger door. "Are we still going to your place later?"

"Yeah."

"Then pick me up when you finish with the Burgesses. Good luck." She waved at Echo. "Take good care of her."

He flashed a smile. "I plan to."

The exchange between them had weird undertones that didn't surprise me. Raine had just lied to me, her face turning red. Raine Cooper couldn't lie if a life depended on it.

"How long do you think Mr. C has?" I asked as I pulled out.

Echo paused in the process of biting his sandwich and frowned. "Mr. C?"

"Raine's father."

"I don't know. I'm actually surprised he's still alive. Something is stopping him from dying." He didn't sound concerned.

"Love."

Echo chuckled. "Norns."

"What would they gain by preventing his death?"

"That's the question, isn't it? Norns are twisted. That's why I don't like dealing with them." He took a bite of his sandwich and chewed with gusto. "So, what are you going to tell the Burgess family?"

"I don't know yet." The closer I got to Newfort, the more nervous I became. Maybe this wasn't such a good idea.

12. Answers

Newfort was half-an-hour's drive from Kayville. It was considered a town, though it had one streetlight and one elementary school. Most of their children attended junior high and high school in Kayville. Defoe Funeral Home served several towns, so it wasn't surprising the family had used it for the wake.

"Turn left at the next stop sign," Echo said. His arm rested on the back of my seat and a slight tug of my hair told me he was playing with a lock of it. How long had he been doing that?

"Eyes on the road, sweetheart. Left turn coming up."

I followed his directions. By the time I pulled up in front of a yellow bungalow with a wraparound porch and a white picket fence, he was stroking my hair.

"You'll be fine," he said reassuringly.

I blew out a breath and reached over my shoulder for his hand. How had he known I was stressing about the meeting? I wished Raine had come with us. She was good at this sort of thing. When the rest of the swim team had refused to volunteer to give a eulogy after one of our swimmers died, Raine was the only who'd stepped up.

"You want me to do it?" Echo asked.

I wished I could let him do it, but this was my problem. If I relied on him, I'd never face relatives of the souls I was trying to help. "Thanks, but I think I can do it."

I let go of Echo's hand and got out of the car. Gripping the envelope, I headed to the front of the house, rang the doorbell, and waited. When no one answered, I glanced toward the car and found Echo leaning against it, arms crossed, eyes watchful. He looked relaxed, but I knew he'd be beside me in seconds if I were in danger.

I pressed on the doorbell again.

The door opened and Victoria Burgess, the girl from my school, stared at me with puzzled eyes. "Cora?" she asked, frowning.

I smiled. "Hey, Victoria."

She stepped outside, closed the door, and crossed her arms. "What are you doing here?"

"I, uh, was hoping I could talk to your mother?" It came out as a question, a telltale sign that I was nervous.

"Oh." She glanced toward my car. "Why?"

I followed her gaze to Echo. He smiled. It was reassuring.

"I have something for her, but I'd rather give it to her in person." I lifted the envelope.

She studied the envelope, but didn't seem eager to invite me inside. "My mother is grieving right now, so if this is about school—"

"No, it's not."

The door opened behind her and an older hulk of a man peered at me. He looked wasted. "Vicky, what's going on out here? Who is this pretty girl?"

"She's a friend from school, Uncle Reed." Once again, she glanced behind me.

"And who are you?" her uncle asked, following her gaze.

"Echo." He sounded close. A glance over my shoulder showed him standing guard behind me.

Uncle Reed let out a loud belch. "What kind of name is Echo?"

"The kind a mother gives a son who's so fast no one can see him coming or leaving," Echo said. "All you hear is an echo."

"It's a stupid name. So are you fast on your feet or with your fist?"

There was silence, but I felt the change in the air behind me.

"You ask stupid questions," Echo said, enunciating his words.

"And you are too smart-mouthed, boy." Vicky's uncle glared. He was tall and beefy and looked like he could snap Echo's backbone in half, but I knew that Echo could hurt him with one blow.

I stepped back until my back touched Echo. I reached behind me and took his hand before he did something we'd both regret. My eyes went to Vicky. "Maybe we'll come back some other time, Vicky."

"Yeah, you do that," her uncle said.

Vicky closed her eyes and sighed. "It's okay. Come this way."

She led us away from the front door, along the wraparound porch to the back, and into the kitchen. Several adults and kids were visible through a doorway leading to their living room. From the sound of the sportscaster, they were watching a football game on TV.

Once again, Victoria's eyes went to the envelope in my hand. "Wait here."

Echo and I stood awkwardly in the tiny kitchen. No wonder Victoria had appeared reluctant to invite us inside. The place was a mess.

"Was that true what you said about your mother?" I asked.

Echo grinned. "Nah. When we were living in the forest, we would run out of food at times and had to visit nearby villages in the dead of the night to steal some. We had to be fast."

I stared at him with wide eyes. "You stole?"

"Day and night. When I got older, my routine changed. A little charm goes a long way with the ladies, especially the wealthy ones."

Bet they couldn't resist him either. I tried to imagine him in a Roman society, wearing a toga and tunica, and smiled. Echo wasn't a conformist. He probably dressed like his priestly Druid master to piss off the Romans.

"So why were you named Echo?"

"I was named Eocho. After I became a Valkyrie and decided to help my people, I changed it to Echo. Because that's all the Romans heard whenever I paid them a visit."

Could he get any more fascinating? Victoria entered the kitchen and I stopped staring into Echo's eyes like a besotted idiot.

"Come with me. Just Cora," she added.

"I'll be fine," I reassured Echo. I untangled our interlocked fingers then followed Vicky. He didn't look happy being left behind.

Vicky took me to a medium-sized bedroom with drawn curtains. A bedside lamp was on. Her mother sat up on the bed with pillows piled behind her. From her ravaged face, she must have been crying for days.

"Mrs. Burgess, I'm so sorry for your loss," I started.

She nodded, blew her nose on a tissue, and crumpled it. "You go to school with my Vicky?"

I moved closer. "Yes, ma'am. My name is Cora Jemison."

She gave me a shaky smile. "What can I do for you, Cora?"

Now that I was in front of her, the lie Raine had come up with seemed so lame. I scrambled to come up with a better explanation. "Uh, last weekend, I was at a bistro across the street when a man walked out of Key Bank and dropped a piece of paper on the ground. By the time I picked it up, he was gone. I didn't know what to do with it until I heard about the accident and realized the man was your husband."

Her eyes went to the envelope, so I gave it to her. She ripped it open and eagerly reached inside for the single sheet of paper. She read it and frowned.

"This is my Bill's handwriting. He likes… He liked to send home greeting cards when he was on the road." She waved toward a stack of cards. "But I don't understand what these words and letters mean," she said.

I moved closer. "I wasn't sure what they meant either, but I think these initials, KB, stand for Key Bank, because he left the one on Main Street when he dropped the papers. The numbers must be for a safety deposit box, because they are written right next to SDB. And he wrote Clare Bear over and over again and PW. It is probably the password for the safe."

She studied me as though I had morphed into a psycho. Then she sighed. I recognized the look on her face. A few nurses at PMI would look at patients like that.

"Clare Bear was your nickname, right?" I asked, desperate to convince her.

"Yes." She smiled again. "Thank you for bringing this, but I don't know how you've reached these conclusions about a safety deposit box. My Bill could not have rented a safety deposit box without discussing it with me first."

She didn't believe everything I had told her. "Will you at least check the bank to see if I'm right?"

"I will, dear. Thank you." She smiled, sliding lower to rest her head on the pillows. "Could you close the door behind you and send my daughter to me."

She didn't believe me. What had I expected? I backed out of the room, almost bumping into Vicky. "She wants to see you."

"I heard. I also overheard what you told her. If Dad opened an account…" she glanced toward the bedroom. "Wait for me outside," she whispered.

While she disappeared inside her mother's bedroom, I hurried back to the kitchen and practically dragged Echo out of there.

"She didn't believe me. I mean, she looked at me like I was crazy. *I* would look at me like I was crazy. What was I thinking?"

"Whoa!" Echo gripped my arms and turned me to face him. "Don't beat yourself so hard. If she doesn't look into it, it won't be your fault. You've done your part."

"And I'll do mine," Vicky said, walking toward us. "Tell me again what you told my mother."

I quickly went over my lie and what was in the paper as we walked to the car. "I know it might sound farfetched, but I know what the initials stand for."

At least, Victoria didn't look at me like I'd lost my marbles. "I'll stop by the bank on Monday, so thank you for bringing the note."

I shrugged like it was nothing then slid behind the wheel.

"You do know there's no restaurant or café across the street from Key Bank," Echo said as Victoria walked back to her house.

"Are you sure?"

He grinned. "I'm a reaper, doll-face. I know every city, town, farm, road, and back road in this realm. Once she finds whatever her dad stashed in that safety deposit box, she won't care about your convoluted lie."

"Oh, I suck at lies." I dropped my head on the steering wheel.

"I'm an expert. Next time, let me come up with one."

Next time? I glanced at him and shook my head. "I don't know if I want to do it again. It was awful. Her mother looked at me like I had lost my mind. Maybe I should just tell them I can communicate with the dead people."

Echo chuckled, but he didn't say anything.

"You're not going to say anything?" I asked.

"Nope."

"Am I doing the right thing by quitting?"

"Are you quitting?"

He was no help. "Some friend you are." I started the car. "I need to think."

"Good. Can we stop by Kip's Frozen Yogurt while you think?"

"Why?"

"Because I need to feed my sweet tooth and you refused to have lunch with me."

"What does your sweet tooth have to do with lunch?"

"I had planned to take you to this amazing Italian restaurant that serves the best gelato."

"There are no gelato shops in Kayville."

He smirked. "Who said the restaurant was in Kayville."

"Okay, we'll go to Kip's on one condition," I said.

"Deal."

"You don't know what I want yet."

"Getting you to agree to anything is a step forward, so I'm being generous."

Not for long. "Okay. Remove Burgess' soul from Torture Island and put him with the general public in Hel. He doesn't deserve to be tortured when I'm the one who gave him the green light to possess me. And if I hadn't, I would never have known how to help him."

Echo chuckled. That sexy sound never failed to send shivers up my spine.

"A soul for frozen yogurt, hmm?"

"So will you do it?" I asked.

"For you, sure. And it's called Corpse Strand, or Naastrand, not Torture Island."

"Isn't it an island where souls are tortured?"

"Yes."

"Then Torture Island it is."

Once I reached Main Street, I headed north, turned at the light on 5th North, and pulled up across from Kip's. The place was packed.

"Come on. My treat." Echo jumped out and stared at me expectantly.

I glanced at the crowded shop. This friendship thing just didn't work for me. I understood and accepted he had to protect me. Knew he had to be around, but doing things like this together wasn't smart.

My door opened, and Echo offered me his hand. "Please?"

"I can wait for you here—"

He squatted and studied me. "What's wrong, doll-face? Have I done or said something to hurt you? Tell me and I'll fix. I want this friendship to work."

How could he be so blind? I wanted to scream at him. Shake him. But one look into his gorgeous wolf eyes and my reluctance melted away. Argh, he didn't play fair. "It's nothing. I'm just tired. You know, the swim meet and the fiasco at Victoria's."

He reached out and ran his knuckles up my cheek. Then he pushed a lock of hair behind my ear. "I'll take you home."

"No. We go in, you get your yogurt, and we leave. We don't stay."

The corners of his lips lifted in an irresistible, sexy smile. "Okay. We'll eat in the car." He stood and held the door. "You get some, too."

I didn't bother to argue. He'd win anyway. He grabbed my hand as we crossed the street. Eyes followed us inside. The tables and the counters lining the walls were all occupied, but my eyes found Drew, Pia, and Leigh. The fourth person at their table had his back to us, but there was something familiar about the wavy brown hair.

Silence fell in the room as most of them, majority of them girls, forgot about their frozen treats and stared. Echo seemed oblivious to the attention he was getting. He was back to wearing leather pants, a dark grey sweater underneath his coat, and boots. His chin was unshaven, and his hair messy as though he'd run his fingers through it. He stood out no matter what he wore.

He pulled me to the cups area and selected the largest. I chose a smaller one and cradled it with my injured right hand. The stainless steel yogurt dispensers covered one wall while the toppings were by the cashier.

He moved behind me, his hand resting on my hip. "What's your favorite flavor?"

"Luscious lemon," I said, trying to warn my heart to behave. Being this close to him really played havoc with my head.

"I try three to four new flavors every time and mix them up. You should try it some time."

"No, thanks. Once I find something I love, I stick with it."

He lowered his head and whispered, "Live a little, doll-face. I'll even let you choose the flavors for me."

"Cora?"

I turned, and my eyes widened. "Blaine? What are you doing here?"

Blaine Chapman had been the QB before Torin took over. Raine said his family had moved. He flashed his famous I-know-I'm-hot smile.

"I'm back," he said. "The team needs me to take them to state."

I chuckled. "We have a quarterback."

"St. James is too flaky. Yesterday he took off in the middle of practice. Today, he didn't even show up. Coach Higgins believes he might disappear during a game, so he called my parents and they said it was okay. Where's my hug?"

He ignored Echo and gave me a hug. A long hug, which didn't make sense because he and I had never been that close. Before his family moved, he'd been dating Casey Riverside. Before Raine and Torin, he and Casey had been Kayville High's perfect couple.

I wiggled out of his arms, since he didn't seem to want to let go, stepped back, and met a hard, immovable wall. Echo. His hand snaked around my waist, anchoring me to him. I wanted to lean back and savor the feel of him, but I didn't dare let my guard down.

I glanced over my shoulder and groaned. His eyes were narrowed on Blaine like he wanted to snap his head. The last thing I needed was Echo going psycho on a human because of me. But it gave me hope. Maybe there was hope for us.

"Uh, Blaine, this is—"

"Echo," Blaine said, the smile disappearing from his topaz eyes. "We've met."

"Get lost, Chapman," Echo said.

"Cora and I are old friends, reaper," Blaine said, his eyes turning to me. "Can we connect later? I need to run something by you."

"Uh, sure. Text me first." Was Blaine a Valkyrie, too? And why was he acting like we were tight? We might have hung out a few times, but he never had eyes for anyone except Casey. "And, uh, sorry about Casey."

Anger flashed in his eyes. "Yeah, she didn't need to die." He nodded and went back to join Drew and the others.

It was my fault Torin had missed practice on Friday and today. How could the coach call Blaine back after everything Torin had done for the team?

"How well do you know him?" Echo asked.

"Obviously not well enough. He was the QB before Torin, and his girlfriend, Casey, died during the last home game. You seem to know him well."

"Our paths have crossed. He comes from a long line of Immortals, and like them, he thinks he's better than us because he serves the gods."

So Blaine was an Immortal. It explained his prowess in sports. I tried to wiggle out of Echo's arm, but he refused to let me go.

"What are you doing?" I whispered.

"Keeping you close. I'll choose the flavors and you press the buttons."

I was growing impatient with his behavior. Worse, I knew he was doing this because of Blaine. "You don't need to hold me for that."

He lowered his head, his cheek brushing mine. "But I do. I like holding you. You are my cuddlebunny."

Instead of causing a scene, I gave in and pushed the dispensing buttons. When we reached the toppings, I chose fruit—strawberries and blueberries—while he piled candy, gummy bears, and crumbled Oreos on top of his.

"You have a serious sweet tooth," I said.

"Guilty." He chuckled, but he sounded distracted. We weighed the cups, paid, and headed outside, whispers following us. Blaine waved. I smiled and waved back.

"I don't like the way he's looking at you," Echo said, following me to the car.

I ignored him and slid behind the wheel. I was not doing this jealousy thing with him. He'd made it clear we could never be together.

"Did you hear what I said?" he asked, sliding beside me.

He wasn't going to let this go. "I didn't think you wanted an answer."

"Why are you agreeing to meet with him?"

"Because he asked me to." I scooped my yogurt and tried it. Tart. Perfect.

Echo watched me with a frown. "I don't trust him. Don't like him." He glared through the windscreen as he ate his yogurt. "His eyes are too shifty, his hair too gelled up."

I laughed. "You are being ridiculous. Blaine is a handsome guy."

He rolled his eyes.

"Try this." Echo fed me a scoop of his treat.

"What flavor is that?"

"Chocolate macadamia." He licked his spoon. His eyes narrowed. "Chapman walks kind of funny, doesn't he? And his ears stick out of his head like that elephant… uh, you know, the one that could fly."

"Dumbo? Seriously?"

He smirked.

"Yeah, Dumbo. He's probably stupid, too."

I tried hard not to laugh. "Blaine wants to discuss something with me, Echo, not date me. Besides, it's none of your business who I date."

His smile disappeared. "So you think he's hot?"

I used to think Blaine was perfect. Not anymore. I shrugged.

"Do you like him?"

I sighed. Echo was acting like I had to want only him and no one else. "I'm not doing this with you, Echo. I'm dealing with enough crap without you giving me grief over a friend who just wants to talk. Do you know that it's my fault Coach Higgins contacted Blaine's family? Torin missed practice today because he went to search for Maliina. And he left in the middle of one yesterday when Raine contacted him after the soul possessed me."

"Torin's problems are his business. Yours are mine. Blaine is not right for you."

I shook my head, getting impatient again. "Why not? After all, he's not a Valkyrie or a Grimnir. And he dated a Mortal before. Casey. Your lofty laws don't apply to him."

"Oh, but they do. He just chose to ignore them, and look at what happened. The Norns took Casey from him. Idiot. The only ones above the law are the gods, and even their destinies are controlled by the Norns. Don't waste your time with a shithead like Blaine. In fact, none of the dimwits at your school are good enough for you."

He spoke with such glee I wanted to smack him. How could he be so possessive of me yet refuse to give us a chance?

"Eirik is a god," I said before I could stop myself.

Echo scowled. "So?"

"So he promised to come back."

"He can't come back here."

I frowned. "Why not?"

"Remember the unfinished discussion you didn't want to hear yesterday?"

"You mean the one you wanted to discuss after you told me you don't date puny Mortals? Which, by the way, I'm okay with that now. I've moved on. I'll find someone who thinks I'm worth breaking a few stupid rules."

Silence filled the car, the kind that came before an explosion.

I stole a glance at Echo and wished I hadn't. His eyes flashed with fury. I must have hit a nerve. Instead of feeling triumphant, I wanted to take my words back. He'd broken enough rules and paid the ultimate price—eternal servitude to Hel. He couldn't afford to break rules anymore.

Echo pushed open the door, marched to the garbage by the entrance of Kip's, and dumped his leftover yogurt. He had barely touched it. Hand fisted, he aimed for the can as though to flatten it. I braced myself, sure he'd destroy the entire sidewalk with a punch. He caught himself and froze.

I sighed with relief when he stepped back, turned, and walked back to the car. He buckled up and snarled, "Let's go."

I felt worse. Not sure which part of the crap I'd spewed had ticked him off, I said, "I'm sorry. I shouldn't have mocked your position. I know what would happen to you if you broke any more rules."

He whipped around. "You think I care about Hel's wrath if I turned you? I would accept a century on Corpse Strand if it meant coming back to you." He shook his head. "But I refuse to put you through what I've seen Mortals endure when they choose one of us. I won't let it happen. So, yes, I may hate hearing that you've moved on and will find someone else, but it is for the best. You can never be mine. You can never love me."

Too late. "Don't worry, Echo. That's never going to happen." I put my leftover yogurt in the cup holder and started the car.

The drive to Raine's was uncomfortable, the silence oppressive. I hated fighting with Echo but, but I wished he'd stop treating me like a child. I wasn't asking for forever with him, just a chance to be with him for as long as I could. I brought the car to a stop and switched it off.

"Cora—"

"Don't. I have one question. Why can't Eirik come back here?"

"Because I will capture him and personally escort him to Hel."

My stomach dropped. Sometimes I wasn't sure whether he said things to get a rise out of me or because he let his reckless side take over. I studied his face. "Why would you do that?"

"The conversation we never finished yesterday involves Eirik. Luring him back to Earth is the reason I came to your house after we met at the store."

Now I was confused. "I thought you came because you and Maliina were lovers."

Echo rubbed his nape. "No, I was on a mission, Cora. The plan was to use the girl Hel's son loved as bait and lure him back to Earth. That girl was Maliina the last time I checked. Or should I say, Maliina impersonating you. The fact that Maliina and I had sex a few times just made things easier for me than the other Grimnirs."

"Bait?"

"Yes. Except I found you, not Maliina. And I put you in harm's way." He went silent and then glanced at me. "Torin and Andris were right. I always have an agenda and I'm good at what I do. I lie, bend the laws, and play dirty to win. That's who I am, and I've never had a reason to change."

"I don't believe you. You're not that manipulative."

"Oh, but I am. I was planning to sleep with you, or the person I thought was Maliina pretending to be you, and make sure the Valkyries knew about it so they could contact Eirik to come to your rescue. He's in love with you. Everyone knows it, including Goddess Hel. She knows that anyone who has you can lure Eirik out of hiding."

I couldn't believe what I was hearing. Could Echo really be that cold-hearted? "So when you said that the goddess wanted me dead because Maliina had failed to lure Eirik to her, you lied?"

"Yes."

He didn't even flinch. "But that was before you knew that I wasn't Maliina."

"Does it matter? I was going to do it up to the point when I learned the truth from Torin that you were not Maliina. That I was dealing with two different women. The truth changed everything, except the objective. I will *never* use you as bait. You're the innocent person in all this, and because of that, I'll protect you from my brothers and sisters eager to please the goddess. But if Eirik comes here, I'll take him to his mother. Why? Because it is a job. It is my objective. My mission. And I never fail to deliver." He paused, but his eyes didn't leave mine. "Like I told you before, I'm not good for you, Cora. I will not lose sleep over handing Eirik to his mother or lying to the Valkyries, but when it comes to you, I can't—"

I pressed a finger to his lips. "Shh. I know."

Silence filled the car.

"So you are saying that you're mean, ruthless, a liar, a manipulator, and basically a badass guy I shouldn't associate with?"

He grinned, but his eyes were sad. "That about covers it."

Yet he was being honest with me. Just like when he'd opened up and told me about his Druid background and why he'd ended up on Hel duty. He was a good guy. He just didn't see it.

"Were you really searching for Maliina last week?"

"Oh yeah. I want to know what runes she etched on you so we can fix you, but I also have other plans for her. She's not getting away with what she did to you."

If he couldn't see what an amazing guy he was, I would find a way to show him. I didn't believe he'd hand over Eirik to his mother, either.

"I think Raine is trying to get your attention," Echo said, his gaze on the second floor of the Cooper's house. I followed his eyes and saw Raine on her window seat. She waved.

"Just one more question, then I'll leave. Why are you telling me the truth about your mission?"

"I hate lying to you. I told you yesterday that I'd always tell you the truth."

"What if I told you that taking Eirik to Hel would hurt me?"

Echo gave me a sad, resigned look. "I'd ask for your forgiveness and then take him anyway. Remember, both his parents are there. And being alive, he cannot be trapped behind the halls of Hel like his father."

Funny, I hadn't looked at it that way. Still, I didn't believe he'd do it, knowing it would hurt me.

He scowled. "Don't look at me like that."

"Like what?"

"Like you think I wouldn't do it. I would. I mean, I will."

He sounded like he was trying to convince himself. I wanted to wrap myself around him, kiss him, and love him, and never let go. He might have done terrible things in the past, or what others perceived as terrible, but I was behind him one hundred percent. If I were in his shoes, I would have rescued my Druid sisters and brothers.

"I believe you'd do the right thing," I said.

"Damn straight. Right by me because if I get a chance to take him and let him go, his mother would lock me up with the souls of the worst criminals until Ragnarok. I'm not willing to go through that for him." He twirled a lock of my hair around his finger. "Go. If you have any more questions, ask me later. I'll see you tonight."

When he let go of my hair, I did something so bold I shocked myself. I leaned forward, gently cupped his cheek, and pressed my lips to his in a whisper of a kiss.

He froze.

I rubbed my lips across his, loving the tingling sparks the contact generated and hoping he'd kiss me back. He didn't pull back, but neither did he kiss me back. In fact, I think he held his breath, his body stiff. I could make him want me. Make him kiss me, but it wouldn't be the same.

I sat back and looked into his eyes, hoping he saw that I believed in him. That I wanted him. That I loved him. Nothing he said or did would ever stop me from wanting and loving him.

If I had taken an artavus and stabbed him in the chest, he wouldn't have looked more tortured. He lifted his hands as though to grab me, stopped, and balled his hands.

"Please," he whispered.

I wasn't sure whether the plea was for me to leave or love him. I'd like to think it was the second one. Smiling, I stepped out of the car.

13. Brokenhearted

"Someone seems pleased with herself," Raine said when I entered her room.

"I am. Sort of. I'm optimistic about… lots of things." Echo. I plopped on her bed, put my hands behind my head, and grinned at the ceiling. "Thanks for not coming with us. By the way, you are still a sucky liar. I knew your mom didn't really need you."

She made a face. "So you two 'talked'? I noticed the steaming windows."

I grinned. Oh, I wanted to steam windows with that reaper, but it was going to take some maneuvering. "We just talked. Nothing delicious or naughty."

"You two going to date?"

"No."

She joined me, lying on her stomach. "Then what's with the Chesire Cat grin?"

I propped myself on my elbows, not wanting to jinx things between Echo and me by talking about my hopes. "We are going to be friends."

"Friends? With benefits?"

I laughed. Raine Cooper of six months ago would not have said that. "You have a dirty mind. Are you and Torin reaping the benefits of being perfectly matched?"

She blushed. "We're not discussing me."

"Then I'm not discussing Echo. I saw Blaine Chapman at Kip's, and he had the nerve to say he's come back to lead the Trojans to state."

Raine made a face. "He's kind of right. Torin called his family a few days ago and talked to his dad. Immortals are supposed to be Valkyries' support team. Remember I told you Andris, Maliina, and Ingrid stayed with his family when they first got here?"

I nodded.

"That's because they are Immortal. Torin knew things were about to get complicated as soon as Echo appeared interested in you. Protecting you became more important than playing ball."

Okay. My opinion of Torin just went up several notches. "He's something else."

She grinned. "Dedicated is more like it. Valkyrie business always comes first."

"Even ahead of your well-being?" I teased.

Her cheeks grew red again, but she didn't need to respond. I'd seen them together. They couldn't keep their hands off each other. "Blaine seemed angry when we spoke. He said we needed to talk."

"He and Andris almost destroyed the viewing when he came to Casey's funeral. He blamed Andris and Torin for not warning him." She grimaced. "As if they know for sure who's going to die before it happens. The lists they are given changes every second, so they're never sure who is going to die and who isn't. Anyway, enough talking about Blaine. How did it go with the Burgesses?"

I scooted to the edge of the bed. "Let's talk on the way to my place."

We stopped by the den and both parents looked up when she opened the door. Her father looked a lot better. His color was back, and he was sitting up, playing a game of chess with Raine's mother.

"Hi, Cora," Mrs. C said when she saw me.

I waved, but stayed by the door.

"How are things, Cora?" Mr. C added.

"Good." I wasn't sure whether Raine had told him about my first possession. I'd forgotten to warn her not to. "How are you feeling?"

"Much better. Are you two going out?"

Raine kissed his forehead. "To Cora's. Do you want me to pick up dinner?"

Her parents exchanged a glance and smiles.

"No, we are going to cook tonight," her mother said.

"Are you sure that's a good idea? Dad just—"

"I know," her mother said. "He'll sit and tell me what to do. Have some fun." Her mother practically threw us out of the den.

Raine was still frowning when we drove off. I headed toward town. "You think your dad is not ready to be up and about?"

"I think Mom is worried. If he's not back on his feet, he can't go to Valhalla. The sick go to Hel. There's no way around it. Worse, Mom might leave at any moment. She's been summoned to appear before the Council and Forseti."

"Who's that?"

"The God of Justice. Sometimes I think prolonging Dad's life is some sort of punishment for what we did."

That sounded too close to what Echo had said. Then, I'd thought he was just making up excuses. "You mean your mother trading her Norn wand for your dad?"

Raine smiled. "Nah, sparing Dad's life. It was supposed to be temporary. You know, so we could say our goodbyes, but now…" She sighed. "I feel like the Norns are prolonging his suffering to punish us. When he flat lined, Mom said his soul didn't leave his body. Usually the soul leaves the body and hangs around, waiting to be reaped, or takes off, like the souls you see. But she didn't see his. It is trapped. I just know it." Her hands were clenched, and her voice had risen. "As long as it doesn't leave his body, he'll not die. He'll continue to suffer."

I reached for her hand and squeezed. "No, Raine. I did."

She looked at me. "You did what?"

"I saw your father last week at the cafeteria. He tried to talk to me. We hadn't discussed everything, so I couldn't tell you. His soul appeared to me, Raine."

A frown creased her forehead. "Why you?"

"I didn't know, but remember when he wanted to see me? He told me he was in total darkness when he saw me. Or rather, he saw the glowing runes Maliina had etched on me, followed them, and found me. That's why he wanted to talk to me when he came back from the hospital."

"That's why he asked you to try to show compassion to the souls."

I nodded. "He said it was dark and scary until he saw my runes. Maybe you are right to believe he was trapped somewhere. Wherever it was, he saw me." I pulled up outside a grocery store.

"We should tell Torin and Lavania. They might have an explanation." She peered at the store. "What are we doing here?"

"We need snacks, and you know my mother." I got out of the car, and Raine followed. My mother hated processed foods.

"I like her pies," Raine said.

"So do I, but I eat them all the time, so if I need foods smothered in sugar and fried in saturated fat, I sneak them into my room."

"She always knows," Raine said.

True. I giggled. Mom's sighs and head shakes whenever she found soda cans and empty Twizzler or potato chips packets in my room didn't bother me. Dad had a thing for chocolates too, so I wasn't the only one who got in trouble.

I snatched a basket when we entered the store. The cashier who'd served us the last time Mom and I were in the store smiled when our eyes met. He didn't have the female soul stroking his hair anymore. I wondered what she'd wanted to tell him. Had I let her possess me, I would have known.

I entered the aisle with snacks, grabbed a couple of bars of chocolate for Dad, and then stopped as an idea popped into my head. Raine bumped into me.

"What is it?" She peered at my face then along the aisle. "You see some? Souls?" she asked in a whisper. I'd told her about my first meeting with Echo.

"No." As though my denial had conjured one, a soul of a buff man in a muscle shirt and cargo pants appeared at the end of the aisle. He stared at me strangely. A female in her mid-twenties walked through the shelf on my left. "Scratch that. Two of them are here."

"Do you want to leave?" Raine said, her voice rising.

"No. I came for Twizzlers and Baked Lays, and I intend to get some." I started forward, my heart pounding. The souls moved closer. I picked up a large bag of Twizzlers, dropped it in the basket, and kept walking. "Besides, I've decided to help them."

"What?"

"I'm going to let souls possess me. I helped the Burgesses, Raine. On Monday, Victoria is going to the bank. So I figure, why not help others?"

"Now?"

I chuckled at the panicked pitch in her voice.

"No. But I need to practice so I can learn to deal with the eek factor."

"Then we're going to need Echo or Torin to order them out of you. I'm still working on my incantations and can't do an exorcism."

"I know." Trying to stay calm, I looked into the eyes of the woman. She was yapping, and I was still soul-deaf. "I will come back and help you," I said, speaking slowly, looking directly into her eyes.

She stopped talking and tilted her head.

"I promise to come back and help you," I added.

She turned and disappeared. The buff guy had stopped walking and talking, too. "I will help you, too. Later. I promise."

He shuffled away backwards. I released a sharp breath and glanced at Raine. She was staring at me with wide eyes, while chewing on her lower lip. Behind her stood Echo. He winked, and then he disappeared.

Raine glanced over her shoulder. "Are they behind me?"

"No. They're gone. Echo was behind you."

"Oh. Yeah, I felt his presence when we left the house."

"Really?" I was a bit disappointed she'd felt his presence. I wasn't one of them, yet I always knew when Echo was around. I'd thought it made us special.

"It's nothing special," Raine continued. "We have this ability to sense the essence of the others like us. It's stronger when you are linked to that person, but it's there, so I'll know if a Grimnir is nearby."

Okay, not so bad. Stronger when linked. Was I linked to Echo? "Linked how?"

"It's kind of hard to explain. Ask Echo about it. About the souls, I think you are crazy to want to help them."

"I know. I'm learning to live a little. Come on, worrywart. The salty snacks are in the next aisle." I looped my arm through hers and laughed. "You've battled the most powerful beings in the world and you are freaking out over souls?"

"You didn't see how you reacted to the possession, smarty pants. You'd be freaking out, too. Besides, you know what they say about fear of the unknown. Until I actually see a soul, I have the right to be wary and scared."

"Some Valkyrie you're going to make."

"Shut up."

I paid for the snacks and a liter bottle of root beer. Then we headed to the car.

***

Dad was in the zone and didn't look up when we entered the house. Mom wasn't in the kitchen, which meant she was finishing her chores in the barn. We grabbed cups and disappeared upstairs.

"I haven't been here in weeks," Raine said.

"Don't remind me. What did you two do when you visited?"

Rained shrugged. "Painted my nails. She blow-dried her hair."

I glared at her. "And that wasn't a clue enough for you that you were dealing with a psycho bitch?"

"Cora Jemison!" Mom snapped from the doorway. "Watch your mouth. Raine." She walked to where Raine sat near my desk and gave her a hug. "How are you doing?"

"Good, Mrs. Jemison."

"Your dad?"

Raine shrugged. "Better than last week. He's planning on making dinner tonight."

Mom smiled. "That's wonderful. It's nice to see you two girls back together. What are you up to tonight? I'm making chili for dinner."

"Raine is going to help me with homework, Mom."

Mom blinked and cocked her eyebrows. "On a Saturday night? That's nice." Her eyes went to the bags of snacks on the bed, and she shook her head. "Make sure you leave room for my chili, girls."

"Okay." I walked to the door and held it. "Bye, Mom."

She chuckled and touched my cheek as she walked out. I closed the door. "We should do something tonight."

Raine scowled. "No."

"Why not?"

"Uh, one word. Grimnirs."

I walked toward the bed. "So I'm supposed to stop living because they're after me?"

"It's called lying low. What are we starting with?" she asked as though the subject was closed.

"Chips." I threw her a bag.

She snatched it. "I meant what subject."

For an hour, we worked on one subject after another. Raine started to read my English paper and made a face. I snatched it from her. "I'm still working on it."

She grinned. "Good. Because it's—"

"Shut up. I don't want to hear how bad it is. I know it needs a rewrite."

"Or two," she added.

I stuck out my tongue. I'd missed her.

The ringtone of my cell phone went off, and I dove for my jacket. I pulled my cell from the pocket and saw the number. Unknown. Frowning, I bought it to my ear.

"Yes?" I said slowly.

"Cora, it's Blaine."

I glanced at Raine and mouthed, "Blaine," then spoke into the phone. "Hey, Blaine. What's going on?"

"Are you busy?"

I made a face. "Uh, not really. We are hanging out at home."

"We?"

"Raine's here."

There was silence. "Why don't I pick you two up, say, in an hour? A bunch of us are going to check out that new club, Xanavoo. We need to talk. It's important."

"Just a second." My watch said it was a quarter to seven. I pressed the phone to my chest. "We are going out, Raine."

She scribbled on a notepad and showed me what she'd written. "NO!!!"

"YES! He wants to talk," I wrote on the back of my crappy English paper and showed her.

"About?" she wrote back.

I grinned and brought the phone back to my ear. "You don't need to pick us up. We'll be there at…" I cocked my eyebrows at Raine. She glared back. "Eight."

"Sweet," Blaine said. "See you later." The line went dead.

"I am not going out, Cora," Raine said, standing.

"Why not? Because Torin is not around to hold your hand?"

Her cheeks grew warm. "That's not it and you know it. Grimnirs—"

"Want a piece of me, I get it. I'm going out. You can come and help me find out what Blaine wants or stay at home and worry yourself to death."

"Whatever it is, he can tell you tomorrow or at school on Monday."

"Come on, Raine." I gripped her arms, peered at her, and pouted. "Please. I need to do something normal. Hang out with normal high school students."

She threw me a disgusted look. "He's far from normal. He's an Immortal with a chip on his shoulder."

I sighed and let her go. "Look. For weeks, I thought I was crazy, thought that life as I knew it was over. Then I got better—no faked that I was better so they would let me go, only to come home to Echo and a new perception of reality. I need to spend one evening being a normal teenager." I waited with a brilliant smile. Raine had never been into clubbing, even before she met Torin. I was a social creature and needed to be out there.

"Cora. Raine. Dinner." Mom's voice reached us, but I didn't move.

"Please, Raine."

She sighed. "Fine. Let's eat dinner first, and if anything happens while we are at this… this new club, you do whatever you always do to summon Echo."

I laughed and gave her a hug. "I don't do anything. He just pops up." We left my room. "At the store, I thought they left because they heard what I'd told them, but now that I've thought about it, I think they left because they saw him."

Downstairs, Mom was removing freshly-baked dinner rolls from the oven. Cora and I set the table.

"Dig in," Mom said when we sat, pouring homemade apple cider into our glasses.

The rolls were moist and hot. Dad broke a roll in half and smothered it with butter. "I've got a question for you two young ladies. One of my main characters, a princess, has just been discovered living among the commoners. She grew up being called Lumae, but her real name is Luminous Pendgaryn. What do you think? Is the name cheesy?"

"Luminous is pretty," I said.

"I like it, too," Raine chimed in. "Is she a Dorganian or one of the Paladins?"

"A Paladin," Dad said.

Raine winced. "Poor girl. The Dorganians won't let her live."

Dad wore a mysterious smile as he served himself chili.

"Is she *the* Paladin Warrioress?" Rained asked. She loved books, and she'd read all my father's sci-fi novels. "The savior of her people?"

"I'm not saying another word," Dad said.

"Can I get an advance copy?" she asked.

"Whoa? Who are the Dorganians?" I asked, my gaze swinging between them.

Mom chuckled. "That's what you get for refusing to read your father's books."

"I did read the first two books," I said defensively and then glared at Dad. "Until he killed my favorite character."

Dad laughed. "I know. You started a petition on my fan page."

"So? Is he back?"

Dad, Mom, and Raine just smiled.

"Fine. I'll read the next two books before your new release hits the shelves. I want to meet this Paladin Warrioress."

For the rest of the meal, we discussed plots, heroes, and villains. Or rather, Raine and Dad did and Mom chimed in while I tried to keep up. I had to go back to reading his books. After dinner, Raine followed Dad to his writing cave, while I cleared the table.

"Mom, is it okay if Raine and I go out for a few hours? A bunch of our friends are meeting at that new club, Xanavoo, in half an hour."

Mom looked at her watch, and then her eyes narrowed on my face. "Okay. But I want you back by midnight."

"Thanks, Mom." I kissed her cheek and dragged Raine upstairs. When she started talking books, she tended to get carried away. "It's time to get ready."

"I have to go home and change," she griped, making it sound like a chore.

"I'll change then apply makeup at your… What are you doing?" I closed the door, but my eyes stayed on her. She was etching runes on the mirror with an artavus.

"Creating a portal to my room," she said nonchalantly.

There must be a gazillion ways of creating portals. Before, at her place, she hadn't used an artavus. Echo didn't even need a surface. He used the scythe to open his dark portal to Hel.

I inched closer as the mirror changed texture and became grainy. The surface churned, coiling in circles until a portal appeared. The floor and walls looked like they were covered with a swirling, white cloud. Raine's room was visible at the other end.

I touched the wall. Solid. Tested the floor. Solid.

"Go ahead and try it," Raine said.

I stepped through the portal, the ground solid under my feet. I didn't realize I was holding my breath until I was in her bedroom. Grinning, I walked back to my room.

"How come you didn't use an artavus at your house? The portal just appeared."

"The runes are already etched on the frame of my mirror, making it a portal. I'll be back in half an hour."

As I watched her walk into her room, I wondered if I should mention what Echo had told me about Grimnirs using me as bait to get to Eirik. Maybe someone would warn Eirik not to ever come back.

***

"It looks packed," Raine said.

It was. We were lucky someone backed out just as we pulled up. I clasped my bag, wrapped my arm around Raine's, and hurried into the building. My red sweater dress was sexy and didn't need a bra. I had topped it with a leather jacket and added knee-length black boots.

Raine looked amazing in print jeggings and an emerald top. She'd curled her hair, and her makeup was flawless. The Raine I'd known before I went to the psych ward was gone. Maybe it was discovering her destiny or having Torin in her life that had caused the change. Whatever the reason, my best friend was now a total knockout.

We entered Xanavoo and looked around. Other than the jocks and their girlfriends occupying several tables, I recognized a few faces from our school in the crowd, including Ingrid. Majority of the patrons were from Walkersville University. A few whistles followed us, while others turned and ogled us as we walked past.

Drew saw us first. His eyes widened and then narrowed. Was he still sulking about last weekend? Pia and another cheerleader sat on either side of Blaine. Sat was being nice. Both were practically on his lap. He'd dated a Mortal before, so I knew he had no problem with human girls. He didn't realize we'd arrived until someone yelled, "Hey, Raine. Where's St. James?"

"Family emergency," Raine answered without missing a beat.

"When is he coming back?" someone asked.

"Tonight," she said.

Blaine, ever the gentleman, stood and gave up his seat for Raine. Then he practically pushed Pia in Heath Kincaid's lap and offered me her seat. Heath was a running back with dreadlocks and walnut-brown skin. He changed girlfriends often, so I wasn't surprised when I caught him staring at my chest when I removed my jacket and draped it on the back of my chair.

"I was about to give up on you two," Blaine said. "What can I get you to drink? Soda? Beer?"

"Root beer," Raine and I said at the same time and exchanged a smile.

Silence descended on the table.

"What happened to Torin?" Heath asked. "He wasn't at practice yesterday or today."

"His aunt is still sick again." Raine glanced at me and added, "Lavania's mother."

I nodded, joining in the charade. Raine must come up with excuses every time Torin went missing.

"Poor Lavania. No wonder she quit school after only a few weeks," Leigh said, and then she looked at me. "I remember you two didn't get along."

I didn't rise to the bait. I simply shrugged and said, "We made up."

The waitress brought our drinks and placed them on coasters in front of us. Blaine pulled up a chair, so he sat between Raine and me, his arm resting on the back of my chair. Drew's annoyance and the way his gaze volleyed between Blaine and me didn't escape me. What was I? The one that got away? It was only one kiss. Or Maliina had done something to screw with his head.

I sipped my drink and half listened to the conversation around the table. As usual, they were talking about football. Raine must hang out with these guys a lot because she jumped right in. She even teased the guys, including Drew, who seemed to thaw just for her. This was no longer my scene.

"Dance with me, Cora," Blaine whispered in my ear.

Since the whole purpose of tonight was to do something normal, I was relieved to get up and get on the dance floor. The club was like all the others scattered around town. Dance floor on one side, bar and sitting area on the other, and pool tables in the back room.

Blaine pulled me into his arms. Funny how I used to think he was hot. Six months ago, I would have loved this—my head on his shoulder, getting lost in the music, the envy of every girl in the room.

Things were different now. His arms weren't the ones I wanted. His scent, masculine and spicy, didn't send my pulse racing. Only one man, one Grimnir, had the power to make my pulse leap like that. I should not have come here tonight. Echo might even be in my room right now, wondering where I was.

"I know everything about you, Cora Jemison," Blaine whispered in my ear.

My stomach dropped. I leaned back to study his face. "What do you mean?"

"I know about PMI and why you ended up there."

My feet faltered, but I recovered. "Since you are an Immortal, I expected you would."

"I know that Maliina marked you. She lived with us for a few weeks when they first arrived here. I don't know the details, but I know she went rogue, joined the evil Norns, and tried to hurt Eirik."

I relaxed a bit. I wasn't sure where the conversation was headed, but he didn't sound like he was about to scream my secret at the top of his lungs.

"Be careful with Valkyries and Grimnirs, especially Echo," Blaine said. "None of them can be trusted." He stiffened. "They are here."

Echo? I turned to look.

"Hey, St. James," reached me before I saw them. Andris headed for the bar, while Torin knocked fists with other jocks, walked to Raine, and claimed her. The man didn't care that the whole room's attention was on them. He kissed Raine like he was starved for the taste of her.

Blaine noticed that I was distracted. "You can't trust these people, Cora," he whispered harshly. "They take and never give back. Use people and never look back."

I remembered what Raine had said about Immortals offering Valkyries support. "I thought you worked with them?"

"My parents do, but you are an Immortal now, and we Immortals must stick together."

"Blaine—"

"Let me finished. Valkyries and Grimnirs think they can boss us around, make us do their bidding whenever, yet when we need them, they ignore us."

That didn't sound right. "What happened?"

"I asked Andris to make my girlfriend Casey Immortal, but he refused. We Immortals can't turn humans. *They* can. She'd still be alive today if he'd done it."

"So you have a problem with Andris?"

"And Torin. He told Andris not to do it."

I sighed. "Torin wouldn't even turn Raine, Blaine. And look what happened to Maliina when Andris turned her. He used his own artavus and she went psycho."

"Ingrid is fine," he retorted.

I felt sorry for him. He must have really loved Casey. "I think their decision not to turn Casey wasn't personal. There are laws."

"Bullshit. Andris had turned two Mortals. Echo is rumored to have turned hundreds. I lost the girl I love because of them. My family is earth-bound. I want to be in Asgard to serve the gods."

And to be with Casey. Wow, when these people loved, they went all in. Body and soul. No holding back. I wanted that same all-consuming love.

My glance touched Torin and Raine, who were now on the dance floor, cheek to cheek. I wanted what they had. I wanted someone to kiss me like he couldn't get enough of me. Touch me like he'd die if we didn't. Look at me like he was seeing me for the first time every time we were together. I wanted Echo. Not just now. I wanted him always. Forever.

"That's where you come in," Blaine said. He must have been talking while I'd spaced out. "Only a powerful Valkyrie or Grimnir can finish my training, or a god can request my service. Torin and Andris won't help, so that leaves…"

"Echo?"

Blaine laughed. "No. I tried talking to him and he laughed in my face. I want you to talk to Eirik. Ask him to send for me."

A warm tingling shot up my back, and I turned my head to find Echo. More people were on the dance floor, and someone had turned on colored LED lights, but I knew he was in the room.

"As his aide, I could move freely around Asgard."

My eyes found Echo standing by the door. His eyes were locked on me. He looked pissed. Then he turned and pushed open the door. Where was he going?

Panicking, I pushed Blaine's arms away.

"Did you hear what I said?" he asked, following me.

"I don't know where Eirik is or if I'll ever see him again." I pushed through the crowd, yelling to be heard above the music. "If I do, I'll tell him." I hurried toward the entrance. I pushed open the door and stepped outside.

Blaine grabbed my arm. "Wait. Where are you going?"

"Hey." I tried to wrestle my arm free. The next second, a blast of cold whipped past me and Blaine was gone

14. Bad Grimnirs

A thud came from my left, and my head whipped around. Echo gripped Blaine's neck. Blaine's back was against the wall.

"Don't ever put your hand on her, Chapman. You don't look at her wrong, raise your voice, or give her a reason to cry. You laugh and cry with her. Worship the fucking ground she walks on. If she's hurting, you'd better be hurting ten times worse because her pain is too much to bear. Get it?"

Blaine shook his head and tried to talk.

"Wrong response, Chapman." He slammed Blaine up against the wall. His feet were now off the ground.

I ran toward them. "Echo, stop."

"If she's sad, you find out why and fix it," he continued as though I hadn't spoken. "If she gets scared, you find the bastards responsible and you annihilate them. You slay her dragons and chase away her demons."

I gripped Echo's arm. "Put him down. He didn't hurt me."

"He did. You cried out." His voice was curt, and he still didn't look at me, his focus on Blaine. "If you ever hurt her in any way or form, there won't be a place or realm for you to hide because I will find you, Chapman, rip out your heart, and feed it to the serpents of Naastrand. Understand?"

Blaine nodded.

"Good." He dropped Blaine. No, threw him, since Blaine landed in the gutter a few feet away. The sound of concrete cracking sounded like a sledgehammer.

Echo glanced at me. Then his gaze shifted to someone behind me, and he smirked.

Caught between knocking some sense into his thick head and going after Blaine, I peered at Blaine. "Are you okay?"

He staggered to his feet, one hand rubbing his neck. "The bastard is crazy!"

A chuckle came from behind me and I turned, expecting to see Echo. He had already disappeared. Instead, Andris, Ingrid, Torin, and

Raine watched me with varied expressions. Ingrid's boyfriend was by the door and I wondered how much he'd seen.

"No, you pissed him off, Chapman," Andris said. "What were you thinking messing with Cora?"

"I didn't mess with her," Blaine snapped. "We were talking, so when she took off, I followed. And that Neanderthal nearly snapped my neck."

"Actually, he could have snapped it." Andris moved closer to where I stood with Blaine. "You grabbed her, dude. That's just wrong."

"Stop giving him a hard time, Andris," I said. "I'm so sorry, Blaine. I'll explain things to Echo."

"You do that. And tell him to stay away from me." Instead of going back to the club, Blaine disappeared in the darkness. A car engine started, and within seconds, a red sports car shot past us.

I turned and faced the others. Torin and Raine still hadn't spoken. Andris looked like he was dying to say something, but I didn't want to hear it.

I started past them. "I'm done. I'm going home."

"I'll drive," Raine said. She had my purse and jacket.

"Can I hitch a ride?" Andris asked.

I didn't care. I just wanted to go home and wait for Echo. He'd better stop by. The things he'd told Blaine were from the heart. I wanted to hear them again. Spoken directly to me.

I was lost in my world and didn't realize we weren't heading home until the car stopped. We were at Eirik's house. "I thought you said they lived next door."

"We're moving." Andris headed for the entrance. "Come inside. We want to show you something."

Torin pulled up behind us on his Harley, switched off the engine, and headed for the entrance. The security light at the front of the house had turned on, so I caught the look he exchanged with Raine. Something was going on.

"Come on," Raine said, taking my hand.

I refused to budge. "What's going on?"

"They want to talk to you," Raine said.

I narrowed my eyes. "About?"

"Echo."

I shook my head. "I'm not listening to any more 'he's a bad guy' speeches from you guys."

"Don't lump me with them," Raine said. "I don't know what's going on either. Torin said…" She glanced at him. He stood in the doorway, but Andris was already inside. "You tell her."

"We want to show you something. That's all," Torin said walking toward us.

I didn't like the look in his eyes. "And if I said I wasn't interested?"

Something lethal flashed in his eyes. "I'd carry you inside and show them to you anyway."

"You'd force me?"

He smirked.

"Do you know how fast Echo would you get here if you so much as touch me?"

Torin sighed. "I don't want to fight him, but I will if it helps us get to the bottom of this mess and how he's connected to it. I guaranteed he's deep in it."

"There's a perfectly good reason why," I snapped, ready to defend Echo, even though I had no idea what was going on.

"There always is. Please, just hear us out."

"No. Whatever you have to say, you say it in front of Echo so he can defend himself. I'm going home." I took my keys from Raine. "Goodnight."

"We have the two Grimnirs who chased you this morning," he said.

Was that this morning? So much had happened since then. I turned and studied Torin. "You told Echo you killed them."

"We are not in the business of killing, Cora. We told him they were taken care of, and they were. We snapped their necks, but like any Immortal, a broken neck is a bruise. It took them hours without fresh runes, but they self-healed. Now they're our prisoners. We've tried to interrogate them to find out why they're after you, but they keep telling us to ask Echo."

"Then find Echo and ask him," I snapped.

"We tried. He only appears when you are in trouble."

"So you brought me here as bait? Do you know what the goddess will do to him once the Grimnirs go back and report that he is working with you?"

Torin studied me and frowned. "You know why they are after you, don't you?"

"Yes. Echo told me." I walked past Torin. Raine followed while he took the rear. Andris, who'd been waiting by the door, closed it. "Where are they?"

"In the pool," Andris said. "We drained it and runed it, so they can't create portals. Come to the kitchen."

We followed him into the kitchen. Eirik's home was still the same. A few vases and pictures were missing here and there, but it was the same grand foyer, the same expensive furniture, and the same kitchen. We sat around the counter while Andris distributed drinks. No one, except him, touched their drink.

"Tell us what you know," Torin said.

"The Grimnirs are not here for me. I am just the bait. They are really after Eirik. Whoever has me can use me to lure Eirik out of hiding."

"Is Echo after Eirik, too?" Raine asked.

"He *was*, but not anymore. He chose to tell me instead, so I can tell you guys and you can warn Eirik," I fibbed, not feeling an ounce of shame. "If he comes here, they'll grab him. So you need to decide what to do with your prisoners because they're exactly where they want to be. Close to me and inside Eirik's house."

Andris and Torin exchanged a glance.

"Raine, keep her out of sight." Torin's gaze touched me then Raine. "Stay here." He followed Andris out of the room.

"Where are they going?" I asked.

"To take care of the two Grimnirs. Come on." Raine started out of the room.

I frowned. "But Torin said—"

"Yeah, he says a lot of things. Doesn't mean I listen. Besides, how are you going to tell Echo what they've done without seeing them do it?" She peered out the door. "This way."

Torin and Andris were headed left toward the pool. We went right. "What makes you think they're doing something?"

"The Grimnirs are fishing for information," Raine explained as we went upstairs. "Torin said they kept saying to ask Echo, a sneaky way of checking if we're working with him. I don't think Hel would be pleased to learn that her favorite reaper has betrayed her."

We entered the den. The glass wall had a spectacular view of the pool. Like Andris had said, they'd drained and runed it. We found the perfect spot to watch them unobserved. Two huge men dressed in leather, like Echo, were immobile on the pool floor. If they'd worn coats, Torin and Andris must have removed them.

"Where're the guys?" I asked.

"Probably plotting their plan of action," Raine murmured.

We were seated on the floor behind a bench when they entered the pool deck. We crouched lower and peered at them. Torin looked up as though he knew we were watching. Maybe he knew Raine was watching him. We ducked, looked at each other, and grinned.

I glanced below again just as Torin leaned down and, moving so fast, thrust his hand toward the Grimnir's chest. The Grimnir rolled out of the way on the blue tiles. Torin's fist connected with the pool wall, and the house shook. The tiled wall cracked like fine china, chucks shooting through the air and raining down to the floor.

Raine and I staggered to our feet, panicked eyes connecting briefly before returning to the scene below. My breath stalled as Torin rolled on to his haunches and the Grimnir rushed him, moving from a speed of zero to category-ten hurricane in fractions of a second. He slammed into Torin with the force of a wrecking ball, and the two flew backwards, hitting one side of the pool. More cracks ran across the pool wall like a spider web.

The other two shadows—Andris and his attacker—met in the middle of the pool and skidded along the floor, leaving behind fissures so deep I couldn't see their legs. They were going to bring the house down, with us in it.

"They are going to kill each other," Raine whispered.

A blast of frigid air cut across room, and I whipped around in relief. Echo stood behind us looking like the angel of death.

"Are you two okay?" he asked.

I nodded, my jaw locked. Speech had long deserted me.

"Help them," Raine said.

One second he was with us; the next he was in the midst of the mayhem. The house shook and shuddered with each hit. When a Grimnir connected with the wall of the den, fingers of tiny fissures spread across the glass. We jumped up and dove behind the couch for cover just in time before the glass exploded. With no barrier between us, every word, crush, and groan from downstairs reached us.

"You are mine now," Echo snarled.

"Not in this lifetime, you traitorous son of a—" A gagging sound followed.

I closed my eyes and hoped it wasn't Echo making that sound. The sound of death. My heart pounded and my lungs burned. A loud roar rumbled through the house. Then there was silence.

I sucked air into my starved lungs and lifted my head. Raine was already standing where the wall had been. I got up, picked my way through the shards of glass, books, and broken bookshelves, and joined her. The scene below was chilling.

I sigh of relief escaped my lips. Echo was okay. On a good day, I would have been repulsed by how he looked and what he'd done, but this wasn't a good day.

He held a heart in his hand, blood dripping onto the floor. At his feet lay one of the Grimnirs, a gaping hole in his chest, his body still twitching. A few feet away, the second Grimnir was halfway inside the fissure on the floor, his head missing. Torin stood a few feet from him, blood still dripping from the tip of his artavus.

"I'll get rid of the bodies," Echo said and opened a portal. He threw the heart, lifted the two men like they were rag dolls, and tossed them inside. A quick glance at me and he was gone.

Andris bent down and pulled something from the fissure. It was the head. He threw it through the portal before it closed. As though my senses had been out of sync, a floodgate opened and everything came crashing down. I started to shake. Nausea churned my stomach. I staggered away and barely managed to contain the contents of my stomach. Taking deep breaths, I searched for Raine.

She was gone. One glance told me she was downstairs. Since she had her runes engaged, she must have shifted to super speed. I followed slowly, still trying to wrap my head around what I'd seen. It was one thing to hear Echo and Torin threaten to rip out hearts and decapitate each other and quite another to actually see them do it. I was trembling so hard I had to grip the banister and stop every few steps.

"We can repair the room tonight," Torin was saying when I approached the pool deck on unsteady legs. The wall was gone, and shards of glass were everywhere.

"Before Lavania comes back," Andris said, taking inventory of the damage.

"I'll help," Raine said. She had her arms around Torin's waist. The two Valkyries looked a mess, their clothes ripped, splattered with blood and dust.

We are not in the business of killing, Torin had said. Right.

I released a ragged breath. Whether I liked it or not, I was part of their world. The world of Immortals, Valkyries, Grimnirs, gods, Norns, and seeresses, or Vol-whatever name Raine uses. Didn't mean I liked it.

Hysteria bubbled to the surface and an insane urge to laugh hit me. Disjointed thoughts slammed into my head. I needed the safety of my home. Things I considered normal. The scent of my mother's cooking. Apple pies with apple cider. I was never going to complain about Mom's pies and organic dishes again. I was going to feast on spinach lasagna like it had layers of Twizzlers dipped in chocolate.

"I'm going home now," I said, the sound of my calm voice surprising me.

The three supernatural beings, because that was what they were, even my best friend, stared at me as though they'd forgotten my existence.

"I'll drive you," Andris said.

Raine and Torin exchanged a glance, and then she said, "No, I'll do it. Torin needs you here."

The Valkyries didn't argue. I didn't argue. Just turned and walked away.

The drive home was a blur, the images and sounds of death playing in my head. I shivered. Outside my house, I switched off the engine and peered at Raine.

"Is it always like that with them?" I asked.

She smiled. She was glowing with runes so if my parents glanced out the window, they'd only see my silhouette.

"No. I've never seen them actually *kill* one of their own. Fight, yes. Snap necks, yes. You okay?"

I started to nod but ended up shaking my head. "You?"

She shrugged. "I've accepted that their world, *our* world, is violent."

I sighed. "I don't know if I ever will."

"You must. Whether you like it or not, you are one of us now, Cora. Echo loves you, and knowing him, he'll find a way to make you Immortal."

"No, he can't." I shook my head, not sure whether I was responding to Echo loving me or making me an Immortal.

"It's the only way to protect you, Cora."

"I don't know if I want him to. He's trying to find Maliina so he can fix me. Maybe then I will stop seeing souls."

"Oh, Cora. Runes are not erasable. If that were the case, the gods would have fixed Eirik by now. Unless Echo knows something we don't, whatever Maliina etched on you can't be changed either. But they'll fade with time and their effects will disappear. In the meantime, just learn to live with them. You are already doing it. You're even willing to help the lost souls, which I think is brave and nice of you."

After tonight, I didn't know what I wanted anymore. I didn't even know if I wanted to help souls. How could I want Echo and reject one aspect of what made him who he was.

"Ask yourself one thing. Once the effects of the runes fade, are you willing to walk away from Echo? Because if you are, we'll use bind runes to make you forget and keep doing it for the rest of your natural life."

I had no answer for Raine. "I gotta go before my parents notice that I'm talking to myself. Do you need to come inside and use the mirror?"

"No." She reached inside her boot and pulled out an artavus. "Go. I'll be fine."

"Okay. Goodnight." I grabbed my jacket, purse, and keys and exited the car. When I looked back, she was gone.

Dad was still working and looked up. "Home early?"

"The club was boring." I locked the door and went to the kitchen, turning on the lights as I went. I cut a large slice of apple pie and poured a glass of milk. Now that I was calmer, I couldn't imagine washing down the pie with cider. And I was never ever going to like spinach lasagna. Bitching about it was normal. My normal.

"Cut a slice for me too, hun," Dad called out when he saw me heading toward the stairs.

Grinning, I placed my slice and milk on a side table and got his. I hugged him and pressed a kiss to his temple. "Goodnight, Dad."

He patted my arm. "Night, sweetheart."

I'd been hoping he'd hug me back, but Dad was Dad when he was writing. Upstairs, I went in search of Mom. She was in bed reading. She tended to read organic farming books and magazines, with the occasional historical romance thrown in.

"Just coming in to say goodnight," I said, putting my snack and drink on the table by the door.

She put the magazine aside and patted the bed. As soon as I sat, she took my hands and peered at me. "You okay?"

A sudden urge to cry washed over me. "Yes."

Mom's grip tightened. "Honey, I know you. What's going on? You're home early."

"I wasn't feeling the club."

She nodded, but I could tell she saw through the lie. "And last weekend? You sounded awful when you called us from Raine's. And this," she added, turning over my right hand with the now healing cut.

I sighed. "Mom, I'm fine. I told you I cut my hand by accident. It's going to take me a while to get back into my old routine."

She shuddered. "No, an acceptable routine. Your old routine was nerve-racking. Too much partying, online activities, and boys."

I rolled my eyes.

Mom laughed. "Come here."

I hugged her tight and fought the urge to cry again.

"Goodnight, hun," she said and kissed my temple.

I left her and hurried to my room, but Echo wasn't there. An hour later, my pie eaten, I crawled in bed. He was still a no show.

Tears slipped under my eyelids. I wasn't even sure why I was crying. My lost innocence? Not really. I lost it the moment I accepted the fact that I could see souls and I wasn't crazy.

Maybe it was because I felt alone. Disconnected from everything familiar. My parents' hugs and love often eased my pain and made my world right when it tilted. I now belonged to a different world they didn't know about. They couldn't chase away all my demons.

Warm air brushed across my cheeks, and my heartbeat spiked. I looked over my shoulder and smiled. Echo stood by the mirror portal he'd just used. The warmth said he hadn't come from Hel. Not that I cared. He was here now.

I didn't say anything or turn on the lights. Just watched him as he walked to my bed. He took me in his arms, coat, boots, and all, and cradled me closer. His intoxicating scent was familiar and reassuring. He was my new normal.

I inhaled him and sighed.

His hand was gentle as he brushed the wetness from my cheek. He didn't ask why I was crying, just held me until I was calm. I closed my eyes, nestled on his chest, and listened to his heartbeat, savoring the feel of him. It didn't matter that the blanket was between us. He was here.

15. Fantasies

"I know today was hard on you," Echo whispered. "Our world can be brutal."

I didn't have a response. I was more concerned for him. "Won't their souls report you to Hel? That you and Torin killed them?"

He chuckled, the sexy sound vibrating through his chest and making my body stir. "They won't. Those two Grimnirs were ancient and bent on reclaiming their glory by grabbing you. I wasn't going to let that happen, and neither were the Valkyries. When a Valkyrie or Grimnir dies, they are doomed to roam this world as shadows. Purposeless phantoms."

I knew I should feel bad for the dead Grimnirs, but I couldn't. They would have killed Torin and Andris had they won.

"We lose a little bit of our humanity when we become reapers, Cora. The longer we reap, the more our souls wither."

Echo sounded sad.

I slipped my arms around him, wedging my hands between him and the bed. "That's terrible."

"Nothing in this world is free, Cora. Immortality comes with a price tag. That's why we try to stay earthbound. Valkyries naturally spend more time here and reap less. We are not so lucky. We have more souls to escort. Not just to Hel's Hall, but to Corpse Strand. Unlike most Grimnirs, I spend as much time as I can on Earth. Interacting with Mortals nourishes our souls. We can love them, without turning them, and suffer as our chosen mates grow old while we stay young forever. It's worse than a stint on Corpse Strand. Or we turn them and get punished for it."

I heard the frustration and the acceptance in his voice. There could never be forever for us. I wanted to ask him if he'd ever been in love. Ever been tempted to turn a Mortal, but I was afraid of the answer.

"So what are you supposed to do? Stay alone forever?"

He chuckled, his warm breath fanning my forehead. "Love them for as long as you can; then walk away. If you are lucky like Torin, your chosen mate turns out to be one of us."

"Tell me more about Corpse Strand?"

"There are many mansions for the sick and the elderly in Hel, but there's only one Corpse Strand. It has huge chambers where the souls of criminals are kept and tortured until the end of the world."

"You, uh, torture them?"

"No. Serpents feed on them. They call it a second death—bitten and chewed on by snakes and dragons, and burned by the venomous poison dripping from their fangs, their screams echoing in the darkness." He shuddered. "Others die a second death during the journey to the island on the river separating it from Hel's Hall, a river of knives, daggers, and swords. When a Grimnir is punished, they are sent to Corpse Strand for a few years. If the goddess is fond of you, you get a few months, maybe a year. Otherwise she leaves you there for decades."

"Have you ever been tempted to turn someone other than your Druid brothers and sisters?" I asked. I couldn't help myself.

"No. Never."

There was no hesitation in his voice, which told me he wasn't lying. Part of me was hurt that he didn't think I was worth going to Corpse Strand for, but another part was relieved.

"Until now," he added softly. "Until you."

Air rushed out of my lungs, and my body relaxed. "Echo—"

"But I can't have you. I will not make you wait for me."

"Then don't." I pressed my fingers to his lips when he tried to protest. "Don't tell me you can't have me when I am giving myself to you."

Echo went very still, glowing runes appearing on his face. I didn't want to give him a chance to reject me, so I went on, speaking fast, tongue tripping, heart pounding.

"And don't tell me I can't want you, because I already do. Nothing you say or do will ever change that."

More runes appeared on his face, his unusual eyes dazzling.

"I don't want anyone else to slay my dragons or chase away my demons. I want you to do it. With me by your side. I want to laugh, and cry, and fight with you."

The yellow in his eyes had swallowed the outer green, making him look both feral and otherworldly. He cupped my face. I was lying on his chest, our faces a few inches apart.

"You are giving yourself to me?" he asked, his voice low and sexy.

"Yes," I said without hesitation.

"Even when I can't give you forever?"

"Forever is overrated."

He grinned. "Then I'll give myself to you for as long as I can." He meshed our lips.

The taste of him went straight to my head. My senses responded, sending my heart off the chart. I slipped both hands around his neck and held him, scared he'd change his mind and start talking about forever and Corpse Strand.

Growling, Echo angled his head to deepen the kiss. One hand moved down to yank the blanket from my lower torso and pull my leg across his hips so my legs straddled him. My pajamas were skimpy shorts and a tank top, the material so thin I might as well be naked. I felt his hardness from my chest to my thighs as I pressed against him, pleasure shooting through my body.

We both moaned.

His mouth left mine to nibble my jaw and my neck. He took my earlobe in his mouth and nipped. I shuddered even as he soothed it with his tongue. I gripped his head and brought his mouth to mine, needing to taste him again.

Letting me take charge of the kiss, his hands slid down my back, caressing the skin between my tank top and my shorts, over my hips to my thighs.

The feel of his hands on my skin was electrifying. Sensations scuttled coursed through me. Cupping my butt cheeks, he pulled me higher and ground against me, his arousal nestling between my legs. I pressed down hard, and he mumbled something into my mouth.

In one smooth move, he rolled to the side of my bed, sat up with me, and wrenched his mouth from mine, his breathing labored.

"Wrap your legs around my waist," he ordered.

I barely complied when he stood and strode to the door. "Where are we going?"

Instead of answering, he went into super speed mode. When he slowed down, runes covered my door. "Your parents won't open your door while we are gone."

"Gone where?"

"To my place."

"No. Not Italy." It was where he used to take Maliina.

"Not there. Already sold it." He captured my mouth in a searing kiss and headed toward the mirror, my room becoming a blur. The next second, we were in a large bedroom dominated by a large round bed. A single bedside lamp stood on the nightstand. I didn't know where we were, didn't really care. I had all that I wanted within my reach.

Echo.

He lowered me to his bed, broke the kiss, and moved back. Cold air rushed in to replace his warmth, but I didn't feel cold. The heat in his eyes as he knelt between my legs was enough to melt the arctic.

"Do you know how often I've wanted to bring you here? Fantasized about you in this bed?" In a fraction of a second, he removed his coat and threw it aside. The boots and socks followed, leaving him with just the dark-brown leather vest, white long-sleeved pirate shirt, and the leather pants.

"I have fantasies, too." I tried to sit up, but he nudged me back.

"No, don't move. I want the memory of you lying there etched in my brain." He undid the vest, one button at a time.

"Only one memory?" I teased.

"One of many to come." He forgot his vest and reached down to run his fingers along my stomach, the part left bare between my shorts and tank top. "Tell me about your fantasies, Cora."

Heat crawled up my face. I shook my head.

He leaned down, shifted his weight on one elbow, and kissed the skin above my tank top. He left a heated trail as his lips moved to my shoulder, one hand slipping under my tank top and caressing me intimately. I shivered. I didn't know what to do with my hands, so I stroked his hair and shoulders. His muscles spasmed as though my touch sent a shock through him.

"If you tell me yours, I'll tell you mine," he whispered against my neck, and I shuddered at the sensation. "Please, Cora. Tell me about your darkest, juiciest fantasies."

I tried to focus on the conversation, but my mind was slow to respond. "I want to undress you. Slowly."

I couldn't believe I'd actually said it. He went still, and I was sure he was going to laugh.

"Okay, doll-face. Undress me." He jumped off the bed and waited, hands on his hips, stance cocky, and an intense sensual gleam in his eyes.

Heart pounding, anticipation making me dizzy, I slid off the bed and went to stand in front of him on wobbly legs. Biting my lower lip in concentration, I undid the next button on his vest.

"Look at me," he ordered.

Our eyes met, and my hand went still. Heat leaped in his wolfish eyes. He brushed my lower lip, forcing me to relinquish it. Muttering a curse, he cupped the back of my head and captured my lips, his tongue slipping inside my mouth to find mine.

Stunned, I forgot about undressing him. The kiss was fierce. Hot. Mind-numbing. I grabbed his arms and hung on.

He lifted his head to growl, "You have thirty seconds, sweetheart. Then I'm taking over."

My movements clumsy, I undid the last buttons and pushed the vest off his broad shoulders. I tugged the shirt tucked into his pants, bunched it, and pushed it up, revealing his lower abs and the thin line of dark hair snaking from his belly button. Echo was pure perfection.

I drooled at the six abs, the wide chest, and the broad shoulders. His chest was right there, begging me to kiss it, so I did, and he groaned. Best fantasy ever. I pulled his shirt over his head and tugged until his arms were free. I threw the shirt aside.

"You are so beautiful," I whispered in awe.

He chuckled. "You say things like that and this fantasy of yours is over."

Smiling, my hand went his belt buckle, unhooked it, and yanked the belt off. It joined his shirt on the floor. I undid the button and lowered the zipper.

He sucked in a breath.

"That's it. I can't take it anymore." He pulled me to him and kissed me. "Off." He gripped the edge of my top and pulled it off, his eyes darkening as he drank me in. "Magnificent," he whispered and ran his fingers across my chest, teased me while I moaned and shivered. "You never fail to take my breath away."

"You did from the first moment we met. I need to see you," I whispered.

"Really?" He scooped me up and threw me on the bed. "What else?" He knelt between my legs and rained kisses on my belly button, his hands gentle as a feather as he caressed my thighs and hips. He moved upwards, driving me crazy with his touch and kisses. The worst part was he watched my every reaction. When I gasped, he grinned.

"You like that?" he asked in a husky voice, the hungry gleam in his eyes mesmerizing and exciting.

"Yes."

My body ceased to be mine. He was in control, taking cues from my responses. I grabbed his shoulder and let him love me, my cries of pleasure filling the room. Without stopping, he reached down and stroked my stomach, my hips, and my thighs. He went on his haunches and stripped me completely.

He ran his eyes over me and gave me a slow wicked smile. "Doll-face, if I were a lesser man, I'd explode from just looking at you."

"I want to see you, too." And touch him and kiss him.

He hooked his fingers under the waistband of his leather pants and pulled them down.

The gorgeous hunk didn't believe in underwear and... wow, he was splendid in his nakedness. I'd seen enough swim team guys in their Speedos, but he was my first. My first naked guy. The first to render me speechless.

"Quit looking at me like that," he teased, kneeling between my legs.

I giggled. "Like what?"

Echo lifted my leg and planted a kiss on my calf. Then he moved lower and planted another on my inner thigh. "Like you can't wait to do wicked things to my body."

My entire body flushed. There was no point denying it. I wanted to do really naughty things to him. "I do."

"Do what?" He stroked his way to my stomach, past it to find me. "Do what?" he asked again, tormenting me with his fingers.

"Wicked things to you." I pulled him to me, loving his weight, his hot body against mine.

Echo kissed my neck then my mouth, our tongues caressing, his fingers pushing me higher and higher. The pleasure was so intense I went a little crazy with each stroke. I rained kisses all over his face, my hands caressing his shoulders and arms, anywhere I could reach.

I went over the edge as my world disintegrated. I was still catching my breath when he went into hyper-speed. I didn't understand until he was back before the cold could replace his warmth. He'd gotten protection. Funny I never even thought of that. Heat flooded my face.

Echo nestled perfectly between my legs. "Look at me."

I tensed. Should I remind him this was my first time?

"Cora, look at me. Please."

I looked into his eyes and remembered this was Echo. The guy who could be so hard and harsh one second and gentle and sweet the next. The guy I loved.

He pulled me closer, his body tense as though he was holding back. I cupped his face, kissed him, and pushed against him, wanting the painful part to be over, but he froze and started to withdraw.

"Don't stop," I begged, wrapping my legs around him.

He hands gripped my hips. "You really are a virgin."

Heat flooded my face again. "Don't let that stop you. I'm ready. Please, make me yours, Echo." I was begging and didn't care.

"Why?" He shifted, breaking the fragile contact. He reached up to caress my cheek with his knuckles.

Tears rushed to my eyes. He'd stopped. "Why what?"

"Why didn't you before me?" He kissed my lips and then moved down to my neck.

"I don't know."

"You know. Tell me," he said, his breath warm on my neck.

It finally dawned on me that he hadn't stopped. He was starting over again, his movements gentler.

"I was waiting for the right person." I'd been waiting for him. He moved lower, teasing me with his teeth, lips, and tongue. I gasped and arched my back.

"Your birthday is next month," he whispered against my skin.

"Yeah," I responded, forking my fingers through his hair, wishing he'd stop talking.

"You'll be eighteen."

I didn't like where this was going.

"We can wait until you are officially an adult, doll-face. I don't mind."

"I do."

He lifted his head and studied me through heavy-lidded eyes. "Are you sure?"

I nodded.

He chuckled and kissed me, moving lower and introducing me to a different kind of intimacy. All I could do was hang on as he took control of everything I thought I knew about myself and flipped it. As my world exploded, he moved fast and we were joined. The pain was there, but it was soon forgotten as I stared into his eyes.

"Are you okay?" he whispered.

"Yes." I never wanted to move.

Then I noticed he was stiff, as though afraid to move.

"Are you okay?" I whispered.

"Yes. Just don't move. Hel's Mist, this is as perfect as it gets." He covered my mouth with his, and then he started to move.

Nothing he had done before had prepared me for this. The intensity. The sensations. The feeling of utter completeness. His runes glowing, his kisses intense, our union so beautiful and soul shattering I knew I had found the man I was destined to love—my soul mate.

***

I was alone in bed when I woke up. The pillow beside mine still had the indentation of Echo's head. I brought it to my face, inhaled, and smiled. Then I noticed the sunlight seeping through the corners of the heavy gold curtains. What time was it?

I looked around the room, searching for a clock. The room was decorated in hunter-green and gold, and everything—from the thick carpet to the chandelier—looked expensive.

Where was I?

The door opened, and Echo walked in. Shirtless. Shoeless. Leather pants and that irresistible sexy smile. Would I ever get tired of staring at him? Wanting to touch him, kiss him, to love him?

Remembering last night and this morning, my face warmed.

"Keep looking at me like that and we won't leave this room," he warned.

I grinned. "What time is it?"

"Almost ten o'clock."

"Oh, no." I scooted to the edge of the bed and searched for my clothes, which seemed to have disappeared. "I have to go home. My parents probably broke down my door, found me missing, and called the police." I crossed my arms and looked everywhere but at Echo. "Where are my clothes?"

He stopped in front of me, cupped my face, and forced me to look at him. His eyes twinkled. "Is my tigress shy?"

"No," I said, but I still couldn't look at him without remembering last night or this morning.

He pulled my arms down and knelt in front of me. His hand moved up and caressed my lower lip. "Your clothes are right behind you."

Sure, enough, my pajamas and panties were neatly folded and placed on top of the headboard.

"Where are we?"

"La Gorce, North Miami Beach. It might be ten here, but it is only seven in Kayville." He kissed me.

Hmm, I could kiss him for hours. He tasted of coffee, mint, and his unique intoxicating flavor.

"Your parents are still asleep. I'll show you." He straightened, walked backwards, runes appearing on his skin, and he turned when he was close to the mirror. He was sheer perfection. Nice butt, narrow waist, broad...

My eyes widened. Scars crisscrossed his back, some thin and narrow as though from lashes. Others were short and ragged. Probably from deep cuts or stab wounds. I couldn't believe this was the first time I was seeing them. I'd felt the uneven skin while we were making out in the car a week ago, but that was it. Who dared to hurt him like this?

I caught his grin and realized he could see me watching him through the mirror.

"I don't mind," he said naughtily, eyes twinkling. "I love your eyes on me."

"You're beautiful."

"No, I'm not, but I'm happy you think so." The mirror responded to his nearness and a portal formed. Part of my room was visible, pre-dawn light slipping through the edges of the curtains.

I slipped on my panties and tank top and followed him, my eyes drawn to him as he stood by my window. The silence in my house meant my parents were still asleep. They often slept late on Sundays, and whenever I could, I made them breakfast. A quick glance out the window said the sun would be rising soon.

Up close, the old scars on Echo's back were barely noticeable. Without the runes lighting up his skin, I would never have noticed them earlier.

I stopped behind him and ran a hand over his back. "Who did this to you?"

He tensed. "It doesn't matter."

With my throat tight with so many emotions, the uppermost anger, I kissed one ragged scar and then another. His chest was flawless, which meant someone had deliberately done this to him while he covered his front. Who? I kissed another scar.

"I told you I wasn't beautiful," he said in a low throbbing voice as though my reaction touched him somehow.

"No. You're much more. You are perfect."

Echo whipped around and pulled me into his arms. Instead of kissing me, he just held me tight. I slipped my arms around his waist, amazed I hadn't felt the edges of some of the jagged scars when we'd made love. I was probably too caught up in the moment.

"Who hurt you, Echo?" So I could kick some ass.

He chuckled and ran his knuckles along my cheek. "You sound like you are ready to wage a war."

"If they are alive…"

He lifted me up so high I had to brace myself against his shoulders. Looking into my face with an expression I couldn't explain, he said, "I don't have recent scars, doll-face. These are old. They don't matter anymore because I forgave them."

"Well, I don't. When you are ready, tell me about them."

"I already did." He walked with me back to his bedroom, the portal closing behind us. He lowered me until I could circle his waist and our lips were closer. "I just skipped the details."

Was he talking about the Romans who'd hunted his kind? He kissed me again, slowly yet so thoroughly I pushed aside the matter of his scars.

"I meant to wake you up with a kiss," he said in a voice gone husky.

I wrapped my arms around his neck. "Do it next time."

"I plan to."

I kissed him this time, my fingers burrowing in his hair and holding it in place. His shaggy hair was soft. "You taste good."

He chuckled. "So do you. Every inch of you."

Heat flooded my face, remembering. "Not fair. I can't say the same. Next time."

Echo groaned.

"Now I won't think of anything else." He lowered me down to the floor, our bodies touching. I wiggled, teasing him. He groaned and wrapped his arms around my waist. "Behave or we'll head back to bed, which is a bad idea because you are still sore."

I was, but I didn't care. "I'm fine."

He chuckled. "What do you want first? Shower or breakfast?"

"Shower. In my bathroom."

He scowled. "It's too small."

"Mom will be up soon, and I usually cook breakfast on Sundays. She'll come looking for me."

"Wait here." He disappeared through the portal to my bedroom then entered my bathroom. Within seconds, I heard the water running. Then he was striding back.

"Now she'll hear the water running and assume you are in the shower. Let's get rid of these." He removed his pants, pulled off my tank top, and hauled me over his shoulders like a caveman.

I giggled. He had the cutest butt ever. I swatted him

"Behave, woman, or you won't like the consequences."

"Promise?"

He laughed.

The bathroom was huge and done in black marble. Through a window, I could see a gazebo and beyond it a dock with a boat and palm trees. The shower stall was spacious, too, with two showerheads.

I lost interest in the property. He looked so adorable with his shaggy hair plastered to his scalp. We shampooed each other's hair.

"Turn around," he ordered. He kissed my shoulder, water raining down on his head. "I'm so happy I'm your first, *Cora-mio*."

"Me too." I wanted him to be my last, and me his. For now, I was enjoying the ride. He turned me around and kissed me long and hard.

"Your turn," I said.

He shook his head. "No way."

"Turn around."

He hesitated.

"I'm not going to hurt you, Echo."

He laughed as though to say that was impossible, but he turned, braced himself against the wall, and rested his head on his crossed arms.

I lathered the sponge and ran it across his broad shoulders. Unable to help myself, I kissed his scars. "Turn around."

"Uh-mm, I don't think that's a good idea."

"Chicken," I teased.

He glanced over his shoulder and grimaced. "Do you know that every time I see you, hear your voice, or even think about you, I want you?"

"No, I didn't." I pressed against his back and sponged his chest. "But I'm happy to hear it."

By the time we finished in the bathroom, the water was lukewarm.

16. Souls

"I plan to help the souls this afternoon. Are you game?" I texted Raine, before starting on breakfast. I should be eating breakfast with Echo instead of cooking it.

My cell phone beeped. It was Raine. "Sure. What time?"

"After lunch. I'll pick you up."

"I'll be at Eirik's old house."

Mom wandered into the kitchen, and I grinned. She was still wearing her pajamas and robe, her hair going every which way. I poured her a cup of coffee.

"Thank you, hun. What did you do with the hot water? I tried to have a shower, but the water was barely warm."

My face warmed. "I, uh, sorry about that. I washed my hair then took a long, hot bath."

"I guess it's okay. I can wait." She sipped her drink and glanced at the waffle iron. "Something smells good. What are we having?"

"Waffle iron hash brown and sausages."

"Good. Your father will enjoy that." She pressed a kiss to my temple. "He was up late last night, so we'll have to keep his warm."

After breakfast, I took my laundry upstairs and put it away. Then I decided to do something with my hair. Afternoon didn't come soon enough.

The gate to Eirik's old house, or should I say the Valkyries' new home, was open when I pulled up. Inside, I noticed a few changes. More colorful paintings on the walls. Plants and flowers. There was no evidence of the mayhem from last night. No cracks. No broken wall. Not a single shard of glass.

Even the pool had water. Ingrid had a few friends over, mainly cheerleaders and their jock boyfriends. Her date from last night was there too.

"How?" I asked Raine.

"Powerful bind runes. Come on." She led the way upstairs to the den, where we'd stood and watched Echo and Torin kill the two Grimnirs. Like downstairs, everything was perfect and neat.

"Cora! How nice to see you again," Lavania said, entering the room. She enveloped me in a hug and kissed me on the cheek. "Sit with me."

I glanced at Raine, but she just wiggled her fingers. "I'll be downstairs when you're ready to leave."

I followed Lavania to the couch. She sat with her back straight, legs crossed at the ankle. Today, she wore leggings and a dress shirt, her hair pinned up. She could wear anything and still look regal, like a throwback to princesses and ladies-in-waiting. I wasn't sure what she wanted, but it couldn't be good. She wasn't smiling.

"So…" she said, studying me with narrowed eyes. "Raine tells me you plan to help lost souls."

She didn't sound like she approved. "Yes. That's okay, right?"

"Only if it's okay with you. Raine told me what happened when one possessed you. Were you not scared?"

I nodded. "Oh, I was."

"Then why are you doing it?"

I shrugged. "I don't know. It's something to do." I sighed. "No, that's not true. I feel sorry for them, and if I can help them find closure, why not? This way I can turn what Maliina did to me into something positive."

Lavania surprised me when she smiled with approval. "Now I understand why Raine values your friendship. You are strong and compassionate." She leaned back. "When I met Maliina, after she took over your image and personality, I knew there was something evil in her. I didn't like her and told Raine she shouldn't encourage her association with Eirik. Of course, you know Raine and how stubborn she can be. She insisted Eirik had a right to court you. You were her best friend and her best friend could not possibly be evil. Now that I've met the real you," she reached out and patted my cheek, "I agree with her. You will make a wonderful consort to our young god."

I blinked. "Consort?"

"Mate. Wife. I think Eirik chose well."

I shook my head. "Oh, no. Eirik and I… no. I don't feel like that toward Eirik. I mean, I had a crush on him, but that's in the past. It's gone."

Lavania just laughed. "Time will tell. You'll see what I mean when he comes back."

"Comes back? When is he coming back?"

"Soon, I hope." Lavania stood. "He wanted to come earlier, but his grandparents wouldn't let him. They didn't think he was ready. He had to learn to control the runes on his body. He kept saying you were in danger. I reassured him that you were fine, and you and Raine were as tight as ever."

Crap. Didn't Raine and the others tell her anything?

Lavania took my arm and led me toward the stairs. "He also insists on finishing your transformation into an Immortal. I offered to help, even told him I had several artavo he can choose from, but he can be stubborn, too."

I didn't know how to respond. The thought of being an Immortal was intriguing, but it didn't appeal to me if Echo wasn't part of it.

"To stop the souls from taking over, this is what you need to do," Lavania said as we started down the stairs. "First, you…"

***

Raine and I left the compound, and the gate closed behind us. "How come you guys haven't told Lavania about Hel's Special Forces?" I asked.

"Are you kidding? She'd tell Eirik, and as soon as he heard you're in danger, he'd rush down here. No, he's training and studying, and that's good. As long as he knows you are fine, he'll stay put."

"According to Lavania, he plans on coming anyway. To court me."

Raine grinned.

I scowled. "It's not funny."

Raine just shrugged. "I know. But it's just like you to have two hot guys chasing you at the same time."

I rolled my eyes. "Do you mean like when Torin and Eirik were after you at the same time?" I sighed, not in the mood to tease her. "Listen, I just think we should warn him."

"Then he'll think we are all in danger because of him and still come anyway. You know Eirik, Cora. He won't care about himself. He'll only think of us and get nabbed by the Grimnirs."

She was right. I just wish there was a way I could let him know about Echo so he would move on. Echo. Even thinking about him sent a thrill through me. I couldn't wait to see him again.

I turned right on 2nd East and headed into downtown Kayville. What were we discussing? Ah, Eirik. "Why does he need to train?"

"All the gods train. Valkyries and Grimnirs too, since they will fight in Ragnarok. In Eirik's case, he'll get a special weapon. You know, like Thor's hammer and Odin's spear. He's also studying runes, which is mandatory for all gods."

"Is he happy?"

"Torin thinks so, though he's only seen him once. They haven't been reaping as much the last several weeks."

Probably because of me. "Sorry about that. I guess they can't keep an eye on me and—"

"No, it's not you. Healthy people haven't been dying lately. I know that sounds weird, but it's true. Last week, Torin and Andris were in Calgary where a ski team was hit by an avalanche. Four of them were buried in the snow for about thirty minutes. Their body temperatures dropped to below twenty-nine degrees, and they shouldn't have survived, yet they all did. Minus a few broken ribs and hypothermia. Everyone is calling it a miracle. One incident is a miracle; several in the last month is too much of a coincidence."

"What do you mean?"

"An NFL guy with the Seahawks totaled his Lamborghini outside Seattle and was banged up pretty badly, but he's going to be okay. A triathlete jogging in the suburbs of Philly was shot by a bunch of bored teenagers. He was in surgery for ten hours and made it. He might never run again, but he will live. More stories like that are coming from all over the world every day, and it doesn't make sense. No one destined for Asgard has died."

"The Hel ones?"

"Dropping like roaches. The Valkyries are having a conference right now. That's why Torin and Andris are gone. Lavania doesn't reap anymore, but she's headed there, too. Something is out of sync, and I bet the Norns have something to do with it."

That explained her father surviving a major stroke. "What do they hope to gain by changing destinies?"

"I don't know, but somehow I know it has a something to do with me. They are always screwing with me."

"I'm so sorry." I reached over and gripped her hand.

She chuckled. "It's not your fault. Mom warned me it wouldn't be easy going against them. I just wish I knew what they're plotting this time."

Before I could respond, not that I knew what to say, a sudden blast of cold air filled the car. Echo. Raine turned and gasped.

"Echo. You scared the beegeebees out of me," she said in a screechy voice. "Where did you come from?"

"Hel." He smirked. Our eyes met in the rearview mirror, and he winked. He leaned closer, lifted my hair, and dropped a kiss on my neck.

His lips were cold, but not for long. I reached back and cradled his face as he nuzzled my neck. My body hummed in response. Words were not necessary between us anymore, and I was becoming really good at this kind of multitasking. Unfortunately, my body didn't always agree with my head. And remembering last night didn't help. The car swayed.

"Do you guys think you should be doing that now?" Raine asked.

I grinned and entered the parking lot of Harvest Foods.

Echo glanced at her. "No, but she likes it, and I'm here to indulge her every wish. Unless, you'd rather come back here and warm me, Raine Cooper."

Raine blushed, but I wasn't amused. Echo was such a flirt. I smacked him on the head.

"I was just kidding," he protested. "No one is allowed to warm me but you, doll-face."

I switched off the engine and glared at him. "And you'd better not forget it, you—"

His lips swallowed the rest of my words. By the time he lifted his head, I didn't care if he flirted with a gazillion women. Raine wore a knowing grin, which I pretended not to see. Flustered, I picked up the notebook and pen.

"Uh, Raine, this is what we'll do. We'll go inside first. When the souls appear, I'll agree to be their host and bring them back to the car. I'll allow them to possess me one at a time and write down whatever messages they have for their loved ones. Lavania suggested that you hold my hand so I stay connected to the physical world."

Raine nodded, but she looked worried.

"May I make a suggestion?" Echo asked, but he didn't wait for my response before adding, "You two stay here, while I get my lost charges and bring them to you after I have a little chat with them."

I heard him, but my attention had shifted to the entrance of the store. The two souls I'd seen two days ago were standing by the entrance, and they weren't alone.

"That's not good," I murmured.

"Why? I think his suggestion is wonderful," Raine said.

"No, they've appeared. Lots of them." I pointed at the storefront. Raine sighed with disappointment because she couldn't see them.

"Stay here," Echo said and was gone. He appeared by the souls, his scythe out, runes on every visible part of his body.

"What is he doing?" Raine asked.

"Talking to the souls, probably threatening them. There are at least a dozen of them." He started toward the car, and the souls followed. "They are coming."

"Now what?"

I blew out air. "Now, I hope I survive this séance."

"If one can call it that," Raine added. She sounded worried. That made two of us.

***

An hour later, I was numb and exhausted. Each soul seemed to take forever. I was done with seven and ten more waited because more kept arriving. We were in the back seat with the window rolled down so I could talk to Echo. He stood guard outside the door and let in one soul at a time.

With his engaged runes, we didn't have to worry about people noticing him. Raine and I gave them something to stare at and smile— two girls seated in the back seat of a car holding hands and talking quietly. That was one thing I loved about Kayville. Despite being a small town, same sex couples didn't bother most people.

Echo peered at me with a creased brow. "Ready?"

"She should stop, Echo," Raine said. It wasn't the first time she'd said that.

With each possession, I swore it was the last one. "I can't, Raine."

"But you're exhausted and," she touched my forehead, "your skin is clammy and greyish."

I was tired, but one girl about my age, a scarf covering her bald head like most cancer patients, was next. She looked miserable. I made eye contact with Echo and nodded.

"This is the last one," he said firmly.

I didn't respond. I could do more.

He stared into the girl's eyes. "Make it quick or you know the consequences."

The soul entered the car. Like others before, she invaded my senses, her presence stifling and suffocating. Her thoughts slammed into mine. Her parents' marriage was falling apart, and she blamed herself. Or rather her illness. She'd been diagnosed with an aggressive cancer a year ago and died within six months. Her mother gave up on life and never left the house anymore, and her father became married to his job. They didn't talk anymore. They fought. By the time she finished and let me go, I was crying.

Echo took one look at me and crawled in the back seat. "You're done."

"Just give me a second, and I'll do a few more."

"No." Echo lifted my chin and studied my face. "You are not going to make yourself sick for them. You're going home. I'll see you tonight." He pressed a kiss to my forehead, and then he was gone.

When I looked outside, he was escorting the souls through a portal, his hood up, scythe in hand. The remaining nine souls were still outside, staring at me. I had nothing left to give them, despite what I'd told Echo. I was drained.

Raine, already behind the wheel, started the engine. "We'll go to my place."

"No. Take me home." I closed my eyes.

"Are you sure? Your mother will take one look at you and rush you to the nearest hospital."

"I look that bad?" I asked without opening my eyes.

"Like crap warmed over."

I tried to smile, but I couldn't pull it off. "No, don't worry about my mother." I didn't open my eyes until she parked outside my house. "You want to come inside?"

"I have to make sure you make it to your room. I think if you do this again, limit it to three or four souls."

"I know." Lucky for me, my parents weren't around, so we went straight upstairs, where I crawled into bed. Raine asked me something about the runes on my door. I mumbled a response. At least, I think I did.

***

When I woke up, it was pre-dawn and Echo was curled behind me, one arm around my waist and the other under my head. I turned and peered at his face.

"I'm awake," he whispered, his hand reaching up to stroke my face. "How are you feeling?"

"Rested."

"I don't think you should do it again," he said, pulling me to his chest and rolling onto his back. "Ever."

He was so cute when he was being protective. I slipped a hand between his body and the bed and listened to his heartbeat.

"You don't owe them anything, Cora," Echo said, stroking my hair.

"I know, but they look so miserable, and the messages will help their relatives find closure."

"I still say it's not your problem. If Mortals didn't spend so much time keeping secrets from each other, they wouldn't bitch about it when their time is up."

"You're not that hard-hearted, Echo. Surely—"

"When it comes to keeping you safe, screw them." He cupped my face and kissed the corner of my mouth. "Are you hungry?"

My clock said it was four in the morning. Seven in Miami. "Famished."

He rolled over and lifted me in his arms. "And afterwards?"

"I have school."

He chuckled. "We have plenty of time."

***

"What's going on?" I asked, coming up behind Raine near our lockers. She was with Torin and a bunch of jocks.

"Assembly," Raine said. "The principal probably wants to talk about the pep rally planned for Friday. Let's go." She wrapped an arm around mine. She and I hadn't had a chance to talk since she dropped me off at home yesterday. "How are you feeling?" she asked.

"Better than last night. I slept until this morning. Mom was totally freaked out. She insists I've been pushing myself since I came home."

"You have. Partying every weekend, running around with a certain Grimnir—"

"Shut up."

"Seriously though, you really shouldn't be helping you-know-who if it has such a terrible effect on you."

"Echo had said the same thing, just more callously."

"Then you won't do it again?"

I rolled my eyes. "Of course, I will. Oh, you have to be careful next time you decide to use a portal to get home. Mom saw us drive up and walk to the house together, but she couldn't remember anyone picking you up. I lied that Torin did. She still wore a skeptical expression because she didn't hear an engine start or stop."

Raine grimaced. "Yikes."

"Exactly."

Blaine, Drew, and two other ball players were by the auditorium doors when we reached the front hall. Blaine's eyes flickered to me. I smiled and nodded, but I might as well be invisible. Drew let his eyes speak for him. Sheesh, how long was he going to hold a grudge?

"Who is starting the game on Saturday?" I asked when we sat inside the auditorium, my gaze moving from Raine to Torin.

Torin smirked. "That depends."

"On what?" Raine and I asked at the same time.

"On whether you've seen any Grimnirs today," he said.

Raine's jaw dropped. She elbowed him. "You are such a jerk. You shouldn't be reminding us of them."

"Why not? I'd rather fight them than play ball." He winked at me. "Have you seen Echo?"

"This morning. Why?"

Before he could answer, Principal Elliot and the head football coach, Jim Higgins, walked to the podium. The noise gradually died until silence filled the auditorium. At the same time, a familiar tingle shot up my spine.

Echo was around. I glanced toward the entrances, but I couldn't see him. This morning, we'd prepared breakfast together and eaten on his patio while listening to waves and seagulls. Echo was a sucky cook, but I didn't care. I wasn't into him for his cooking. Then we'd made out. Now that was an area where he knew exactly what to do.

"What is it?" Raine asked.

"Echo is around here somewhere, but I can't see him." The last few students were trickling in. Others headed upstairs to the balcony. He wasn't up there either.

"Do you want me to find him?" Torin asked.

"No. It's okay. I'm sure he'll appear when he wants to."

"He's probably making his rounds," Torin said.

I cocked my brow. "Rounds?"

"Making sure there're no Grimnirs around."

He was always looking out for me. No wonder I was crazy about him. It wasn't a crush or a passing thing either. I loved Echo. The auditorium erupted in whistles and applause as though giving its approval, and I giggled.

Raine shot me a questioning look. Since she was leaning against Torin, I let my head rest on her. She put her arm around my shoulder. I bet if I told her about my feelings for Echo she'd understand. My eyes met with Drew, who seemed more interested in me than Principal Elliot's speech.

Move on already.

He smirked like he knew something about me. Frowning, I ignored him and focused on the principal.

"We want Kayville represented at Jeld-Wen on Saturday," he said. "The mayor is urging the people of Kayville to come out and show the team their support. If you can, head to Jeld-Wen and show the team that we are proud of them. A pep rally is planned for Friday." He glanced at Coach Higgins, who nodded. "But for the rest of the week, classes will be held as usual and attendance is mandatory. No one, including members of the football team, is exempt from learning. Because the bottom line is we are here to learn and..."

I ignored the rest of his speech and the coach's and tried to find Echo. My eyes met Drew's a few times. He still wore that creepy smirk. Maybe Blaine told him about my stay at PMI.

Assembly over, we piled out of the auditorium and I headed to my English class. Echo was a no show. I don't know why I'd expected him to follow me around school like a love-struck idiot. One stalker was enough. I couldn't turn around without seeing Drew staring at me. What was his problem?

At lunch, he, Blaine, and a few jocks stood by the cafeteria entrance when I walked past with Kicker and Naya. Our eyes met, then mine drifted to Blaine. He didn't return my smile. I wished I could tell him the truth—that I wasn't Immortal like him.

If he'd told Drew about my stay at the psych ward, people would be talking about it. So far, I hadn't heard anything. News like that traveled fast, and Kicker, info guru and general busybody, hadn't said anything either, so Drew's smirk didn't make sense.

Throughout lunch, I felt his eyes on me.

"Cora, wait up," someone called as I walked toward my car.

I turned to see Victoria hurrying across the street. She was smiling, which meant good news.

"Thank you for bringing that note. Mom and I went to the bank today during lunch, and we found all these papers Dad had left behind. He took out a life insurance policy in case of an accident, and we now have the deed to the house. He'd even opened an account for me."

The shiver of awareness told me Echo was behind me before his arm wound around my waist and nudged me against him.

Victoria glanced at him and color flooded her cheeks. "Thank you, too."

"Don't thank me," Echo said. "It was all her doing."

"She's awesome," Victoria said, waved, and took off.

I turned around, taking in his chiseled features, and grinned. I reached up and finger-combed his shaggy hair. It had grown longer since I first saw him. "I'm awesome."

He chuckled. "In more ways than she knows."

Our lips met, and the world ceased to exist. I dropped my backpack and looped my arms around his neck. When he lifted his head, he whispered, "Want to get out of here?"

"Yes. I have swim practice."

He groaned. "Do you have to go?"

"Yes. You can watch me. Like you did this morning."

He gave me a blank look. "I have no idea what you are talking about."

"You are not that sneaky. You were in the auditorium."

He chuckled, grabbed my bag from the ground, and followed me to the car. Just before we drove off, my eyes met Drew's across the parking lot. He wasn't smiling anymore.

"What is it?" Echo asked.

"Nothing."

"Is Drew bothering you?"

The change in his voice told me he'd rip Drew apart if I said the word. "No. He's friends with Blaine and that bothers me."

"Why?"

"Blaine is angry about his girlfriend Casey's death, and he blames you guys for not warning him and saving her."

A snicker escaped Echo. "It's not our job to warn people before they die."

"So if a reaper comes for *my* soul and—?"

"No one would dare," he snapped.

Didn't he realize how ridiculous he sounded? "I am going to die someday, Echo."

He glowered.

Okay, wrong topic. "Anyway, Blaine thinks I'm an Immortal like him and seeing me with you or Torin seems like a betrayal. He warned me to stay away from you guys."

Echo laughed. "It's none of his business who you date."

"So we are dating?" I asked.

"What do you think?"

I shouldn't have mentioned dying. It had put him in a funky mood. I reached for his hand and squeezed. "It's okay. I want to date you."

"Why? I'm an ass."

I grinned. "Yes, you are. Sometimes."

"So why are you with me?"

Because I love you. If I told him the truth, he'd bolt. He'd already told me not to fall for him. I thought about that for a moment then threw him a smile. "I've always gone after what I want, and I want you *and* like you."

"I like you, too." He kissed my shoulder then took my hand and interlaced our fingers. He wore several of the Gothic rings he'd worn the first time we met.

After a while I needed my hand back, so I reached inside the glove compartment and removed the notebook with the information from the souls. "Here. Make yourself useful."

He flipped through the messages. "What do you want me to do?"

"I need suggestions. How to tell them. What lies to use. The cancer girl, I can text her parents the link to her online video. She's a vlogger like me, but her vlog is set to private."

"Text messages can be traced back to your phone."

"Oh. I hadn't thought of that." I brought the car to a stop in the parking lot across the street from the Draper Building.

"I can help find their addresses and go talk to them," Echo said.

"That's a great idea. I mean, finding their addresses. But I don't trust you to be nice and polite."

"I can be nice." He lifted my chin and studied my face. "Especially when I have a reason."

"And what's that?"

"You'd be nicer to me afterwards." He nuzzled my cheek. "Several times."

Oh yes I would. I forced myself to focus. It wasn't easy with his hand on my nape and his breath on my skin. "Okay. You can help, but I have to be there."

He sighed. "That defeats the purpose, doll-face."

"Which is?"

"To protect you. This is a small town. People talk. When I'm gone, you'll still live here."

Something clasped my chest at his words. I didn't want him to leave. And why was it okay for him to talk about leaving, yet when I mentioned my death he acted like he wanted to punch someone?

"They won't remember me, but they will remember you. You are unforgettable."

"Yeah, right." I reached in the back for my swim bag. He caught my wrist and stopped me from leaving the car.

"What's wrong, babe?" he asked, studying me under heavy lidded eyes. I loved that look on him. Made me want to tell him how much I loved him.

"Nothing." I planted a kiss on his lips. "See you inside."

He stepped out of the car as I walked away. When I looked back, he was staring after me with a frown. I entered the building and saw a familiar tall figure, a computer bag on his shoulder.

"Dad! What are you doing here?"

"I thought I'd watch you practice. It's been months since I did that."

Months? How about years? My parents never attended high school swim practice. Mom had put him up to this. "Okay. See you inside."

"Who was that young man?"

My feet faltered. "What?"

"The young man with you in the car."

Had he seen us kiss? "He's, uh, a friend. I have to go, Dad." I hurried to the swim desk, showed them my student ID, and disappeared inside the changing room. Explaining Echo to Dad would only complicate things. My parents were big on meeting any guy I dated.

When I appeared on the deck, Dad was already seated. I kept glancing at the bleachers nervously. He waved a few times. When Echo appeared, Dad noticed him right away. In that duster, he was hard to miss.

Halfway through practice, they were seated next to each other. Talking. About what? I tried to catch their attention several times with little results. Finally, Echo looked at me and winked.

He was too bold.

The practice passed in a blur. I showered quickly and raced outside, expecting to find Echo waiting for me. Instead, Dad stood by my car. Alone. I wasn't sure whether that was good or bad.

"You seemed distracted," he said.

I made a face. "I was the only one with a parent on the bleachers."

He grinned. "Don't worry. After a few days you won't even notice I'm there."

"What? You mean you plan on coming—"

"I'm joking, muffin. I have to go now. I promised your mother I'd pick up a few things from the store. See you at home."

"Okay. I have to stop by Jenny's for my hair."

"What's wrong with your hair? It's perfect the way it is."

Considering his long gray hair was always messy or in a ponytail, he wouldn't know anything about perfect hair. "I need a trim." I threw my bag in the back seat of my car. "Oh, Dad?"

He turned.

"Did I see you talk to Echo?"

Dad frowned. "Who?"

"The guy I gave a ride. I thought I, uh, saw you two talking during practice."

His eyes narrowed as he shook his head. "You gave some guy a ride? Is he someone special? Someone I should meet? I would remember if I talked to him."

Oh no, Echo had put a whammy on him. "No, never mind. Must have been a trick of the light."

He frowned, his eyes filled with concern. "You are not seeing things again, are you?"

"No." I shook my head. "Not anymore."

His frown intensified. Somehow I had expected him to be relieved. "If you do, come and talk to me. I never want to send you to PMI again. It was wrong of us to do it the first time. Sometimes things happen that we can't explain."

If only he knew. I hugged him tight. "Love you, Dad."

17. An Amazing Guy

Mom was waiting for me when I walked through the doors. She studied my hair and smiled. "Oh, I was worried you'd do something drastic with your hair."

I chuckled. "No. I needed to take care of the split ends. That's all. Is Dad home?"

"Not yet. He stopped by Raine's to see Tristan. So who was this boy you gave a ride?"

I rolled my eyes. "He's just a friend, Mom. Do you need help in the kitchen or—"

"No. Dinner is ready. We are having pot roast. This boy—"

"Is just a friend," I added again. There was no way I'd discuss Echo with her. Where would I begin? Uh, he's centuries old or he's a reaper? "Can I eat upstairs? Please. I have homework and Dad is not here."

She chuckled. "Okay. Go ahead. I hope we get to meet this young man some time."

"Sure, Mom." More like "never, Mom". I got a bowl, served myself, and headed upstairs.

Echo wasn't in my bedroom. Disappointed, I sat at my desk and got online while I ate. Maliina had spoiled vlogging for me, but my videos were still up.

I removed the book with the messages from the souls and typed the link the Cancer Soul had given me. After five minutes of watching, I couldn't stand it. It was a dying girl's private message to her parents, sad and heartbreaking. Somehow, I had to get the message to them.

I did what Raine had done and checked the obituaries to locate the families. Most of them had died in the last year. A few the last two years. I finished dinner and started on my homework.

The sound of a car pulling up outside my house drew my attention. Dad was finally home. The conversation we'd had earlier flashed through my head, and I smiled. If I ever decided to tell my family the truth about my ability to see souls, I'd start with Dad. I peeked through the window, but it wasn't our truck I saw beside my car. It was Drew's SUV.

What was he doing at my house this late? My watch said it was almost nine. I stepped away from the window and hurried downstairs. Mom's voice mixed with a familiar deep voice reached me before I got downstairs. That wasn't Drew's voice. It was Blaine's. Now I was really confused.

"Oh, there you are," Mom said when she saw me. "You didn't tell me Blaine was back in town."

Dad loved football and watched everything, from local high school games to NFL, so of course Mom knew who Blaine was. "I only just found out."

"Well, come inside, Blaine," Mom said, stepping back.

"If you don't mind, Mrs. Jemison, I'd like to talk to Cora privately. I know it's late, so I won't keep her for long. We'll just be outside."

"But it's cold and—"

"It's okay, Mom. I'll use this." I grabbed her heavy coat from the coat rack by the door and shrugged it on. She still wore a worried expression when I squeezed past her.

Blaine was dressed for the weather in an expensive coat and boots. His father was an investment banker, and they'd lived in one of the mansions on the east side of town, where Kayville's elite resided. In fact, his former home wasn't far from Eirik's.

Now I couldn't help wondering just how old his parents were, how long they'd been investors, how often they moved so people wouldn't notice they didn't age. Then there was Blaine. Was he only eighteen?

There was a bench on the porch, but Blaine kept walking, so I followed him. When he moved past the SUV and started toward the orchard, I frowned. A soul moved from tree to tree a few feet away. Since Andris and Torin etched runes on my house, they kept their distance.

"Where are we going?" I asked.

"Away from your mother. She's peering at us."

I glanced back, and Mom let the curtain fall back. When I turned to face Blaine, the soul was closer. "Go away."

She paused, blinked, and walked away.

"You still see souls?" Blaine asked.

"Yeah. How did you know?"

He grinned. "I felt it. You do know that with the right runes, you can block them."

"Really?"

"Yeah. I can etch them on you if you'd like." He pulled an artavus from the inner pocket of his coat.

I stared at the blade and thought of all the possibilities. No more souls. My life would go back to normal. No more seeing runes. No more seeing Echo when he was invisible. No, normal was overrated.

I shook my head. "No, thanks."

He frowned. "Are you sure? Most Immortals choose to go that route."

"I'm not most Immortals." Heck, I wasn't even an Immortal. Besides, my runes were special, inerasable, and irreversible if Raine was right. "So what's going on?"

"Stop screwing with Drew's head."

I blinked. "What?"

"Do you know he ditched Leigh for you?"

"I haven't encouraged him," I protested.

"Yes, you have. I've seen you, Cora. And ignoring him at school is beyond cruel. Don't screw with him like that. Too many of our people treat Mortals like play things. They are the ones who get hurt. Decide who you want. Drew or Echo, but you can't have both. Echo is a whack job. If he knows you are two-timing him, he'll hurt Drew. While that might seem cool or romantic, killing a Mortal has consequences."

I rolled my eyes. "Echo would not kill him."

"He would have snapped my neck if I wasn't Immortal."

"Okay, I hear you, but you are wrong about me and Drew. I flirted with him—"

"You've done more and you know it."

Maliina must have really messed with his head. What else had she done? Slept with him? "Blaine, I don't want to fight with you over this. Do you want me to officially tell Drew there's nothing between us? Set him straight?"

"Yeah, do that. I'm staying at his place, and I'd appreciate a night of uninterrupted sleep, if you know what I mean."

What did Drew do? Play loud music in the middle of the night and scream my name? Keep Blaine awake at night with stories about me?

"Echo is in your room?" Blaine said, and I turned, my eyes meeting Echo's.

I waved and started for the house. Blaine fell in step with me.

"Don't forget to break things with Drew," he reminded me. Blaine Chapman was actually a sweet guy.

"How long are you staying with his family?"

"Until graduation." He stopped by the SUV and glanced at my house then back at me. "I don't know how you do it, but... be careful."

I waved and hurried to the house. Inside, Mom was finishing in the kitchen, but I knew she'd been peering at us. "Goodnight, Mom."

"So you and Blaine are—"

"Friends. Night, Mom." I ran upstairs. I entered my room and locked the door, but it was all for nothing. Echo was gone.

Disappointed and a little angry, I glared at the mirror and got ready for bed. He'd better not have thought I was with Blaine and gotten mad. I was brushing my teeth when I felt his presence. Then he appeared in the mirror. He must have showered because his hair was wet and he only wore a towel around his waist. The chain with the heavy pendant I'd seen him wear the first day we met was back around his neck.

I studied him through the mirror. He stared back with heavy-lidded eyes. I loved that look on him. It said he wanted me. I turned and smiled. His eyes ate me up.

I was wearing a two-piece, silk lingerie camisole.

My heart slammed against my chest as he drew closer. "Take it off."

"No. I just put it on and I like it."

"You don't need to wear it for me. You are naturally beautiful." He lifted my chin and brushed his lips across mine. "Take it off for me."

He was in a strange mood. I stepped back, pulled at the string holding the two sides together, and the silk camisole came open. I let it fall to the floor.

He sucked in a breath.

I'd worn it with a matching thong. I started to remove it, but Echo said, "No. Leave those on."

"Okay." I stepped back. "Take the towel off. For me."

He flashed a wicked grin then whipped it off.

His magnificence never failed to amaze me.

Chuckling, he lifted me up. I wrapped my legs around him, leaned down, and kissed him. He kissed me back. There was something different about his kiss.

"I want you to love me, doll-face," he whispered.

I wasn't sure whether he meant make love to him or just love him. "Then let me in."

"You *are* in. You have me. All of me. In ways I never imagined. You are all I think about. All I've ever wanted. I want you to want me." He marched out of the bathroom, runes appearing on his skin. The mirror responded, and we crossed into his bedroom. He sat on the bed with me on his lap. "I want you to love me."

I cupped his face, kissed his temple, cheek, and lips. "I do."

"Show me." He ran his hands up and down my legs, eyelids lowered as he studied me.

I wasn't sure what was going on, but he wanted something from me tonight. Maybe he needed me to show him that I wanted him. Him and no one else. As if there was ever a doubt about what he meant to me. But maybe he needed reassurance or something.

I kissed him, and he let me take the lead. My kisses were soft, timid at first. Then I got bolder, remembering everything I'd learned from him. I discovered something about myself—I was a quick learner and there was nothing I wouldn't do to show this man what he meant to me.

As runes covered his body and sensation after sensation swelled through me, something weird started to happen. It was as though I could *feel* what he felt. Every kiss and caress, every stroke flowed into me, increasing the magnitude of the sensations. From his shocked expression, he was feeling it too.

"Hel's Mist," Echo ground out.

Looking into each other's eyes, our souls blended and became one. There was no other way to describe it. This confirmed it. He was my soul mate. He and I completed each other.

"*Cora-mio,*" he whispered, wrapped his arms around me, and held me tight as though to absorb me into him. I grabbed onto his shoulder and curled around him. Never wanting to let go.

***

It seemed like forever before the world came into focus. Echo nibbled my shoulder. I smiled, turned his face to mine, and whispered, "Did you feel that?"

"Yes." He grinned, looking boyish. "I've never felt anything like it before. Everything you felt flowed into me. Want to do it again?"

I laughed. "With me on top again? Yes."

He chuckled. "Anything for you, babe. You have me."

I stroked his face. "Do I really?"

He rolled onto his back, taking me with him. His hands slid down my back. "Do you what?"

"Have you? All of you?"

He chuckled. "My soul is too dark and my heart is too damaged for you. They're no good for anyone, let alone you. You deserve better. But my body is yours. To do with as you please." He kissed me long and hard. "I'm happy you don't mind that it's scarred."

"You have a beautiful soul and a generous heart. As for your body, you're perfect." I slipped my hands between his body and the bed and caressed the scars. I stared into his unusual eyes. "These scars help shape who you are, Echo."

He buried his face in my hair and shuddered.

"Tell me the story behind the scars."

He ran his knuckles up and down my back as though memorizing the curve of my back. "You know the story."

"I know that your people, the Druids, were hunted by Roman soldiers. Your group went into hiding in the forest, but the soldiers caught up with you, and your sisters were killed. Then Valkyries came and recruited you."

His hand stopped caressing my back. "You were listening."

I smiled. Didn't he know anything he'd ever told me about him was etched in my brain? "Of course I was. So when did you get the scars? From the soldiers?"

Silence followed, and I was sure he wouldn't say anything. But then he started to talk, and my heart felt like it was being crushed.

"I had gone to a village to steal some food when the soldiers caught me. They decided to use me to draw out my people. Every day, they tied me to a post and humiliated me. Flogged me. The villagers used whatever they could find. Sticks. Rocks. Hot water. They figured if I cried out for help, my people would come out of the forest and attempt a rescue."

Tears filled my eyes, and I squeezed him tight, wanting to absorb his pain. "The bastards."

"I didn't. Not once, did I make a sound. It infuriated them. The more I resisted, the more they came up with new ways to torture me. I'd pass out only to be revived the next day for even more."

Tears raced down my face and fell on his chest. At that very moment, I knew I would love Echo forever. I wanted a chance to love him for hundreds and thousands of years.

"What I didn't know was my people were watching and plotting a rescue. They waited until the villagers came with their usual rounds of rotten vegetables, sticks, and stones, mingled with them, and attempted a rescue. But the soldiers were waiting for them. What followed was a massacre." A shudder rocked his body. "It was horrible. Only a few of us made it out alive. My sisters didn't. My mother died in my arms. And my uncle, the mastermind, somehow managed to get me to safety. A few months later I met a Valkyrie, my maker."

I was sobbing so hard my body shook. How could one person endure so much and still manage to smile and laugh? I had never been subjected to real pain before. Except for my stay at PMI and losing my grandma, my upbringing had been charmed compared to his.

"I'm sorry I made you cry," Echo whispered, lifting my face to kiss my tears away. "I didn't mean to. And I don't want you to feel sorry for me. I actually had it better than some."

As if possible, I cried harder. I hurt for him and had nothing but hatred for those who'd hurt him. I wished I could find the people responsible and make them pay.

"Please, don't cry. You're killing me."

The pain in his voice forced me to reign in my anger. "If I could find the people who did this to you—"

"I did, *Cora-mio*." The smile that curled his lips was smug. "I made it my mission to find them and made sure they paid for what they did. For eternity."

As I looked into his eyes, everything fell into place. "You deliberately turned your people so you'd end up on permanent Hel duty."

He smirked. "Damn right. And I found them, every last one of them. I told you, my soul is dark and—"

"No, it's beautiful," I cut in. "You are amazing and wonderful." I punctuated each word with a kiss. "I don't care what you say or what anyone says. You are the avenging angel. Those soldiers deserved what they got, and you made it happen. If I had been there, I would have proudly been by your side. Your soul is beautiful. It's pure. And it belongs with mine. Your heart… Oh, Echo. I want you to give it to me so I can keep it safe and never do anything to hurt it." I stopped kissing him and stared into his eyes. "I love you."

He touched my face. "Cora—"

"No, don't say anything. This is not a contest. I'm not telling you this so you can say it back to me. This is me giving you my heart because I know you will keep it safe. I know you'll slay any dragons and monsters that threaten me. I want you to because I love you. I love your craziness. Your cockiness. Impulsiveness and even the way you kick ass. I don't care what you've done or will do. That won't change how I feel about you. All I ask is one thing—give me a chance to love you. Not just now. Forever. I want to spend eternity by your side. Fighting with you. Laughing. Crying. I want to love you for the next century or two or three. I want to love you for eternity. Make me Immortal."

There. I had said. I waited with abated breath.

Echo sat up, but his expression wasn't that of a lover. He looked worried. "Your dad is coming upstairs."

My eyes flew to the mirror. "How do you know?"

"The runes I placed on your door are connected to the ones in the portal and your hallway. Go. Tell him goodnight or something." He lifted me off his lap.

I frowned and stared at him. "Are you trying to push me away because I told you that I love you?"

"No, sweetheart."

"That I want to be Immortal?"

He stood and planted a hard kiss on my lips. "No. Come on. Your father is really upstairs." Echo took my arm and led me toward the mirror, runes appearing on his skin. The portal formed.

I reached up and kissed him. "I'll be back."

Racing to my room, I grabbed the robe on the back of my chair, shrugged it on, and tied the belt. A glance back told me Echo had followed me. He crossed the room, picked up his towel from the floor where he'd dropped it, and wrapped it around his waist. He sauntered closer, a wicked smile curling his lips.

"He's outside your door," he warned.

The runes on his body made him invisible but still...

"Behave," I mouthed. Then I unlocked the door. Dad was just about to knock. "Hi, Daddy."

"Hi, sweetheart. I just came up to say goodnight." He frowned, his eyes searching my face and probably seeing that I'd been crying. "Are you okay?"

"Oh, yes. Couldn't be better." I reached up and kissed his cheek. "Goodnight, Dad."

"I think he wants to talk," Echo said from behind me.

"Can we talk?" Dad asked.

"Told you," Echo said.

I stepped back, almost bumping into Echo. "Sure. Come in."

But Dad didn't come inside. Instead, he stood in the doorway, gave my room a sweeping glance, and focused on me. "Your mother said Blaine Chapman is back."

"Yeah. He, uh, might start the game on Saturday."

"Did he do or say anything to hurt you?"

"No." I shook my head. "Blaine is a sweet guy."

"He's not," Echo retorted. "He's a self-serving shithead."

Dad peered at my face. "Muffin, I can tell you've been crying."

I laughed. "I was watching a sad movie. You know me, Dad. I forgot it was just a movie."

Echo chuckled.

Dad touched my cheek. "As long it's not Chapman breaking my little girl's heart. Then I'd have to pay him a visit. I always thought he was a decent kid and a decent ballplayer, but St. James is a much better quarterback. With the two of them at the helm, you might just win state this year. I promised Tristan I'd watch Saturday's game at his place. He has a bigger screen, and he could use some company. He looks a lot better than I expected." Dad smiled sheepishly as though he realized he had gotten off topic. "Anyway, remember what we talked about. I'm here if you need to talk."

I nodded. "Thanks, Dad."

"Your mother said I, uh, called her and mentioned seeing a boy in your car, but I don't remember making the call or seeing anyone. But then I remembered you mentioned a friend after swim practice."

"That's my fault." Echo said behind me. "I didn't know he'd called home."

Once again, I ignored Echo and focused on my father. "That was my fault. There was a student behind you and I assumed you were talking to him."

"So you didn't give anyone a ride this afternoon?"

"I'll make him forget about me," Echo said, appearing on my right, a runic blade in his hand. I didn't realize he'd gone and gotten one.

"No," I said, blocking his path when he could have slipped past me.

"No? Are you sure?" Dad asked, assuming I was talking to him.

I shook my head. "I mean, no, you weren't wrong. I was with a guy in the car. He's a friend." I grinned. "Actually, he's my boyfriend and an amazing guy. And when I'm ready and he's ready, I'd like to bring him home for dinner or something, so you and Mom can meet him and see how wonderful he is."

Dad chuckled. "That's nice."

I knew what he was thinking—another one. I'd gushed over every boy I'd ever dated.

"Goodnight, sweetie." Dad planted a kiss on my forehead.

"'Night, Dad."

I watched him walk to the end of the hallway. Then I closed the door and exhaled. Echo was already seated on my bed, a strange look on his face—a cross between amazement and worry.

"You etched forgetful runes on my father," I said.

"He remembered me and was giving me the third degree." He tugged on the belt of my robe and smiled when it fell apart. "Mortals are not supposed to remember us."

"He's my dad, Echo. One runed person in my family is enough."

"Okay." He circled my waist, nuzzled my stomach, and kissed my belly button. Then he pulled me down on his lap. His hand slipped under my robe to stroke my skin. He loved to touch me and I loved his touch, so I wasn't complaining.

"You would invite me to your home for dinner?" he asked in a strange voice.

Ah, that explained the look on his face. "Yes, and to meet my parents. If I could, I'd tell them everything about you so they can understand why I love you."

"*Cora-mio*," Echo whispered, tilted my chin, and claimed my lips. It was a soft kiss. A gentle kiss filled with reverence and promises. He might not be able to say it yet, but I knew he loved me.

"What did Blaine want?" he asked in a calm voice, drawing circles on my stomach with the tips of his fingers.

"I don't want to talk about Blaine." I stood and straddled him. "I want to make love to you again."

He chuckled and pulled me down to his lap, the towel around his waist the only barrier between us.

"I plan to, but first, let's talk about Blaine. He wants you."

"No. He thinks Drew is obsessed with me."

Echo went still. "Has Drew said or done something to show that? Because if—"

"No. He just stares at me with a lost puppy expression, like I broke his heart or something. I went to his party and left with you. That's it." I tugged at the towel.

He grabbed my hands. "Focus, Cora. Tell me exactly what Blaine said."

Something in his voice set off warning bells in my head. "He told me to stop screwing with Drew's head. He said he'd seen me and that ignoring Drew at school was cruel, both of which didn't make sense. Oh, and he'd like to get a decent night's sleep." I rolled my eyes. "Maybe Drew's been moaning my name in his sleep."

Echo frowned. "Or while he's awake."

Why would he be moaning—oh! Masturbating. "Ew."

"She's back," Echo said, his expression bleak.

I frowned, not getting what he meant. "Who?"

"Maliina."

18. A Surprise Visitor

My stomach dropped. Echo was right. It explained everything Blaine had said about seeing me and ignoring Drew at school. She was obviously sleeping with him.

"What does she want now?" I asked.

"I don't know, but she's up to something or she wouldn't have stolen your identity again."

Why couldn't she choose someone else? Why me? Unless... "Do you think she knows that Hel still wants Eirik?"

"I'm sure she does and that the only way for her to make things right with the goddess is to find Eirik and take him to his mother." Echo's hands tightened on mine. "But she won't use you. I'll make sure of that."

I didn't think I could sleep after that, yet I did, thanks to Echo. And the next morning, he woke me up with a kiss.

"Morning, *Cora-mio*," he whispered. "I gotta go, but I'll see you later."

Cora-mio.

He'd used it before here and there, but more often now. I didn't know what it meant, but I loved the sound of it. I Googled it as soon my laptop rebooted.

In Italian, it meant "my Cora". Echo was now calling me his.

Grinning, I changed for school. I knew I shouldn't be this happy with Maliina's presence hanging over my head. I stared at my reflection and debated whether to ditch school until Echo caught her. I didn't doubt for one minute that he would. He was unstoppable.

No, I wasn't hiding. I refused to let her take over my identity again. I grabbed my bag and hurried downstairs. Two male voices reached me before I stepped off the stairs. When I did, my eyes widened at the scene around my kitchen counter. Mom was serving breakfast to Blaine Chapman, while he and Dad discussed football.

Blaine saw me first, stood, and smiled. "Good morning, Cora."

"Morning." I was confused. What was he doing in my house?

Mom beamed with approval as though she was planning my wedding. Blaine's clean-cut appearance would appeal to her. Dad's expression was watchful. He was probably wondering if Blaine was the Mr. Amazing I'd mentioned last night.

"What are you doing here?" I asked.

Blaine flashed his famous smile. "I thought we'd ride to school together."

Really? Drew's farm was on the other side of town. Something was going on. "Sure."

"Sit and eat, sweetie," Mom said, scooping eggs and bacon onto a plate.

"I was just telling your parents that I'm back to help the Trojans win state, but Torin will be starting next weekend."

Okay, something strange was definitely going on. Last week, he was all about taking back *his* team. Now he was happy playing second fiddle to Torin? Did Echo put a whammy on him? Could Immortals be influenced by runes? I had a lot to learn.

"That's nice." I picked up a piece of toast and munched on it as I poured coffee into a travel mug. My eyes met Dad's. I saw the question in his eyes. I smiled and shook my head.

"Okay, let's go, Blaine," I said, turning the lid on the mug.

"You barely ate anything," Mom protested.

I raised my coffee mug. She shot me a pointed look. I rolled my eyes. She knew I wasn't a breakfast person. I ripped a sheet from the paper towel roll, took one more piece of toast, and showed her. She sighed. Blaine said his goodbyes and grabbed my swim bag. Outside, I turned and faced him as soon as the door closed.

"What's up?"

"Let's talk in the car." He led the way to the SUV, which looked familiar. It wasn't Drew's though. I threw my bag in the back and slid in the front passenger seat, too aware of my parents watching us through the window.

Blaine started the car, backed up, and drove away from the farmhouse. "There was a meeting last night, and it was decided I should be your designated driver today."

"What meeting? Why wasn't I invited, and who made the decision without checking with me?"

"Echo."

"Oh."

Blaine chuckled. "Actually, you were there, just sound asleep. Echo wasn't too thrilled about leaving you alone in your little farmhouse in case Maliina showed up and traded places with you, so he carried you to the meeting."

Sounded like something he'd do. I frowned. "Where was this meeting, and who was there?"

"The Seville mansion. All of us—Lavania, Torin, Andris, Ingrid, Raine, Echo, and me. Basically, we are to keep an eye on you until Maliina is taken care of." He glanced at me from the corner of his eyes. "You should have told me you were a Mortal, Cora."

"Is that why you're my bodyguard instead of Echo or one of the others?"

"Yes and no. Your parents know me and already think I'm interested in you, so I was the only choice." He grinned. "Echo went to Hel to make sure Maliina wasn't tattling on him. The last thing he needs is the goddess knowing he's working with the Valkyries. She might put two and two together and conclude he was the one who killed the missing Grimnirs. How did he put it? If Hel came after him, he would have to go underground and he wasn't putting you through that." Blaine glanced at me again. "So you two are together?"

"Yeah. And before you ask if I love him, the answer is yes."

"He'll have to turn you."

"No. I won't let him do it." The conversation we'd had flashed in my head. If Echo turned me, he'd end up on the very island where he'd sent the souls of the ones who'd slaughtered his people. "But we'll find a way to be together."

"I felt the same way about Casey."

And now she was dead. Panic gripped my stomach. If Maliina caught up with me, I'd be just like Casey. I couldn't imagine life without Echo. No, he wouldn't let anything happen to me.

"Since when do you go along with whatever Echo and Torin decide?" I asked. "Last I heard, you told me to stay away from them."

"That changed when I learned that you, a Mortal, was involved. Immortals don't just serve the gods. We help them by taking care of people, too. If you knew how many wars I have…" He smiled. "Just know it is my duty to watch over you now."

"So how old are you?"

Blaine grinned. "Old enough. Can we talk about something else?"

Was I ever going to get used to this age thing with these people? Blaine looked like any eighteen year old. Forever young. The lure was too much, especially when you were in love with one of them.

"Where are we going?" I asked when I realized we weren't heading toward school.

"To the mansion to return the SUV to Andris."

No wonder the SUV had looked familiar. It was the one Andris often drove. Blaine took short cuts and was soon headed east. "Why can't they just create a portal that opens in the car and land in the back as you drive?"

Blaine laughed. "No one sane does that. It's too dangerous."

I grinned. *Oh, Echo. The things you do.*

"You really should have told me you were not an Immortal," Blaine said.

"I know. My life became complicated after I learned about your world, so I'm never sure who to trust. But it looks like Echo decided to trust you."

Blaine snickered at the idea. "He doesn't. He had no choice. Torin explained a few things to him. You know how things work in this world." Blaine rubbed his chest. "Needless to say, he didn't like hearing them and promised to yank out my heart and feed my soul to the serpents of Corpse Strand if anything happens to you."

I grinned.

Blaine glanced at me and grimaced. "It's not funny. No Immortal, Valkyrie, or even Grimnir should ever end up on that island. Unfortunately, that's where Echo stashes everyone who pisses him off."

"And they deserve it."

"Your boyfriend has anger issues."

I laughed. "Echo is perfect."

"Yeah, love makes us believe anything." He stopped smiling, and I wondered if he was thinking about Casey. Silence filled the car for the rest of the drive.

"Do you still want to be stationed in Asgard?" I asked as we entered the Seville compound.

"More than anything. Andris said he'll try to locate Casey next time he's there." He parked beside the silver Mercedes he'd driven a few nights ago, jumped down, and came around the car to open the door for me.

"Nice car," I said, eyeing the expensive sports car.

"Beautiful, isn't it?" He grinned. "I'm just your designated driver from your house. Andris will take it from here. Drew is not supposed to see us together or suspect I'm working with you guys, so it's okay to ignore me at school." Blaine made a face. "I'm supposed to keep an eye out for Maliina at Drew's, too."

A shiver slithered up my skin, and I crossed my arms. Which if she suspected something? Then what?

"Are you going to be okay? I mean, aren't you worried she might find out and turn on you?"

He smirked. "What can she do? I'm an Immortal."

And there was the arrogance inherent in all of them. Ingrid came out of the house, dressed in trendy clothes, blonde hair perfectly styled. She smiled and waved. I wondered how she felt about all this mess with her sister. She was probably wishing she had a different sister.

Andris followed her, hair messy as though a lover had run his or her fingers through it. It was a style Echo had perfected with his hair. As usual Andris looked like he was going to a photo shoot for some magazine cover instead of school.

Blaine threw him the car keys, and Andris snatched them in mid-air. "So I'm babysitting you again, Mortal," Andris teased.

I grinned at his disgruntled voice. "Sucks for you, doesn't it, Valkyrie? But then again, what do you expect. We Mortals are weak and helpless. We need you big and strong Immortals to survive," I said sarcastically.

Ingrid giggled.

Andris made a face. "Nice comeback for someone who's Grimnir bait. Chapman, when are you moving in?"

"When this mess is over," Blaine said. He didn't sound happy about it.

"You're moving in with them?" I asked.

Blaine nodded. "My father insisted."

"Why do you say it like that?" Andris asked, glaring at him then me. "Living with us is fun. He won't have to worry about using portals or switching to super speed. Plus, we throw killer pool parties."

"With or without water?" I asked.

Andris grimaced. "You just had to bring that up."

"Bring what up?" Ingrid asked.

"Yeah, what does pool party 'with or without water' mean?" Blaine asked.

"It's on a need-to-know, and you two Immortals," he pointed the key at Blaine then Ingrid, "don't need to know."

"She's Mortal and she knows," Ingrid said, pouting.

"She's linked at the hip with our resident Hel boy, so she outranks you." He winked at me. "You know how to pick the crème de la crème, don't you? Gives new meaning to sleeping your way to the top."

Andris could be so crude sometimes. I ignored him and got in the back seat while Ingrid sat in front. Blaine took off ahead of us.

"Text, Raine," Andris told Ingrid as he gunned the engine. "Tell them we're leaving."

"Torin is not staying at the mansion?"

Andris chuckled. "Nope. He likes to be close to his ladylove. Look out his window and see her. Doesn't matter that they'd only be a portal away if he moved here. He's so whipped."

"It's called love," Ingrid said.

Andris took her hand and kissed her knuckles. "It's called whipped, sweetheart. Love means learning to let go."

I tuned out at their conversation and stared ahead, worrying about Echo. If Hel found out he was protecting me, what would she do to him? Or to me? Down the street, Torin and Raine followed us to school. Then we moved as a group across the street into the school building.

Drew, Blaine, and a few jocks were talking and laughing when we entered the foyer. Blaine didn't even miss a beat. He said something to the others while staring at Torin and snickered. We ignored them, though I felt Drew's eyes on me. It was hard not to look back.

Poor guy.

We all went to put our bags away. Then Andris walked me to my class while Torin and Raine disappeared upstairs.

"Looks who's waiting for you," Andris whispered when we reached the doorway of my class.

My heart tripped when I saw Echo waiting by my chair. Minus his duster. He was also dressed casually in jeans and a long-sleeved sweater. No man looked good in Levis like Echo, and the sweater hugged his masculine chest. I couldn't keep from ogling him.

The runes said he was invisible, so I couldn't kiss him without looking like an idiot. He played with a lock of my hair, then traced a line down my cheek to my lips and ran his thumb across my lower lip, teasing me. He gave me that slow, sexy smile I loved. He knew I was lusting after him, the naughty guy.

"You look amazing," he whispered huskily, his eyes on my mouth.

I covered his hand. It was killing me not to kiss him, and he wasn't helping. Faking indifference, which was hard because his delectable lips were only a few inches away, I flipped my hair over my shoulder and lifted my chin. His hand moved to my nape.

I put my phone to my ear so anyone who saw me wouldn't think I was talking to the wall. "What are you doing here?" I asked.

"Checking on things. Would you like a kiss, *Cora-mio*?"

I forgave him. When he called me his Cora, he could get away with anything. "Yes."

He chuckled, lifted my chin and took his time. The kiss was sweet and way too brief. I fisted my hands to stop myself from reaching up and grabbing his face. I growled in frustration.

"Nod or shake your head," he whispered against my lips. "Did everything go smoothly this morning?"

I nodded.

"Good. I'm not staying, just doing rounds." He caressed my cheek. "Maliina is not here, but I'll check again. Want to have lunch with me?"

"Yes!" I said. Then, remembering I was supposed to nod, I glanced around. Thankfully, no one in class seemed to be paying attention to me.

"I'll be outside the school." This time the kiss was deeper, lingering. Then he swaggered out of the class. Nice walk. Nice ass. All mine. It was unfair for a guy to look that good so early in the morning. On the other hand, I had seen him with nothing on earlier.

I couldn't wait for lunchtime, but the morning dragged. Worse, Echo wasn't outside when the bell rang. Andris, Ingrid, Raine, and Torin were.

"Where's Echo?" I asked.

"At the mansion," Torin said. "He went to get lunch."

Lunch turned out to be quite festive. The guys were entertaining as they argued about the number of souls they'd poached from each other. I had no idea souls could be stolen. Whatever problem the Valkyries had with Echo, and vice versa, didn't seem important anymore. Or maybe they'd put it aside to protect me. Lavania peeked inside the kitchen, smiled, and disappeared again.

Later that evening, Andris and Raine watched me swim, but she drove me home. We grabbed snacks and disappeared in my bedroom to do homework. When we were done, we started on the mail for relatives of the souls I'd communicated with.

"Did you know there are runes that can stop you from seeing souls?" I asked.

Raine, lying on my bed, cocked an eyebrow. "Really? Lavania never mentioned them."

"Blaine told me most Immortals use them."

"Use what?" Echo asked, entering the room.

"Runes that stop them from seeing souls," I said.

"Where did you come from?" Raine asked.

"Florida." Echo walked to where I sat on the chair and lifted my chin. "Why are you discussing soul-block runes with him?"

His display of jealousy was sweet and unnecessary. "There was a soul in the trees when he was here and Blaine mentioned the runes. He said most Immortals use them to stop seeing souls. Of course, he thought I was an Immortal at the time. Anyway, I told him I wasn't interested." I waited for Echo to respond, but all he did was frown.

"And they probably wouldn't work on me anyway," I added.

I didn't know if Echo believed me. He lifted me, took my seat, and put me on his lap. Without speaking, he ran the tip of his fingers up and down my bare arm. I shivered. From the slow smile that curled his sculptured lips, he liked my reaction.

"You'd tell me if you wanted out, wouldn't you, doll-face?" he asked.

I nodded. "But I don't."

He pressed a kiss to my shoulder. "Good, because if Blaine or anyone else ever marks you, I'd kill them."

I rolled my eyes. "Yeah, right."

"Uh, I think he means it," Raine said. She'd been so quiet I had forgotten her presence.

I leaned back and studied Echo's face. He looked the way he always did. Sexy. Eyes twinkling. I pushed the hair from his forehead. "She's kidding, right? I mean, you wouldn't."

He smiled. "I would. You see, if anyone is going to mark you, it's going to be me."

Yikes. If he knew Torin had after my hand got hurt, would he go after him? "Okay."

"Good. So what are you girls up to?"

"We were finishing these," Raine waved the letters. "So why Florida?"

"I own a place there." He lifted my hair and burrowed into my neck.

Raine sat up. "Can I see it?"

"Go ahead." He waved toward the mirror.

Still trying to wrap my head around what Echo had said, I shifted to selective listening mode. If he wouldn't allow anyone to turn me and he'd already made his position obvious, didn't that mean I'd never be Immortal?

***

"Can I snap his scrawny neck?" Andris asked Friday morning when Blaine dropped me off at their house. We were discussing Drew who was becoming more obsessed with me as the days crawled by without Maliina. To him, *I* had ditched him after sleeping with him for several nights. I kind of felt sorry for him.

"Are you forgetting something, Valkyrie?" Blaine snapped.

"I'm sure you will enlighten me, Champion-of-all-Mortals," Andris said while waving rooter pom. We had pep rally day, and we all wore something crimson or gold.

Blaine's eyes narrowed. "He's innocent in all this. He and Cora are victims here."

"Have you always been this melodramatic?" Andris asked. "So not attractive."

"Screw you, Andris," Blaine snapped.

Andris laughed. "Sorry, you're not my type. Although I could be persuaded if you begged."

Blaine looked ready to punch him. I took his arm and pulled him away, wishing Torin and Echo were around. They were pushing themselves, trying to find Maliina. Andris only ever behaved when those two were around, and Blaine still hadn't forgiven them for Casey's death. He'd become testy the last few days. Actually, everyone had become grumpy since Maliina went underground.

"Stop messing with him, Andris," Ingrid scolded, and then she glanced at us. "Don't worry, guys. He's just talking. Torin would go ballistic if anything happened to Drew." She looped an arm through Andris'. "Come on." They continued toward the SUV.

Blaine and I followed slowly.

"How can you stand them?" he asked. "They are arrogant, rude, and act like they are invincible."

"They *are* invincible. *You* are invincible, too. You are just… nicer. But since you're going to live with them, you need to know a few things. Ingrid is sweet and will always be neutral."

Blaine snickered. "She always takes Andris' side."

"But stops him from being a jackass. Torin's word is the law. When he says no, Andris might complain and bitch about it, but he'll listen."

"Except when it involves some girl or guy he's sleeping with. Do you know he's now dating a local college girl?"

I didn't bother to keep up with who Andris slept with since Raine told me he was bisexual and changed preferences on a whim.

"I didn't know that, but he says and does things to get a reaction. Don't let him get to you. Ignoring him doesn't work either, so give him as good as you get." I patted his arm. "See you at school."

"And tonight, I'm moving out of Drew's after school." He sounded relieved.

I waved as he took off. The drive to school had followed the same routine since we'd discovered Maliina was sleeping with Drew. My parents were now convinced I was dating Blaine since he picked me up and dropped me off in the evenings. Torin and Echo were busy searching the entire valley, Hel, and places they'd refused to disclose every morning and evening. With her Norn runic powers, she could be anyone, and we wouldn't know it. Raine, with her ability to feel and hear the Norns, hadn't had any luck feeling her either.

The school was abuzz with pep rally activities. The rooter pom-poms had gone on sale a week ago and most students carried theirs as we streamed into the school building.

"See you guys," Ingrid said and went to join the cheerleaders.

Almost everyone wore school colors—crimson, black, and gold. A recording of our school fight song blasted from the speakers. Banners, flyers, balloons, and streamers decorated the halls and the lockers of football players. Cheerleaders and our dancers performed in the hall as students arrived. Others sold leftover pom-poms and gave out water bottles with coins for noise.

Cheerleaders separated Torin from our group, putting beads around his neck. The players were being treated like royalty, which they justly deserved. If they won the game tomorrow, they'd make history.

"The pep rally will start during the last two periods of school," the principal announced between songs. Despite my problems, I was caught in the moment.

As per every pep rally day, the classes were shorter and cheers and contests were held between classes. All the teachers were dressed in wacky costumes. An invisible Andris followed me from class to class and sat in the back with a stack of comic books as he'd done the last three days. He'd stopped grumbling about babysitting me.

Just before lunch, Raine walked into my history class and handed the teacher a note. She didn't look too good. I was out of my chair with Andris close behind before the teacher finished saying, "Cora Jemison, report to the front office."

"What is it?" I asked as soon as we moved away from the door.

"We have a problem," Raine said without slowing down.

"What?" Andris and I asked at the same time.

"We're going to the mansion." She pushed open the door to the girls' bathroom, and we followed her inside. There was already a portal, and through it, we could see the foyer of the mansion.

"We have a visitor," she whispered, leading the way.

"Maliina?" I asked, hurrying after her. I was now used to treating portals as doorways.

"No." Before she could explain, I was staring at the back of familiar Chex Mix hair.

"Eirik?"

He whipped around and grinned. "Surprise!"

"What are you doing here?" I asked, staring.

He wasn't alone. A guy a few inches shorter than him with copper hair stood to his right. They both wore a uniform of some kind—long-sleeved black shirts, matching pants, and knee-length boots. Weapon belts hung low around their waists.

Torin stood a few feet to their left with his back to the wall. He didn't look happy. My senses picked up on Echo's presence. Where was he? I glanced around and tried to find him.

"You can't be here," I said, walking towards him. "Didn't they tell you the danger you're in?"

Eirik laughed. "I came all this way to see you and you meet me with a lecture. I've missed you." He swept me into a hug, lifted me off the ground, and turned around. When he stopped, he looked into my eyes. "I thought I was too late."

"For what?" I still couldn't see Echo.

"This." His head swooped down and he crushed my lips with his.

For a brief moment, I was too shocked to react. Just when I reached up to push him away, a roar filled the foyer. Echo. I saw a blur from the corner of my eyes. Then Eirik was yanked from me.

19. Bad to Worse

The force of the attack sent Eirik flying across the room. He hit the wall, the thud reverberating around the room, a dent appearing on the wall. Echo was on him before he hit the ground, grabbing him by the collar.

"You touch her again and you are a dead man," he growled, arm raised.

Eirik hit Echo in the solar plexus. Since Echo still held him by his collar, the two rolled on the floor. Torin grabbed Echo, while the copper-haired man grabbed Eirik, his dagger drawn.

"Who in Hel's Mist is he?" Eirik yelled, trying to break free from his friend's grip.

"Your executioner if you so much as look in her direction," Echo snarled.

"Stop it!" I yelled, but my words were drowned by another. "ENOUGH!"

We all looked at the top of the stairs, where Lavania stood, looking regal in an ankle-length white dress. "Echo, I told you to stay out of the way until Cora talked to Eirik."

"And I don't recall agreeing," Echo snapped, pushing Torin away. "He kissed her. I ought to haul his ass to Hel for that alone."

"What's stopping you?" Lavania asked, moving down the stairs.

He glanced at me, his eyes narrowing. I saw the answer in his eyes. He would do it if Eirik touched me again. Sighing, I crossed the foyer and looked him straight in the eyes. "Eirik and I need to talk."

Echo stiffened, and his eyes shifted to Eirik. "No. I'm not leaving you alone with him."

I glanced at Eirik and wondered what was going on in his head. He'd have to be an idiot not to realize that Echo's behavior was that of a lover. First Raine ditched him for Torin, and now I was following in her footstep, ditching him for Echo. My news was going to hurt him, but first things first.

I took Echo's hand and sandwiched it with mine. "Look at me. Please?"

He did.

"Trust me."

"I do." He glared at Eirik. "It's him I don't trust."

"Who is he?" I heard Eirik ask angrily, and I knew we needed to talk before he lost it. Raine had told me what happened to people whenever Eirik went ballistic. The others were safe, but I wasn't sure about me.

"Then trust me to do the right thing," I said softly to Echo and turned.

He caught my wrist, and I was sure he was going to pull me into his arms and show Eirik who he was—my boyfriend, but something in my eyes must have convinced him to behave because he smiled.

"Okay, doll-face. Have your talk. I'll be out here when you are done." His voice rose during the last sentence, and I knew he was warning Eirik. He let go of me, crossed his arms, and fixed his narrowed eyes on Eirik.

Eirik still wore a puzzled expression. The others all looked tense. The faster I sorted this out, the sooner he could leave. He shouldn't be here. "Let's talk in the kitchen."

"Living room is closer," Echo suggested, steel in his words.

Yeah, right, He was only suggesting it because it didn't have a door and he would hear us. "No. We're going to the kitchen. Eirik."

I left without checking to see whether he was following me. The dining room opened into the foyer and the kitchen was on its other side. I used that entrance instead of the one that led to the hallway and the pool.

I was reaching for bottled water in the fridge when Eirik appeared.

"Do you want something to drink?" I asked while I rearranged my thoughts.

"No." Eirik leaned against the counter and crossed his arm. "Who was that guy?"

I took my time twisting the lid and sipping water while studying him. He looked different. More mature. His hair was shorter than I recalled, his features more chiseled. The things Raine had told me about him zipped through my head. He had gone through so much crap, and it showed. Eirik wasn't the fresh-faced innocent boy I'd known months ago. He'd changed.

"His name is Echo," I said.

The way his eyes widened, I knew he'd heard of him.

I swallowed, hating what I had to say next. Part of me wanted to delay the inevitable, but another part knew I had to do it now. "Echo is my boyfriend."

A spasm crossed Eirik's face, eyes sharpening as emotions churned in their depth. For a moment, he didn't speak. He just stared at me, his hand clenching and unclenching.

He shook his head. "No, he can't be. He's a Grimnir. I know because I saw him in your room weeks ago and knew I had to rescue you. If my grandparents hadn't delayed me—"

"You saw me?"

"I used my grandfather's chair, but that's beside the point. I missed you, and I wanted to make sure you were okay." He moved closer. "I'd meant to tell you everything about me, who I was and why I'd left, and the most important of all, how I feel about you, Cora." He reached up and touched my cheek, a sad smile tugging his lips. "How I've always felt about you."

Oh, God. This was bad. "Eirik—"

"I'm not saying you were supposed to wait for me, Cora. I'm not even angry about the Grimnir. You are beautiful and always dated other guys, but that never stopped me from wanting you. I told my grandfather I would bring you to Asgard. That you're the one I've chosen."

This was beyond bad. "Eirik—"

"Let me finish. My grandmother was convinced that I'd never go back to Asgard if I left. I told them if they made me stay and didn't let me get you, I'd leave for good. We don't need to live with them. I can make you Immortal with Lavania's help, and we can finish high school and do whatever we—"

"No." I interrupted him this time. "I can't be with you, Eirik. I'm so sorry." Our friendship was important, but Echo was my life. I couldn't live without with him. "I love him."

Eirik blinked, disbelief in his amber eyes. "You can't love him."

The way he disregarded my feelings annoyed me. I put the bottle down, feeling better that I was telling him the truth now. "I do love him. I didn't mean to, but it happened. If I could spare you—"

"Don't." He moved away from me, yet I felt his pain. "I'm an idiot."

"Don't say that."

"First I thought I had a chance with Raine, but then Torin happened and I ceased to matter. Then I thought I had a chance with you. I believed Raine when she told me you had feelings for me. I believed we had a chance." He sounded so defeated tears rushed to my eyes.

"I did have feelings for you. I still do, but it's different with Echo." The counter separated us now.

"Just like it was different with Torin." A sarcastic laugh escaped him. "I guess I'm truly my mother's son."

I frowned, not liking the bitterness that had crept into his voice. "What do you mean?"

He smiled, the emotions churning in his eyes hard to watch. "My mother couldn't find anyone to love her either. She had to trap my father in Hel with her. Maybe I'm destined to be alone like her. Doomed to never feel loved."

I closed the gap between us. "Don't say that. You'll meet someone."

"I have no interest in meeting someone." He turned and punched the counter. The marble top split and edges lifted up as it collapsed into the cupboards underneath it. The sound was echoed by another from the foyer.

Echo.

"I have to go and so do you. I don't want you and Echo fighting over me because it won't make any difference. Go back to Asgard, Eirik. Go home. You really shouldn't be here with Grimnirs looking for you." I closed the gap between us and touched his arm. He stiffened. More sounds came from the other room, telling me the others were trying to stop Echo. "Please, go."

I turned to leave, but he grabbed me, pulled me into his arms, and buried his face in my hair. I didn't know what to do or say to him. He was shaking, which only made me feel bad. I put my arm around his waist and hugged him.

"I'm so sorry, Eirik. I never meant to hurt you."

"I wish you had waited for me, Cora. Why didn't you wait for me?"

More thuds shook the house.

"I must go to Echo before they hurt him." I wiggled out of Eirik's arms, looked up, and gulped. Eirik's eyes had a weird glow in them. I had no idea what that meant. Raine had explained, but for the life of me I couldn't remember whether it was a good thing or not. I had no time to calm him or help him deal with his pain. The sounds coming from the foyer were getting louder and coming faster.

I ran to the door between the kitchen and the dining room and pushed. The door wouldn't budge. Something was blocking it from the other side. I spun around, raced past Eirik, and gunned for the door leading to the hallway. I burst through the swinging doors to see Raine and Eirik's copper-haired buddy running toward me.

"Where's Eirik?" Raine asked.

"In the kitchen. What's happening?"

"Grimnirs are here." Raine rushed past me. "They know he's here. We must get him out. They also know that Echo is working with us."

"No," I whispered in horror.

"He'll be okay. Just don't go in there, Cora. He said to keep you away."

I hesitated, not sure what to do. I had no superpowers and couldn't fight these people, but I couldn't cower in the hallway while they killed Echo either.

A roar came from the kitchen followed by thumps and crashes. Without looking back, I raced toward the foyer. My stomach dropped at the scene.

The wall separating the foyer from the living room was gone. From the number of long-coated blurs zipping around the room, the Grimnirs outnumbered our people two to one. Even Lavania in her fancy flowing gown was fighting.

Not sure what I could do to help, heart pounding, I searched for Echo in the chaos. I ducked behind the wall as half the stairs crumbled to my left, plaster and debris crashing to the floor. I felt a presence behind me and whipped around, expecting Raine.

A pale-blonde woman dressed in all black, including knee-length boots, and a belted leather jacket stood behind me. I'd never seen her before.

"So we meet again, Cora," she said with an accent.

"Maliina," I whispered.

"Echo is going to rot in Hel's island for disobeying the goddess. And for what? You? A mere Mortal?"

"Stay away from her," Echo roared, and I saw him, or the blur that was him, zip toward us. Two Grimnirs intercepted him, and the three took down the rest of the dining room wall.

"Echo," I screamed and started toward him, reaching for a slab of plaster.

"You really think you can fight us?" Maliina said with a sneer. "They could snap your neck like that." She snapped her fingers.

"You're forgetting something. I'm Mortal. If they touch me, they will be punished for eternity."

"Not if they say they couldn't tell the difference," Maliina said with malice. Then her face, hair, and clothes shifted and transformed until I was staring at my double. "Just like Echo couldn't tell the difference. He's only with you because I looked like you when we met. I bet when he touches you, it's me he sees."

I'd moved passed those insecurities a long time ago. "For an Immortal, you're stupid. Why don't you ask yourself why he has stayed *after* learning I'm not you?"

"Because he knows I'll be waiting to replace you once your body withers and dies."

I lost it and hit her with the slab. It broke into tiny pieces while she laughed mockingly. I jumped her, grabbing a chunk of her hair and yanking. She shook me off like I weighed nothing. I landed on my ass and pain shot up my spine. The battle in the foyer wasn't slowing down, but I heard Echo yell my name above the noise.

Maliina grabbed my arm and pulled me up. "Walk or I'll snap your arm."

"If you think I'll let you distract Echo—"

Her hand moved to my back. "One punch and I'll snap your spine into two, Mortal. Now walk. We are going to the portal near the entrance. Eirik will follow us once he realizes I have you."

Swallowing, I started forward across the war zone.

"Watch out, Cora!" Raine screamed.

I whipped around to see Eirik boring down on us, a medieval spiked flail dangling from his hand. Raine and his friend hurried beside him, yelling at him like they were trying to reason with him.

Eirik slowed down when he saw me and Maliina, his eyes volleying between my face and Maliina's. They were still unfocused.

"Cora?" he asked.

"Yes," Maliina and I said at the same time.

Maliina's hand dropped from my back. "She's trying to hurt me, Eirik. Destroy her."

He raised the flail, the chain wrapping around his wrist, the spiked head coming to rest on the back of his arm. Instead of confusion, his eyes now burned with rage. I was sure he didn't care who the real me was anymore. His anger was probably directed at me for not waiting for him, for not loving him. My heart stopped.

"Eirik, it's me," I whispered.

"Eirik, it's me," Maliina imitated me.

Eirik shook his head, his breathing labored, eyes starting to glow eerily. His friend and Raine tried to pull him away. From Raine's expression, she couldn't tell us apart either.

A bloodied Echo appeared in my periphery, and I turned, relief slamming through me. He would stop Eirik.

"She hurt me, Echo," Maliina begged. "Finish her."

Echo didn't even slow down, he grabbed my hand and pushed me behind him. "Think I can't tell the difference, you evil bitch? She's all yours, Eirik."

Eirik's fist slammed into Maliina, sending her flying across the room. He followed, his friend behind him. Echo pushed me toward Raine and snapped, "Get her out of here."

One second he was beside me; the next, he barreled into a Grimnir and the two of them disappeared inside what used to be the dining room.

"Let's go," Raine urged.

I know I was completely useless here, but still… "We have to stop this somehow."

"Eirik can, but I must help him," Raine said. "Go to his old bedroom and wait there while…"

Something sharp pierced my back, and I sucked in a breath. I didn't hear the rest of Raine's words. The pain was gone fast, but the warmth at the spot told me I was bleeding. I tried to reach where the pain had originated, even as the warmth radiated. Across the room, Maliina slowed down and smirked at me.

She'd done this to me. Had she snapped my spine as she'd promised?

"Go, Cora," Raine yelled. "Run." Then she was gone.

I tried to call her back, tell her that something was wrong with my back, but whatever I said, if I said anything at all, was swallowed by the crashes and thuds reverberating around us. Numbness replaced the warmth, spreading up and down my spine. Black dots appeared in my vision. I tried to move away from the carnage, but I couldn't move my hands, legs, or head.

I tried to find Echo, but the fighters all looked the same—blurry masses of black and gray. My eyes found Raine and Eirik. She was yelling at him. My vision blurred, and they swung out of focus. I was going to black out.

No, I will not. I. Will. Not. My vision sharpened.

The battle still raged on, but Eirik stood in the middle of the room with his right hand raised, the chain and the spiked ball at the end of his flail whipping the air with a whooshing sound. My heartbeat slowed down, each beat loud in my ears. I rolled my eyes down and gulped at the blood pooling at my feet. *My* blood.

Tears filled my eyes. Someone yelled my name. Was it Echo? I couldn't tell, but I wanted to see him. Even if it was to say goodbye.

"Duck, Cora!" Raine yelled and raced toward me. Eirik had let go of the flail.

She tackled me, and we both went down. I couldn't break my fall and landed face down in my own blood, probably bruising my cheeks and chin. I still couldn't feel pain. But the numbness spread. It was kind of surreal. Raine must have realized I was hurt because I heard her scream.

She appeared in my line of vision, her mouth opening and closing. I didn't hear a thing. She disappeared. Then a few of her words filtered through the surreal haze cocooning me. "Too deep... can't pull it... bleed out..."

I watched Eirik's flail act like a boomerang, spinning and whistling as it sailed around the room, smashing everything it its path without slowing down. Everyone dived out of its way. He raised his hand and caught it by the handle. The chain wrapped around his wrist, the spiked top stopping as though he had some power over it.

Silence followed.

People pulled themselves from the floor and behind shattered walls and furniture, but the fighting had stopped. Eirik had gotten everyone's attention. I closed my eyes with relief.

"I am Eirik, son of Baldur, grandson of Odin, father of the gods," he bellowed. "When I speak, you listen. When I ask a question, you answer, or you will answer to me and the gods."

I didn't see or hear the response from the others because Raine yelled, "Help me!"

In the silence, her voice carried. Echo was the first to arrive. I didn't see him. I felt him. Felt his hand on my face. Heard him as he bellowed his rage. "MALIINA!" he roared.

"No, she is mine!" Andris yelled.

A few thuds followed. Then there was silence. The eerie kind. I knew the moment Echo came back. I felt his breath on my face, the only place that seemed to have feelings on my entire body. I couldn't feel anything from my neck down.

"Open your eyes, *Cora-mio*. Look at me," Echo begged.

I was determined to obey him, so I focused hard until I opened my eyelids. His beloved face was only a few inches away, yet I couldn't touch him. He lay on the floor on his side, his eyes bright. I knew it was killing him to see me so helpless. Tears filled my eyes.

"Cold," I whispered. At least I think I did.

"It's okay," he said and showed his artavus. The other one, not the scythe. "I'm going to etch healing runes on you."

"Nnn-no," I managed to say. "Love. You. Let. Me. Go."

"No. You and I, *Cora-mio*, are meant to be together."

"Take her to the hospital," I heard Torin say.

"She won't make it," Raine said.

"Step back," Echo snarled.

"Echo, you can't," Raine protested. "You know what will happen to you if you do." Then her voice lowered. "*They* stopped fighting because Eirik ordered them to, not because of some love they have for you. If you mark her, they'll report you to your goddess."

"Let them. I'm not letting her die." He touched my face, his warmth reassuring. "I will accept whatever punishment Hel throws my way, but she must live."

"She will. Step aside." I recognized Lavania's voice. "I spoke to the goddess about the work Cora's been doing with lost souls, and she gave her approval. Cora is compassionate and caring. Her love for her fellow humans will make her a perfect Immortal." She knelt next to Echo. "Go to sleep, Cora Jemison. When you wake up, your new life will begin."

I didn't feel anything, but my eyelids grew heavy.

"I love you, Cora."

Maybe I wanted to hear it or imagined it, but it sounded like Echo just told me he loved me.

***

Voices reached me from afar. I strained to hear them, to understand what they were saying. They grew stronger and became one.

"Come back to me, *Cora-mio*," Echo begged. "I need you to love me, to make my life complete." He stroked my face.

His voice faded, and I struggled to hold on to it through the foggy darkness that threatened to swallow me.

"I had my unhappy existence," Echo said, his voice stronger. "Reaping. Sleeping around. Buying things on a whim and selling them. Then I kissed you and my life changed. You gave me a reason to laugh. To love. I now look forward to coming back from Hel because I know you'll be waiting for me."

His voice faded again. I wanted to tell him I'd willingly wait for him, but once again, there was silence. I tried to move, searched for him in the darkness. Then his voice returned.

"You've shown me that what's on the outside doesn't matter. That my heart might be damaged but it's okay to give it to you. It's yours, doll-face. You've had it from the moment you looked into my eyes and showed me I was worthy of your love. The moment I held you in my arms, you became mine and I became yours. You need to come back and complete me."

A knock interrupted his beautiful monologue. Then Raine said, "How is she doing?" Raine sounded bad. Like she'd been crying.

"She's still out," Echo said in a low voice filled with anguish.

"And the others?" Raine asked tentatively.

What others? I struggled to open my eyes, move my fingers, toes. I could feel them now, like someone was filling me with adrenaline, breathing life into my limbs.

"Damned souls," Echo snarled. "I threatened them, but they won't leave. Your Valkyrie mentor did something wrong. I should have checked every rune she etched on Cora. Where's the damn book? If she made a mistake—"

"Lavania didn't make a mistake, Echo," Raine said gently. "She never does. Maliina severed Cora's spinal cord with that dagger. She might need a while to heal. Or you could add more runes on her if you want."

Add more? He'd get in trouble. I struggled through the fog, opened my eyes, and found him. He was kneeling by the bed, his head bowed over my hand, his shoulders hunched in defeat. No wonder I couldn't move my hand. He held it in a tight grip.

I glanced around and saw the souls. There were so many. I recognized a few from outside the grocery store. One by one, they drifted out of the room. They must have been waiting to see if I would make it. With them gone, I could now see that I was on Raine's bed.

"I can't live without her, Raine," Echo mumbled. "I refuse to live without her."

Echo wasn't the type to open up to someone. That he'd admitted his innermost feelings to Raine said he was really scared. Scared of losing me, and I'd never loved him more. My eyes met Raine's. They were red-rimmed. She grinned, touched her lips, and backed out of the room.

"And I don't want to live without you either, Echo," I whispered.

Echo's head whipped up before I finished the sentence. He scrambled to his feet and sat on the edge of the bed. He reached out as though to pull me in his arms, but then he stopped. "How are you feeling? Are you in pain? Can you move? Can I hold you?"

"Yes. I feel great." I moved my arms and wiggled my toes. "No pain." I started to sit up.

"No. Don't move." He slid beside me. "I just want to hold you. The last two hours were the worst of my life."

I curled in his arms and inhaled. He smelled so good. Felt even better. When he buried his face in my neck, I wrapped one arm around his broad shoulder and pressed the other against his chest. His heart was pounding hard.

"I'm never letting you out of my sight. Never."

That was a useless vow since he was a reaper and I had school, but it was nice to hear him say it.

"I'm going to enroll in your school until you finish."

"You hate hanging around Mortals," I reminded him.

He laughed, his warm breath on my sensitive neck sending sweet sensations down my back. "I'll be hanging around you, not them. Don't ever scare me like that. Every second you didn't wake up, my heart wilted."

"I still want it. Wilted or damaged. It's mine."

"Then you have it. And my dark soul. And scarred body."

"I love your scarred body."

He chuckled, the sexy sound rumbling through me. "I love you, Cora Jemison," he whispered in my ear. Then he trailed hot kisses along my neck. I tilted my head, giving him better access. "I promise to love and cherish you for the rest of our lives and beyond."

He claimed my lips and sealed the promise. His warmth surrounded me as he took over my senses until nothing else mattered but kissing him. Holding him. I almost hadn't made it. Almost missed this chance to be with him. To hold and kiss him. To touch him. Tears rushed to my eyes and raced down my face. He must have tasted them because he lifted his head.

"Whoa, sweetheart," he murmured, cupping my face and wiping the wetness with his thumb. "What is it?"

"I almost missed out on us," I murmured, feeling ridiculous to be crying over nothing. "On loving you."

"I would not have let it happen. You are mine, *Cora-mio*. I'm never letting you go. Alive or dead, you are mine," he said in a fierce voice.

I studied his beautiful face, his incredibly sexy, long eyelashes, his sensual lips. I couldn't imagine a life without him, and now we had eternity. "Forever."

He grinned. "I couldn't have it any other way."

Then a thought occurred to me. "What about Eirik?"

Echo frowned. "He wants to visit his parents. He sent the other Grimnirs with a message after Andris finished off Maliina. He is going home."

I frowned. "That is not good."

"It is brilliant. He realized his mother would never leave him, you, or Raine alone until she had him, so he decided to make himself available. You can't kidnap someone who willingly walks right to your door and demands entrance. And since he's not dead, he can just waltz right out of the gates of Hel. The gates of Hel cannot hold him in."

This was a new development, and I wasn't sure how I felt about it.

"I don't know if he'll want to leave," I said slowly. "He was so angry and bitter when we spoke. He even said he wasn't interested in love because he's been burned twice. That maybe he wasn't meant to find love, like his mother. He might decide to stay there."

"Then it will be his choice. He has issues to work through, Cora, and he's chosen to work through them in Hel, not here or in Asgard. His friend is going with us."

"With you?"

"Eirik told the Grimnirs that he'd already agreed to leave with me. He also told them Maliina was responsible for the deaths of the other Grimnirs, which ties the loose ends rather nicely." Echo chuckled. "My Grimnir brothers were terrified of him. They were convinced he might tell Hel they were working with Maliina, so they'll do and say whatever he tells them. I might not like the fact that he's in love with you, but I have to give it to him. He's Odin's grandson. Wise and smart for his age. He'll be okay, so stop worrying."

He nipped my shoulder, and I trembled. Smirking at my reaction, he soothed it with his tongue. For a moment, we were lost in each other. He pulled me onto his chest and settled against the pillows. "He wants to see you."

Echo didn't seem ready to let me go yet. I didn't mind. I loved cuddling with him. "Okay." The clock on the side table said it was two in the afternoon. "When do you leave?"

"We were waiting for you to wake up." He rolled and pinned me to the bed, his leg between my legs. "I don't want to leave you."

"I'm not going anywhere. I'll be here waiting. Always."

His eyes caressed my face, and he smiled. "You have no idea how happy you make me. There's so much I want to share with you, show you…"

A knock rattled the door.

"Go away," Echo said.

Eirik walked into the room. Seeing us together was still painful for him, and it showed in his eyes. He walked to the window and gave us his back.

"We'll need to leave soon," he said firmly.

Echo sat up.

"I'll leave you two alone, but if you make her cry, it won't matter that you are the goddess's son. You will have to deal with me." He touched my cheek, his fingers lingering. Then he shifted to super speed and left the room.

I caught my reflection in the mirror when I swung my legs to the edge of the bed and sat up. Funny I hadn't thought about it until now, but before they brought me here, I'd been lying face down in my own blood. I still wore the same clothes, yet there was not a spec of caked blood on me. They must have used runes to clean me up.

Eirik didn't turn from the window. "You know that was an empty threat."

He was allowed to brag. After all, he'd saved the day and was still hurting because of me. "I know. You are Odin's grandson *and* you have a special flail like Thor's hammer."

Eirik looked at the metal handle peeking out from the sheath hanging on his waist. "That's not it. I know the truth about what happened here. I know he and Torin killed the Grimnirs. One word from me and I could condemn both of them."

My stomach dropped. He wouldn't dare. I stared at his broad back. Dressed in black with that belt around his waist, he looked distant. I wanted to get angry at him, but I knew he was lashing out.

"What's stopping you?" I asked.

"I love Raine and would never do anything to hurt her. Taking Torin from her would do that." He turned. His face was expressionless, and when he smiled, his eyes remained flat. "And I love you, Cora. It might not be close to what Echo feels for you, but I've always loved you, always wanted you to look at me the way Raine did."

"She adored you."

"Like a brother. We didn't see it. All I knew was I could do no wrong in her eyes, but everything I did and said made you angry."

"I wanted you to want and love me. Only me. I always came second. You might not want to hear this, but you were my first crush and it hurt me when you chose her."

Eirik sighed, pulled up a chair, and sat. He leaned forward and propped his elbows on his knees, beautiful amber eyes fixed on me. A lock of his hair had fallen over his forehead. I remembered how I used to want to run my fingers through his hair. He was so beautiful, and one day, he'd meet someone who deserved him.

"I blew it, didn't I?" he said, speaking slowly.

I shook my head. Echo was my soul mate. I'd like to think we would have found each other no matter what. "Sometimes we can't fight destiny."

"I don't believe that. I think you choose your path and shape your own destiny. If I hadn't put Raine first, we would have had a chance."

"That's true." I reached out and pushed the hair back from his forehead. He inhaled sharply but shifted so I wouldn't touch him. I let my hand fall to my lap. "Sorry. I'll always love you in my own way, Eirik. Please, believe that."

He shrugged. "It doesn't matter now. I don't want you to think that I'm going to Hel just to save your men. I want to meet my parents, get to know them. I told Raine the same thing and she's not happy with my decision, but it's my decision."

I reached for his hands and held on when he tried to pull away. "Promise me one thing."

"I don't owe you—"

"Please, Eirik. Just listen." He glared, but I didn't back down. "Don't stay there too long. Come back. The sooner the better."

"Come back to what?"

I was sure there was someone out there for him. It didn't matter whether she was human, Immortal, Valkyrie, or Grimnir. "Come back to Earth, or Asgard if you like, because you need to find that path and shape your destiny."

The smile that touched his lips was bitter, but he didn't blow me off. He wiggled his hands free from mine and stood. "I have to go. Maybe someday our paths will cross, Cora. Who knows?"

No hug. No kiss. No goodbye. I stood and watched him leave the room, feeling terrible and helpless. Echo entered the room seconds later. Well, swaggered into the room was more like it. He wore his duster with the hood up, gloves, and the Gothic rings with weird etchings. He looked like he did the first day we met. Maybe hotter since I knew him better. I walked into his arms for a hug and a kiss.

"Watch Eirik's back while you are down there," I whispered.

Echo rolled his eyes. "Raine demanded the same thing. The guy is a freaking god and can take care of—"

"Please," I added.

Echo sighed. "How can I refuse you anything?"

I smiled and kissed him. "Thank you. Come back soon."

"To you? Always." He touched my cheek and left.

THE END

TO MY READERS

First, I want to thank you for your amazing support: the shout-outs on social media, the endless e-mails, reviews (good and bad), word-of-mouth PR, and posts about Runes series. The response to this series has been amazing and the support heartwarming. You, my loyal fans, have made this series successful. Because of you, Torin was nominated for the YA Crush Tourney a month after the release of Runes and did amazingly well for a new book crush. I sincerely hope you enjoyed meeting Echo in Grimnirs.

The things I have planned for this series are big and exciting, and I can't wait to share them with you. SEERS, (book #3-Raine and Torin's story), will be out in spring of 2014. In between the next installments in Raine and Torin's saga, I will write a book focusing on a secondary character. I call them my guilty pleasures. These will be full-length romance novels like Grimnirs, Cora's story. Just like Echo, there's so much about these guys we don't know about (I'm serious. They only reveal things to me when I write about them). I still have Blaine, Eirik, Viggo, Ingrid, and Andris stories to write, so stop by my discussion group on Goodreads and let's discuss whose story is next and why.
I love you, guys.
Merry Christmas, Happy Kwanzaa, Happy Hanukkah, and Happy New Year.
Ednah Walters

BIOGRAPHY

Ednah is the author of The Guardian Legacy series, a YA fantasy series about children of the fallen angels, who fight demons and protect mankind. AWAKENED, the prequel was released in September 2010 with rave reviews. BETRAYED, book one in the series was released by her new publisher Spencer Hill Press in June 2012 and HUNTED, the third installment, was released April 2013. She's working on the next book in the series, FORGOTTEN.

Ednah also writes Young Adult/New Adult paranormal romance. RUNES is the first book in her new series. IMMORTALS (book 2) was released three months later. GRIMNIRS (book 2.5) is the bridge between book 2 and 3. Ednah is presently working on book 3, SEERESS.

Under the pseudonym E. B. Walters, Ednah writes contemporary romance. SLOW BURN, the first contemporary romance with suspense, was released in April 2011. It is the first book in the Fitzgerald family series. Since then she has published five more books in this series. She's presently working on book seven.

You can visit her online at www.ednahwalters.com or www.ebwalters.com. She's also on Facebook, twitter, ya-twitter, Google-plus, and RomanceBlog, YAblog.

CPSIA information can be obtained at www.ICGtesting.com
Printed in the USA
LVOW11s1520180615

442981LV00006B/970/P